MAN AND BOY

Tony Parsons

HARPER

This novel is entirely a work of fiction. The names, characters and incidents portrayed in it are the work of the author's imagination. Any resemblance to actual persons, living or dead, events or localities is entirely coincidental.

Harper
An imprint of HarperCollins*Publishers*
77–85 Fulham Palace Road,
Hammersmith, London W6 8JB

www.harpercollins.co.uk

This paperback edition 2008
1

First published in Great Britain by
HarperCollins*Publishers* 1999

ISBN 978-0-00-785588-9

Typeset in Postscript Linotype Minion by
Palimpsest Book Production Limited,
Grangemouth, Stirlingshire

Printed and bound in Great Britain by
Clays Ltd, St Ives plc

MAN AND BOY

Man and Boy won the Book of the Year Prize, and has been translated into 38 languages. Tony Parsons' subsequent novels – *One For My Baby, The Family Way, Man and Wife, Stories We Could Tell* and *My Favourite Wife* – were all bestsellers. He lives in London.

Visit www.AuthorTracker.co.uk for exclusive information on Tony Parsons.

Praise for *Man and Boy*

'As ever, [Tony Parsons] is in impressively depth-charging, straight-talking form. A broadsheet mind with a tabloid tongue, he remains one of the few male writers prepared to look beyond his own navel in search of answers'

GQ

'As tautly plotted as a thriller and its rich cast of characters defy stereotype . . . Like Kern or Gershwin, he touches the universal via the specific and we weep'

Irish Times

'Unashamedly touching . . . funny and well-written'

Telegraph magazine

'I sobbed my way shamelessly through this book'

Woman's Journal

'Superb. *Man and Boy* is as witty and sharp as you would expect from Parsons but it is not at all bitter – rather profoundly moving. It will strike chords with many readers'

Yorkshire Post

'Entertaining. Hugely so. Parsons has thc skill to grip you by the collar and drag you into the heart of the story'

Manchester Evening News

'Parsons is a brisk and punchy writer, moving the story on in a series of jaunty episodes and comic vignettes'

Times Literary Supplement

'Anyone expecting Parsons' trademark razor-sharp mockney one-liners will find something altogether more subtle. It might sound a bit Nick Hornby but I'd liken it to *Kramer v Kramer*. A surprising tear-jerker'

Mirror

'What distinguishes Parsons's effort from a shelfful of "male identity" outings is his ability to take the traditional framework of the genre . . . and work within it to produce a series of wholly unexpected twists and eddies . . . If this is the direction in which British chaps' fiction is heading, then no one who cares about contemporary writing can seriously complain'

Literary Review

BY THE SAME AUTHOR

One For My Baby
Man and Wife
The Family Way
Stories We Could Tell
My Favourite Wife

For my mother

part one: *skylarking*

The Most Beautiful Boy in the World

It's a boy, it's a boy!

It's a little boy.

I look at this baby – as bald, wrinkled and scrunched up as an old man – and something chemical happens inside me.

It – I mean he *– looks like the most beautiful baby in the history of the world. Is it – he – really the most beautiful baby in the history of the world? Or is that just my biological programming kicking in? Does everyone feel this way? Even people with plain babies? Is our baby really so beautiful?*

I honestly can't tell.

The baby is sleeping in the arms of the woman I love. I sit on the edge of the bed and stare at the pair of them, feeling like I belong in this room with this woman and this baby in a way that I have never belonged anywhere.

After all the excitement of the last twenty-four hours, I am suddenly overwhelmed, feeling something – gratitude, happiness, love – well up inside me and threaten to spill out.

I am afraid that I am going to disgrace myself – spoil everything, smudge the moment – with tears. But then the baby wakes up and starts squawking for food and we – me and the woman I love – laugh out loud, laugh with shock and wonder.

It's a small miracle. And although we can't escape the reality of everyday life – when do I have to get back to work? – the day is glazed with real magic. We don't really talk about the magic. But we can feel it all around.

Later my parents are there. When she is done with the hugs and kisses, my mother counts the baby's fingers and toes, checking for webbed feet. But he is fine, the baby is fine.

'He's a little smasher,' my mum says. 'A little smasher!'

My father looks at the baby and something inside him seems to melt.

There are many good things about my father, but he is not a soft man, he is not a sentimental man. He doesn't gurgle and coo over babies in the street. My father is a good man, but the things he has gone through in his life mean that he is also a hard man. Today some ice deep inside him begins to crack and I can tell he feels it too.

This is the most beautiful baby in the world.

I give my father a bottle I bought months ago. It is bourbon. My father only drinks beer and whisky, but he takes the bottle with a big grin on his face. The label on the bottle says 'Old Granddad'. That's him. That's my father.

And I know today that I have become more like him. Today I am a father too. All the supposed landmarks of manhood – losing my virginity, getting my driving licence, voting for the first time – were all just the outer suburbs of my youth. I went through all those things and came out the other side fundamentally unchanged, still a boy.

But now I have helped to bring another human being into the world.

Today I became what my father has been forever.

Today I became a man.

I am twenty-five years old.

one

Some situations to avoid when preparing for your all-important, finally-I-am-fully-grown thirtieth birthday.

Having a one-night stand with a colleague from work.

The rash purchase of luxury items you can't afford.

Being left by your wife.

Losing your job.

Suddenly becoming a single parent.

If you are coming up to thirty, whatever you do, don't do any of that.

It will fuck up your whole day.

Thirty should be when you think – *these are my golden years, these are my salad days, the best is yet to come* – and all that old crap.

You are still young enough to stay up all night, but you are old enough to have a credit card. All the uncertainties and poverty of your teens and twenties are finally over – and good riddance to the lot of them – but the sap is still rising.

Thirty should be a good birthday. One of the best.

But how to celebrate reaching the big three-oh? With a collection of laughing single friends in some intimate bar or restaurant? Or surrounded by a loving wife and adoring small children in the bosom of the family home?

There has to be a good way of turning thirty. Perhaps they are all good ways.

All my images of this particular birthday seemed to be derived from some glossy American sitcom. When I thought of turning thirty, I thought of attractive thirty-nothing marrieds snogging like teens in heat while in the background a gurgling baby crawls across some polished parquet floor, or I saw a circle of good-looking, wisecracking friends drinking latte and showing off their impressive knitwear while wryly bemoaning the dating game. That was my problem. When I thought of turning thirty, I thought of somebody else's life.

That's what thirty should be – grown-up without being disappointed, settled without being complacent, worldly wise, but not so worldly wise that you feel like chucking yourself under a train. The time of your life.

By thirty you have finally realised that you are not going to live forever, of course. But surely that should only make the laughing, latte-drinking present taste even sweeter? You shouldn't let your inevitable death put a damper on things. Don't let the long, slow slide to the grave get in the way of a good time.

Whether you are enjoying the last few years of unmarried freedom, or have recently moved on to a more adult, more committed way of life with someone you love, it's difficult to imagine a truly awful way of turning thirty.

But I managed to find one somehow.

The car smelled like somebody else's life. Like freedom.

It was parked right in the window of the showroom, a wedge-shaped sports car which, even with its top off, looked as sleek and compact as a muscle.

Naturally it was red – a flaming, testosterone-stuffed red.

When I was a little bit younger, such blatant macho corn would have made me sneer, or snigger, or puke, or all of the above.

Now I found it didn't bother me at all. In fact, it seemed to be just what I was looking for at this stage of my life.

I'm not really the kind of man who knows what cars are called, but I had made it my business – furtively lingering over the ads in glossy magazines – to find out the handle of this particular hot little number. Yes, it's true. Our eyes had met before.

But its name didn't really matter. I just loved the way it looked. And that smell. Above all, that smell. That anything-can-happen smell. What was it about that smell?

Amidst the perfume of leather, rubber and all those yards of freshly sprayed steel, you could smell a heartbreaking newness, a newness so shocking that it almost overwhelmed me. This newness intimated another world that was limitless and free, an open road leading to all the unruined days of the future. Somewhere they had never heard of traffic cones or physical decay or my thirtieth birthday.

I knew that smell from somewhere and I recognised the way it made me feel. Funnily enough, it reminded me of that feeling you get when you hold a newborn baby.

The analogy was far from perfect – the car couldn't squint up at me with eyes that had just started to see, or grasp one of my fingers in a tiny, tiny fist, or give me a gummy little smile. But for a moment there it felt like it just might.

'You only live once,' the car salesman said, his heels clicking across the showroom floor.

I smiled politely, indicating that I would have to think that one over.

'Are you in the market for some serious fun?' he said. 'Because if the MGF is about one thing, it's about fun.'

While he gave me his standard sales pitch, he was sizing me up, trying to decide if I was worth a test drive.

He was pushy, but not so pushy that it made your flesh crawl. He was just doing his job. And despite my weekend clothes – which because of the nature of my work were not really so different from my weekday clothes – he must have seen a man of substance. A fast-track career looking for some matching wheels. Young, free and single. A life as carefree as a lager commercial. How wrong can you be?

'This model has the Variable Valve Control system,' he said, with what seemed like genuine enthusiasm. 'The opening period of the inlet valves can be varied by altering the rotational speed of each cam lobe.'

What the fuck was he going on about? Was it something to do with the engine?

'A total babe magnet,' he said, noting my dumbfounded expression. 'Plenty of poke. A young single guy couldn't do any better than the MGF.'

This was my kind of sales pitch. Forget the technical guff, just tell me that you can lose yourself in a car like this. Let me know you can lose yourself. That's what I wanted to hear.

The salesman was distracted by something on the street, and I followed his gaze out of the showroom's plate-glass wall.

He was looking at a tall blonde woman holding the hand of a small boy wearing a Star Wars T-shirt. They were surrounded by bags of supermarket shopping. And they were watching us.

Even framed by all those plastic carrier bags and chaperoning a little kid, the woman was the kind that you look at more than once.

What you noticed about her child – and he was certainly her child – was that he was carrying a long, plastic tube with a dull light glowing faintly inside.

If you had been to the cinema at any time over the last twenty years you would recognise it as a light sabre, traditional weapon of the Jedi Knights. This one needed new batteries.

The beautiful woman was smiling at me and the salesman. The little kid pointed his light sabre, as if about to strike us down.

'*Daddy*,' he mouthed from the other side of the plate-glass wall which divided us. You couldn't hear him, but that's what he was saying.

'My wife and son,' I said, turning away, but not before I caught the disappointment in the salesman's eyes. 'Got to go.'

Daddy. That's me. Daddy.

'You don't even like cars,' my wife reminded me, edging our old VW estate through the thick early-evening traffic.

'Just looking.'

'And you're too young for a mid-life crisis,' she said. 'Thirty is much too young, Harry. The way it works, you wait for fifteen years and then run off with a secretary who's young enough to be your second wife. And I cut off the sleeves of all your suits. Not to mention your bollocks.'

'I'm not thirty, Gina,' I chuckled, although it wasn't really all that funny. She was always exaggerating. 'I'm twenty-nine.'

'For one more month!' she laughed.

'It's your birthday *soon*,' our boy said, laughing along with his mother, although he didn't have a clue why, and tapping me on the back of the head with his sodding light sabre.

'Please don't do that, Pat,' I said.

He was back there with the week's shopping, strapped into his little car seat and muttering under his breath, pretending to be in the cockpit of the Millennium Falcon with Harrison Ford.

'I've lost my starboard engine,' he jabbered away to himself. 'Fire when ready.'

I turned to look at him. He was four years old with dirty

blond hair that hung down over eyes that were the same shade of blue as his mother's. Tiffany blue. Catching my eye, he grinned at me with pure childish delight.

'Happy birthday, dear Daddy,' he sang. 'Happy birthday, birth-day.'

To Pat, my birthday was a chance to finally give me the home-made card he had hidden under his bed (Luke Skywalker decapitating a space monster with his trusty light sabre). To me it meant that the best might already be over. It really did.

When would I feel the way I felt the night my wife said that she would marry me? When would I feel the way I felt the morning my son was born? When would life be that – I don't know – *real* again? When?

'When did you become interested in cars?' Gina asked. She wouldn't let this car thing rest. 'I bet you don't even know what kind of petrol this one uses, do you?'

'Oh, come on, Gina.'

'What is it, then?'

Fucking hell.

'The green kind,' I said, taking a wild guess. 'You know – non-leaded. The one that saves a rain forest every time you fill her up.'

'It's diesel, you doughnut,' she laughed. 'I never knew a man less interested in cars than you. What happened?'

What could I tell her? You don't tell a wife that some inanimate object somehow represents all those things you know you are never going to have. The places you are never going to see, the women you are never going to love, the things you are never going to do. You can't tell a wife all that stuff. Not even a wife you love very much. Especially not a wife like that.

'It only carries one passenger,' she said.

'What does?' I said, playing dumb.

'You know very well what I'm talking about,' she said. 'It only carries one passenger – one thin, female passenger.'

'You're still pretty thin and female,' I said. 'Or you were the last time I looked.'

'What's brought all this on, Harry? Come on. Tell me.'

'Maybe I'm compensating for becoming an old git,' I said. 'I'm joining the old gits' club, so, pathetically, I want to recapture my glorious youth. Even though I know it's ultimately futile and even though my youth wasn't particularly glorious. Isn't that what men do?'

'You're turning thirty,' she said. 'We're going to open a couple of bottles and have a nice cake with candles.'

'And balloons,' Pat said.

'And balloons,' Gina said. She shook her lovely head. 'We're not having you put down, Harry.'

Gina was a couple of months older than me. She had breezed through her thirtieth birthday surrounded by friends and family, dancing with her son to Wham's greatest hits, a glass of champagne in her hand. She looked great that night, she really did. But clearly my own birthday was going to be a bit more traumatic.

'You don't regret anything, do you?' she said.

'Like what?'

'You know,' she said, suddenly deadly serious. 'Like us.'

We had married young. Gina was three months pregnant with Pat on our wedding day and it was, by some distance, the happiest day of my life. But nothing was ever really the same again after that day. Because after that there was no disguising the fact that we were grown-ups.

The radio station where I was working gave me the week off and we spent our honeymoon back at our little flat watching daytime television in bed, eating M&S sandwiches and talking about the beautiful baby we were going to have.

We talked about eventually taking a proper, grown-up

honeymoon – Gina wanted us to snorkel among the tropical fish of Okinawa. But by the time there was a bit of money and a bit of time, we had Pat and the course of our lives seemed set.

Gina and I found ourselves separated from the rest of the world by our wedding rings. The other married couples we knew were at least ten years older than us, and friends our own age were still in that brief period between living with their mothers and living with their mortgages. Our little family was on its own.

While our friends were dancing the night away in clubs, we were up all hours with our baby's teething problems. While they were worrying about meeting the right person, we were worrying about meeting the payments on our first real home. Yet I didn't regret any of it. Yes, we had given up our freedom. But we had given it up for something better.

I loved my wife and I loved our son. Together, the two of them made my world make sense. My life without them was unimaginable. I knew I was a lucky man. But I couldn't help it, I just couldn't help it – lately I found myself wondering when I had stopped being young.

'I just really hate the way that life starts to contract as you get older,' I said. 'The way your options narrow. I mean, when did owning a car like that become ridiculous for me? When exactly? Why is it such a joke? I would love to know. That's all.'

'The Force is strong in this one,' Pat said.

'A red sports car,' Gina said to herself. 'And you don't even like *driving*.'

'Listen, I was just looking, okay?' I said.

'Happy birthday to *you*,' Pat sang, smacking me across the ear with his light sabre. 'Squashed tomatoes and glue. You-look-like-a-monkey-and-you-act-like-one-too.'

'That's not nice,' I told him, as the traffic ground to a halt and my ear began to throb.

Gina put the handbrake on and looked at me, as if trying to remember what she had liked about me in the first place. She seemed a bit stumped.

I remembered what I had liked about her. She had the longest legs I had ever seen on a woman. But I still didn't know if that was the best basis for the love of your life.

Or the worst.

two

When I could no longer stand the sight of the rusty white van dawdling along in front of me, I swung the MGF into the oncoming traffic and smacked my foot down.

My new car squirted past the old van with a confident, throaty roar. As I cut back in front of it I caught a glimpse of the driver – a blur of bad teeth, tattoos and loathing – before he disappeared in my rear-view mirror. I felt good. The MGF meant that I no longer had to look at rusty white vans or their drivers. All that was behind me now. I could look forward to a future full of open-top motoring and admiring glances. Then the van pulled up alongside me at the very next red light.

Jesus, I thought. Road rage.

'You stupid little git,' he told me, winding down his window to reveal a face like a Big Mac in a bucket of beer. 'Get out and push it.'

After he had driven off at the green light, I sat shaking for a while, thinking about what I should have said to him.

If I get out, pal, it will be to push your crappy van up your tattooed back passage! If I pushed this thing, pal – it would have been really good to call him pal – I'd still be going faster than you. You lager-bellied moron! You fat fuck!

I saw myself delivering some perfect put-down and then pulling away in a squeal of rubber, an infuriating little smile on my face. But what actually happened was that I just sat there trembling and dreaming until all the cars behind me started sounding their horns and shouting stuff about the lights having changed.

So I drove off, thinking about what my dad would have done.

He certainly wouldn't have sat there and said nothing. And he wouldn't have wasted time cooking up some devastating response worthy of Oscar Wilde at his pithy best.

My father would simply have got out of the MGF and punched that van driver's lights out. He really would.

Not that my dad would ever be seen dead in a fancy sports car, to tell you the truth. He thought they were for wankers.

My dad would have felt much more at home in one of those white vans.

Gina had been incredibly understanding about the MGF. She had encouraged me to go back and talk to the salesman when even I was starting to find the idea of buying a sports car a bit stupid.

And there were plenty of reasons why buying it was crazy. Its boot was smaller than a supermarket trolley. We really didn't need two cars. A soft top in London is a hate object for any spotty fourteen-year-old cretin with a chip on his shoulder and a blade in his sock. But Gina just wasn't interested.

She told me to buy the thing and to stop thinking that my life was over just because I was turning thirty. She told me I was being pathetic, but she laughed when she said it and put her arm around me, giving me a little shake. Trying to force some sense into me. Fat chance.

At any other time during the seven years we had been together, we wouldn't have been able to afford a good second car. In fact, at any other time we wouldn't have been able to afford an incredibly crappy second car. We hadn't even owned our crappy first car for very long.

But we no longer practically had to have a heart attack every time we received a red-topped bill. At last my job was going well.

I was the producer of *The Marty Mann Show*, a late-night talk show that went out every Saturday on terrestrial television. For the six years before that I had been the producer of *The Marty Mann Show* back when it was on local radio and most of the country had not even heard the first rumours about its mad bastard presenter. It seemed a long time ago now.

Over the last twelve months Marty and I had turned a no-budget radio show into a low-budget TV show. The line between the two was surprisingly thin. But crossing that thin line was enough to make Marty Mann some sort of star.

If you walked into a restaurant with him, everybody stopped eating and talking just so they could look at him. Girls, who a few years earlier wouldn't have touched him wearing surgical gloves, now thought he was a love god. He got photographed even when he wasn't doing anything special. Marty had arrived big time and he had been decent enough to bring me along with him.

The critics, or at least the ones who liked him, called Marty child-like – meaning he was open, frank and intuitive. They thought he asked the kind of questions other interviewers decided it was best not to even think about. And it was true – the editing process that exists in most of us seemed to be completely missing from Marty's brain. And he got answers, even when what he really deserved was a punch in the mouth.

The critics who didn't like Marty also called him child-like – meaning he was selfish, immature and cruel. But Marty wasn't really child-like at all. Sometimes I watched our Pat peacefully play for hours with his little plastic Star Wars toys. *That* was child-like. Marty's attention span was nowhere near that long. Marty wasn't child-like. He was just undeveloped.

We had met at a local radio station where the staff were either on their way up or on their way out. It was a grotty little building full of curdled ambition and stale cigarette smoke, and most of our regular callers were either hopelessly lonely or borderline barking. But I always sort of missed the place. Because that was where I met Gina.

The station was always desperate to get guests – for some reason there was never a mad rush for our cheques, which were so small they were invisible to the naked eye – and so there was often an improvisational element to our bookings.

For instance, when the first Japanese banks started to go bust, the person we booked to talk about what it all meant was not an economist or a financial journalist, but the professor who taught Japanese at the college across the street.

Okay, so he was a language teacher, but like any language teacher he was in love with the country whose lingo he taught. Who better to discuss why the Asian tigers were turning into neutered pussycats? Well, lots of people, probably. But he was the best we could get. Except he didn't show up.

As if in sympathy with the exploding Japanese bubble, the professor's appendix burst on the morning he was due to come in, and coming off the bench as his substitute we got his star pupil – Gina.

Tall, radiant Gina. She was fluent in Japanese, apparently an expert on the culture, and she had legs that went on for weeks. I took her into the studio and couldn't even find the courage to talk to her, couldn't even look in her eyes. She was beautiful, charming, intelligent. But most important of all, she was also way, way out of my league.

And then when the red light came on in the studio, something happened. Or rather, nothing happened at all. Gina became paralysed with nerves. She couldn't speak.

When I had first seen her I had thought she was unapproachable. But as I watched her stuttering and sweating her way through her incoherent tale of economic decline, she was suddenly human. And I knew I had a chance. A slim chance, maybe. A snowball's chance in hell, perhaps. But a chance all the same.

I also knew exactly how she felt. The red light always did that to me too. I was never comfortable in front of a microphone or a camera, and the very thought of it can still make me break out in a cold sweat.

So when it was over and Marty had put her out of her misery, it was not difficult for me to commiserate with her. She was very good about it, laughing at her nerves and vowing that her career in broadcasting was over.

My heart sank.

I thought – *then when will I see you again?*

The thing that got me about Gina is that she didn't make a big deal about the way she looked. She knew she was good-looking, but she didn't care. Or rather, she thought it was the least interesting thing about her. But you wouldn't look twice at me if you saw me in the street. And someone as ordinary-looking as me can never be that casual about beauty.

She took me for sushi in Sogo, the big Japanese department store on Piccadilly Circus, where the staff all knew her. She talked to them in Japanese and they called her 'Gina-san'.

'Gina-san?' I said.

'It's difficult to translate exactly,' she smiled. 'It sort of means – honourable, respected Gina.'

Honourable, respected Gina. She had been in love with Japanese culture ever since she was a little girl. She had actually lived there during her year out between sixth form and college, teaching English in Kyoto – 'The happiest year of my life' – and she was planning to go back. There was a job offer from an American bank in Tokyo. Nothing was going to stop her. I prayed that I would.

Desperately racking my brain for my little knowledge of Japan, I mentioned Yukio Mishima. She dismissed the novelist as a right-wing fruitcake – 'It's not all raw fish and ritual suicide, you know' – and told me I should read Kawabata if I really wanted to understand Japan. She said she would lend some of his stuff to me, if I wanted. I saw my chance and grabbed it.

We met for a drink and she brought a book called *Snow Country*. I read it as soon as I got home – a jaded playboy falls in love with a doomed geisha in a mountain resort, it was actually pretty good – dreaming of Gina's eyes, her legs, the way her whole face seemed to light up when she laughed.

She cooked dinner back at her flat. I had to take my shoes off before I came in. We discussed Japanese culture – or rather Gina talked and I listened, dropping bits of chicken teriyaki on the carpet with my chopsticks – until it was time to call a cab or brush my teeth. And then we were making love on the floor – or the futon, as Gina called it. I was ready to bomb Pearl Harbor for her.

And I wanted her to stay with me forever. So I promised her everything – happiness, endless love and, crucially, a family. I knew the family thing would get her – her dad had buggered off when Gina was four years old, and she had grown up pining for the security of family life. But she still cried when she told the bank that she wouldn't be going to Tokyo after all.

Instead of living in Japan, she worked as a freelance translator for Japanese companies in the City. But many of them were going under or going home by now. Her career wasn't what it should have been. I knew she had given up a lot to be with me. If I hadn't been so deliriously happy, I might even have felt a bit guilty.

After we were married and Pat was born, she stayed home. She said she didn't mind giving up work for Pat and me – 'my two boys,' she called us.

I suspected that the fact her career had disappointed her had as much to do with staying home as wanting a real family life. But she always tried to make it sound like the most natural thing in the world.

'I don't want my son brought up by strangers,' she said. 'I don't want some overweight teenager from Bavaria sticking him in front of a video while I'm in an office.'

'Fine,' I said.

'And I don't want him eating all his meals fresh from the microwave. I don't want to come home from work too tired to play with him. I don't want him growing up without me. I want him to have some sort of family life – whatever that is. I don't want his childhood to be like mine.'

'Right,' I said. I knew this was a touchy subject. Gina looked like she was ready to start bawling at any minute. 'What's wrong with being a woman who stays home with her kid?' she said. 'All that ambition stuff is so pathetically eighties. All that having-it-all crap. We can get by with less money, can't we? And you'll buy me sushi once a week, won't you?'

I told her I would buy her so much raw fish she would sprout gills. So she stayed home to look after our son.

And when I came back from work at night I would shout,

'Hi honey, I'm home,' as though we were characters in some American sitcom from the fifties, with Dick Van Dyke bringing home the bacon and Mary Tyler Moore making bacon sandwiches.

I don't know why I tried to make a joke of it. Maybe because in my heart I believed that Gina was only pretending to be a housewife, while I pretended to be my father.

three

Marty grew up eating dinner with the TV on. Television had been his babysitter, his best friend, his teacher. He could still recite entire programming schedules from his childhood. He could whistle the theme tune to *Dallas*. His Dalek impersonation was among the best I have ever heard. The Miss World contest had taught him everything he knew about the birds and bees, which admittedly wasn't very much.

Although I was nothing like him, Marty took to me because I came from the same sort of home. That doesn't sound like much of a basis for friendship, but you would be surprised at how few people in television come from that kind of background. Most of the people we worked with came from homes with books.

When we first met at the little radio station we were both what was laughingly referred to as multi-skilled. Marty was mostly skilled in fetching sandwiches, sorting mail and making the tea. But even then his grinning, pop-eyed energy was such that everyone noticed him, even if nobody took him seriously.

I was in a more elevated position than Marty, writing items, producing shows and sometimes very nervously reading the news. As I said, I was always lousy at coming alive when the red light came on – only slightly better than Gina. The red light came on and, instead of coming alive,

I went sort of dead. But it turned out to be what Marty was born to do.

When we suddenly lost the regular presenter of our late-night phone-in – the nut shift, we called it – to a job in cable television, I persuaded the station to give Marty a shot. Partly because I thought he would be good at it. But mostly because I was terrified of having to do it myself.

Amazingly, he worked wonders with the most unpromising material imaginable. Five nights a week Marty took calls from hangers, floggers, conspiracy theorists, alien watchers and assorted loony tunes. And he turned it into good radio.

What made it good radio was that Marty sounded like there was nowhere else he would rather be than chatting to the mouth-foaming denizens of nut nation.

We slowly started to build what they call a cult following. After that, we very quickly began to get offers to put the show on television. People bought us lunch, made flattering noises and made big promises. And very soon we abandoned our successful radio show, a rare case of rats deserting a floating ship.

But it was different on television. We couldn't just let our guests practically wander in off the street as they had done on radio. Amusing lunatics who had been impregnated by randy aliens were no longer quite enough.

After a year fronting his own show, Marty still looked like he was exactly where he wanted to be. But the strain was starting to tell, and every week he needed a little more time in make-up to cover the cracks. It wasn't just the seven-day stress of finding good guests that was putting those licks of grey in his bottle-blond hair. When we were on radio, Marty had nothing to lose. And now he did.

He was in the chair of the make-up room when I arrived at the studio, brainstorming about future guests to the group of young women who surrounded him, hanging on to his every wishful thought while the make-up girl attempted to make his skin look vaguely human for the cameras. He dubiously sipped the glass of water which had been placed in front of him.

'Is this Evian?'

'Did you want sparkling?' asked a sweet-faced young woman in combat trousers and army boots.

'I wanted Evian.'

She looked relieved. 'That's Evian.'

'I don't think so.'

'Well, it's Badoit.'

Marty looked at her.

'But there wasn't any Evian in the vending machine,' she said.

'Try the green room,' he suggested with a little sigh.

There were murmurs of assent. The green room – the holding pen for the show's guests – was definitely the place to find Marty's Evian. Crestfallen but smiling bravely, the girl in combat trousers went off to find the right water.

'I'm thinking classic encounter with Hollywood legend,' Marty said. 'I'm thinking Michael Parkinson meets the stars with his clipboard. I'm thinking Tinsel Town. I'm thinking Oscar nominee. I'm thinking . . . Jack Nicholson?'

'Jack's not in town,' our researcher said. She was a small, nervous girl who wouldn't be doing this job for much longer. Her fingernails were already chewed to the knuckle.

'Leonardo DiCaprio?'

'Leo's unavailable.'

'Clint Eastwood?'

'I've got a call in with his office. But – doubtful.'

'Robert Mitchum? James Stewart?'

'They're dead.'

Marty shot her a vicious look.

'Don't ever say that,' he said. 'They are merely unable to commit to the show at this moment in time.'

He looked at me in the mirror, his beady eyes blinking inside a cloud of orange foundation.

'Why can't we get any of these fucking screen greats, Harry?'

'Because none of the people you mentioned have any product out,' I told him, as I had to tell him every week. 'And when they do, we still have to fight for them with all the other talk shows.'

'Did you see the news tonight?' the make-up girl said dreamily, the way make-up girls do, completely oblivious to the nervous breakdowns that were happening all around her. 'It was really interesting. They showed you those protesters out at the airport. The ones chaining themselves to the trees? Protesting against the new terminal?'

'What about them?' Marty asked. 'Or are you just making conversation?'

'I really like their leader,' she said. 'You know – Cliff. The one with the dreadlocks? He's *gorgeous*.'

Every woman in the room muttered agreement. I had seen this Cliff character up his tree – skinny, well-spoken, dreadlocks – but I had had no idea he was considered a sexual entity.

'That's who you should have on the show,' the make-up girl said triumphantly, dabbing Marty's face with a powder puff. 'He's much more interesting than some old superstar with a hair transplant and an action thriller on general release.'

'Cliff's not a bad idea,' I said. 'But I don't know how to reach him. Although he can't be as difficult as Clint Eastwood.'

'Well, I've got a mobile number for him,' someone said from the back of the make-up room. 'If that's any use.'

We all turned to look at her.

She was a slim redhead with that kind of fine Irish skin that is so pale it looks as though it has never seen the sun. She was in her early twenties – she looked as though she had been out of university for about forty-five minutes – but she still had a few freckles. She would always have a few freckles. I had never seen her before.

'Siobhan Kemp,' she said to no one in particular, blushing as she introduced herself. 'I'm the new associate producer. Well – shall I give Cliff a call?'

Marty looked at me. I could tell that he liked the idea of the tree man. And so did I. Because, like all television people, what we worshipped above all else was authenticity. Apart from genuine, high-octane celebrity, of course. We worshipped that most of all.

We were sick of junior celebs pushing their lousy product. We hungered after real people with real lives and real stories – stories not anecdotes. They offered us great television at rock-bottom prices. We offered them therapy, a chance to get it all off their chest, an opportunity to let it all just gush out over a million carpets.

Of course, if Jack Nicholson had suddenly called up begging to appear on the show then we would have immediately called a security guard to escort all the real people from the building. But somehow Jack never did. There were just not enough celebrities to go round these days.

So we revered real people, real people who felt passionate about something, real people with no career to protect. And someone up a tree with police dogs snapping at his unwashed bollocks sounded about as real as it gets.

'How do you know him?' I asked her.

'I used to go out with him,' she said.

Marty and I exchanged a glance. We were impressed. So this Siobhan was a real person too.

'It didn't work out,' she said. 'It's difficult when one of you is up a tree for so much of the time. But we managed to stay close and I admire him – he really believes in what he's doing. The way he sees it, the life-support systems of the planet are nearing exhaustion, and all the politicians ever do is pay lip service to ecological issues. He thinks that when man enters the land, he should leave only footprints and take only memories.'

'Fucking brilliant,' Marty said. 'Who's his agent?'

I was up in the gallery watching a dozen screens showing five different shots of Marty interviewing a man who could inflate a condom with it pulled down over the top half of his head – he was actually pretty good – when I felt someone by my side.

It was Siobhan, smiling like a kid on her first day at a new school who has suddenly realised that she is going to be okay.

In the darkness of the gallery her face was lit by the monitors on the wall. They are TV sets, that's all, but we call them monitors. They provide the director with a choice of shots for transmission. Monitors don't only show the image that is going out, but all the images that could be. Siobhan smiled up at them. She had a beautiful smile.

'I thought that this Cliff didn't do interviews,' I said. 'Not since he was stitched up by that Sunday paper who said he was just in it for the glory and the hippy chicks.' Then I remembered she had gone out with him. 'No offence meant.'

'None taken,' she said. 'That's true, but he might do this one.'

'Why? Because of you?'

'No,' she laughed. 'Because he likes Marty. He doesn't consider him part of the media establishment.'

I looked at Marty on the monitors, almost gagging with laughter as the condom exploded on the guy's head. If anyone was part of the media establishment, it was Marty. He would have considered it a compliment.

'And most of all,' said Siobhan, 'because we're live.'

It was true that we were practically the last live show on television. By now most shows were what are called 'as live' – meaning they faked the excitement of live television while always having the safety net of recording. Phoney as hell.

But *The Marty Mann Show* was the real thing. When you watched that guy with a condom on his head, it was actually being inflated at that very moment.

'The way these eco-warriors see it,' Siobhan said, 'the only place in the media where there's no censorship is live television. Can I ask you something?'

'Go ahead.'

'Is that your MGF down in the carpark? The red one?'

Here it comes, I thought. The lecture about what cars do to the muck in the air and the hole in the sky. Sometimes I despair for the young people of today. All they ever think about is the future of the planet.

'Yeah, that's mine,' I said.

'Nice car,' she said.

They were both asleep by the time I got home. I brushed my teeth and undressed in the darkness, listening to my wife softly breathing in her sleep.

The sound of Gina sleeping never failed to stir an enormous tenderness in me. It was the only time she ever seemed vulnerable, the only time I could kid myself that she needed me to protect her. She stirred when I slid into bed and wrapped my arm around her.

'Good show tonight,' she murmured.

She was warm and sleepy and I loved her like that. She

had her back to me, her usual sleeping position, and she sighed as I snuggled up against her, kissing the back of her neck and letting my hand trace the length of one of those long legs that had knocked me out when I first met her. And still did.

'Oh, Gina. My Gina.'

'Oh, Harry,' she said softly. 'You don't want to – do you?' She brushed me with her hand. 'Well. Maybe you do.'

'You feel great.'

'Pretty frisky, aren't you?' she laughed, turning to look at me, her eyes still half-closed with sleep. 'I mean, for a man of your age.'

She sat up in bed, pulled the T-shirt she was wearing over her head and tossed it to the floor. She ran her fingers through her hair and smiled at me, her long, familiar body lit by the street light seeping through the blinds. It was never really dark in our room.

'Still want me?' she said. 'Even after all these years?'

I may have nodded. Our lips were just about to touch when Pat began to cry. We looked at each other. She smiled. I didn't.

'I'll get him,' Gina said, as I flopped back against the pillow.

She returned to the bedroom with Pat in her arms. He was sort of gasping for breath and tearfully trying to explain his nightmare – something about big monsters – while Gina soothed him, rolling him into bed between us. As always, in the warmth of our bed his sobbing immediately stopped.

'Make spoons,' Gina told us.

Pat and I obediently rolled over, his warm little legs in their brushed cotton pyjamas tucked up inside the back of mine. I could hear him sniffing, but he was okay now. Gina threw one of her long thin arms over the pair of us, nestling up against Pat.

'Go to sleep now,' she whispered. 'Everything's going to be all right.'

I closed my eyes, the boy between us, and as I drifted away I wondered if Gina was talking to me, or to Pat, or to both of us.

'There are no monsters,' she said, and we slept in her arms.

four

Gina's thirtieth birthday had not been completely painless.

Her father had called her in the early evening to wish her a happy birthday – which meant she had spent all of the morning and all of the afternoon wondering if the worthless old git would call her at all.

Twenty-five years ago, just before Gina had started school, Glenn – as her dad insisted everyone call him, especially his children – walked out the door, dreaming of making it as a rock musician. And although he had been working behind the counter of a guitar shop in Denmark Street for a couple of centuries, and all the dreams of glory had receded along with his hippy hairline, he still thought he was some kind of free spirit who could forget birthdays or remember them as the mood took him.

Glenn had never made it as a musician. There had been one band with a modest recording contract and one minor hit single. You might have glimpsed him playing bass on *Top of the Pops* just before Ted Heath left 10 Downing Street forever.

He was very good-looking when he was younger – Glenn, not Ted Heath – a bit of a Robert Plant figure, all blond Viking curls and bare midriff. But I always felt that Glenn's true career had been building families and then smashing them up.

Gina's little family had been just the first in a long line of wives and children that Glenn had abandoned. They were scattered all over the country, the women like Gina's mother, who had been considered such a great beauty back in the sixties and seventies that her smiling face was sometimes featured in glossy magazines, and the children like Gina, who had grown up in a single parent family back when it was still called a broken home.

Glenn breezed in and out of their lives, casually missing birthdays and Christmases and then turning up unexpectedly with some large, inappropriate gift. Even though he was now a middle-aged suburban commuter who worked in a shop, he still liked to think he was Jim bloody Morrison and that the rules which applied to other people didn't apply to him.

But I can't complain too much about old Glenn. In a way he played Cupid to me and Gina. Because what she liked about me most was my family.

It was a small, ordinary family – I'm the only child – and we lived in a pebble-dashed semi in the Home Counties which could have been in almost any suburb in England. We were surrounded by houses and people, but you had to walk for half a mile before you could buy a newspaper – surrounded by life, yet never escaping the feeling that life was happening somewhere else. That's the suburbs.

My mum watched the street from behind net curtains ('It's my street,' she would say, when challenged by my dad and me). My dad fell asleep in front of the television ('There's never anything on,' he always moaned). And I kicked a ball about in the back garden, dreaming of extra time at Wembley and trying to avoid my dad's roses.

How many families are there like that in this country? Probably millions. Yet certainly a lot less than there were. Families like us, we're practically an endangered species. Gina acted as though my mum and my dad and I were the last of the nuclear families, protected wild life to be cherished and revered and wondered over.

To me, of course, my family was on the staid side. All that car-washing, all that peeking from behind net curtains, all the nights spent in front of the television, all the B&B holidays in Devon and Cornwall or a caravan in Frinton. I envied Gina's exotic background – her mum a former model, her dad a would-be rock star, the pictures in the glossy magazines, even though the pictures were fading now.

But Gina remembered the missed birthdays of her childhood, a father who was always preoccupied with his more recent, more exciting attachments, the promised holidays that never happened, and her mother going to bed alone, growing old alone, getting sick alone, crying alone and finally dying alone. Gina could never be cavalier about an ordinary family. It wasn't in her.

The first Christmas I took Gina home, I saw her choking up when my mum gave her a little present – just some smelly stuff in a basket from the Body Shop, some soap in the shape of polar bears covered in cling film – and I knew I had her. She looked at those polar bears and she was hooked.

You should never underestimate the power of the nuclear family. These days coming from an unbroken home is like having independent means, or Paul Newman eyes, or a big cock. It's one of life's true blessings, given to just a lucky few. And difficult to resist.

But those unbroken homes can lull their children into a false sense of security. When I was growing up, I took it for granted that every marriage would be as stable and everlasting as my mum and dad's – including my own. My parents made it look easy. But it's not easy at all.

Gina would probably have washed her hands of Glenn years ago if her mother had lived. But she died of breast cancer just before Gina walked into the radio station and my life, and suddenly she felt the need to salvage the few ragged bits of family she still had left.

So Glenn came to our wedding, and rolled a joint in front of my mum and dad. Then he tried to get off with one of the bridesmaids. Pushing fifty, he seemed to be under the impression that he was nineteen years old and everything was still before him. He wore leather trousers that went creak-creak-creak when he danced. And, oh, how he danced.

Gina had been so upset that Glenn couldn't manage even the vaguest impersonation of a father that she didn't want to send him any photographs of Pat when he was born. But I had put my foot down, insisting the man had a right to see pictures of his only grandchild. And I secretly thought that when Glenn saw our beautiful boy, he would be instantly smitten. When he forgot Pat's birthday for the third year in a row, I realised that I now had reasons of my own to hate the old hippy bastard.

'Maybe he's terrified of being a grandfather,' I said. 'Freaked out – isn't that what he'd call it?'

'Yes, there's that,' Gina said. 'And there's also the fact that he's a selfish arsehole who never grew up. Let's not forget that.'

Unlike Gina's mother and father, nobody had ever thought my parents were a golden couple. Nobody had ever thought that their union summed up the spirit of an era. My mum's picture had never appeared in a glossy magazine – although her prize-winning tomatoes had once been prominently featured in the local rag. But my parents had stayed together for a lifetime. And Gina and I were going to do the same.

Since our wedding day, we had friends who had met someone, fallen in love, married, divorced and started to hate their ex-partner's guts. That would never happen to us. Though our backgrounds were different, they meant we wanted the same thing.

I wanted a marriage that would last forever because that's what my parents had. Gina wanted a marriage that would last forever because that was exactly what her parents had never had.

'That's what is so good about us,' Gina told me, 'our dreams match.'

Gina was mad about my parents and the feeling was mutual. They looked at this blonde vision coming up the garden path with their little grandson, and the pair of them seemed to visibly swell with pleasure, smiling shyly behind their reading glasses and geraniums.

None of them could believe their luck. My parents thought they were getting Grace Kelly. Gina thought she was getting the Waltons.

'I'm going to take Pat to see your mum and dad,' she said before I went to work. 'Can I borrow your mobile phone? The battery's flat on mine.'

I was happy to lend it to her. I can't stand those things. They make me feel trapped.

A shiver of panic ran through the gallery.

'The fly's back!' the director said. 'We got the fly!'

There it was on the monitor. The studio fly.

Our fly was a huge beetle-black creature with wings as big as a wasp's and a carcass so bloated that it seemed to have an undercarriage. On a close-up of Marty reading his autocue, we watched the fly lazily circle our presenter's head and then bank off into a long slow climb.

The fly lived somewhere in the dark upper reaches of the studio, up there among the tangle of sockets, cables and lights. The fly only ever put in an appearance during a show, and up in the gallery the old-timers said that it was responding to the heat of the studio lights. But I always thought that the fly was attracted to whatever juice it is that human glands secrete when they are on live television. Our studio fly had a taste for fear.

Apart from the fly's aerial display, Marty's interview with Cliff was going well. The young green started off nervously, scratching his stubble, tugging his filthy dreadlocks, stuttering his way through rambling sentences and even committing television's cardinal sin of staring directly into the camera. But Marty could be surprisingly gentle with nervous guests and, clearly sympathetic to Cliff's cause, he eventually made the young man relax. It was only when Marty was winding up the interview that it all began to go wrong.

'I want to thank Cliff for coming in tonight,' Marty said, unusually solemn, brushing away the studio fly. 'And I want to thank all his colleagues who are living in trees out at the airport. Because the battle they are fighting is for all of us.'

As the applause swelled, Marty reached out and shook his guest's hand. Cliff held it. And continued to hold it. Then he reached inside the grubby, vaguely ethnic coat he was wearing and produced a pair of handcuffs. While Marty watched with an uncertain smile, Cliff snapped one metal ring around his own wrist and the other around Marty's.

'Free the birds,' Cliff said quietly. He cleared his throat.

'What – what is this?' Marty asked.

'Free the birds!' Cliff shouted with growing confidence. 'Free the birds!'

Marty shook his head. 'Do you have the key for this thing, you smelly little shit?'

Up in the gloaming of the gallery we watched the scene unfold on the bank of screens shining in the darkness. The director carried on choreographing the five cameras – 'Stay on Marty, two . . . give me a close-up of the handcuffs, four . . .' – but I had the feeling that you only get when live television is going very wrong, a feeling which somehow combines low-grade nausea, paralysis and terrible fascination, as it sits there in the pit of your stomach.

And suddenly there was the fly, hovering for a few seconds by Cliff's hair, then executing a perfect landing on the bridge of his nose.

'Free the birds!'

Marty considered his arm, unable to quite believe that he was really chained to this scruffy young man whose make-up was starting to melt under the lights. Then he picked up the water jug that was on the table between them and, almost as if he were trying to swat the studio fly, smashed it into Cliff's face. There was an eruption of blood and water. Marty was left holding just the jug's broken handle.

'Fuck the birds,' he said. 'And bugger the hole in the ozone layer.'

A floor manager appeared on camera, his mouth open with wonder, his headphones dangling around his neck.

Cliff cradled his crushed nose. Someone in the audience started booing. And that's when I knew we were stuffed. Marty had done the one thing he wasn't allowed to do on our kind of show. He had lost the audience.

Up in the gallery the telephones all began to ring at once, as if to commemorate my brilliant career going straight down the toilet. Suddenly I was aware of how hard I was sweating.

The studio fly appeared briefly on all the monitors, seemed to perform a victory roll, and then was gone.

'I'm so stupid,' Siobhan said hours later in the deserted gallery. 'It's all my fault. I should never have booked him. I should have guessed he wanted to use us to do something like this. He always was a selfish little bastard. Why did I do it? Because I was trying to impress everyone. And now look what's happened.'

'You're not stupid,' I told her. 'Marty was stupid. It was a good booking. Despite what happened, it's still a good booking.'

'But what's going to happen now?' she asked, suddenly seeming very young. 'What will they do to us?'

I shook my head and shrugged. 'We'll soon find out.' I was tired of thinking about it. 'Come on, let's get out of here.'

I had sent Marty home, smuggled out of the back of the building into a minicab which was waiting by the freight entrance, telling him to talk to no one. The press would tear him to pieces. We could count on that. I was more worried about what the station would do to him. And us. I knew they needed *The Marty Mann Show*. But did they need it this badly?

'It's so late,' Siobhan said, as we got into the lift. 'Where can I get a cab?'

'Where do you live?' I asked.

I should have guessed that she would say Camden Town. She just had to be living in one of those old working-class neighbourhoods that had been colonised by the people in black. Actually, she was not that far from our little house by Highbury Corner. We were at opposite ends of the same road. But Siobhan was at the end of the Camden Road where they aspired to Bohemia. I was at the end where they dreamed of suburbia.

'I can give you a lift,' I said.

'What – in your MGF?'

'Sure.'

'Great!'

We laughed for the first time in hours – although I couldn't quite work out why – and took the lift down to the underground carpark where the little red car was standing completely alone. It was late. Almost two. I watched her slide her legs under the dashboard.

'I'm not going to go on about it,' she said, 'but I just want to say you've been really sweet about tonight. Thank you for not being angry with me. I appreciate it.'

It was a gracious apology for something that she really didn't have to apologise for. I looked at her pale Irish face, realising for the first time how much I liked her.

'Don't be silly,' I said, quickly turning on the ignition to cover my embarrassment. 'We're on the same side, aren't we?'

It was a warm summer night and the city streets were as close to empty as they were ever going to get. Within twenty minutes we were driving past the shuttered flea market, the funky ethnic restaurants and all the second-hand stores with their grotesquely oversized signs – there were giant cowboy boots, colossal rattan chairs and monster slabs of vinyl, all of them looming above the street like the visions caused by some bad drug. Gina and I used to shop around here on Saturday afternoons. It was years ago now.

Siobhan gave me directions until we pulled up in front of a large white town house that had long ago been converted into flats.

'Well,' I said, 'goodnight then.'

'Thanks,' she said, 'for everything.'

'You're welcome.'

'Listen, I don't think I can sleep yet. Not after tonight. Do you want to come in for a drink?'

'A drink might keep me awake,' I said, hating myself for sounding like a pensioner who had to scurry back to the cocoa and incontinence sheets of his sheltered accommodation.

'You sure?' she asked, and I was ridiculously flattered that she seemed a bit disappointed. I also knew that she wouldn't ask again.

Go home, a voice inside me said. *Decline with a polite smile and go home now.*

And maybe I would have if I hadn't liked her so much.

Maybe I would have if it hadn't been such a rough night.

Maybe I would have if I wasn't coming up to thirty.

Maybe I would have if her legs had been a couple of inches shorter.

'Okay,' I said, far more casually than I felt. 'Sounds good.'

She looked at me for just a moment, and then we were kissing each other, her hands on the back of my neck, tugging at my hair with small, urgent fists. That's strange, I thought. Gina never does that.

five

A child can change in a moment. You turn your back for a couple of seconds, and when you look again you find they have already grown into someone else.

I can remember seeing Pat smile properly for the first time. He was a little fat bald thing, Winston Churchill in a Babygro, howling because his first teeth were pushing through, so Gina rubbed some chocolate on his sore gums and he immediately stopped crying and grinned up at us – this big, wide, gummy grin – as if we had just revealed the best secret in the world.

And I can remember him walking for the first time. He was holding himself up by the rail of his little yellow plastic stroller, swaying from side to side as if he were caught in a stiff breeze, as was his custom, when without warning he suddenly took off, his fat little legs sticking out of his disposable nappy and pumping furiously to keep up with the stroller's spinning blue wheels.

He bombed off out of the room and Gina laughed and said he looked as though he was going to be late for the office again.

But I can't remember when his games changed. I don't know when all his toddler's games of fire engines and Postman Pat videos gave way to his obsession with Star Wars. That was one of the changes which happened when I wasn't looking.

One minute his head was full of talking animals, the next it was all Death Stars, stormtroopers and light sabres.

If we let him, he would watch the three Star Wars films on video all day and all night. But we didn't let him – or rather Gina didn't let him – so when the television was turned off, he spent hours playing with his collection of Star Wars figures and grey plastic spaceships, or bouncing on the sofa, brandishing his light sabre, muttering scraps of George Lucas storylines to himself.

It seemed like only the day before yesterday when nothing gave him more pleasure than his collection of farmyard animals – or 'aminals', as Pat called them. He would sit in his bubble bath, a little blond angel with suds on his head, parading his cows, sheep and horses along the side of the tub, mooing and baaing until the water turned cold.

'I'm taking me bath,' he would announce. 'I need me aminals.'

Now his aminals were collecting dust in some forgotten corner of his bedroom while he played his endless games of intergalactic good and evil.

They were a lot like the games I could remember from my own childhood. And sometimes Pat's fantasies of brave knights, evil warlords and captured princesses sounded like echoes from a past that was long gone, as if he were trying to recover something precious that had already been lost forever.

Siobhan slept like someone who was single.

She edged right into the middle of the bed, her freckled limbs thrown out every which way, or she rolled over on her side, taking my share of the duvet with her. I lay there in that strange bed wide awake, clutching a scrap of sheet the size of a handkerchief as the room got light.

It was too soon to feel really bad. Pushed to the back of

my mind there was the thought of Gina and all the promises I had ever made to her – promises from the days when I was trying to persuade her to love me, the promises we made on our wedding day, and all the promises of all the days beyond, all that stuff about undying love and never wanting anyone else that I had really meant at the time. And still did, I discovered. Now more than ever, in a funny sort of way.

Later, this would all really get to me, and driving home I would look in the mirror wondering when I had become the kind of man I used to hate. But now was too soon for all that. I lay there as the night faded away thinking to myself – *well, that seemed to go okay.*

The reason that most men stray is opportunity, and the joy of meaningless sex should never be underestimated. It had been a meaningless, opportunistic coupling. That's what I had liked most about it.

What I liked least about it was that already I was starting to feel like a traitor.

And it was far from great. You try too hard with someone new. You try too hard to truly enjoy yourself. Sex with someone new is too much like taking your driving test. Yet when I thought of all the things that could have gone wrong – and all of them seemed to involve timing – it was okay.

Thank God, thank God, thank God.

But all the time I was with Siobhan, while half of me thought that this was probably the woman I hadn't realised I had been looking for all my life, this pale Irish beauty who would have lovely red-headed children, the other half of me sort of missed my wife.

I missed the easy familiarity you get with someone who you have been with for years. If I was going to be unfaithful, then I kind of wished it could have been with Gina.

Still, you can get tired of always being the man who pays the mortgage and calls the plumber and can't put together the self-assembly furniture. You get tired of being that man because in the end you don't feel like much of a man at all, more of a domestic appliance.

So you go home with some stranger who doesn't let you have your share of the duvet and end up feeling more tired of yourself than ever. Now what did I do with my trousers?

Daylight was creeping into the room as I got dressed, and glimpses of Siobhan's life floated into view. It was a good flat – the kind of comfortable, ordered flat I had always wanted but never had. I seemed to have gone straight from student squalor to domestic disorder.

The only photographs I could see were of Siobhan as a teenager, laughing as she held on to grinning dogs or some sweet-looking old people. Pictures of pets and parents.

There were some Japanese prints on the walls, of peasants struggling through a rainy landscape – stuff Gina would have liked. Shelves neatly stacked with books and CDs revealed a taste for literature that had made it to the movies and a weird mix of rock groups and mellow jazz – Oasis and U2 next to Stan Getz, Chet Baker and the softer side of Miles.

Looking at her books and records made me like her more. But probably looking at anyone's books and records will make you feel that way, even if they have lots of rubbish. Because what they like, and what they used to like, reveals things about them that they wouldn't normally choose to advertise.

I liked it that Siobhan had probably grown out of white rock bands and was now looking for something a bit more cool and sophisticated (it seemed unthinkable that she might have started out on Chet Baker and Miles Davis then later switched to U2 and Oasis). It showed she was still really young and curious, still discovering what she wanted from the world. Still inventing her life rather than trying to recover it.

It was very much a young single woman's apartment, the flat of a girl who could please herself. Despite the magazines and clothes that were strewn around, there was none of the real mess and clutter that you get in a place with a child, none of the homely chaos I was used to. You could make it all the way to the door without stepping on a Han Solo figurine.

But I sort of missed all of the clutter and mess that I knew from my home, just as I already missed being the kind of man who knows how to keep his promises.

Gina was crying when I got home.

I sat on the side of the bed, afraid to touch her.

'It was crazy after last night's show,' I said. 'I had to stay at the station.'

'I understand,' she said. 'It's not that.'

'Then what is it?'

'It's your mum, Harry.'

'What about her?'

'She's so good with Pat,' Gina choked. 'It just comes so easily to her. I'll never be like her. She's so patient, so kind. I told her that I sometimes feel like I'm going crazy – at home all day with nobody to talk to but a little boy. And when he's at his nursery school, it's even worse.' She looked up at me, her eyes brimming. 'I don't think she even understood what I was talking about.'

Thank Christ for that. For a moment there I thought she knew everything.

'You're the best mother in the world,' I said, taking her in my arms. And I meant it.

'No, I'm not,' she said. 'You want me to be. And I want to be, I really do. But just wanting something doesn't make it true.'

She cried some more, although her sobs had lost that

desperate edge. It happened sometimes, this crying, and I never knew what might start it off. To me it always looked as though she was crying about nothing. Not a good mother? I mean, what was all that about? Gina was a brilliant mother. And if she was feeling a bit isolated during the day, she could give me a call at work. My secretary would always take a message. Or there was an answering machine on my mobile. How could she ever be lonely? I just didn't get it.

I cuddled her until the tears were gone and then I went downstairs to make us some coffee. There were about a million messages on the machine. The world was going crazy about Marty. But I wasn't too worried about the newspapers and the station.

I had heard somewhere that a problem at work is like a plane crash that you can walk away from. It's not like your home life, where you can't get away from your problems, no matter how far you run.

six

Every father is a hero to his son. At least when they are too small to know any better.

Pat thinks I can do anything right now. He thinks I can make the world bend to my will – just like Han Solo or Indiana Jones. I know that one day soon Pat will work out that there are a few differences between Harrison Ford and his old dad. And when he realises that I don't actually own a bullwhip or a light sabre, he will never look at me in quite the same way again.

But before they grow out of it, all sons think their dad is a hero. It was a bit different with me and my dad. Because my father really was a hero. He had a medal to prove it and everything.

If your saw him in his garden or in his car, you would think he was just another suburban dad. Yet in a drawer of the living room of the pebble-dashed semi where I grew up there was a Distinguished Service Medal that he had won during the war. I spent my childhood pretending to be a hero. My dad was the real thing.

The DSM – that's important. Only the Victoria Cross is higher, and usually you have to die before they give you that. If you saw my dad in a pub or on the street you would think you knew all about him, just by looking at his corny jumper or his balding head or his family saloon or his choice of newspaper. You would think that you knew him. And you would be dead wrong.

I picked up the phone. I could ignore all the messages from the station and the papers. But I had to call my parents.

My old man answered the phone. That was unusual. He couldn't stand the phone. He would only pick it up if my mum was nowhere near it, or if he happened to be passing on his way from *Gardener's World* to the garden.

'Dad? It's me.'

'I'll get your mother.'

He was gruff and formal on the phone, as if he had never got used to using one. As if we had never met. As if I were trying to sell him something he didn't want.

'Dad? Did you see the show last night?'

I knew he had seen it. They always watched my show.

There was a pause.

'Quite a performance,' my father said.

I knew he would have hated it all – the swearing, the violence, the politics. I could even hear him bitching about the commercials. But I wanted him to tell me that it didn't matter. That I was forgiven.

'That's live television, Dad,' I said with a forced laugh. 'You never know what's going to happen.'

The old man grunted.

'It's not really my scene,' he said.

At some point during the nineties, my father had started using the vernacular of the sixties.

His speech was peppered with 'no ways' and 'not my scenes'. No doubt in another thirty years he would be collecting his pension and hobbling about in a zimmer frame while proclaiming that he was 'sorted' and 'mad for it'. But by then the world wouldn't know what he was going on about.

'Anyway,' I said, 'there's no need to worry. Everything's under control.'

'Worried? I'm not worried,' he said.

The silence hummed between us. I didn't know what to say to him. I didn't know how to bridge the gap between our separate worlds. I didn't know where to start.

'I'll get your mother.'

While he went to get my mum, Pat wandered into the room. He was in his pyjamas, his mass of dirty yellow hair sticking up, those eyes from Tiffany still puffy with sleep. I held out my arms to him, realising with a stab of pain how much I loved him. He walked straight past me and over to the video machine.

'Pat? Come here, darling.'

He reluctantly came over to me, clutching a tape of *Return of the Jedi.* I pulled him on to my lap. He had that sweet, musty smell kids have when they have just got up. He yawned wide, as I kissed him on the cheek. His skin was brand new. Freshly minted. The softest thing in the world.

And he still looked like the most beautiful thing in the world to me, like a little blond angel who had dropped off a cloud on his way to the celestial video shop.

Was he really that pretty? Or was that just my parental gene kicking in? Does every child in the world look like that to its parent? I still don't know.

'Did you have a nice time at Nanny and Granddad's house?' I asked.

He thought about it for a moment.

'They don't have any good films,' he said.

'What kind of films do they have?'

'Stupid ones. Just with . . . pictures.'

'You mean cartoons?'

'Yeah. Just pictures. For babies.'

I was indignant.

'Pat, they're not for babies. You don't like Dumbo? The elephant with the big ears? The poor little elephant who everyone makes fun of?'

'Dumbo's stupid.'

'Dumbo's great! What's wrong with Dumbo? Jesus Christ, I grew up with Dumbo!'

I was going to give him a lecture about the genius of Walt Disney and the glory of animation and the magic of childhood, but my mum came on the line.

'Harry? We were so worried. What on earth's going to happen? Will you lose your job?'

'Mum, I'm not going to lose my job. What happened last night – that's what we call good television.'

'Really, dear? I thought you once told me that it was good television if the guest attacked the host. I didn't know it worked the other way round.'

'It'll be fine,' I said, although she had a point. All the talk show punch-ups I could remember involved the presenter getting twatted. And not the other way around. 'They're giving me a new contract soon. Don't worry, Mum – we don't have to send Pat up a chimney just yet.'

'And what's wrong with Gina? She seems so – I don't know – down.'

'Gina's fine,' I said. 'What's Gina got to be down about?'

After I'd hung up, Pat beetled over to the video machine and stuffed in *Return of the Jedi*. The film began where he had left it – Princess Leia dressed as a slave girl at the feet of Jabba the Hutt. Drool slipped from Jabba's filthy lips as he considered his nubile concubine. My four-year-old son watched the scene impassively. This couldn't be good for him, could it?

'Why don't we have a game?' I suggested.

His face brightened.

'Okay!'

'What do you want to play?'

'Star Wars.'

Grinning from ear to ear, he hauled his favourite toy box in from his bedroom and emptied its contents on to the carpet. Out spilled all the things that made George Lucas famous. I sat on the floor with Pat while he carefully manoeuvred Han, Luke, Chewie and the two 'droids around his grey plastic Millennium Falcon.

'Princess Leia is being held captured on the Death Star,' Pat said.

'Captive,' I said. 'She's being held captive.'

'Being held captured,' he said. 'We have to rescue her, Daddy.'

'Okay.'

I sat playing with my son for a while, something I knew I didn't do nearly enough. Then after about five or ten minutes I decided I had better get in to work. It was going to be a long day.

Pat was disappointed that I was cutting our game short, but he cheered up when I switched his video of Princess Leia as a beautiful slave girl back on. He really liked that bit.

We were all over the papers.

The broadsheets saw the Cliff incident as symptomatic of a medium in terminal decline, desperate for cheap sensation in a world of visual overload and limited attention spans. The tabloids were going barmy about the blood and bad language.

All of them were calling for the head of Marty Mann. I was going to call him from the car, but I remembered that I had lent Gina my mobile phone.

Marty's company – Mad Mann Productions – had a floor in a building on Notting Hill Gate, a large open-plan office where self-consciously casual young people in their twenties worked on *The Marty Mann Show* or spent months planning future Mad Mann projects. The office was currently working on a game show for clever people, an alternative travel programme, a scuba diving series that would allow Marty to spend six months in the Maldives, and lots of other ideas which would almost certainly never actually happen.

We called it development. The outside world would call it farting around.

Only Marty and I had offices at Mad Mann. Actually they were more like little private cubbyholes, full of tapes and shooting scripts and a few VCRs. Siobhan was waiting for me in mine.

She had never been in my room before. We sort of blushed at each other. Why is it so easy to talk to someone before you go to bed with them for the first time and then suddenly so difficult?

'You should have woken me up before you left,' she said.

'I was going to,' I said, 'but you looked so . . .'

'Peaceful?'

'Knackered.'

She laughed. 'Well, it was a bad night. The only good thing about it was you.'

'Listen, Siobhan –'

'It's okay, Harry. I know. I'm not going to see you again, am I? Not like last night, I mean. You don't have to pretend. You don't have to say anything that isn't true. I know you're married.'

'You're a great girl, Siobhan. You really are.'

And I meant it.

'But you love your wife. I know, I know. Don't worry. I would prefer to hear it now than six months down the line. I would rather get it over with before I start to really like you. At least you're not like some of them. You didn't tell me that your wife doesn't understand you. You didn't tell me that you're probably going to break up. You didn't spend months sneaking out of the house to phone me. You're not a stinking hypocrite.'

Not a hypocrite? I spent last night with you and I'll spend tonight with my wife. Surely a hypocrite is exactly what I am?

'You're no good at all this, Harry. That's what I like about you. Believe me, there are not many around like you. I know. The last one – Jesus! I really thought he was going to leave his wife and that we were actually going to get married. That's how stupid I am.'

'You're not stupid,' I said, putting my arms around her.

We held each other tight, with real feeling. Now we were splitting up, we were getting on brilliantly.

Then she started to get choked up about how difficult it is to find a good man, while I thought to myself – *well, that's a relief. We aren't going to star in a remake of* Fatal Attraction *after all.*

I knew I was getting off lightly. Siobhan was going to let me go without pouring acid on my MGF or putting our pet rabbit in a pot. Not that we had a rabbit. But after the relief had subsided I was surprised to find that I felt a little hurt. Was it so easy to say goodbye to me?

'This always happens to me,' Siobhan laughed, although her eyes were all wet and shining. 'I always pick the ones who have already been picked. Your wife is a lucky woman. As I believe I said on that message I left you.'

'What message?'

'The message on your mobile.'

'My mobile?'

'I left a message on your mobile phone,' Siobhan said, drying her eyes with the back of her hand. 'Didn't you get it?'

seven

Gina was packing her bags when I got home. Stuffing a suitcase and a weekend bag up in our bedroom, pale-faced and dry-eyed, doing it as quickly as she could, taking only the bare essentials. As if she couldn't stand to be there any more.

'Gina?'

She turned and looked at me, and it was as if she were seeing me for the very first time. She seemed almost giddy with contempt and sadness and anger. Especially anger. It scared the shit out of me. She had never looked at me like that before.

She turned again, picking something up from the little table by her side of the bed. An ashtray. No, not an ashtray. We didn't have any ashtrays. She threw my mobile phone at me.

She had always been a lousy shot – and we had had one or two arguments where things had been thrown – but there wasn't the room to miss, and it smacked hard against my chest. I picked it up off the floor and a bone just above my heart began to throb.

'I'll never forgive you for this,' she said. 'Never.' She nodded at the phone. 'Why don't you listen to your messages?'

I pressed the icon on the phone which showed a little envelope. Siobhan's voice came crackling through, wry and sleepy and completely out of place in our bedroom.

'It's always a bad sign if they go before you wake up . . . but please don't feel bad about last night . . . because I don't . . . your wife is a lucky woman . . . and I'm looking forward to working with you . . . Bye, Harry.'

'Did you sleep with this girl, Harry?' Gina asked, then shook her head. 'What's wrong with me? Why am I even bothering to ask? Because I want you to tell me that it isn't true. But of course it's true.'

I tried to put my arms around her. Not hugging her. Just trying to hold on to her. Trying to calm her down. To stop her getting away. To stop her from leaving me. She shook me off, almost snarling.

'Some little slut at the office, is she?' Gina said, still throwing clothes into her suitcase. She wasn't even looking at the clothes she was packing. She didn't look as though she thought she was a lucky woman. 'Some little slut who thinks you can do her a few favours.'

'She's actually a really nice girl. You'd like her.'

It was a truly stupid thing to say. I knew it the second the words left my big mouth, but by then it was already too late. Gina came across the bedroom and slapped me hard across the face. I saw her wince with pain, her eyes suddenly brimming with tears. She didn't really know how to hit someone. Gina wasn't like that.

'You think it was romantic or passionate or some such bullshit,' Gina said. 'But it's none of those things. It's just grubby and sordid and pathetic. Really pathetic. Do you love her?'

'What?'

'Are you in love with this girl?'

'It wasn't like that.'

'If she wants my life, she can have it. All of it. Including you. Especially you, Harry. Because it's all a lie.'

'Please, Gina. It was a mistake. A terrible mistake, okay?'

I scrambled for words. 'It didn't mean a thing,' I told her.

She started laughing and crying at the same time. 'Don't you understand that makes it worse?' she said. 'Don't you understand anything at all?'

Then she really started to sob, her shoulders all hunched up and shaking, not even trying to wipe away tears that seemed to start somewhere deep inside her chest. I wanted to put my arms around her. But I didn't dare touch her.

'You're just like my father,' she said, and I knew it was the worst thing in the world she could ever say. 'Just like him.'

'Please, Gina,' I said. 'Please.'

She shook her head, as if she could no longer understand me, as if I had stopped making any kind of sense.

'What, Harry? Please? What? You're like a fucking parrot. Please what?'

'Please,' I said, parrot-like. 'Please don't stop loving me.'

'But you must have *known*,' she said, slamming shut the suitcase, most of her clothes still unpacked and scattered all over our bed. The other bag was already full. She was almost ready to leave. She was nearly there now. 'You must have known that this is the one thing I could never forgive,' she said. 'You must have known that I can't love a man who doesn't love me – and only me. And if you didn't know that, Harry, then you don't know me at all.'

I once read somewhere that, in any relationship, the one who cares the least is the one with all the power.

Gina had all the power now. Because she didn't care at all any more.

I followed her as she dragged her suitcase and bag out into the hall and across to Pat's bedroom. He was carefully placing Star Wars figures into a little Postman Pat backpack. He smiled up at us.

'Look what I'm doing,' he said.

'Are you ready, Pat?' Gina asked.

'Nearly,' he said.

'Then let's go,' she said, wiping away the tears with her sleeve.

'Okay,' Pat said. 'Guess what?' He was looking at me now, his beautiful face illuminated by a smile. 'We're going on a holiday.'

I let them get as far as the door and then I realised that I couldn't stand losing them. I just couldn't stand it. I grabbed the handle of Gina's bag.

'Where are you going? Just tell me where you're going.'

She tugged at the bag, but I refused to let go. So she just left me holding it as she opened the front door and stepped across the threshold.

I followed them out into the street, still holding Gina's bag, and watched her strap Pat into his child seat. He had sensed that something was very wrong. He wasn't smiling any more. Suddenly I realised that he was my last chance.

'What about Pat?' I said. 'Aren't you going to think about him?'

'Did you?' she said. 'Did you think about him, Harry?'

She heaved her suitcase into the back of the estate, not bothering to get the other bag back from me. She let me keep it.

'Where will you stay?'

'Goodbye, Harry.'

And then she left me. Pat's face was small and anxious in the back seat. Gina stared straight ahead, her eyes hard and shining. She already looked like someone else. Someone I didn't know. She turned on the ignition.

I watched the car until it had turned the bend in the street where we lived, and only then was I aware of the curtains that were twitching with curiosity. The neighbours were watching us. With a sinking feeling, I realised that's the kind of couple we had become.

I carried Gina's bag back into the house, where the phone was ringing. It was Marty.

'Can you believe what these fuckers are saying about me in the papers?' he said. 'Look at this one – BAN MAD MANN FROM OUR TELLY. And this one – A MANN OF FEW WORDS – ALL OF THEM ****ING OBSCENE. What the fuck are they implying? These people want my *job*, Harry. My mum is really upset. What are we going to do?'

'Marty,' I said. 'Gina's left me.'

'She's left you? You mean she's walked out?'

'Yeah.'

'What about the kid?'

'She's taken Pat with her.'

'Has she got someone else?'

'Nothing like that. It was me. I did something stupid.'

Marty chuckled in my ear. 'Harry, you dirty dog. Anyone I know?'

'I'm frightened, Marty. I think she might be gone for good.'

'Don't worry, Harry. The most she can get is half of everything you own.'

He was wrong there. Gina had already walked out with everything I had ever wanted. She had got the lot.

eight

Barry Twist worked for the station. Over the past year, I had been to dinner at his home, and he had come to dinner at mine. But, the way our world worked, we weren't exactly friends. I couldn't tell him about Gina. It felt like I knew a lot of people like that.

Barry had been the first of the television people to take Marty and me out to lunch when we were doing the radio show. He had thought the show would work on television and, more than anyone, he had been responsible for putting us there. Barry had smiled all the way through that first lunch, smiled as though it was an honour to be on the same planet as Marty and me. But he wasn't smiling now.

'You're not a couple of kids dicking about on the radio any more,' he said. 'These are big boys' rules.' His conversation was full of stuff like 'big boys' rules', as though working in television was a lot like running an undercover SAS unit in South Armagh. 'We had nine hundred phone calls complaining about the fucking language.'

I wasn't going to roll over and die just because he was our commissioning editor.

'Spontaneous TV, Barry, that's what you pay him for. On this kind of show it's not what the guests say that makes news. It's what they do.'

'We don't pay him to assault the guests.' Barry indicated

the papers on his desk with a thin little smile. I picked up a fistful of them.

'Front page of the *Mirror* and the *Sun*,' I said. 'A two-column story on page one of the *Telegraph* . . . Nice colour picture of Marty on page three of *The Times* . . .'

'This is the wrong kind of news,' Barry said. 'And you know it. I repeat – this isn't talk radio any more. You're not just being listened to by a couple of cranks and their cats. And it's not as though we're some crappy little satellite outfit scratching in the dust for viewers. There are advertisers, there are broadcasting authorities, there are viewers' associations, there is the man upstairs. And please take my word for it, Harry – they are all going fucking ape shit.'

I put the papers back on his desk, my fingers black with print. As nonchalantly as I could manage, I rubbed my hands together. But the print wouldn't come off.

'Let me tell you what's going to happen, Barry. Marty is going to be called every name in the book – and next week we will get our biggest ratings ever. That is what's going to happen. And they are going to be talking about that last show for years – that's going to happen too.'

Barry Twist shook his head.

'It was too much. It's not just Marty. The man upstairs is getting called every name in the book – and he doesn't like it. Over the last twelve months *The Marty Mann Show* has had drunken guests, abusive guests and guests who have tried to remove their clothes. But this is the first time you've had a guest who has been beaten up. It's got to stop. We can't have a manifestly unstable man going out live on national television.'

'What are you suggesting?'

'No more live shows, Harry. Record the show on the afternoon of transmission. That way, if Marty assaults anyone else – or decides to beat them to death with his ego – we can edit it out.'

'As live? You want us to go as live? Marty will never stand for it.'

'Make him stand for it, Harry. You're his producer – do some producing. Doesn't your contract come up for renewal soon?'

I knew they couldn't drop Marty. He was already too big for that. But for the first time I understood that it wasn't Marty's hide that was on the line.

It was mine.

Despite all his games of death and destruction, Pat was a very loving child. He was always hugging and kissing people, even total strangers – I had once seen him embracing the old geezer who cleaned our street – in a way that was no longer permissible, or even wise, in the lousy modern world.

But Pat didn't know or care about any of that. He was four years old and he was full of love. And when he saw me on the doorstep of his other grandfather's home he went crazy, holding my face in his hands and kissing me on the lips.

'Daddy! Are you staying with us? Staying with us on our – on our – on our holiday at granddad Glenn's?'

I found them the day after they left. It wasn't difficult. I made a few phone calls to Gina's friends from college, the ones who had turned up for her thirtieth birthday party, but it had been years since she had been really close to any of them. She had let them drift out of her life, kidding herself that she could get everything she needed from me and Pat. That's the trouble with a relationship as close as ours – when it comes undone, you're left with no one.

It didn't take me long to work out that Gina had been so desperate for somewhere to stay that she had gone home to her father, who was currently between marriages.

Glenn lived in a small flat right on the edge of the *A to*

Z, among golf clubs and green belts, a neighbourhood that he must have thought looked a bit like Woodstock when he first moved in. But instead of jamming with Dylan and The Band, every day Glenn took the commuter train to his guitar shop in Denmark Street. He was home when I knocked on his door, greeting me with what seemed like real warmth as I stood holding my son.

'Harry, how are you doing, man? Sorry about your troubles.'

In his early fifties now, what was left of Glenn's hair was carefully arranged to approximate the Viking feather cut of his prime. He was still snake-hip thin, and still wore clothes that would have looked appropriate on a Jimi Hendrix roadie. And he was still good-looking, in a faded old roué kind of way. But he must have looked pretty funky walking down the King's Road in 1975.

For all his faults – the missed birthdays, the forgotten promises, the fact that he tended to fuck off and leave his wife and kids every few years – Glenn wasn't really an evil man. He had a friendly, easy charm about him, flashes of which I could see in Gina. Glenn's fatal flaw was that he had never been able to see further than the end of his own gratification. Yet all the wounds he inflicted were unintentional. He wasn't a cruel man, not unless weakness is another kind of cruelty.

'Looking for Gina?' he said, putting an arm around me. 'She's inside.'

Inside Glenn's modest flat, The Verve were booming from the speakers. He wasn't one of those classic rock freaks with a copy of *Mojo* and his gramophone needle stuck forever on the music of his youth. Glenn's devotion to the cause was so great that he always liked to keep up with the big new bands. I didn't know how he managed it.

Gina came out of the little guest room, serious and pale. Very pale. I felt like kissing her. But I didn't.

'Hello, Harry.'

'Can we talk?'

'Of course. There's a park nearby.'

We took Pat. Glenn pointed out that, for all the surrounding greenery, the park was actually a fair distance away, past a sad little string of shops and endless big posh houses. So I suggested we took the MGF. Pat almost squealed with delight. Although she wasn't a four-year-old boy, I hoped Gina might also be impressed – from the moment I had seen that car I knew I wanted to drive around with some special person by my side. Now I saw with terrible clarity that the special person had always been Gina. But she didn't say anything until we arrived at the park.

'No need to worry about recapturing your youth, Harry,' she said, swinging her legs out of my new car. 'You never really lost it.'

Pat skipped on ahead of us, brandishing his light sabre and howling. When he arrived at the climbing frame he stood there in silence, shyly watching two bigger boys clamber around on the higher part of the frame. He was always full of admiration for bigger boys. Gina and I watched our son watching them.

'I miss you like crazy,' I said. 'Please come home.'

'No,' she said.

'It wasn't some mad, passionate affair. It was just one night.'

'It's never just one night. If you can do it once, you can do it again. Again and again and again. And next time it will be easier. I've seen it all before, Harry. Seen it all with Glenn.'

'Jesus, I'm nothing like your dad. I don't even wear an earring.'

'I should have known,' she said. 'The romantic ones are always the worst. The hearts and flowers brigade. The ones who promise never to look at another woman. Always the worst. Because they always need that new fix. That regular shot of romance. Don't you, Harry?'

I didn't like the way she was talking about me, as though I were indistinguishable from every other man in the world, as though I were just one of the hairy adulterous masses, as though I were just another sad salary man who got caught fucking around. I wanted to still be the one.

'I'm sorry I hurt you, Gina. And I'll always be sorry about it. You're the last person in the world I would want to hurt.'

'It can't always be a honeymoon, you know.'

'I know, I know,' I said, but deep down inside what I thought was – *Why not? Why not?*

'We've been together for years. We have a child together. It can never be all that Romeo and Juliet crap again.'

'I understand all that,' I said, and most of me really did. But a tiny, tiny part of me wanted to say – *Oh, I'm off then.*

Gina was right – I wanted us to be the way we were at the start. I wanted us to be like that forever. And you know why? Because we were both so happy then.

'You think it's been easy living in our house?' she said, suddenly flaring up. 'You think it's easy listening to you whining about not being a teenager any more, getting Pat to stop watching Star Wars for five minutes, taking care of the house? And you're no help. Like every man on the planet, you think that as long as you do your little job, your work is done.'

'Well,' I said, taken aback. 'I'm surprised you didn't leave years ago.'

'You didn't give me a reason. Until now. I'm only thirty,

Harry. Sometimes I feel like an old woman. You *tricked* me,' she said. 'You tricked me into loving you.'

'Just come back home. You and me and Pat. I want it to be the way it was before.'

'It can never be that way again. You changed it all. I trusted you and you broke my trust. You made me feel stupid for trusting you.'

'People don't break up because of a one-night stand, Gina. It's not what grown-ups do. You don't chuck it all away because of something like that. I know it hurts. I know what I did was wrong. But how did I suddenly go from being Mr Wonderful to Mr Piece of Shit?'

'You're not Mr Piece of Shit, Harry.' She shook her head, trying to stop herself from crying. 'You're just another guy. I can see that now. No different from the rest. Don't you get it? I invested so much in you being *special.* I gave up so much for you, Harry.'

'I know you did. You were going to work abroad. You were going to experience another culture. It was going to be incredible. And then you stayed here because of me. I know all that. That's why I want to make this marriage work. That's why I want to try again.'

'I've been doing a lot of thinking,' Gina said, 'and I've worked out that nobody is interested in a woman who stays at home with her child. Not even her husband. Especially not her husband. I'm so boring, he has to sleep around.'

'That's not true.'

'Looking after your child – it should be the most respected job in the world. It should be worth more than going to any office. But it's not. Do you know how many people at your fucking little television dinners and parties and launches have made me feel like nothing at all? *And what do you do?*' She made it sound like a sneer. '*And what do you do?* Me? Well, I don't do anything. I just stay at home and look after my little boy. And they stare right through you – the women as well as the men, in fact the women are probably worse – as though you're some kind of moron. And I'm twice as smart as half of these people you work with, Harry. Twice as smart.'

'I know you are,' I said. 'Listen, Gina – I'll do anything. What do you want?

'I want my life back,' she said. 'That's all, Harry. I want my life back.'

That sounded like trouble.

nine

Things hadn't quite worked out how my dad had planned. Not with his home. And not with me.

When my parents had bought the place where I grew up, the area had been countryside. But the city had been creeping closer for thirty years. Fields where I had roamed with an air rifle were now covered with ugly new houses. The old High Street was full of estate agents and solicitors. What my parents had thought would always be a living, breathing episode of *The Archers* started being swallowed by the suburbs from the moment we moved in.

My mum didn't much mind the changes – she was a city girl, and I can remember her complaining about our little town's lack of shops and a cinema when I was a kid – but I felt for my dad.

He didn't like the army of commuters who clogged the railway station on weekdays and the golf courses at the weekend. He didn't like the gangs of would-be yobs who drifted around the estates pretending they were getting down in South Central LA. He hadn't expected to be so close to crowds and crime this late in life.

And then there was me.

My parents came to the door expecting to see the three of us arriving for dinner. But there was only their son. Bewildered, they watched me drive past their gate, looking for somewhere to park. They didn't get it.

When I was a kid, there were no cars parked on this street – one garage for every family had been more than enough. Now you practically had to give yourself a double hernia looking for a parking place. Everything had changed.

I kissed my mum and shook my dad's hand. They didn't know what was happening. There was going to be too much food. They were expecting Gina and Pat. They were expecting happy families. And what they got was me.

'Mum. Dad. There's something I have to tell you.'

The old songs were playing. Tony Bennett live at Carnegie Hall was on the stereo, although it could just have easily been Sinatra or Dean Martin or Sammy Davis Junior. In my parents' home the old songs had never stopped playing.

They sat in their favourite chairs staring up at me expectantly. Like a couple of kids. I swear to God they thought I was going to announce the imminent arrival of another grandchild. And I stood there feeling the way I so often felt in front of my parents – more like a soap opera than a son.

'Well, it looks like Gina's left me,' I said.

The tone was all wrong – too casual, too glib, too uncaring. But the alternative was getting down on all fours and weeping all over their shag carpet. Because after yesterday's trip to the park and a second sleepless night in a bed that was far too big for just me, I was finally starting to believe that she might not be coming back. Yet I felt I was too old to be bringing my parents bad news. And they were too old to have to hear it.

For a few moments they didn't say a word.

'What?' said my father. 'Left you where?'

'Where's the baby?' my mother said. She got it immediately.

'Pat's with Gina. At her dad's place.'

'That punk rocker? Poor little thing.'

'What do you mean she's left you?' the old man demanded.

'She's walked out, Dad.'

'I don't understand.'

He really didn't get it. He loved her and he loved us and now all of that was finished.

'She's buggered off,' I said. 'Done a runner. Gone. Scarpered.'

'Language,' my mother said. She had her fingers to her mouth, as if she were praying. 'Oh, Harry. I'm so sorry.'

She came across the room towards me and I sort of flinched. It would be okay if they weren't kind to me. I could get through it if they didn't put their arms around me and tell me that they understood. But if they were going to be kind, I didn't think I could take it. I knew it would all get clogged up inside me. Luckily, the old man came to the rescue. Good old Dad.

'Walked out?' my dad said angrily. 'What – you're getting a divorce? Is that what you mean?'

I hadn't really thought about that. Getting a divorce? Where do you start?

'I guess so. Yes. That's what people do, isn't it? When they split up.'

He stood up, the colour draining from his face. His eyes were wet. He took off his glasses to wipe them. I couldn't stand to look at him.

'You've ruined my life,' he said.

'What?'

I couldn't believe what I was hearing. My marriage falls apart and he becomes the victim? How did that happen? I was sorry that his precious daughter-in-law had walked out of his life. I was sorry that his grandson had seen his parents break up. And most of all, I was sorry that his son had turned out to be just another dumb schmuck bumbling towards the divorce courts. But I wasn't going to let my father hog the starring role in our little tragedy.

'How have I managed to ruin your life, Dad? If anyone's the victim here, it's Pat. Not you.'

'You've ruined my life,' he said again.

My face burned with shame and resentment. What was he so bitter about? His wife had never left him.

'Your life is over,' I told him angrily.

We looked at each other with something approaching hatred and then he walked out. I could hear him shuffling around upstairs. I was already sorry about what I had said. But I felt that he had given me no choice.

'He doesn't mean it,' my mum said. 'He's upset.'

'Me too,' I said. 'Nothing bad ever happened to me before, Mum. I've had it easy. Nothing bad ever happened to me before now.'

'Don't listen to your father. He just wants Pat to have what you had. Two parents. Somewhere settled and stable to build his life. All that.'

'But it's never going to be like that for him, Mum. Not if Gina's really gone. I'm sorry, but it's never going to be that simple.'

My dad came back down eventually and I tried to give them some background as we waded through dinner. There had been trouble at home, things hadn't been too good for a while, we still cared about each other. There was hope.

I left out all the stuff about me fucking a colleague from work and Gina feeling that she had thrown her life away. I thought that might make them choke on their lamb chops.

When I left, my mum gave me a big hug and told me that things would turn out all right. And my dad did his best too – he put his arm around me and told me to call if there was anything they could do.

I couldn't look at him. That's the trouble with thinking

your father is a hero. Without saying a word, he can make you feel that you are eight years old again, and you have just lost your first fight.

'Our guest next tonight no needs introduction,' Marty said for the third time in a row. '*Fuck* . . . *fuck* . . . *fuck* . . . what is wrong with this pigging autocue?'

There was nothing wrong with the autocue and he knew it.

Up in the gallery, the director murmured soothing words into his earpiece about going for the rehearsal again when he was ready. But Marty tore off his microphone and walked off the floor.

When we were live, Marty had always been fearless in front of an autocue. If he made a mistake, if he stumbled over the words rolling before him, he just grinned and kept going. Because he knew that he had to.

Recording was different. You know you can always stop and start again if you are taping. This should make things easier, of course. But it can paralyse you. It can do things to your breathing. It can make you start to sweat. And when the camera catches you sweating, you're dead.

I caught up with him in the green room where he was ripping open a beer. This worried me more than the tantrum on set. Marty was a screamer, but he wasn't a drinker. A few beers and his nerves would be so steady he wouldn't be able to move.

'Recording a show is a different rhythm,' I told him. 'When you're live, the energy level is so high that you just zip through it from beginning to end. When you're recording, the adrenaline has to be more controlled. But you can do it.'

'What the fuck do you know about it?' he asked me. 'How many shows have you presented?'

'I know that you don't make it easier by ranting about the autocue girl.'

'She's moving that thing too fast!'

'Yes, to keep up with you,' I said. 'If you slow down, so will she. Marty, it's the same girl we've been using for a year.'

'You didn't even try to keep the show live,' he sulked.

'As soon as you smacked Tarzan, all this was inevitable. The station can't take a chance on that happening again. So we do it live on tape.'

'Live on fucking tape. That says it all. Whose side are you on, Harry?'

I was about to tell him, when Siobhan stuck her head around the door of the green room.

'I've managed to find a replacement for the autocue girl,' she said. 'Shall we try again?'

'We're watching telly-vision,' Pat told me when I arrived at Glenn's place.

I picked him up and kissed him. He wrapped his arms and legs around me like a little monkey as I carried him into the flat.

'You're watching TV with Mummy?'

'No.'

'With granddad Glenn?'

'No. With Sally and Steve.'

In the little living room there was a boy and a girl in their mid teens tangled around each other on the sofa. They were wearing the kind of clothes that don't look quite right without a snowboard.

The girl – thin, languid, blank – looked up at me as I came into the room. The boy – podgy, spotty, blanker – tapped the TV's remote control against his lower teeth and didn't take his eyes from a video of an angry man with no shirt on, a singer who looked as though he should be helping police with their enquiries. Glenn would know who he was. Glenn would have all his records. He made me wonder if music was getting crap or I was getting old. Or both.

'Hi,' the girl said.

'Hi. I'm Harry – Pat's dad. Is Gina around?'

'Nah – she went to the airport.'

'The airport?'

'Yeah – she had to, you know, what do you call it? Catch a plane.'

I put Pat down. He settled himself among the Star Wars figures that were scattered over the floor, shooting admiring glances at the spotty youth. Pat really did love big boys. Even dumb, ugly big boys.

'Where did she go?'

The girl – Sally – frowned with concentration.

'To China. I think.'

'China? Really? Or was it Japan? It's very important.'

Her face brightened.

'Yeah – maybe Japan.'

'There's a big difference between China and Japan,' I said.

The boy – Steve – looked up for the first time.

'Not to me,' he said.

The girl laughed. So did Pat. He was only little. He didn't know what he was laughing about. I realised that his face was dirty. Without a bit of encouragement, Pat had a very cavalier attitude to personal hygiene.

Steve turned back to the television with a satisfied smirk, still tapping the remote control against his lower teeth. I could have cheerfully stuffed it down his throat.

'Do you know how long she'll be gone?'

Sally grunted a negative, absent-mindedly squeezing Steve's beefy leg.

'Glenn not around?' I said.

'Nah – my dad's at work,' said Sally.

So that was it. The girl was one of Glenn's abandoned kids, from a marriage or two after Gina's mother.

'You visiting?' I asked.

'Staying here for a while,' she said. 'Been getting a lot of hassle from my mum. Whining about my friends, my clothes, the time I come home, the time I don't come home.'

'Is that right?'

'"You're treating this place like a hotel,"' Sally screeched. '"You're too young to smoke that stuff. Blah blah blah."' She sighed with the weariness of the very young. 'The usual. It's not as though she didn't do it all herself back in the dark ages, the hypocritical old bitch.'

'Bitch,' said Steve.

'She's a bitch,' smiled Pat, a Star Wars figure in each tiny fist, and Steve and Sally laughed at him.

This is how it works, I thought. You break up and your child becomes a kind of castaway, set adrift in a sea of daytime television and ducked responsibilities. Welcome to the lousy modern world where the parent you live with is a distant, contemptible figure and the parent you don't live with feels guilty enough to grant you asylum any time things get too tense at home.

But not my boy.

Not my Pat.

'Get your coat and your toys,' I told him.

His dirty little face brightened.

'Are we going to the park?'

'Darling,' I said, 'we're going home.'

ten

We were meant to be celebrating.

Barry Twist had come up with the idea of a fifteen-minute delay system for the show, meaning we would go back to doing the thing live, but with a short time-lag before transmission as insurance against either the host or the guests going bananas.

The station was happy because it meant there was still time to edit out anything that was really going to give the advertisers the running squirts, and Marty was happy because it meant he no longer got paralysis of the lower autocue.

So Marty took me to lunch at his favourite restaurant, a fashionably spartan basement where well-fed people in television put authentic Italian peasant food on their expense accounts.

Like most of the places we went to, its bare floorboards and white walls made it look more like a gym than a restaurant, possibly to make us feel that we were doing ourselves some good in there. When we arrived just after two – I was running late after delivering Pat to my parents, leaving him with them because with Gina gone there was no one to pick him up after nursery – the place was already crowded, but the reception desk was empty.

A waitress approached us. She was clearly not having a good day. She was hot and flustered and there was a red wine stain on her white uniform. She kept doing this thing with her hair, which was shiny and black and cut in one of those old-fashioned bell shapes that you imagine on women in an F. Scott Fitzgerald novel, or on Hong Kong girls in the fifties. A bob. That's what you call it. The fringe kept flying up as she stuck out her bottom lip and blew some air through it.

'Can I help you?' she said.

'We have a table,' Marty said.

'Sure,' she said, picking up the book of reservations. 'Name?'

'Marty Mann,' he said, with that special little emphasis that indicated he expected her to recognise him now and practically faint with excitement. But Marty didn't mean a thing to her. She was American.

'Sorry,' she said, consulting the book. 'Can't see your name on the list, sir.'

Then she gave us a smile. She had a good smile – wide, white and open. One of those smiles that just shines.

'Believe me,' Marty said, 'we do have a table.'

'Not here, you don't.'

She slammed the book shut and moved to walk away.

Marty blocked her path. She looked pissed off. She stuck out her bottom lip and blew some air through her fringe. 'Excuse *me*,' she said.

She was tall and thin with a dancer's legs and wide-set brown eyes. Good-looking, but not a kid. Maybe a couple of years older than me. Most of the people working in this restaurant that looked like a gym were cool young things who clearly thought they were on their way to somewhere better. She wasn't like that at all.

She looked at Marty and massaged the base of her spine as though it had been aching for a long time.

'Do you know how important I am?' Marty asked.

'Do you know how busy I am?' she replied.

'We might not be on the list,' Marty said very slowly, as though he were talking to someone who had just had part of their brain removed, 'but one of my people called Paul – the manager? You do know Paul?'

'Sure,' she said evenly. 'I know Paul.'

'Paul said it would be okay. It's always okay.'

'I'm real glad that you and Paul have got such an understanding relationship. But if I don't have a spare table, I can't give you one, can I? Sorry again.'

This time she left us.

'This is fucking stupid,' Marty said.

But Paul had spotted us and quickly crossed the crowded restaurant to greet his celebrity client.

'Mr Mann,' he said, 'so good to see you. Is there a problem?'

'Apparently there's no table.'

'Ah, we always have a table for you, Mr Mann.' Paul's Mediterranean smile flashed in his tanned face. He had a good smile too. But it was a completely different smile to the one she had. 'This way, please.'

We walked into the restaurant and got the usual stares and murmurs and goofy grins that Marty's entrance always provoked. Paul snapped his fingers and a table was brought from the kitchen. It was quickly covered with a tablecloth, cutlery, a wedge of rough-hewn peasant bread and a silver bowl of olive oil. A waitress appeared by our side. It was her.

'Hello again,' she said.

'Tell me this,' said Marty. 'Whatever happened to the good old stereotype of the American waitress? The one who serves you with a smile?'

'It's her day off,' the waitress said. 'I'll get you the menu.'

'I don't need the menu,' Marty said. 'Because I already know what I want.'

'I'll get it anyway. For your friend here. We have some interesting specials today.'

'Shall we have this conversation again once you've turned on your hearing aid?' Marty asked. 'Read my lips – we eat here all the time. We don't need the menu.'

'Give her a break, Marty,' I said.

'Yeah.' She looked at me for the first time. 'Give me a break, Marty.'

'I'll have the twirly sort of pasta with the red stuff on top and he'll have the same,' Marty said.

'Twirly pasta.' She wrote it down on her little pad. 'Red stuff. Got it.'

'And bring us a bottle of champagne,' Marty said, patting the waitress on her bum. 'There's a good girl.'

'Get your sweaty hand off my butt before I break your arm,' she said. 'There's a good boy.'

'Just bring us a drink, will you?' Marty said, quickly removing his hand.

The waitress left us.

'Christ, we should have ordered a takeaway,' Marty said. 'Or got here a bit earlier.'

'Sorry about the delay,' I said. 'The traffic –'

'Doesn't matter,' he said, raising a hand.

'I'm glad you agreed to the fifteen-minute delay system,' I told him. 'I promise you that it's not going to harm the show.'

'Well, that's just one of the changes we're making,' Marty said. 'That's why I wanted to talk to you.'

I waited, at last registering that Marty was nervous. He had a set of breathing exercises which were meant to disguise him having the shakes, but they weren't working now. And we weren't celebrating after all.

'I also want Siobhan more involved with the booking of guests,' Marty said. 'And I want her up in the gallery every week. And I want her to keep the station off my back.'

I let it sink in for a moment. The waitress brought our champagne. She poured two glasses. Marty took a long slug and stared at his glass, his lips parting as he released an inaudible little belch. 'Pardon me,' he said.

I let my glass stand on the table.

'But all those things – that's the producer's job.' I tried on a smile. 'That's *my* job.'

'Well, those are the changes I want to make.'

'Wait a minute. I'm not getting a new contract?'

Marty spread his hands as if to say – what can I do? It's a crazy world!

'Listen, Harry. You don't want me to move you sideways into some little nothing job that you could do with your eyes closed. That would look terrible, wouldn't it?'

'Marty,' I said. 'Marty. Hold on. Hold on just a minute. I really need this job. Now more than ever. There's the thing with Gina – I've got Pat living with me – and I don't know what's going to happen. You know all that. And I can't lose my job. Not now.'

'I'm sorry, Harry. We need to make some changes.'

'What is this? Punishment for not being available twenty-four hours a day when my marriage is breaking up? I'm sorry I wasn't in the office this morning, okay? I can't leave my son alone. I had to –'

'Harry, there's no need to raise your voice. We can do this in a civilised fashion.'

'Come on, Marty. You're Mister fucking Controversy. You're not worried about a little scene, are you?'

'I'm sorry, Harry. Siobhan's in. You're out. And you'll thank me for it one day. This could be the best thing that's ever happened to you. No hard feelings?'

The little shit actually held out his hand. I ignored it, getting up as quickly as I could and smacking my thighs against the side of the table.

He shook his head, all disappointed in me.

I began to walk out of the restaurant, my legs aching and my cheeks burning, only turning back when I heard Marty shriek with pain.

Somehow the waitress had spilled an entire plate of pasta in his lap.

'Boy, I'm sorry,' she said. 'Would you like a little parmesan on that?'

My parents drove Pat home. My mother went around turning on all the lights while my father asked me how work was going. I told him that it was going great.

They stayed with Pat while I did our shopping at the local supermarket. It was only a five-minute drive away, but I was gone for quite a while because I was secretly watching all the women I took to be single mothers. I had never even thought about them before, but now I saw that these women were heroes. Real heroes.

They were doing it all by themselves. Shopping, cooking, entertaining, everything. They were bringing up their children alone.

And I couldn't even wash Pat's hair.

'His hair's filthy,' my mum said as my parents were leaving. 'It needs a good old wash.'

I knew that already. But Pat didn't want me to wash his hair. He had told me so when I had casually dropped hair-washing into the conversation after we had come back from Glenn's. Pat wanted his mother to wash his hair. The way she always did.

Yet we couldn't put it off any longer. And soon he was standing in the middle of the soaking wet bathroom floor wearing just a pair of pants, his dirty blond hair hanging down over eyes that were red from tears and the baby shampoo that Gina still used on him.

It wasn't working. I was doing something wrong.

I knelt by his side. He wouldn't look at me.

'What's wrong, Pat?' I asked him.

'Nothing.'

We both knew what was wrong.

'Mummy's gone away for a little while. Won't you let Daddy wash your hair?'

Stupid question. He shook his head.

'What would a Jedi Knight do at a time like this?' I asked him.

He didn't reply. Sometimes a four-year-old doesn't bother to reply.

'Listen,' I said, fighting back the urge to scream. 'Do you think that Luke Skywalker cries when he has his hair washed?'

'Don't know, don't care.'

I had tried to wash his hair with him leaning into the bath, but that hadn't worked. So now I helped him out of his pants, scooped him up and placed him sitting down in the tub. He wiped snot from his little nose while I ran the water until it was the right temperature.

'This is fun, isn't it?' I said. 'We should do this together more often.'

He scowled at me. But he leaned forward and allowed me to run the water over his head. Then he felt my hands applying more shampoo and something snapped. He stood up, throwing one of his legs over the side of the bath in a pitiful attempt to escape.

'Pat!' I said. 'Sit down, please.'

'I want Mummy to do it!'

'Mummy's not here! Sit down!'

'Where is she? Where is she?'

'I don't know!'

He blindly tried to climb out of the bath, howling as the suds dripped into his eyes. I pushed him back down and held him there, quickly hosing off the shampoo and trying to ignore his screams.

'This is not how a Jedi Knight acts,' I said. 'This is how a baby acts.'

'I'm not a baby! You are!'

I towelled him down, took him by the hand and dragged him back to his bedroom, his little legs moving quickly to keep up with me. We glared at each other while I put him in his pyjamas.

'Making such a fuss,' I said. 'I'm really disappointed in you.'

'I want *Mummy*.'

'Mummy's not here.'

'But when will I see her again?' he said, suddenly plaintive. 'That's what I want to know.'

'I don't know,' I said. 'I don't know, darling.'

'But what did I do?' he said, and it broke my heart. 'I didn't mean it, I didn't mean it at all.'

'You didn't do anything. Mummy loves you very much. You'll see her soon. I promise.'

Then I took him in my arms, smelling the shampoo that I had missed, holding him close for a long time, and wondering how two flawed adults had ever managed to make something so perfect.

I read him *Where The Wild Things Are* until he fell asleep. When I came out of his room there were three messages on the answer machine. All of them were from Gina.

'I'm sorry, but I had to get away for a while. You'll never know how much you hurt me. Never. It was supposed to be for life, Harry. Not until one of us got a bit bored. Forever

– not until one of us decided that things were getting a bit dull in the old marital bed. It doesn't work like that. It can never work like that. Do you think I could let you touch me when I know you've been touching someone else? Your hands, your mouth . . . I can't stand all that. The lying, the sneaking around, the sound of someone crying themselves to sleep every night. I had enough of that when I was growing up. If you think –'

The machine cut her off. It only let you talk for a certain amount of time. There was a beep and then her second message. She was calmer now. Or trying to be.

'I just spoke to Glenn. He told me that you collected Pat. That really wasn't necessary. He was perfectly happy there. And I know how busy you are at work. But if you are going to look after him until I get back, then you need to know that he has his hair washed every Sunday. And don't let him put sugar on his Coco Pops. He can go to the toilet by himself – you know that already – but sometimes he forgets to lift the lid. Make sure he cleans his teeth. Don't let him watch Star Wars videos all the time. If he doesn't sleep in the afternoon then make sure he's in bed by no later than –'

Another beep. A final message. Not so calm any more, the words tumbling out.

'Just tell Pat I love him, okay? Tell him I'll see him very soon. Take good care of him until then. And don't ever feel too sorry for yourself, Harry. You're not Mr Wonderful. Women all over the world look after children alone. Millions of them do it. Literally millions. What's so special about you?'

Long after I had turned off all the lights, I stayed there watching our boy sleep. And I saw that I had let everyone down.

Gina. My mother and father. Even Marty. I hadn't been strong enough, I hadn't loved them enough, I hadn't been the man they wanted me to be, or the man that I wanted myself to be. In different ways, I had betrayed them all.

I pulled the blanket that Pat had kicked off up to his shoulders, making one final promise, which this time I would keep – I would never betray this child.

Yet there was a distant voice, like someone calling on a bad line from the other side of the world, and it kept on saying – *you did, you did, you already did.*

eleven

Children live in the moment. The good thing about falling out with them is that they have forgotten all about it the next day. At least that's what Pat was like at four years old.

'What do you want for breakfast?' I asked him.

He considered me for a moment.

'Green spaghetti.'

'You want spaghetti? For breakfast?'

'Green spaghetti. Yes, please.'

'But – I don't know how to make green spaghetti. Have you had it before?'

He nodded. 'In the little place across the big road,' he said. 'With Mummy.'

We lived on the wrong side of Highbury Corner, next to the Holloway Road rather than Upper Street, the side where there were junk stores rather than antique shops, pubs rather than bars, quiet little cafés instead of trendy restaurants. Some of these cafés were so quiet that they had the air of the morgue, but there was a great one right at the end of our street, a place called Trevi where they spoke English at the counter and Italian in the kitchen.

The beefy, good-humoured men behind the counter greeted Pat by name.

'This is the place,' he said, settling at a table by the window.

I watched the waitress come out of the kitchen and approach our table. It was her. She still looked tired.

'What can I get you boys?' she said, smiling at Pat. There was a trace of the south in her voice which I hadn't noticed when I was with Marty.

'Do you do anything that could be described as green spaghetti?'

'You mean spaghetti pesto? Sure.'

'Isn't that too hot for you?' I asked Pat.

'Is it green?' he said.

I nodded. 'It's green.'

'That's what I have.'

'How about you?' she asked.

'I'll have the same,' I replied.

'Anything else?'

'Well, I was wondering how many jobs you've got.'

She looked at me properly for the first time.

'Oh, I remember you,' she said. 'You were the guy with Marty Mann. The one who told him to give me a break.'

'I thought you didn't recognise him.'

'I've been here for almost a year. Of course I recognised the little dickhead.' She glanced at Pat. 'Excuse me.'

He smiled at her.

'I don't get to watch much TV – you don't in this job – but his ugly mug is always in the papers. Doing not very much, far as I can see. Funnily enough, you were my last customers. Paul didn't like my style.'

'Yeah, well. If it's any consolation, I lost my job around the same time as you.'

'Yeah? And you didn't even get to drop a plate of pasta on Marty's shrivelled little –' She looked quickly at Pat. 'Head. Anyway. He deserved it.'

'He sure did. But I'm sorry you lost your job.'

'No big deal. A girl can always get another job as a waitress, right?'

She looked up from her pad. Her eyes were so far apart

that I had trouble looking at them both at the same time. They were brown. Huge. She turned them on Pat.

'Having lunch with your dad? Where's your mom today?'

Pat glanced at me anxiously.

'His mother's in Tokyo,' I said.

'That's Japan,' Pat said. 'They drive on the same side of the road as us. But when it's nighttime there, it's daytime here.' I was surprised he remembered so much of what I had told him. He knew almost as much about the place as I did.

She looked at me with those wide-set brown eyes and I thought that somehow she knew that our little family was all broken and scattered. Which was absurd. How could she have possibly known?

'She's coming back soon,' Pat said.

I put my arm around him.

'That's right,' I said. 'But it's just us for a while.'

'That's unusual, isn't it?' the waitress said. 'I mean – you looking after your boy. Not many men do that.'

'I guess it happens,' I said.

'I guess it does,' she said.

I could see that she liked me a little bit now that she knew I was taking care of Pat. But of course she didn't know me. She didn't know me at all. And she had me all wrong.

She saw a man alone with a child and she thought that somehow that must make me better than other men – more kind-hearted, more compassionate, less likely to let a woman down. The new, improved male of the species, biologically programmed for child-caring duties. As if I had planned for my life to work out this way.

'How about you?' I asked her. 'What brought you to London from – where?'

'Houston,' she said. 'Houston, Texas. Well, what brought me was my partner. Ex-partner. This is where he's from.'

'That's a long way to come for some guy, isn't it?'

She seemed genuinely surprised. 'Do you think so? I always thought that, if you really love someone, you'll follow them anywhere.'

So she was the romantic kind.

Under that tough, touch-me-again-buster-and-you'll-get-linguini-in-your-lap exterior, she was one of those women who was willing to turn her world inside out for some man who almost certainly didn't deserve it.

Maybe my wife was right. The romantic ones are the worst.

Gina came home late the next day.

Pat and I were playing on the floor with his toys. Neither of us reacted to the diesel rumble of a black cab pulling up outside. But we looked at each other as we heard the rusty clank of our little gate, then a key turning in the front door, and finally the sound of her footsteps in the hall. Pat turned his face to the door.

'Mummy?'

'Pat?'

And suddenly there she was, smiling down at our son, bleary from the twelve-hour flight from Narita and lugging her old suitcase that still had a scarred sticker from our distant holiday in Antigua.

Pat flew into her arms and she held him so tight that he disappeared inside the folds of her light summer coat, all of him gone, apart from the top of his head and a tuft of hair that was exactly the same shade of blond as his mother's. Their faces were so close that you couldn't see where Gina ended and Pat began.

I watched them feeling something better than happy. I was sort of glowing inside, believing that my world had been restored. And then she looked at me – not cold, not angry, just from a great distance, as though she was still somewhere far away and always would be – and my spirits sank.

She hadn't come back for me.

She had come back for Pat.

'You all right?' I asked her.

'Bit tired,' she said. 'It's a long flight. And you get back the same day that you leave. So the day never seems to end.'

'You should have told us you were coming. We would have met you at the airport.'

'That's okay,' she said, holding Pat out to inspect him.

And I could see that she had come back because she thought I couldn't do it. She thought I wasn't up to looking after our child alone while she was away. She thought that I wasn't a real parent, not the way that she was a real parent.

Still holding Pat, her eyes took in the squalid ravages of the living room, a room which seemed to confirm that even her own lousy father was a better prospect than me.

There were toys everywhere. A video of *The Lion King* playing unwatched on the television. Two takeaway pizza boxes – one large, one small – from Mister Milano squatting on the floor. And Pat's pants from yesterday sitting on the coffee table like a soiled doily.

'Goodness, look at your dirty hair,' Gina said brightly. 'Shall we give it a good old wash?'

'Okay!' Pat said, as if it were an invitation to Disneyland.

They went off to the bathroom and I made a start on clearing up the room, listening to the sound of running water mixing with their laughter.

'I've been offered a job,' she told me in the park. 'It's a big job. As a translator for an American bank. Well, more of an interpreter, really. My written Japanese is too rusty for translating documents. But my spoken Japanese is more than good enough for interpreting. I would be sitting in on meetings, liaising with clients, all that. The girl who's been doing the job – she's really nice, a Japanese-American, I met her – is leaving to have a baby. The job's mine if I want it. But they need to know now.'

'Wait a minute,' I said. 'This job's in Tokyo?'

She looked away from Pat's careful negotiation of the lower reaches of the climbing frame.

'Of course it's in Tokyo,' she said sharply. Her eyes returned to our boy. 'What do you think I've been doing out there?'

To be honest, I thought she was having a break. Seeing a few old Japanese and expatriate friends from her year out, shooting about on the bullet train, taking in a few temples in Kyoto, just getting away from it all for a while.

I had forgotten that she wanted her life back.

That's what she had been doing after moving into her father's flat – making a few international calls, reviving some old contacts, seeing if she still had an option on all the things she had given up for me.

I knew her well enough to realise that she was dead serious about this job. But I still couldn't quite believe it.

'You're really going to take a job in Japan, Gina?'

'I should have done it years ago.'

'For how long? Forever?'

'The contract is for a year. After that, well, we'll see.'

'What about Pat?'

'Well, Pat comes with me. Obviously.'

'Pat goes with you? To Tokyo?'

'Of course. I'm not going to leave him here, am I?'

'But you can't just uproot him,' I said, trying to keep the note of hysteria out of my voice. 'Where are you going to live?'

'The bank will sort that out.'

'What's he going to eat?'

'The same things he eats here. Nobody's going to make him have miso soup for breakfast. You can get Coco Pops in Japan. You don't have to worry about us, Harry.'

'I am worried. This is serious, Gina. Who's going to look after him when you're working? What about all his stuff?'

'His stuff?'

'His bike, his toys, his videos. All his stuff.'

'We'll ship it over. How hard can it be to crate up a four-year-old's possessions?'

'What about his grandparents? You going to crate them up and ship them out? What about his friends at the nursery? What about me?'

'You can't stand the thought of me having a life without you, can you? You really can't stand it.'

'It's not that. If this is really what you want, then I hope it works out for you. And I know that you can do it. But Pat's life is here.'

'Pat's life is with me,' she said, a touch of steel in her voice. Yet I could tell that I was getting through to her.

'Leave him with me,' I said. Pleaded, really. 'Just until you get settled, okay? A few weeks, a couple of months, whatever it takes. Just until you're on top of the job and you've found somewhere to live. Let him stay with me until then.'

She watched me carefully, as if I were making sense but still couldn't be trusted.

'I'm not trying to take him away from you, Gina. I know I could never do that. But I can't stand the thought of him being looked after by some stranger in some little flat while you're at the office trying to make a go of your new job. And I know you can't stand it either.'

She watched our boy slowly clamber to the top of the climbing frame. He carefully turned so that he could grin at us.

'I have to take this chance,' she said. 'I have to know if I can do it. It's now or not at all.'

'I understand.'

'I'd call him every day, of course. And send for him as soon as I can. Maybe you can bring him out.'

'That sounds good.'

'I love Pat. I love my son.'

'I know you do.'

'You really think you can look after him by yourself for a while, do you?'

'I can manage it. I can.' We looked at each other for a long time. 'Just until you're settled.'

We took Pat home and put him to bed. Happy and tired, he was soon asleep, lost in dreams that he wouldn't remember in the morning.

Gina chewed her bottom lip.

'Don't worry,' I said. 'I'll take good care of him.'

'Just until I'm settled.'

'Just until you're settled.'

'I'll be back for him,' Gina said, more to herself than to me.

And eventually, she did come back for him. But things were a bit different by then.

By the time Gina came back for Pat there wouldn't be yesterday's pants on the coffee table and Mister Milano pizza boxes on the floor. By the time she came back for our boy, I would be something like a real parent, too.

That's where Gina got it wrong. She thought that she could change but that I would always remain the same.

The way my parents dealt with Gina going away, they tried to turn Pat's life into a party.

Overnight their non-negotiable 'one Coke a day' rule

was abolished. Suddenly when Pat and I turned up at their house there were gifts waiting for him, such as a special edition *Return of the Jedi* ('New Scenes, New Sounds, New Special Effects'). More and more they wanted him to stay over with them, no doubt hoping to replace my gloomy face and moody silences with their canned laughter, laughter so strained that it made me feel like weeping.

And now one of them always wanted to accompany us to the gates of Pat's nursery school. It was a long drive for them – reaching us took at least an hour going anti-clockwise around the M25 in the rush hour – but they were willing to do it day after day.

'As a special treat,' my dad said, groaning as he folded his old legs into my low-slung car.

I knew what they were doing and I loved them for it. They were trying to stop their grandson from crying. Because they were afraid that if he started crying, then he would never stop.

But Pat's life wasn't a party with his mother gone. And no amount of Star Wars merchandise or good intentions could make it a party.

'What are you doing today then, Pat?' my father said, his grandson perched on his lap in the MGF's passenger seat. 'Making some more Plasticine worms? Learning about Postman Pat and his black-and-white cat? That'll be good!'

Pat didn't reply. He stared at the congealed early-morning traffic, his face pale and beautiful, and no amount of jolly banter from my old man could draw him out. He only spoke when we were at the gates of the Canonbury Cubs nursery.

'Don't want to go,' he muttered. 'Want to stay home.'

'But you can't stay home, baby,' I said, about to use the great parental cop-out and tell him that Daddy had to go to work. But of course Daddy didn't have a job any more. Daddy could stay in bed all day and still not be late for work.

One of the teachers came to collect him, looking at me meaningfully as she gently took his hand. It wasn't the first time that Pat had been reluctant to leave me. In the week since Gina had been gone, he didn't like to let me out of his sight.

With my dad promising him unimaginable fun and games at the end of the day, we watched Pat go, holding on to the teacher's hand, his blue eyes swimming in tears, his bottom lip starting to twitch.

He would probably make it to the little classroom without cracking. They might even get his coat off. But by the time the Plasticine worms were unveiled he would lose it, inconsolable, sobbing his heart out while the other kids stared at him or impassively went about their four-year-old business. We wouldn't have to look at any of that.

'I remember when you were that age,' my dad said as we walked back to the car. 'I took you to the park in the week between Christmas and the New Year. Bloody freezing, it was. You had your little sledge with you. I had to drag you on it all the way from home. And at the park we watched the ducks trying to land on the frozen lake. They just kept coming in to land and – boom! Sliding on their bums across the ice. And you just laughed fit to burst. Laughed and laughed, you did. We must have watched them for hours. Do you remember that?'

'Dad?'

'What?'

'I don't know if I can do it, Dad.'

'Do what?'

'I don't know if I can look after Pat alone. I don't know

if I'm up to it. I told Gina I could do it. But I don't know if I can.'

He turned on me, eyes blazing, and for a moment I thought that he was going to hit me. He had never laid a finger on me in my life. But there's always a first time.

'Don't know if you can do it?' he said. 'Don't know if you can do it? You have to do it.'

It was easy for him to say. His youth might have been marred by the efforts of the German army to murder him, but at least in his day a father's role was set in stone. He always knew exactly what was expected of him. My dad was a brilliant father and – here's the killer – he didn't even have to be there to be a brilliant father. *Wait until your father gets home* was enough to get me to behave. His name just had to be evoked by my mother and suddenly I understood all I needed to know about being a good boy. *Wait until your father gets home*, she told me. And the mere mention of my father was enough to make everything in the universe fall into place.

You don't hear that threat so much today. How many women actually say, *Wait until your father gets home* now? Not many. Because these days some fathers never come home. And some fathers are home all the time.

But I saw he was right. I might not do it as well as he had – I couldn't imagine Pat ever looking at me the way I looked at my old man – but I had to do it as well as I could.

And I did remember the ducks trying to land on the frozen lake. Of course I remembered the ducks. I remembered them well.

Apart from the low wages, unsociable hours and lack of standard employee benefits such as medical insurance, probably the worst thing about being a waitress is that in the course of her work she has to deal with a lot of creeps.

Like a little apron and a notepad, creeps come with the job. Men who want to talk to her, men who ask her for her number, men who just refuse to leave her alone. Creeps, the lot of them.

Creeps from building sites, creeps from office blocks, creeps in business suits, creeps with their bum crack displayed above the back of their jeans, creeps of every kind – the ones who think they're funny, the ones who think they're God's gift, the ones who think that just because she brings them the soup of the day, they're in with a chance.

She was serving a table of creeps when I took my seat at the back of the café. One creep – a business creep rather than a building-site creep – was leering up at her while his creep friends – all pinstripes, hair gel and mobile phones – smiled with admiration at his creepy cheek.

'What's your name?'

She shook her head. 'Now why do you need to know my name?'

'I suppose it's something typically southern, is it? Peggy-Sue? Becky-Lou?'

'It's certainly not.'

'Billie-Joe? Mary-Beth?'

'Listen, are you going to order or what?'

'What time do you get off?'

'Did you ever date a waitress?'

'No.'

'Waitresses get off late.'

'You like being a waitress? Do you like being a service executive in the catering industry?'

That got a big laugh from all the creeps who thought they looked pretty cool talking about nothing on a mobile phone in the middle of a crowded restaurant.

'Don't laugh at me.'

'I'm not laughing at you.'

'Long hours, lousy pay. That's what being a waitress is like. And plenty of assholes. But enough about you.' She tossed the menu on the table. 'You think about it for a while.'

The business creep blushed and grinned, trying to butch it out as she walked away. His creepy friends were laughing, but they were not quite as hearty as before.

She came over to me. And I still didn't know her name.

'Where's your boy today?'

'He's at nursery school.' I held out my hand. 'Harry Silver.'

She looked at me for a moment and then she smiled. I had never seen a smile like it. Her face lit up the room. It just shone.

'Cyd Mason,' she said, shaking my hand. It was a very soft handshake. It's only men who try to break your bones when you shake their hand. It's only creeps.

'Pleased to meet you, Harry.'

'As in Sid Vicious?'

'As in Cyd Charisse. You probably never even heard of Cyd Charisse, did you?'

'She danced with Fred Astaire in Paris in *Silk Stockings.* She had a haircut like the one you've got now. What's that haircut called?'

'A China chop.'

'A China chop, is it? Yeah, Cyd Charisse. I know her. She was probably the most beautiful woman in the world.'

'That's Cyd.' She was impressed. I could tell. 'My mother was crazy about all those old MGM movies.'

I caught a glimpse of her childhood, saw her sitting at the age of ten in front of the TV in some little apartment, the air-con turned up to full blast and her mother getting all choked up as Fred twirled Cyd across the Left Bank. No wonder she had grown up with a warped view of romance. No wonder she had followed some creep to London.

'Can I tell you about the specials?' she said.

She was really nice and I felt like talking to her about Houston and MGM musicals and what had happened between her and the man who had brought her to London. Instead I kept my eyes on my pasta and my mouth shut.

Because I didn't want either of us to start thinking that I was just another creep.

Gina was gone and she was everywhere. The house was full of CDs I would never listen to (sentimental soul music about love lost and found), books I would never read (women struggling to find themselves in a world full of rotten men) and clothes I would never wear (skimpy M&S underwear).

And Japan. Lots of books about Japan. All the classic texts that she had urged me to read – *Black Rain*, *Pink Samurai*, *Barefoot Gen*, *Memories of Silk and Straw* – and a battered old copy of *Snow Country*, the one I had actually read, the love story she said I had to read if I was ever going to understand.

Gina's things, and they chewed up my heart every time I saw them.

They had to go.

I felt bad about throwing it all out, but then if someone leaves you, they really should take their stuff with them. Because every time I saw one of her Luther Vandross records or Margaret Atwood novels or books about Hiroshima, I felt all the choking grief rise up inside me again. And in the end I just couldn't stand it any more.

Gina, I thought, with her dreams of undying love and hard-won independence, Gina who could happily accommodate Naomi Wolf's steely, post-feminist thoughts and Whitney Houston's sweet nothings.

That was my Gina all right.

So I got to work, stuffing everything she had left behind into rubbish sacks. The first one was quickly full – did the woman never throw anything away? – so I went back into the kitchen and got an entire roll of heavy-duty bin-liners.

When I had finished removing all her paperbacks, the book shelves looked like a mouth full of broken teeth.

Throwing away her clothes was much easier because there was no sorting involved. Soon her side of our wardrobe was empty apart from mothballs and wire coat hangers.

I felt better already.

Starting to sweat hard, I prowled the house mopping up what was left of her presence. There were all the Japanese prints from her single days. A painting she had bought on our holiday to Antigua when Pat was a baby. A pink razor on the edge of the bath. A couple of Gong Li videos. And a photograph of our wedding day with her looking like the most beautiful girl in the world and me grinning like a happy, dopey bastard who never believed he could get so lucky.

All trash now.

Finally, I looked in the laundry basket. Among Pat's Star Wars pyjamas and my faded Calvins there was the old Gap T-shirt that Gina liked to sleep in. I sat on the bottom of the stairs holding that T-shirt for a while, wondering what she was sleeping in tonight. And then I threw it into the last rubbish sack.

It's amazing how quickly you can remove the evidence of someone's life from a house. It takes so long to put your mark on a home, and so little time to wipe it away.

Then I spent another few hours fishing it all out of the rubbish sacks and carefully returning the clothes, the CDs, the books, the prints and everything else to exactly where I had found them.

Because I missed her. I missed her like mad.

And I wanted all her things to be just as she had left them, all ready and waiting for her in case she ever felt like coming back home.

twelve

A bit of a panic attack in the supermarket.

Nothing serious, nothing serious. Just the sudden realisation that a man like me, whose little family had broken into tiny pieces, was daring to do his shopping at the feeding trough of the happy family. I felt like an impostor.

Being surrounded by all the grotesques of aisle eight should have made me feel better – the women with tattoos, the men with earrings, the little children dressed like adults, the adults dressed like adolescents – but they didn't.

I was shaking and sweating at the checkout, wanting it to be over with, wanting to be out of there, my breath coming in short, shallow gasps, and by the time the semi-comatose teen on the till handed me my change while idly scratching at his nose ring, I felt on the very edge of screaming or weeping or doing both at once.

I burst out of the supermarket into the open air and just at that moment the bag containing dinner for Pat, the cat and me lost its handle, and my shopping haemorrhaged into the street.

Gina's supermarket bags never broke. We had done our weekly shop together every Saturday for seven years, and I never once saw a carrier bag that she had loaded spring a leak. But maybe Gina didn't buy as many microwave meals as me. They weigh a ton, those things.

Suddenly there were cat tins and ready-in-one-minute

meals everywhere, under the wheels of shopping trolleys, at the feet of a young man selling the *Big Issue* and skittering towards the road. I was on my hands and knees picking up a box that promised, 'A Taste Of Tuscany' when they saw me.

'Harry?'

It was Marty. And there was a girl with him. Siobhan.

Marty and Siobhan. Holding hands!

The shock of seeing them together cancelled out any embarrassment I felt at being caught with my shopping scattered all over the pavement. But only for a moment. Then my face started burning, burning, burning.

It had been a while since I had seen them, although not that long. I had been out for just over a month. But my producer's mind didn't actually think in terms of weeks and months. Five shows, I thought. They have done five shows without me.

They looked good. Even Marty, the ugly little git. They were both wearing dark glasses and white trousers. Siobhan was carrying a supermarket bag containing a French loaf and a bottle of something dry, white and expensive. There might even have been a sliver of pâté in there, too. But their bag wasn't about to break. Two confident professionals doing a little light shopping before returning to their glamorous, high-powered careers, they didn't look like the kind of people who had to worry about stocking up on cat food.

'Here, let me help you,' Siobhan said, bending down to catch a can of beef and heart Whiskas as it rolled towards the gutter.

Marty had the decency to look a little ashamed, but Siobhan seemed glad to see me, if a bit surprised to find me grovelling around on the pavement picking up cans of cat food, toilet rolls and microwave dinners, rather than picking up a BAFTA.

'So – what are you doing these days?' she asked.

'Oh – you know,' I said.

Pacing up and down my living room for hours every day – 'Like a caged tiger', my mum reckoned – after I dropped Pat off at nursery school, worried sick about how he was doing, worried sick that he might be crying again. And waiting for Gina to phone at four o'clock sharp every afternoon – midnight on her side of the world – although I always handed the receiver straight to Pat, because I knew that he was the only reason she was calling.

And what else? Talking to myself. Drinking too much, not eating enough, wondering how my life ever got so fucked up. That's what I'm doing these days.

'Still considering my options,' I said. 'How's the show?'

'Better than ever,' Marty said. A bit defiant.

'Good,' Siobhan said, pleased but neutral, as though she didn't think the old show's fate would really concern a hotshot such as myself. 'Ratings are slightly up.'

I felt like puking.

'That's great,' I smiled.

'Well – we'd better move,' Marty said. It wasn't just me. A few shoppers had started to smirk and point. Was it really him?

'Yeah, me too,' I said. 'Got to run. Things to do.'

Siobhan grabbed me and planted a quick kiss on my cheek. It made me wish that I had shaved today. Or yesterday. Or the day before.

'See you around, Harry,' Marty said.

He held out his hand. No hard feelings. I went to shake it, but he was holding a can of cat food. I took it from him.

'See you, Marty.'

Fucking bastards.

Fucking bastards the lot of you.

* * *

The phone rang when I was in the middle of bathing Pat. I left him in the tub – he could happily stay in there for hours, he was like a little fish – and went down the hall, picking up the phone with wet hands, expecting my mum. But there was a little transcontinental blip as the connection was made and suddenly Gina was in my ear.

'It's me,' she said.

I looked at my watch – it was only twenty to four. She was early today.

'He's in the bath.'

'Leave him. I'll call back at the usual time. I just thought he might be around. How is he?'

'Fine,' I said. 'Fine, fine, fine. You're still there, are you?'

'Yes. I'm still here.'

'How's it going?'

I could hear her taking a breath. Gina taking a breath on the other side of the world.

'It's a lot harder than I thought it would be,' she said. 'The economy is all screwed up. I mean, really screwed up. My company's laying off locals, so there's not much job security for a *gaijin* whose Japanese is a bit rustier than she thought. But the work's okay. Nothing I can't handle. The people are kind. It's everything else. Especially living in a place about the size of our kitchen.' She took another breath. 'It's not easy for me, Harry. Don't think I'm having the time of my life.'

'So when are you coming home?'

'Who said I was coming home?'

'Come on, Gina. Forget all that stuff about finding yourself. This is all about punishing me.'

'Sometimes I wonder if I did the right thing coming out here. But a few words from you and suddenly I know I did the right thing.'

'So you're staying out there, are you? In your flat the size of our kitchen?'

'I'll be back. But just to collect Pat. To bring him out here. I really want to make a go of it, Harry. I hope you can understand.'

'You're kidding, Gina. Pat out there? I can't even get him to eat beans on toast. I can just see him tucking into a plate of sprats on rice. And where's he going to live? In a flat the size of our kitchen?'

'Christ, I wish I'd never mentioned the size of the bloody flat. I just can't talk to you any more.'

'Pat stays with me, okay?'

'For now,' she said. 'That's what we agreed.'

'I'm not handing him over until it's the best thing for him. Not you. Him. That's what I agree to, okay?'

Silence. And then a different voice.

'That's for the lawyers to decide, Harry.'

'You tell your lawyer – Pat stays with me. You were the one who left. Tell him that.'

'And you tell your lawyer that you were the one who was fucking around!'

'I can't – I don't have a lawyer.'

'You should get one, Harry. If the thought of trying to steal my son from me ever crosses your mind, then get a very good lawyer. But you don't mean it. We both know you can't look after Pat permanently. You can't even look after yourself. You just want to hurt me. Look – do you want to talk about it like adults? Or do you want to argue?'

'I want to argue.'

There was a sigh.

'Is Pat there?'

'No – he's out having dinner with a few of his fast-set pals. Of course he's here. He's four years old. Where do you expect him to be? On a hot date with Naomi

Campbell? I told you he's in the bath. Didn't I tell you that?'

'You told me. Can I talk to him?'

'Sure.'

'And Harry?'

'What?'

'Happy birthday.'

'That's *tomorrow*,' I said angrily. 'My birthday is *tomorrow*.'

'Where I am it's almost tomorrow.'

'I'm not in Japan, Gina. I'm here.'

'Happy birthday anyway. For tomorrow.'

'Thanks.'

I got Pat from the bath, dried him down and wrapped him in a towel. Then I knelt in front of him.

'Mummy wants to talk to you,' I said. 'She's on the phone.'

It was the same every day. There was a jolt of surprise in those blue eyes and then something that could have been either joy or relief. By the time I gave him the receiver he looked more guarded.

'Hello?' he whispered.

I guess I was expecting bitter tears, angry recriminations, torrents of emotion. But Pat was always cool and composed, muttering one-word answers to Gina's questions until he eventually handed me the phone.

'I don't need to talk to Mummy any more,' he said quietly.

He walked off to the living room, the towel still wrapped around him like a shawl, leaving a trail of small wet footprints behind him.

'I'll call him again tomorrow,' Gina told me, more upset than I had expected her to be, in fact so unravelled that I felt better than I had for days. 'Is that okay, Harry?'

‘Any time is fine,’ I said, wanting to ask her how we had got to a place where we threatened each other with lawyers, how two people who had been so close could become a divorce-court cliché.

Was it really all my fault? Or was it just random bad luck, like getting hit by a car or catching cancer? If we had loved each other so much, then why hadn’t it lasted? Was it really impossible for two people to stay together forever in the lousy modern world? And what was all of this going to do to our son?

I really wanted to know. But I couldn’t ask Gina any of that stuff. We were on opposite sides of the world.

thirteen

We were halfway to my parents' house when my mobile rang. It was my mother. She was usually a calm, unflappable woman, the still centre at the heart of the family. But not today.

'Harry!'

'What's wrong?'

'It's your dad.'

God, I thought – he's dead. On my thirtieth birthday. Even today he has to be the centre of attention.

'What happened?'

'We were burgled.'

Christ. Even out there. Even that deep into the suburbs. Nowhere was safe any more.

'Is he okay? Are you okay?'

'Please, Harry . . . come quick . . . the police are on their way . . . please . . . I can't talk to him . . .'

'Hang on, okay? Hang on, Mum. I'll be there as quickly as I can.'

I hung up, swinging the car out into the fast lane and slamming the accelerator to the floor. The MGF surged forward, as if this were the moment it had been built for.

On the passenger seat next to me, Pat laughed out loud.

'Wicked,' he said.

Now where did he get that from?

My mother opened the door in her best dress, all dolled

up for her son's birthday. But her party clothes were undermined by the white, shaken look on her face.

'It's awful, Harry. We were burgled. In the living room. Look.'

She took Pat off to the kitchen, gently deflecting his questions about his granddad, and I let myself into the living room, steeling myself for the sight of my father half-dead in a dark puddle of blood. But the old man was standing by the fireplace, his sunburned face creased with pleasure. I had never seen him look happier.

'Hello, Harry. Happy birthday, son. Have you met our guests?'

At his feet were two youths, belly down on the carpet with their hands tied behind their backs.

At first I thought I recognised them – they had exactly the same washed-out menace that I had seen on the face of Sally's boyfriend over at Glenn's place, although they didn't look quite so menacing now – but I only recognised the type. Expensive trainers, designer denim, hair so slick with gel that it looked as sticky and brittle as the skin of a toffee apple. My dad had trussed them up with the pair of silk ties I had bought him last Christmas.

'Saw them out on the street a bit earlier. Skylarking around, they were. But it turned out to be a bit more than skylarking.'

Sometimes it felt like my old man was the curator of the English language. As well as his love for outmoded hipster jive, another peculiarity of his speech was his use of expressions from his youth that everyone else had thrown out with their ration books.

He was always using words like skylarking – his arcane expression for mischief, fooling around and generally just mucking about – words that had gone out of fashion around the same time as the British Empire.

'They came in through the French windows, bold as brass. Thought nobody was home. Your mother was doing the shopping for your birthday – she's got a lovely roast – and I was upstairs getting spruced up.'

Getting spruced up. That was another one he was preserving for the archives.

'They were trying to unplug the video when I walked in. One of them had the cheek to come at me.' He lightly prodded the thinnest, meanest looking youth with a carpet slipper. 'Didn't you, old chum?'

'My fucking brother's going to fucking kill you,' the boy muttered, his voice as harsh in this room where I had been a child as a fart in church. There was a yellow and purple bruise coming up on one of his pimply cheekbones. 'He'll kill you, old man. He's a gangster.'

My dad chuckled with genuine amusement.

'Had to stick one on him.' My father threw a beefy right hook into the air. 'Caught him good. Went out like a bloody light. The other one tried to make a run for it, but I just got him by the scruff of the neck.'

The muscles on my father's tattooed arms rippled under his short-sleeved shirt as he demonstrated his technique for getting a teenage burglar by the throat. He had my mother's name in a heart inscribed on one arm, the winged dagger of the Commandos on the other. Both tattoos were blurred with the ages.

'Got him on the floor. Lucky I was deciding which tie to wear when they appeared. Came in handy, those ties you gave me.'

'Jesus Christ, Dad, they could have had knives!' I exploded. 'The papers are full of have-a-go heroes who get killed for tackling criminals. Why didn't you just call the law?'

My dad laughed good-naturedly. This wasn't going to be

one of our arguments. He was enjoying himself too much for that.

'No time, Harry. Came downstairs and there they were. Large as life, in my home. That's a bit naughty, that is.'

I was angry with him for taking on the two little goons, although I knew he was more than capable of handling them. I also felt the furious relief that comes when you finally find a child who has gone missing. But there was also something else. I was jealous.

What would I have done if I had found these two yobs – or any of the million like them – in my home? Would I have had the sheer guts and the bloody-minded stupidity to take them on? Or would I have run a mile?

Whatever I would have done, I knew I wouldn't have done it with the manly certainty of my father. I couldn't have protected my home and my family in quite the same way that he had protected his home and family. I wasn't like him. But with all my heart, I wanted to be.

The police eventually came, pulling up in a blaze of sirens and twirling blue lights. Pat ran outside to meet them, his eyes wide with wonder.

There were two of them – a fit-looking young cop around my age who regarded my dad's heroics with a quiet exasperation, and an older, heavier officer who immediately struck up a relationship with my old man.

In truth my father had never been much of a fan of the police – I remember him being stopped for speeding a few times when I was a child, and he was invariably lippy, never deferential, never willing to kiss their arses for a quiet life. Whenever he saw a police car screaming through the streets he was always contemptuous. 'They're only going home for their dinner,' he would say. But now he sipped hot sweet tea with the older cop, a pair of *Sunday Express* readers together, two stolid real men wondering what the world was coming to as they surveyed the secured yobs at their feet.

'You can imagine what kind of homes they come from, of course,' said my dad.

'The mother's on benefits,' guessed the old policeman. 'The father probably buggered off years ago. If he was ever there. So the state has to pay to bring up these little charmers. Which means you and me.'

'Too true. And don't think they're grateful for being supported by the taxpayer. It's all rights these days, isn't it? All rights and no responsibilities.'

'You see them all over these estates. Women with a bunch of screaming kids and no ring on their fingers.'

'Amazing, isn't it? You need a licence to drive a car. You need a licence to own a dog. But anyone can bring a child into the world.'

I went out into the kitchen with my mum and Pat, wondering why all the decent citizens in the world have it in for single mothers. After all, I thought, the single mother is the parent who stayed.

Despite being able to eat a couple of burglars for breakfast, my father wasn't a violent man. He wasn't the battle-hardened war veteran of myth and movies. He was the most gentle man I ever met in my life.

It was true that I had seen him explode a few times when I was growing up. There was a sweet shop where my mother worked part-time when I was around Pat's age, and the creep of a manager wouldn't let her take a personal call from the hospital when her father, my granddad, was dying of cancer. I watched my dad grab the manager by the throat – the scruff of his neck, he would have called it – and lift him right off the ground. The man thought my father was going to kill him. So did I.

And there were other occasions – a cocky swimming-pool attendant who said the wrong thing when I was wearing a particularly lurid pair of water wings, a motorist who cut him up on our way to the seaside one steaming Bank Holiday Monday. He had dealt with them all the way he dealt with the two pockmarked burglars. But he never lifted a finger to me or my mother.

The war was always there, as undeniable as the jagged little black lumps of shrapnel which spent a lifetime worming their way out of his hard old body. But the real drama of his life – the friends who died before they were old enough to vote, the men he killed, the unimaginable things he saw and did – was over by the time he was out of his teens. Although I always thought of him as a warrior, a Royal Naval Commando with a silver medal on his chest, my dad had been something else for fifty years.

After the war he worked on a stall selling fruit and vegetables for five years. Then he married my mother and managed a greengrocer's shop directly below the flat where my parents lived, childless for more than a decade, desperately trying for a baby that just wouldn't be born.

I finally came along, when it must have seemed as though I never would, and from the day we moved out of our little flat above the shop until the day he retired, my father was a produce manager for a chain of supermarkets, travelling to stores across Kent and Essex and East Anglia to make sure the fruit and vegetables on sale were up to his demanding standards.

So he wasn't a warrior to the world. But he was to me. And he wouldn't hurt a fly. Quite literally wouldn't hurt a fly. Perhaps it was because he had seen enough blood and gore to last forever, but if anything flew or crawled or crept from his well-tended garden into our small suburban home, my father would forbid my mother and me from touching it.

He would crouch beside some broken butterfly or wandering ant – or wasp or fly or mouse, no creature was too lowly or too filthy for him to rescue – scoop it up in his hands or a matchbox or a jam jar, and escort it to the back door, gently releasing it back into the wild while my mum and I mocked him and sang the chorus of 'Born Free'.

But although we laughed at him, my childish heart reeled with admiration.

My father was a strong man who had learned to be gentle, a man who had seen enough of death to fully appreciate life. And I couldn't compete, I just couldn't compete.

Pat wouldn't eat his dinner. Maybe it was the call from his mother. Maybe it was the attempted burglary. But I don't think so. I think it was just my lousy cooking.

I had started to worry about his diet. Just how much nutrition was there in the takeaway pizzas and microwave meals I fed him on? Not much. The only time he was getting anything that remotely resembled healthy food was when we went to my parents or ate out. So one night I tried boiling up a few vegetables and slipping them into his microwaved pasta.

'Yuk,' he said, examining an orange blob on the end of his spoon. 'What's *that*?'

'That's called a carrot, Pat. You must remember carrots. They're good for you. Come on. Eat it all up.'

He pushed his plate away with a look of disgust.

'Not hungry,' he said, making to get down from the kitchen table.

'Hold it,' I said. 'You're not going anywhere until you've eaten your dinner.'

'I don't *want* any dinner.' He looked at the orange blob swimming in bubbling gruel. 'This tastes *yuk*.'

'Eat your dinner.'

'No.'

'Please eat your dinner.'

'No.'

'Are you going to eat your dinner or not?'

'*No.*'

'Then go to bed.'

'But it's early!'

'That's right – it's dinner time. And if you don't want any dinner then you can go to bed.'

'That's not fair!'

'Life's not fair! Go to bed!'

'I hate you, Daddy!'

'You don't hate me! You hate my cooking! Go and put your pyjamas on!'

When he had flounced out of the kitchen I snatched up his plate of microwaved crap with added overboiled vegetables and tossed it all in the bin. Then I held the plate under the hot tap until the water burned my hands. I didn't really blame him for not eating it. It probably wasn't edible.

When I went into Pat's bedroom he was lying on his bed, fully clothed, quietly sobbing. I sat him up, dried his eyes and helped him into his pyjamas. He was fading fast – eyes half-closed, mouth all puffy, head nodding like a little dashboard dog – so an early night wouldn't do him any harm. But I didn't want him to fall asleep hating my guts.

'I know I'm not a very good cook, Pat. Not like Granny or Mummy. But I'm going to try harder, okay?'

'Daddies can't cook.'

'That's not true at all.'

'You can't cook.'

'Well, that's true. This daddy can't cook. But there are lots of men who are great cooks – famous chefs in fancy restaurants. And ordinary men, too. Men who live alone. Daddies with little boys and girls. I'm going to try to be like them, okay? I'm going to try to cook you good things that you enjoy. Okay, darling?'

He turned his head away, sniffing with disbelief at something so outrageously unlikely. I knew how he felt. I couldn't believe it either. I suspected we were both going to have to develop a profound love for sandwiches.

I took him to the bathroom to brush his teeth, and when we came back I managed to get a reluctant goodnight kiss out of him. But he wasn't really interested in making up. Telling myself that he would have forgotten all about my rotten carrots by the morning, I tucked him in and turned out his light.

I went back to the living room and flopped on the sofa, knowing that I needed to get back to work. A bank statement had arrived that morning. I didn't have the heart to open it.

They had sacked me the modern way – by letting my contract run out and bunging me just one month's salary. It was already gone. So I needed to get back to work because we were desperate for money. But I also needed to get back to work because it was the only thing in this world that I was any good at.

I picked up a trade paper and turned to the situations vacant, circling production jobs in radio and TV which looked promising. But after a few minutes of half-hearted job hunting I laid the paper to one side, rubbing my eyes. I was too tired to think about it right now.

The Empire Strikes Back was still running on the video – a battle between the forces of good and evil in the snow of some faraway planet. Even though this stuff was a constant background noise in our lives and sometimes made me feel like I was losing my mind, I was just too exhausted to turn it off.

The action switched from the frozen wasteland to some

dark, bubbling swamp where the wise old master was lecturing Luke Skywalker on his destiny. And I suddenly realised how many father figures Luke has, father figures who seem to cover the waterfront of parental possibilities.

There's Yoda, the wrinkled elder who has good advice coming out of his pointy green ears. And then there's Obi-Wan Kenobi, who combines homespun homilies with some old-fashioned tough love.

And finally there's Darth Vader, the Dark Lord of the Sith, who is probably more in keeping with the spirit of our time – an absent father, a neglectful dad, a selfish old man who puts his own wishes – in Mr Vader's case, a desire to conquer the universe – before any parental responsibility.

My old man was definitely the Obi-Wan Kenobi type. And that's the kind of father I wanted to be too.

But I fell asleep on the sofa surrounded by the situations vacant, suspecting that I would always be a lot more like the man in the black hat, a father with not enough patience, not enough time, forever lost to the dark side.

fourteen

'I know there've been a few problems at home,' the nursery teacher said, making it sound as though the dishwasher was playing up, making it sound as though I could just pick up Yellow Pages and sort out my life. 'And believe me,' she said, 'everyone at Canonbury Cubs is sympathetic.'

It was true. The teachers at Canonbury Cubs always made a big fuss of Pat when I delivered him in the morning. As the blood drained from his face yet again, as his bottom lip started to quiver and those huge blue eyes filled up at the prospect of being taken away from me for another day, they really couldn't have been kinder.

But ultimately he wasn't their problem. And no matter how kind they were, they couldn't mend the cracks that were showing in his life.

Unless it was to be with my fun-mad parents, Pat didn't like being separated from me. There was high drama when we parted at the gate of Canonbury Cubs every morning and then I went home to pace the floor for hours, fretting about how he was doing, while back at the nursery poor old Pat kept asking the teachers how long before he could go home and crying all over his finger paintings.

Nursery wasn't working. So amid their concerned talk about possibly finding a child psychologist and time healing all wounds, Pat dropped out.

As the other kids started work on their Plasticine worms,

I took Pat's hand and led him out of that rainbow-coloured basement for the last time. He cheered up immediately, far too happy and relieved to feel like any kind of misfit. The teachers brightly waved goodbye. The little children looked up briefly and then returned to their innocent chores.

And I imagined my son, the nursery-school dropout, returning to the gates of Canonbury Cubs in ten years' time, just to sneer and leer and sell them all crack.

The job seemed perfect.

The station wanted to build a show around this young Irish comedian who was getting too big to do the clubs yet who was not quite big enough to do beer commercials.

He didn't actually do anything as old-fashioned as tell jokes, but he had wowed them up at the Edinburgh Festival with an act built completely around his relationship with the audience.

Instead of telling gags, he spoke to the crowd, relying on intelligent heckling and his Celtic charm to pull him through. He seemed born to host a talk show. Unlike Marty and every other host, he wouldn't be dependent on celebrities revealing their secrets or members of the public disgracing themselves. He could even write his own scripts. At least that was the theory. They just needed an experienced producer.

'We're very excited to see you here,' said the woman sitting opposite me. She was the station's commissioning editor, a small woman in her middle thirties with the power to change your life. The two men in glasses on either side of her – the show's series producer and the series editor – smiled in agreement. I smiled back at them. I was excited too.

This show was just what I needed to turn my world around. The money was better than anything I had ever got working for Marty Mann, because now I was coming from another television show instead of some flyblown outpost of radio. But although it would be a relief not to worry about meeting the mortgage and the payments on my car, this wasn't about the money.

I had realised how much I missed going to an office every day. I missed the phones, the meetings, the comforting rituals of the working week. I missed having a desk. I even missed the woman who came around with sandwiches and coffee. I was tired of staying at home cooking meals for my son that he couldn't eat. I was sick of feeling as if life was happening somewhere else. I wanted to go back to work.

'Your record with Marty Mann speaks for itself,' the commissioning editor said. 'Not many radio shows can be made to work on television.'

'Well, Marty's a brilliant broadcaster,' I said. The ungrateful little shitbag. May he rot in hell. 'He made it easy for me.'

'You're very kind to him,' the series editor said.

'Marty's a great guy,' I said. The treacherous, treacherous little bastard. 'I love him.' My new show's going to blow you out of the water, Marty. Forget the diet. Forget the personal trainer. You're going back to local radio, pal.

'We hope that you can have the same relationship with the presenter of this show,' the woman said. 'Eamon's a talented young man, but he is not going to get through a nine-week run without someone of your experience behind him. That's why we would like to offer you the job.'

I could see the blissful, crowded weeks stretching out ahead of me. I could imagine the script meetings at the start of the week, the minor triumphs and disasters as guests dropped out and came in, the shooting script coming together, the nerves and cock-ups of studio rehearsal, the lights, cameras and adrenaline of doing the show, and finally the indescribable relief that it was all over for seven more days. And, always, the perfect excuse to avoid doing anything I didn't want to do – I'm too busy at work, I'm too busy at work, I'm too busy at work.

We all stood up and shook hands, and they came with me out into the main office where Pat was waiting. He was sitting on a desk being fussed over by a couple of researchers who stroked his hair, touched his cheek and gazed with wonder into his eyes, shocked and charmed by the sheer dazzling newness of him. You didn't get many four-year-olds in an office like this.

I had been a bit worried about bringing Pat with me. Apart from the possibility of him refusing to be left outside the interview room, I didn't want to rub their noses in the fact that I was currently playing the single parent. How could they hire a man who had to lug his family around with him? How could they give a producer's job to a man who couldn't even organise a babysitter?

I needn't have worried. They seemed surprised but touched that I had brought my boy to a job interview. And Pat was at his most charming and talkative, happily filling the researchers in on all the gory details of his parents' separation.

'Yes, my mummy is in abroad – in Japan – where they drive on the left side of the road like us. She's going to get me, yes. And I live with my daddy, but at weekends I sometimes stay with my nan and granddad. My mummy still loves me, but now she only likes my dad.'

His face lit up when he saw me, and he jumped down off the desk, running to my arms and kissing me on the cheek with that fierceness he had learned from Gina.

As I held him and all those television people grinned at us and each other, I glimpsed the reality of my new brilliant career – the weekends spent writing a script, the meetings that started early and finished late, the hours and hours in a studio chilled to near freezing point to stop beads of sweat forming on the presenter's forehead – and I knew that I would not be taking this job.

They liked the single father and son routine when it had a strictly limited run. But they wouldn't like it when they saw me buggering off at six every night to make Pat's fishfingers.

They wouldn't like it at all.

fifteen

I called Gina when Pat was staying overnight with my mum and dad. I had realised that I needed to talk to her. Really talk to her. Not just shout and whine and threaten. Tell her what was on my mind. Let her know what I was thinking.

'Come home,' I said. 'I love you.'

'How can you love someone – really love them – and sleep with someone else?'

'I don't know how to explain it. But it was easy.'

'Well, forgiving is not quite so easy, okay?'

'Christ, you really want to see me crawl, don't you?'

'It's not about you, Harry. It's about me.'

'What about our life together? We have a life together, don't we? How can you throw all that away because of one mistake?'

'I didn't throw it away. You did.'

'Don't you love me any more?'

'Of course I love you, you stupid bastard. But I'm not in love with you.'

'Wait a minute. You love me, but you're not *in* love with me?'

'You hurt me too much. And you'll do it again. And next time you won't feel quite so much guilt. Next time you'll be able to justify it to yourself. Then one day you'll meet someone you really like. Someone you love. And that's when you'll leave me.'

'Never.'

'That's the way it works, Harry. I saw it all with my parents.'

'You love me, but you're not in love with me? What's that supposed to mean?'

'Love is what's left when being in love has gone, okay? It's when you care about someone and you hope they're happy, but you're not under any illusions about them. Maybe that kind of love is not exciting and passionate and all those things that fade with time. All those things that you're so keen on. But in the end it's the only kind of love that really matters.'

'I have absolutely no idea what you're going on about,' I said.

'And that's exactly your problem,' she told me.

'Forget Japan. Come home. You're still my wife, Gina.'

'I'm seeing someone,' she said, and I felt like a hypochondriac who has finally had his terminal disease confirmed.

I wasn't surprised. I had spent so long being terrified that finally having my worst fears realised brought a kind of bleak relief.

I had been expecting it – dreading it – ever since she had walked out the door. In a way I was glad it had happened, because now I didn't have to worry about when it was going to happen. And I wasn't so stupid that I thought I had the right to be outraged. But I still hadn't worked out what to do with our wedding photographs. What are you meant to do with the wedding photographs after you split up?

'Funny old expression, isn't it?' I said. 'Seeing someone, I mean. It sounds like you're checking them out. Observing them. Just looking. But that's exactly what you're not doing. Just looking, I mean. When you're seeing someone, well, it's gone way beyond the just looking stage. How serious is it?'

'I don't know. How do you tell? He's married.'

'Fuck me.'

'But it's not – apparently it hasn't been good for ages. They're semi-separated.'

'Is that what he told you? Semi-separated? And you believed him, did you? Semi-separated. That's a suitably vague way of putting it. I haven't heard that one before. Semi-separated. That's very good. That just about covers any eventuality. That should allow him to string both of you along nicely. He can keep the little wife at home making sushi while he sneaks off with you to the nearest love hotel.'

'Oh, Harry. The least you could do is wish me well.'

'Who is he? Some Japanese salary man who gets his kicks by sleeping with western women? You can't trust the Japanese, Gina. You think you're the big expert, but you don't know them at all. They don't have the same value system as you and me. The Japanese are a cunning, double-dealing race.'

'He's American.'

'Well, why didn't you say? That's even worse.'

'You wouldn't like anyone I got involved with, would you, Harry? He could be an Eskimo and you would say – "Ooh, Eskimos, Gina. Cold hands, cold heart. Steer well clear of Eskimos, Gina."'

'I just don't understand why you've got this thing about foreigners.'

'Perhaps because I tried loving someone from my own country. And he broke my heart.'

It took me a moment to realise that she was talking about me.

'Does he know you've got a kid?'

'Of course he knows. Do you think I would hide that from anyone?'

'And how does he feel about it?'

'What do you mean?'

'Is he interested in Pat? Is he worried about the boy? Does he care about his wellbeing? Or does he just want to fuck his mother?'

'If you're going to talk like that, Harry, I'm going to hang up.'

'How else am I meant to put it?'

'We haven't talked about the future. We haven't got that far.'

'Let me know when you get that far.'

'I will. But please don't use Pat as a rod for my back.'

Is that what I was doing? I couldn't tell where my genuine concern ended and my genuine jealousy began.

Pat was one of the reasons I wanted to see Gina's boyfriend dead in a car crash. But I knew he wasn't the only reason. Maybe he wasn't even the main reason.

'Just don't try to poison my son against me,' I said.

'What are you talking about, Harry?'

'Pat tells everyone he meets that you said you love him but you only like me.'

She sighed.

'That's not what I said. I told him exactly what I've just told you. I told him that I still loved you both but unfortunately and sadly I was no longer in love with you.'

'I still don't know what that means.'

'It means that I'm glad for the years we spent together. But you hurt me so much that I can never forgive you or trust you again. And I think it means that you're no longer the man I want to spend the rest of my life with. You're too much like any other man. Too much like my father.'

'It's not my fault that your old man walked out on you and your mum.'

'You were my chance to get over all that. And you messed it up. You left me, too.'

'Come on. It was one night, Gina. How many times are we going to have this conversation?'

'Until you understand the way I feel. If you can do it once, you can do it a thousand times. That's the first law of fucking around. The unified theory of fucking around clearly states that if they do it once, they will do it again and again. You broke my trust and I just don't know how to mend it. And that hurts me too, Harry. I wasn't trying to turn Pat against you. I was just trying to explain the situation to him. How do you explain it?'

'I can't explain it. Not even to myself.'

'You should try. Because if you don't understand what happened to us, you're never going to be happy with anyone.'

'You explain it to me.'

She sighed. You could hear her sighing all the way from Tokyo.

'We had a marriage that I thought was working, but you thought was becoming routine. You're a typical romantic, Harry. A relationship doesn't measure up to your pathetic and unrealistic fantasy so you smash it up. You ruin everything. And then you've got the nerve to act like the injured party.'

'Who's providing the armchair psychology? Your Yank boyfriend?'

'I've discussed what happened with Richard.'

'Richard? Is that his name? Richard. Hah! Jesus Christ.'

'Richard is a perfectly ordinary name. It's certainly no stranger than Harry.'

'Richard. Rich. Dicky. Dick. Old Richard Dicky-dickhead.'

'Sometimes I look at you and Pat, and I honestly can't tell which one is the four-year-old.'

'It's easy. I'm the one who can pee without getting anything on the floor.'

'Blame yourself for all this,' she said, just before she hung up. 'It happened because you didn't appreciate what you had.'

That wasn't true. I was smart enough to know what I had. But too dumb to know how to keep it.

Like any couple living under the same roof, we soon developed our daily rituals.

Just after daybreak, Pat would stagger bleary-eyed into my bedroom, asking me if it was time to get up. I would tell him that it was still the middle of the bloody night and he would climb into bed with me, immediately falling asleep in the spot where Gina used to sleep, throwing his arms and legs about in his wild, childish dreams until eventually I would give up trying to get any more rest and get up.

I would be reading the papers in the kitchen when Pat dragged himself out of bed, and I would immediately hear him sneak into the living room and turn on the video.

Now that Pat was out of nursery and I was out of a job, we could take our time getting ready. But I was still reluctant to let him do exactly what he wanted to do, and what he wanted to do was watch videos all day long. So I would go and turn the video off and escort him to the kitchen, where he would toy with a bowl of Coco Pops until I gave him his freedom.

After we were washed and dressed, I would take him over the park on his bike. It was called Bluebell, and it still had the stabilisers on. Pat and I sometimes discussed removing the stabilisers and trying to ride it with just two wheels. But it seemed like an impossible leap forward to both of us. Knowing when the time was right to remove a bike's stabilisers was the kind of thing that Gina was good at.

In the afternoons my mother would usually collect Pat and this would give me a chance to do some shopping, clean up the house, worry about money, pace the floor and imagine Gina moaning with pleasure in the bed of another man.

But in the morning, we went to the park.

sixteen

Pat liked to ride his bike by this open-air swimming pool at the edge of the park.

The little pool was kept empty all year round apart from a few weeks early in the summer when the council grudgingly filled it with heavily chlorinated water which made the local children smell as though they had been dipped in industrial waste.

Long before the summer was over, the water would be drained from the pool and the odd supermarket trolley fished from the bottom. We were only in the middle of August, but the little pool had already been abandoned for another year by everyone apart from Pat and his Bluebell.

There was something depressing about the almost permanently empty pool. It was in a desolate part of the park, nowhere near the adventure playground where children screamed with delight, or the little café where mums and dads – but they were mostly mums – drank endless cups of tea.

But the little asphalt strip that surrounded the pool was somewhere for Pat to ride his bike without having to plough through the discarded kebabs, used condoms and dog shit that littered most of the park. And to tell you the truth, it suited me to be away from all those mums.

I could see what they were thinking when we entered the park every morning.

Where's the mother?

Why isn't he at work?

Is that really his kid?

And of course I could understand their concern, most of the perverts in this world being the proud owner of a penis. But I was tired of feeling that I should apologise for taking my son to the park. I was tired of feeling like a freak. The empty swimming pool suited me fine.

'Daddy! Look at me!'

Pat was on the far side of the pool, breathing hard as he paused by the stubby little diving board that poked out over the empty deep end.

I smiled from the bench where I sat with my paper, and as soon as he saw that he had my attention he shot off again – eyes shining, hair flying, his little legs pumping furiously as he tore around the pool on Bluebell.

'Stay right away from the edge!'

'I will! I do!'

For the fifth time in five minutes, I read the opening sentence of an article about the collapse of the Japanese economy.

It was a subject that had come to interest me greatly. I felt sorry for the Japanese people because they seemed to be living in a system which had failed them. But mixed with the human sympathy was a kind of relish. I wanted to read about banks closing down, disgraced CEOs bowing and weeping at press conferences, freshly unemployed expatriates heading for Narita airport and the next flight back home. Especially that. But I couldn't concentrate.

All I could see was Gina and Richard, although I couldn't see them very well. Gina was starting to slip out of focus. She wasn't my Gina any more. I couldn't imagine the place where she lived, the office where she worked, the little noodle joint where she had her lunch every day. I couldn't picture any of it. And it wasn't just her new life that was difficult for me to see. I could hardly see her face in my mind any more. But if Gina was a blur, then Richard was a complete blind spot.

Was he younger than me? Richer than me? Better in bed than me? I would have liked to think that Gina was stepping out with an impotent bankrupt on the verge of senility. But I could see that was probably just wishful thinking on my part.

All I knew was that he was married. Yet even that was suspect – what the fuck did semi-separated mean? Was he still living with his wife? Was she American or Japanese? Did they still sleep together? Did they have kids? Was he serious about Gina or just stringing her along? And would I like it more if he saw her as a casual fling or as the love of his life? Which one would hurt me the most?

'Look at me now!'

The sight made me freeze.

Pat had very carefully edged his bike out on to the diving board. He was balanced above a ten-foot drop to the pockmarked concrete at the bottom of the pool. Either side of Bluebell, his legs were at full stretch as he steadied himself with the toes of his dirty trainers. I hadn't seen him looking so happy for weeks.

'Stay right there,' I called. 'Don't move.'

His smile faded when he saw me start running towards him. I should have gone slower. I should have pretended that nothing was wrong. Because when he saw the look on my face, he started trying to back off the diving board. But it was easier to get on than off and the world seemed to slip into slow motion as I saw one of Bluebell's stabilisers slide off the side of the diving board, spin in the air for a moment, and then Pat's little feet inside the dirty trainers were off balance and scrambling for something that wasn't there, and I was watching my boy and his bike falling headfirst into that empty swimming pool.

He was lying under the diving board, the bike on top of him, the blood starting to spread around his mop of yellow hair.

I waited for him to start screaming – just as he had screamed the year before when he was using our bed for a trampoline, bounced right off and smashed his head against the chest of drawers, and just as he had screamed the year before that, when he had overturned his pushchair by standing up in it and trying to turn around to smile at me and Gina, and just as he had screamed on all the other occasions when he had banged his head or fallen flat on his face or grazed his knees.

I wanted to hear him crying out because then I would know that this was just like all the other scrapes of childhood. But Pat was totally silent, and that silence gripped my heart.

His eyes were closed and his pale, pinched face made him look like he was lost in some bad dream. The dark halo of blood around his head kept growing.

'Oh Pat,' I said, pulling the bike off him and holding him far more tightly than I should have. 'Oh God,' I said, taking my mobile phone out of my jacket with fingers which were sticky from his blood, frantically tapping in the PIN number and hearing the beep-beep-beep sound of a flat battery.

I picked up my son.

I started to run.

seventeen

You can't run far with a four-year-old child in your arms. They are already too big, too heavy, too awkward to carry with any speed.

I wanted to get Pat home to the car, but I staggered out of the park knowing that wasn't going to be quick enough.

I burst into the café where we had eaten green spaghetti, Pat still pale and silent and bleeding in my arms. It was lunch time, and the place was full of office workers in suits stuffing their faces. They stared at us open-mouthed, forks twirled with carbonara suspended in mid-air.

'Get an ambulance!'

Nobody moved.

Then the kitchen doors flew open and Cyd came through them, a tray piled with food in one hand and her order pad in the other. She looked at us for a moment, flinching at the sight of Pat's lifeless body, the blood all over my hands and shirt, the blind panic on my face.

Then she expertly slid the tray on to the nearest table and came towards us.

'It's my son! Get an ambulance!'

'It will be quicker if I drive you,' she said.

There were white lines on the hospital floor that directed you to the casualty department, but before we got anywhere near it we were surrounded by nurses and porters who took

Pat from my arms and laid him on a trolley. It was a trolley for an adult, and he looked tiny on it. Just so tiny.

Tears came to my eyes for the first time, and I blinked them away. I couldn't look at him. I couldn't stop looking at him. Your child in a hospital. It's the worst thing in the world.

They wheeled him deeper into the building, under the sick yellow strip lights of crowded, noisy corridors, asking me questions about his birthday, his medical history, the cause of his head wound.

I tried to tell them about the bike on the diving board above the empty swimming pool, but I don't know if it made much sense to them. It didn't make much sense to me.

'We'll take care of him,' a nurse said, and the trolley banged through green swing doors.

I tried to follow them and caught a glimpse of men and women in green smocks with masks on their faces, the polished chrome of medical equipment, and a kind of padded slab where they laid him down, that slab as thin and ominous as a diving board.

Cyd gently took my arm.

'You have to let him go,' she said, and led me to a bleak little waiting area where she bought us coffee in polystyrene cups from a vending machine. She filled mine with sugar without asking if that's how I liked it.

'Are you okay?' she said.

I shook my head. 'I'm so stupid.'

'These things happen. Do you know what happened to me when I was about that age?'

She waited for my reply. I looked up at her wide-set brown eyes.

'What?'

'I was watching some kids playing baseball and I went up and stood right behind the batter. Right behind him.' She smiled at me. 'And when he swung back to hit the ball, he almost took my head off. That bat was only made of some kind of plastic, but it knocked me out cold. I actually saw stars. Look.'

She pushed the black veil of hair off her forehead. Just above her eyebrow there was a thin white scar about as long as a thumbnail.

'I know you feel terrible now,' she said. 'But kids are tough. They get through these things.'

'It was so high,' I said. 'And he fell so hard. The blood – it was everywhere.'

But I was grateful for Cyd's thin white scar. I appreciated the fact that she had been knocked unconscious as a child. It was good of her.

A young woman doctor came and found us. She was about twenty-five years old, and looked as though she hadn't had a good night's sleep since medical school. She was vaguely sympathetic, but brisk, businesslike, as honest as a car wreck.

'Patrick is in a stable condition, but with such a severe blow to the head we have to take X-rays and a brain scan. What I'm worried about is the possibility of a depressed fracture to the skull – that's when the skull is cracked and bony fragments are driven inward, causing pressure on the brain. I'm not saying that's happened. I'm saying it's a possibility.'

'Jesus Christ.'

Cyd took my hand and squeezed it.

'This is going to take a while,' the doctor said. 'If you and your wife would like to stay with your son tonight, there's time to go home and get some things.'

'Oh,' Cyd said. 'We're not married.'

The doctor looked at me and studied her chart.

'You're Patrick's father, Mr Silver?'

'Yes.'

'I'm just a friend,' Cyd said. 'I should go,' she told me, standing up. I could tell that she thought she was getting in the way. But she wasn't at all. She was the only thing keeping me from falling apart.

'And the child's mother?' the doctor asked.

'She's out of the country,' I said. 'Temporarily out of the country.'

'You might want to call her,' the doctor said.

My mother had been crying, but she wasn't going to do it in public. She always saved her tears for behind closed doors, for the eyes of the family.

At the hospital she was all gritty optimism and common sense. She asked practical questions of the nurses. What was the risk of permanent damage? How long before we would know? Was it okay for grandparents to stay the night? It made me feel better having her around. My dad was a bit different.

The old soldier looked lost in the hospital cafeteria. He wasn't used to sitting and waiting. He wasn't used to situations that were beyond his control. His thick tattooed arms, the broad shoulders, his fearless old heart – they were all quite useless in here.

I knew that he would have done anything for Pat, that he loved him with the unconditional love you can probably only feel for a child, a love that's far more difficult to feel when your perfect child has grown into one more fallible adult. He loved Pat in a way that he had once loved me. Pat was me before I had a chance to screw everything up. It gnawed at my father inside that all he could do was sit and wait.

'Does anyone want any more tea?' he said, desperate to do something, anything to make our miserable lot a little better.

'We'll have tea coming out of our ears,' my mum said. 'Just sit down and relax.'

'Relax?' he snorted, glaring at her, and then deciding to leave it.

He flopped into a cracked plastic chair and stared at the wall. There were bags under his eyes the colour of bruised fruit. Then after five minutes he went to get us some more tea. And as he waited for news of his grandson and sipped tea that he didn't really want, my father seemed suddenly old.

'Why don't you try Gina again?' my mother asked me.

I don't know what she was expecting. Possibly that Gina would get on the next plane home and soon our little family would be united once more and forever. And maybe I hoped for that, too.

But it was no good. I went out to the reception area and called Gina's number, but all I got was the strange purring sound of a Japanese telephone that nobody answers.

It was midnight in London, which made it eight in the morning in Tokyo. She should have been there. Unless she had already left for work. Unless she hadn't come home last night. Her phone just kept on purring.

This was how it was going to be from now on. If I had spoken to Gina, I know that her strength and common sense would have got the better of any fear or panic. She would have been more like my mum than my dad. Or me. She would have asked what had happened, what were the dangers and when would we know. She would have found out the time of the next flight home and she would have been on it. But I just couldn't reach her.

I hung up the phone, knowing that the rest of our lives were going to be like this, knowing that things had gone too wrong to ever be the way they were, knowing that we were too far away from each other to ever find our way back.

eighteen

The doctor came looking for me at five in the morning. I was in the empty cafeteria, nursing a cup of tea that had gone cold hours ago. I stood up as she came towards me, waiting for her to speak.

'Congratulations,' she said. 'Your son has a very hard head.'

'He's going to be okay?'

'There's no fracture and the scan is clear. We're going to keep him in for observation for a few days, but that's standard procedure when we've put twelve stitches in a four-year-old's head wound.'

I wanted that doctor to be my best friend. I wanted us to meet up for dinner once a week so she could pour out all her frustrations with the NHS. I would listen and I would care. She had saved my son. She was beautiful.

'He's really all right?'

'He'll have a sore head for a few weeks, and a scar for life. But, yes, he's going to be okay.'

'No side effects?'

'Well, it will probably help him get girls in fifteen years' time. Scars are quite attractive on a man, aren't they?'

I took her hands and held them a bit too long.

'Thank you.'

'That's why we're here,' she smiled. I could see that I was

embarrassing her, but I couldn't help it. Finally I let go.

'Can I see him?'

He was at the far end of a ward full of children. Next to Pat there was a pretty little five-year-old in Girl Power pyjamas with her hair all gone from what I guessed was chemotherapy. Her parents were by her side, her father asleep in a chair, and her mother at the foot of the bed, staring at her daughter's face. I walked quietly past them to my son's bed, knowing that I had been wrong to wallow in self-pity for so long. We were lucky.

Pat was on a saline drip, his face as white as his pillow, his head swathed in bandages. I sat on his bed, stroking his free arm, and his eyes flickered open.

'You angry with me?' he asked, and I shook my head, afraid to speak.

He closed his eyes, and suddenly I knew that I could do this thing.

I could see that my performance so far had been pretty poor. I didn't have enough patience. I spent too much time thinking about Gina and even Cyd. I hadn't been watching Pat closely enough in the park. All that was undeniable. But I could do this thing.

Maybe it would never be perfect. Maybe I would make a mess of being a parent just as I had made a mess of being a husband.

But for the first time I saw that being a man would have nothing to do with it.

All families have their own legends and lore. In our little family, the first story that I featured in was when I was five years old and a dog knocked out all my front teeth.

I was playing with a neighbour's Alsatian behind the row of shops where we had our flat. The dog was licking my face and I was loving it until he put his front paws on my chest to steady himself and tipped me over. I landed flat on my mouth, blood and teeth everywhere, my mother screaming.

I can just about remember the rush to hospital and being held over a basin as they fished out bits of broken teeth, my blood dripping all over the white enamel sink. But most of all I remember my old man insisting that he was staying with me as they put me out with the gas.

When the story was retold in our family, the punch line was what I did when I came home from the hospital with my broken mouth – namely stuff it with a bag of salt and vinegar crisps.

That ending appealed to my old man, the idea that his son came back from the hospital with eight bloody stumps where his front teeth used to be and was so tough that he immediately opened a packet of crisps. But in reality I wasn't tough at all. I just liked salt and vinegar crisps. Even if I had to suck them.

I knew now that my dad wasn't quite as tough as he would have liked to have been. Because nobody feels tough when they take their child to a hospital. The real punch line to that story was that my father had refused to leave my side.

Now I could understand how he must have felt watching his five-year-old son being put out with gas so that the doctors could remove bits of broken teeth from his gums and tongue.

He would have had that feeling of helpless terror that only the parent of a sick or injured child can understand. I knew exactly how he must have felt – like life was holding him hostage. Was it really possible that I was starting to see the world with his eyes?

He was standing outside the main entrance to the hospital, smoking one of his roll-up cigarettes. He must have been the only surviving Rizla customer in the world who didn't smoke dope.

He looked up at me, holding his breath.

'He's going to be fine,' I said.

He released a cloud of cigarette smoke.

'It's not – what did they call it? – a compressed fracture?'

'It's not fractured. They've given him twelve stitches and he'll have a scar, but that's all.'

'That's all?'

'That's all.'

'Thank Christ for that,' he said. He took a tug on his roll-up. 'And how about you?'

'Me? I'm fine, Dad.'

'Do you need anything?'

'A good night's kip would be nice.'

When I was with my father, I sometimes found myself talking his language. He was the only person in the country who still referred to sleep as kip.

'I mean, are you all right for money? Your mum told me you're not going to take this job.'

'I can't. The hours are too long. I'd never be home.' I looked across the almost empty carpark to where the night sky was streaked with light. Somewhere birds were singing. It wasn't late any more. It was early. 'But something will turn up.'

He took out his wallet, peeled off a few notes and handed them to me.

'What's this for?' I asked.

'Until something turns up.'

'That's okay. I appreciate the offer, Dad, but something really will turn up.'

'I know it will. People always want to watch television, don't they? I'm sure you'll get something soon. This is for you and Pat until then.'

My dad, the media expert. All he knew about television was that these days they didn't put on anything as funny as *Fawlty Towers* or *Benny Hill* or *Morecambe and Wise.* Still, I took the notes he offered me.

There was a time when taking money from him would have made me angry – angry at myself for still needing him and his help at my age, and even angrier at him for always relishing his role as my saviour.

Now I could see that he was just sort of trying to show me that he was on my side.

'I'll pay this back,' I said.

'No rush,' said my father.

Gina wanted to get on the next plane home, but I talked her out of it. Because by the time I finally reached her late the following day, getting on the next plane home didn't matter quite so much.

She had missed those awful minutes rushing Pat to the emergency room. She had missed the endless hours drinking tea we didn't want while waiting to learn if his tests were clear. And she had missed the day when he sat up with his head covered in bandages, clutching his light sabre, in a bed next to the little girl who had lost all her hair because of the treatment she was receiving.

Gina had missed all that, she had missed all that through no fault of her own. Personally, I blamed that fucking bastard Richard.

By the time I reached Gina, we knew that Pat was going to be all right. Now I didn't want her to come home.

I told myself that it was because I didn't want her to hold Pat and tell him everything was going to be fine and then leave again. But I knew it was not quite as noble as that. Where the fuck was Gina when we needed her?

'I can be there tomorrow,' she said. 'This job can wait.'

'There's no need,' I said, dead calm. 'It was just a knock. A bad knock. But he's going to be okay.'

'I'll be coming home soon anyway. I'm not quite sure when –'

'Don't change your plans,' I said.

Listen to us – as formal as two people feeling their way at a dull dinner party. Once we could talk all night, once we could talk about anything. Now we sounded like two strangers who had never been properly introduced. Listen to us, Gina.

Cyd was standing on my doorstep holding a takeaway container.

'Is this a bad time?'

'No, it's not a bad time. Come in.'

She came into my home, handing me the container.

'For Pat. Spaghetti pesto.'

'Green spaghetti. His favourite. Thank you.'

'You just need to put it in the microwave. Can you do that?'

'Are you kidding? Even I know how to use a microwave. One minute or two?'

'One ought to do it. Is he awake?'

'He's watching some TV. Just for a change.'

Pat was sprawled all over the sofa, still in his Star Wars pyjamas and M&S dressing gown, watching the director's cut of *Return of the Jedi*. The rule book had been thrown out of the window since he had come home from the hospital.

'Hi Pat,' Cyd said, crouching down beside him and stroking his hair, carefully avoiding the large plaster that now covered one side of his forehead. 'How's your poor old head?'

'It's fine. My stitches are a bit itchy.'

'I bet they are.'

'But – guess what? They don't have to be taken out. My stitches.'

'No?'

'No, they just fade away,' Pat said, looking to me for confirmation.

'That's right,' I said. 'They dissolve. They're the new kind of stitches, aren't they?'

'The new kind,' Pat nodded, turning his attention back to Princess Leia dressed as a scantily-clad concubine in the court of Jabba the Hutt.

'That's some outfit she's got on,' Cyd said.

'Yes, it is,' agreed Pat. 'She's a slave girl.'

'Goodness.'

They watched Princess Leia squirming on the end of her chain for a few moments.

'Well, I'm going to leave you to get better,' Cyd said.

'Okay.'

'Cyd brought you some dinner,' I said. 'Green spaghetti. What do you say?'

'Thank you.' He gave her his most charming, David Niven-like smile.

'You're welcome,' she said.

I walked her to the door and I realised that something inside me felt like it was singing. I didn't want her to go.

'Thanks for coming round,' I said. 'It's made my day.'

She turned and looked at me with those wide-set brown eyes.

'I mean it,' I said. 'This is the best thing that's happened to me all day. Definitely.'

'But I don't understand,' she said.

'What don't you understand?'

'Why do you like me? You don't even know me.'

'Do you really want to know?'

'Yes.'

So I told her.

'I like you because you're strong but you're not hard. I like it that you don't take crap from men, but you still left your country for a man because you thought he was the one for you.'

'Biggest mistake of my life.'

'Maybe. But I like it that you're so romantic from watching all those MGM musicals as a little girl.'

She laughed, shaking her head.

'You see right through men, but you still want to find a man to share your life with,' I said.

'Says who?'

'And I like the way your entire face lights up when you smile. I like your eyes. I like your legs. I like the way you know how to talk to a four-year-old kid. I like the way you were there when I needed someone. Everyone else just stood and stared. You were kind. And you didn't have to be kind.'

'Anything else?'

'You're beautiful.'

'I'm not beautiful at all.'

'You're beautiful and brave and I'm jealous of every man who ever went out with you. Now and again I walk in front of the place where you work in the hope of bumping into you.'

'You miss your wife,' she said. 'You really miss her.'

'That's true,' I conceded. 'But it's also true that you blow me away.'

'Boy,' she said, shaking her head. 'But you still don't know me.'

She didn't say it the way she had said it before. Now she said it gently, kindly, as if it weren't my fault that I didn't know her.

And she moved towards me as she said it, looking at me with those eyes for a moment before they closed as she placed her mouth upon mine.

I kissed her back.

'I know you a little bit,' I said.

'Yes,' she said, giving me that. 'You know me a little bit.'

part two: *the ding-dong man*

nineteen

Pat started school.

The uniform he had to wear should have made him look grown up. The grey V-necked sweater, the white shirt and yellow tie should have made him look like a little man. But they didn't.

The formality of his school clothes only underlined the shocking newness of him. Approaching his fifth birthday, he wasn't even young yet. He was still brand new. Even though he was dressed more grown-up than me.

As I helped him get ready for his first day at school, I was startled to realise just how much I loved his face. When he was a baby I couldn't tell if he was really beautiful, or if that was just my parental software kicking in. But now I could see the truth.

With those light blue eyes, his long yellow hair and the way his slow, shy smile could spread right across his impossibly smooth face, he really was a beautiful boy.

And now I had to let my beautiful boy go out into the world. At least until 3.30. For both of us, it felt like a lifetime.

He wasn't smiling now. At breakfast he was pale and silent in his pastiche of adult's clothing, struggling to stop his chin trembling and his bottom lip sticking out, while over the Coco Pops I kept up a running commentary about the best days of your life.

The Coco Pops were interrupted by a call from Gina. I knew it must have been difficult for her to phone – the working day was still going strong where she was – but I also knew that she wouldn't miss Pat's big day. I watched him talking to his mother, uncomfortable in his shirt and tie, a baby suddenly forced to impersonate a man.

Then it was time to go.

As we drove closer to the school I was seized by a moment of panic. There were children everywhere, swarms of them all in exactly the same clothes as Pat, all heading in the same direction as us. I could lose him in here. I could lose him forever.

We pulled up some way from the school gates. There were cars double-parked and treble-parked everywhere. Tiny girls with Leonardo DiCaprio lunch boxes scrambled out of off-road vehicles the size of Panzer tanks. Bigger boys with Arsenal and Manchester United kitbags climbed out of old bangers. The noise from this three-foot-high tribe was unbelievable.

I took Pat's clammy hand and we joined the throng. I could see a collection of small, bewildered new kids and their nervous parents milling about in the playground. We were just going through the gates to join them when I noticed the lace on one of Pat's brand new black leather shoes was undone.

'Let me get your lace for you, Pat,' I said, kneeling down to tie it, realising that this was the first day in his life he had ever been out of trainers.

Two bigger boys rolled past, arm in arm. They leered at us. Pat smiled at them shyly.

'He can't even do his shoes up,' one of them snorted.

'No,' Pat said, 'but I can tell the time.'

They collapsed in guffaws of laughter, holding each other up for support, and reeled away repeating what Pat had said with disbelief.

'But I *can* tell the time, can't I?' Pat said, thinking they doubted his word, his eyes blinking furiously as he seriously considered bursting into tears.

'You can tell the time brilliantly,' I said, unable to really believe that I was actually going to turn my son loose among all the cynicism and spite of the lousy modern world. We went into the playground.

A lot of the children starting school had both parents with them. But I wasn't the only lone parent. I wasn't even the only man.

There was another solo father, maybe ten years older than me, a shagged out business type accompanying a composed little girl with a rucksack bearing the grinning mugs of some boy band I had never heard of. We exchanged a quick look and then he avoided my eyes, as if what I had might be catching. I suppose his wife could have been at work. I suppose she could have been anywhere.

The kindly headmistress came and led us into the assembly hall. She gave us a brief, breezy pep talk and then the children were all assigned to their individual classrooms.

Pat got Miss Waterhouse, and with a handful of other parents and new kids we were marched off to her class by one of the trusted older children who were acting as guides. Our guide was a boy of around eight years old. Pat stared up at him, dumbstruck with admiration.

In Miss Waterhouse's class a flock of five-year-olds were sitting cross-legged on the floor, patiently waiting for a story from their teacher, a young woman with the hysterical good humour of a game-show host.

'Welcome, everyone!' Miss Waterhouse said. 'You're just in time for our morning story. But first it's time for everyone to say goodbye to their mummy.' She beamed at me. 'And daddy.'

It was time to leave him. Although there had been a

few emotional goodbyes before he dropped out of nursery school, this time felt a bit different. This time it felt as though I were being left.

He was starting school, and by the time he left school he would be a man and I would be middle-aged. Those long days of watching Star Wars videos at home while life went on somewhere else were over. Those days had seemed empty and frustrating at the time, but I missed them already. My baby was joining the world.

Miss Waterhouse asked for volunteers to look after the new boys and girls. A forest of hands shot up, and the teacher chose the chaperones. Suddenly a solemn, exceptionally pretty little girl was standing next to us.

'I'm Peggy,' she told Pat. 'And I'm going to take care of you.'

The little girl took his hand and led him into the classroom.

He didn't even notice me leaving.

I can remember sleeping on the back seat of my father's car. We were driving away from the city, coming back from nights out – the yearly visit to the London Palladium to see a pantomime, the weekly visits to see my grandmother – and I would watch the yellow lamps of East End streets and Essex A-roads blurring high above my dreaming head.

I would stretch out on the back seat of my dad's car – 'You don't have to sleep, just rest your eyes,' my mother would tell me – and soon I would be rocked off to sleep by the motion of the car and the murmur of my parents' voices.

The next thing I knew I would be in my father's arms, the car up our drive, the engine still running as he lifted me from the back seat, swaddled in the tartan blanket that he kept in the car for our trips to the seaside and relatives and the London Palladium.

These days it takes next to nothing to wake me. A drunk staggering home, a car door slammed, a false alarm miles away – they are all enough to snap me out of sleep and leave me staring at the ceiling for hours. But when I was a child sleeping on the back seat of my dad's car, nothing could wake me up. I hardly stirred from my dreams when we arrived home and I was carried up the stairs to bed wrapped up in that tartan blanket and my father's arms.

I wanted Pat to have memories like that. I wanted Pat to feel as secure as that. But with Gina gone and our old VW estate sold to pay the mortgage, these days Pat was by my side in the passenger seat of the MGF, struggling and fighting against sleep even when we were coming back from my parents and there was an hour's worth of empty motorway ahead of us.

I wanted my son to have car rides like the car rides I had known as a child. But we were travelling light.

Cyd called towards the end of the long morning.

'How did it go?' she asked me.

She sounded genuinely anxious. That made me like her even more.

'It was a bit fraught,' I said. 'The chin wobbled when it was time to say goodbye. There were a few tears in the eyes. But that was me, of course. Pat was absolutely fine.'

She laughed, and in my mind's eye I could see her smile lighting up the place where she worked, making it somewhere special.

'I can make you laugh,' I said.

'Yes, but now I've got to get to work,' she said. 'Because you can't pay my bills.'

That was true enough. I couldn't even pay my own bills.

* * *

My father came with me to meet Pat at the end of his first day at school.

'A special treat,' my dad said, parking his Toyota right outside the school gates. He didn't say if it was a special treat for Pat or a special treat for me.

As the children came swarming out of the gates at 3.30, I saw that there was never a possibility of losing him in the crowd. Even among hundreds of children dressed more or less the same, you can still spot your own child a mile off.

He was with Peggy, the little girl who was going to take care of him. She stared up at me with eyes that seemed strangely familiar.

'Did you enjoy it?' I asked him, afraid that he was going to threaten to hold his breath if he ever had to go back.

'Guess what?' Pat said. 'The teachers have all got the same first name. They're all called Miss.'

My old man picked him up and kissed him. I wondered how long it would be before Pat would start squirming under our kisses. Then he kissed my dad on the face – one of those hard, fierce kisses he had learned from Gina – and I saw that we still had a while.

'We've got your bike in the back of Granddad's car,' my dad said. 'We can go to the park on the way home.'

'Can Peggy come?' Pat asked.

I looked down at the solemn-eyed child.

'Of course she can,' I said. 'But we have to ask Peggy's mummy or daddy first.'

'My mum's at work,' Peggy told me. 'So's my dad.'

'Then who meets you?'

'Bianca,' she said. 'My babysitter. Although I'm not a baby any more.'

Peggy looked around her, gazing up at the herd of adults meeting children until she saw the face she was looking for.

A girl in her late teens was pushing through the crowds, sucking on a cigarette and searching for her charge.

'That's Bianca,' Peggy pointed.

'Come on, Peggy,' the girl said, offering her hand. 'Let's go.'

Pat and Peggy stared at each other.

'We're off to the park for an hour or so,' I told Bianca. 'Peggy's welcome to come with us. And you too, of course.'

The babysitter curtly shook her head.

'We've got to go,' she said.

'See you tomorrow then,' Peggy told Pat.

'Yes,' he said.

Peggy smiled at him as Bianca dragged her off through the thinning crowd.

'I'll see her tomorrow,' Pat said. 'At my school.'

There was dirt on his hands, paint on his face and a piece of what looked like egg sandwich by his mouth. But he was fine. School was going to be okay.

Another difference between me and my old man. After Pat fell into the empty swimming pool, I would have been quite happy never to set eyes on his bicycle again. But during one of those endless hours at the hospital, my dad drove to the park and recovered Bluebell.

The bike was exactly where we had left it, on its side at the empty deep end, undamaged apart from a bent handlebar. I would have cheerfully stuck it on the nearest skip. My dad wanted Pat to ride it again. I didn't argue with him. I thought I would leave Pat to do that.

Yet when my father took Bluebell from the boot of his car, my son seemed happy to see it.

'I've straightened the handlebar,' my dad told us. 'It needs a lick of paint, that's all. Shouldn't take a minute. I can do it for you, if you like.'

My dad knew that I hadn't held a paintbrush since I had dropped out of O level art.

'I can do it,' I said sullenly. 'Put your coat on, Pat.'

It was September and the first cold snap of autumn was in the air. I helped Pat into his anorak, pulling up the hood, watching the smile spread across his face at the sight of his bike.

'One more thing,' my father said, producing a small silver spanner from his car coat. 'I think it's time that a big boy like Pat took the stabilisers off his bike.'

This was my old man at seventy – tough, kind, confident, grinning at his grandson with boundless tenderness. And yet I found myself railing against his DIY competence, his manly efficiency, his absolute certainty that he could bend the world to his will. And I was sick of the sight of that bike.

'Jesus, Dad,' I said. 'He just fell off the bloody thing five minutes ago. Now you want him to start doing wheelies.'

'You always exaggerate,' my father said. 'Just like your mother. I don't want the lad to do wheelies – whatever wheelies might be. I just want him to have a crack at riding without his stabilisers. It will do him good.'

My father got down on his haunches and began to remove the little stabilising wheels from Bluebell. Seeing him at work with a spanner made me feel that I had spent my life watching him do odd jobs, first in his home and later at mine. When the lights went on the blink or the rain started coming through the ceiling, Gina and I didn't reach for the Yellow Pages. We called my dad.

The burst boiler, the knackered guttering, the hole in the roof – no task was too big or too difficult for his immaculately kept tool box. He loved Gina's praise when the job was completed – she always laid it on a bit thick – but he would have done it anyway. My father was what my mother would call 'good around the house'. I was exactly the opposite. I was what I would call 'fucking useless around the house'.

Now I watched Pat's face bleaching with fear as my dad finished removing the little stabilising wheels from his bike. For a moment I was about to erupt, but then I kept it in. Because if I started, then I knew all the rows of thirty years would come pouring out – my laziness against my father's can-do capability, my timidity against my old man's machismo, my desire for a quiet life against my dad's determination to get his own way.

I didn't want all that to come out in front of Pat. Not today. Not any day. So I looked on in silence as my dad helped my son on to his bike.

'Just a little try,' my dad said soothingly. 'If you don't like it, we can stop. We can stop straightaway. Okay, baby?'

'Okay, Granddad.'

My father seized hold of the bike's handlebars with one hand and its seat with the other. Pat clung on to both handlebars for dear life, his already scuffed school shoes trailing reluctantly on the pedals as Bluebell's wheels rolled round and round. With me bringing up the sulky rear, we wobbled past the swings and slides and across an empty patch of grass.

'Are you holding on?' Pat asked.

'I'm holding on,' my dad reassured him.

'Could you look after Pat on Saturday night for me?' I said.

'Saturday night?' he repeated, as if it were a strange request, as though I knew very well that was the night he and my mum liked to go out and drop a few Es.

'Yes, I'm going out.'

'Of course,' he said. 'We'll always look after him for you. Something to do with work, is it?'

'Nothing to do with work, Dad. I don't have any work

right now, remember? I'm going out with a girl.' That didn't sound quite right. 'With a woman.' That didn't sound quite right either.

I thought that it might have stopped him. But he carried on in his half-crouch, supporting Pat's bike as we made our way through the daisies and the dog crap.

'Who is she?' he asked.

'Just a friend. We might go to the pictures.'

He finally stopped, rubbing his back as he straightened up to look at me.

'You think that's appropriate behaviour for someone in your position, do you?'.

'Going to the pictures? I don't see why not.'

'I'm not talking about going to the pictures. I'm talking about going out with a strange woman just after –' He nodded at the hood of Pat's anorak. 'You know.'

'There's nothing strange about her,' I said. 'And we're only going to the pictures. We're not eloping.'

He shook his head, dumbfounded at what the world was coming to.

'I don't care what you get up to,' he said. Then he indicated Pat again. 'What I care about is him. This girl – is it serious?'

'I don't know, Dad. Can we get our first date out of the way before we start picking out curtains?'

I was playing the injured innocent. But I knew that if I went out with a woman it would confuse and frighten him. It wasn't my intention to hurt him. I just wanted to show him that I was thirty years old and that he couldn't decide when I took my stabilisers off.

We had come to a ragged scrap of tarmac in front of a tatty stage.

'Are you ready?' my father asked Pat.

'Ready,' Pat said, sounding not very ready at all.

'I'm holding you, okay?' my dad said, increasing his pace. 'I'm going to keep holding you. Just keep your back straight. And pedal.'

'Okay.'

'Are you holding on?'

'I'm holding on!'

They took off across the tarmac, Pat's face hidden by the hood of his anorak and my father bent double by his side, like a little elf being chased by a hunchback. Then my dad let go of the bike.

'You holding on, Granddad?'

'I'm holding on!' he cried as Pat left him behind. 'Pedal! I've got you!'

His little legs pedalled. Bluebell gave a dangerous wobble as Pat splashed through a puddle, but the bike seemed to right itself and gather speed.

'You're doing it!' my dad shouted. 'You're doing it, Pat!'

He turned to look at me and we both laughed out loud. I ran to my father's side and he put his arm around my shoulders. He smelled of Old Spice and Old Holborn.

'Look at him go,' my dad said proudly.

The bike reached the edge of the tarmac, bounced once and skidded on to the grass. Pat was moving more slowly now, but still pedalling furiously as he made a beeline for the trees.

'Don't go too far!' I shouted. But he couldn't hear me. He disappeared into the shadows of some old oak trees, like some hooded creature of the forest returning to his lair.

My father and I looked at each other. We weren't laughing now. We took off after him, our shoes sliding on the wet grass, calling his name.

Then he was nonchalantly riding towards us out of the trees, the hood of his anorak flown off, and grinning from ear to ear.

'Look what I can do,' he said proudly, briefly standing up in Bluebell's stirrups before skidding to a halt.

'That's brilliant, Pat,' I said. 'But don't go off like that again, okay? Always stay where we can see you.'

'What's wrong with Granddad?' he said.

My father was leaning against a tree, clawing at his chest and gasping for air. The blood had drained from his face and there was something in his eyes that I had never seen before. It might have been fear.

'I'll be fine,' he wheezed.

'Granddad?' Pat said.

'Granddad's fine,' he said.

After a long, desperate minute he managed to get some air in his lungs. Still breathing hard, he laughed off the concern of his son and grandson.

'Just getting old,' he said. 'Too old for a jog in the woods.'

And I thought that's exactly what it was – old age catching up on a man whose body had endured so much in his youth. All my life those small pieces of shrapnel, jagged and black, had been squeezing out of his tough old body. Every summer we saw that giant starburst of a scar on his side. All that pain and punishment was bound to catch up on him sooner or later.

But I was wrong. It wasn't the past calling. It was the future.

'Don't worry about me,' my father told us. 'I'm fine. Let's go home.'

We walked back to his car through the lengthening shadows of that September afternoon, Pat riding his bike ahead of us, my old man humming, 'You Make Me Feel So Young', consoled and comforted by his personal Dean Martin, his own private Sinatra.

twenty

When you are deep into a relationship that you expect to last forever, it never crosses your mind that one day you will be taking your third shower of the day and getting ready to go out on a date.

Like getting your mum to do your washing or having to borrow money from your dad, you think that all those nervy bathroom rituals are way behind you.

You never dream that there will again come a time when you are as fanatical about your personal hygiene as a fifteen-year-old with a permanent erection. That you will once more find yourself standing in front of the mirror trying to do something with your hair. That you will be brushing teeth that are already perfectly clean. And that you will do all these things so you can sit in the dark for a couple of hours with a member of the opposite sex who you have only just met.

It's scary. Dating is a young person's game. You get out of practice. You might not be any good at it any more.

You use a different part of your brain for going out with someone you have just met than you use for going out with someone you are married to. You use different muscles. So perhaps it's only natural that when you start using those muscles again, they can feel a little stiff.

Two grown-ups going through all those teenage mating rituals – trying to look nice, meeting at the arranged hour, knowing what it is time to do and what should wait a while and what should wait forever. It should be really difficult to get back into all that stuff after you have been with someone for years. But it didn't feel difficult with Cyd.

She made it feel easy.

'The first film we see together is really important,' Cyd said. 'I know we're just friends and all, but our choice of movie tonight is really important.'

I tried to look as though I knew what she was talking about.

'A lot of people on a first date, they try to play safe. They go for a big summer movie. You know, one of those films where New York gets destroyed by aliens or a tidal wave or a big monkey or something. They think that kind of movie guarantees a good time. But a big summer movie is not a good choice.'

'It isn't?'

She shook her head. 'Nobody really has a good time at those movies apart from thirteen-year-old kids in Idaho. It's the law of diminishing returns. When you've seen the Empire State Building blown up once, you don't need to see it again.'

I was starting to get it. 'You think the earth is going to move. But you end up yawning as the aliens zap the White House.'

'If you choose a big summer movie, it shows you have really low expectations,' she said, shooting me a look as I squeezed the MGF through the afternoon traffic clogging up around the Angel. 'About everything. It means you think life is essentially just a bucket of stale popcorn and a carton of flat Diet Coke. And that's the most that anyone can hope for.'

I tried to remember the first film I had seen with Gina. It had been something arty and Japanese at the Barbican. It was about depressed people.

'Art-house movies are just as bad,' Cyd said, reading my mind. 'It means you are both pretending to be something that you're probably not.'

'And think of all those couples around the world whose first film was *Titanic*,' I said. 'All those budding relationships doomed before they had even really begun. Before they had even left port.'

She gave me a punch on the arm. 'This is serious,' she said. 'I had a friend back home who got married to a guy who took her to see *The Fly* on their first date.'

'And later he turned into a bug?'

'As good as,' she said. 'He certainly changed. For the worse.'

'So what do you want to see?' I asked her.

'Trust me?' she said.

'I trust you,' I said.

She wanted to see one of those films that they put on television every Christmas. One of those films that I somehow imagined I had already seen a dozen times. But I don't think I had ever really seen it at all.

I don't know why they were showing *It's A Wonderful Life* down at the NFT on the South Bank. It might have been a Frank Capra season or a James Stewart season. They might have had a restored, digitally-enhanced, freshly polished print. I don't know and it doesn't matter. That was the movie we went to see on our first night together. And at first it seemed like pretty grim stuff.

The special effects were from the steam age. Up in a starry sky that was clearly just a painted sheet of cardboard with a torch behind it, some angels – or rather, heavenly beings represented by pinpricks in the cardboard – were discussing

George Bailey, pillar of his community, and his date with destiny.

As the action switched to a small American town and their merry little Christmas, I found myself yearning for aliens or a tidal wave or a big monkey to come along and destroy the lot. If Cyd's theory about the omens of your first film were true, then we would be lucky to last the evening.

Then gradually, as all of James Stewart's hopes and dreams began to recede, I found myself drawn into this story of a man who had lost sight of why he was alive.

The film was far tougher than I remembered it when it had been flickering in black and white in the background of my multicoloured childhood, sandwiched between Christmas *Top of the Pops* and my mum's turkey sandwiches.

As his world starts to unravel, James Stewart abuses one of his children's teachers on the phone and gets punched out by her husband in a bar. He bitterly resents the loving wife he gave up his dreams of travelling the world for. Most shocking of all, he is rotten to his children – an irritable, bad-tempered bully. But you know that it's not because he doesn't love them enough. It's because he loves them so much.

In the darkness, Cyd reached over and squeezed my hand.

'Don't worry,' she said. 'Everything works out all right in the end.'

It was still light when we came out of the film, but only just. We bought slices of pizza in the NFT café and ate them at those long wooden tables outside where you have to share with other people and you feel like a student.

The NFT is in an ugly building in a beautiful part of town. It's inside a dumb concrete sixties block plonked down just where the Thames curls south as it passes under the shadow of Waterloo Bridge, and it faces right across the river from the lights of the Victoria embankment and St Paul's. That's where Cyd told me that she had grown up in a home full of women and movies.

'The first film my parents saw together was *Gone with the Wind*,' she said. 'And after my dad died, my mom saw it sixteen times alone. She would have seen it more often. But she was trying to ration herself.'

Cyd was the youngest of four sisters. Her mother worked as a nurse at the Texas Medical Center – 'Where big shots go to get their hearts fixed' – and her father had driven trucks out in the oil fields.

'Houston is an oil town,' she said. 'When oil prices are high, life is sweet. And when oil prices fall through the floor, we tighten our belts. But for better or worse, for richer or poorer, Houston is always an oil town.'

The way she told it, her parents never came off their honeymoon. Even when they had four teenage daughters, they would still hold hands in public and give each other a single flower and leave love notes in lunch boxes.

'When I was twelve, it embarrassed me,' Cyd said. 'Now I love it. Now I love it that they were that much in love. I know what you're thinking – maybe they were never really like that and I just like to remember them that way. Maybe they got on each other's nerves and snapped at each other. But I know what I saw. They were mad about each other. They chose right.'

Then one Sunday she was with her friends in the Dairy Queen at the Galleria shopping mall when her oldest sister came to find her to tell her that their father had died of a heart attack.

'My mom didn't grow old overnight,' Cyd said. 'It wasn't like that at all. She just sort of retreated into the past. Maybe she figured that the best was over. She still went to work.

She still cooked our meals. But now she watched a lot of old movies. And some of her video collection must have rubbed off on me. Because when I met the guy I came to England for, I thought he was Rhett Butler.'

I am never comfortable when the conversation turns to someone's old partners. All those hopes that came to nothing, all those wounds that haven't healed, all the bitterness and disappointment of seeing your love get left out for the dustbin men – it seems to take the shine off the whole evening. And she could feel it too. She changed the subject, veering away from her sad story by playing chirpy tourist guide.

'Did you know that Houston was the first word spoken on the moon?' she said. 'That's a fact. Neil Armstrong said to Mission Control – *Houston, Tranquillity base here. The Eagle has landed.*'

'Until I met you, I never really thought about Houston,' I said. 'It's not one of those American cities that you can see in your head.'

'It's not like here,' she said. 'If it's got a second coat of paint, it's an antique. We have these drinking joints by the side of the road called ice houses where all the women look like they just stepped out of a Hank Williams song. But if you're young you go to the Yucatan Liquor Store on a Saturday night where the girls try to look like Pamela Anderson and the boys can't help looking like Meatloaf.'

'It sounds a bit like Essex,' I said. 'So where did you meet this English guy?'

'At the Yucatan Liquor Store. On a Saturday night. He asked me if I wanted a drink and I said no. Then he asked me if I wanted to dance and I said yes. He was working in Houston as a despatch rider. That's what he does. He delivers stuff on a motorbike. Sort of a glamorous postman. Naturally, I was impressed.'

'And he didn't turn out to be Rhett Butler after all?'

'Well, you know,' she said. 'Not even Clark Gable turned out to be Rhett Butler, did he?'

'But you came to London with him?'

'Yeah.'

'Why didn't you stay over there? Did they kick him out?'

'Oh, no. We were married. He had his Green Card. Did you know a Green Card is really pink?'

I shook my head.

'It surprised us, too. We had to go through those interviews with immigration officials who make sure you're really in love. We showed them our wedding album and it wasn't a problem. We could have stayed there forever.' She thought about it. 'I think he felt like he should be doing more with his life. America can make you feel like a bit of a failure. So we came here.'

'And what went wrong?'

'Everything.' She looked at me. 'He was into the bamboo. Do you know what that means?'

I shook my head. 'Is it some drug thing?'

'No. Well, in a way. It means he liked Asian girls. And still does. And always will.'

'Asian girls?'

'You know – Korean girls. Chinese. Japanese. Filipinas. He wasn't that fussy – which is a bit insulting to Asian women, as they can look as different to each other as a Swede and a Turk. But he genuinely didn't care, as long as they were Asian. The night we met, he was at the Yucatan with a little Vietnamese girl. We have a lot of Vietnamese in Houston.'

'Asian? You mean Orientals.'

'You can't say Orientals any more. It's considered insulting – like Negro or stewardess. You have to say African-American and flight attendant. And Asian instead of Oriental.'

'To me, Asian sounds like Indian.'

'Sorry, mister. That's what you have to say.'

'What did he like about them?'

'Maybe he liked the fact that they didn't look like him. That they looked like something completely different. I can understand that. Heterosexuality – it's all about being attracted to someone who doesn't look like you, isn't it?'

'So if he liked Asian girls – if this guy who wasn't Rhett Butler was into the bamboo – why did he like you?'

'Search me. I think I was an aberration. A working holiday. I don't know.'

She brushed her black bell of hair from her forehead and stared at me with those wide-set brown eyes. Now she mentioned it, I could see how someone who was into the bamboo could fall for her. In a certain light.

'We were together for two years,' she said. 'One year back home and another year over here. Then he reverted to type. Or I found out that he had reverted to type. With a Malaysian student who he met in a park. He showed her London – and a few other things. He wasn't a bad guy. He's still not a bad guy. I just chose wrong. What about you?'

'Me?'

'Yeah, what happened to your marriage?'

I tried to figure out what had happened to Gina and me. I knew that it had something to do with getting older and taking something for granted and feeling that life was slipping away. James Stewart could have explained it to me.

'I don't really know what happened,' I said. 'I lost my moorings there for a while.'

'Oh, I see,' Cyd said. 'You mean you fancied a quick fuck?'

'It was more than that. Although that was a part of it. But I just – I don't know how to explain. I sort of let the light go out.'

She stared at me for a moment and then she nodded.

'Let's go and look at the lights,' she said.

It was dark now. On the other side of the river you could see the illuminations running all the way along the embankment like a string of pearls. In the morning you would be looking across at grey office blocks and another traffic jam and the city scuttling to pay the rent. But tonight it was beautiful.

'Looks like Christmas,' she said, taking my arm.

It did. And it felt like Christmas too.

'I'm going to take a chance on you,' she told me.

twenty-one

When the chain-smoking babysitter realised that we weren't going to steal her away forever, Peggy was finally allowed to come home with Pat for a couple of hours.

'Look what I've got,' she told me, producing a little man made of moulded plastic. He was looking very pleased with himself inside white satin trousers, a spangly silver waistcoat and what looked like a purple tuxedo.

'Disco Ken,' she said. 'Barbie's friend. Going to the disco.'

It was strange watching them play together. Pat wanted to blow up the Death Star. Peggy wanted to hang drapes in the Millennium Falcon.

Excited to the point of hysteria at having his friend in his very own living room – although noticeably unimpressed by Disco Ken – Pat bounced off the furniture waving his light sabre above his head and shouting, 'I'll never join you on the Dark Side!'

Peggy considered him with her solemn dark eyes and then began moving little Star Wars figures around the Millennium Falcon – heavily Sellotaped on one side after crash landing into a radiator – as though they were having tea and buttered scones at the Ritz.

Nature or nurture? I knew that Pat had never been encouraged to play violent games – in fact his never-ending blood baths often drove me up the wall.

Not quite five years old, he was actually a gentle, loving little boy who was too sweet for the rough and tumble of the playground. There had been some bullying because he didn't have a mother waiting for him at the school gates, and neither of us had yet worked out a way to deal with it.

Peggy was completely different. At five-and-a-half, she was a strong, confident little girl who nothing seemed to faze or frighten. I never saw any fear in those serious brown eyes.

Pat wasn't built for hunting and gathering, and Peggy wasn't made for making jam and jumpers. Yet give them a box of Star Wars toys and suddenly they were responding to their gender stereotypes. Peggy just wasn't interested in games of death and destruction. And that's all that Pat was interested in.

It didn't stop them from enjoying each other's company. Pat hung on to the back of the sofa, grinning with love and admiration as Peggy shoved little figures of Princess Leia and Han Solo and Luke Skywalker around grey plastic spaceships which had clocked up a lot of miles in hyperspace.

'Where's your mum?' Peggy asked him.

'She's in abroad,' Pat said. 'Where's your mum?'

'She's at work. Bianca picks me up from school but she's not allowed to smoke in the flat. It makes her grumpy.'

There didn't seem to be a man anywhere near Peggy's life, but that was hardly worth commenting on these days. I wondered who he was – probably some jerk who had fucked off the moment he was asked to buy some nappies.

The door bell rang. It was one of those young men who are out of work but not yet out of hope. I admire that spirit, and I always try to support them by buying some chamois leather or rubbish sacks. But this one didn't have the usual kitbag full of household goods.

‘Really sorry to disturb you,’ he said. ‘I’m Eamon. Eamon Fish.’

At first it didn’t register. Living in the city you get so used to complete strangers knocking on your door that it comes as a shock when someone who has actually touched your life rings the bell.

But of course – this was Eamon Fish, the young comedian who would probably be doing beer commercials and sleeping with weather girls by this time next year. Or next month. Or next week. The same Eamon Fish whose show I was asked to produce and had turned down because of fish finger cooking duties.

I didn’t know what to do with him. I didn’t know why he was here. I was expecting some down-at-heel young man who was going to sell me chamois leather. And here was some down-at-heel young man who would soon be getting pissed at the next BAFTAs.

‘What can I do for you?’ I asked him.

‘What’s that?’ he said, frowning and cocking his head towards me.

‘What do you want?’

‘Can we talk? It would mean a lot to me.’

I let him in. We went into the living room where Peggy and Pat were sitting surrounded by an avalanche of toys. Pat still had his light sabre in his hand.

‘Wow,’ Eamon said. ‘A light sabre! Traditional weapon of the Jedi Knights! Can I have a look?’

A slow smile spreading across his face, Pat stood up and handed the young stranger his light sabre.

‘Good fellow you are,’ Eamon said.

He swept the light sabre back and forth, making a buzzing sound that made Pat’s smile grow even wider.

‘I haven’t held one of these for years,’ Eamon said. ‘But you never forget, do you?’ He grinned at Pat. ‘I come from a little town called Kilcarney. And when I was growing up, I felt a lot like Luke Skywalker felt growing up on Tatooine. You know Tatooine?'

'Luke's home planet,' Pat said. 'With the two suns.'

'What's that?' Eamon said. 'Luke's home planet, you say? Well, that's right. And he felt cut off from the rest of the galaxy, didn't he? Luke felt a long way from the action, stuck out there under the two suns of old Tatooine. And when I was growing up in sleepy old Kilcarney, I also dreamed of escaping and having lots of adventures in faraway places that I could hardly imagine.' He handed Pat his light sabre. 'And that's exactly what I did.'

'Yes,' said Peggy. 'But what happened between then and now?'

'What's that you say?'

Was he completely deaf?

'I said – what happened between *leaving* your home planet and *today*?' Peggy shouted.

'Well, that's what I want to talk to your daddy about,' Eamon said.

'He's not my daddy,' Peggy said. 'My daddy's got a motorbike.'

'The boy's mine,' I said, indicating Pat. He was still staring at Eamon with profound approval for his light sabre technique.

'He's got it,' Eamon said, smiling with what seemed like real warmth. 'Around the chin, I mean. He's got it. He's a handsome lad, all right.'

'Come into the kitchen,' I told him. 'I'll make us some coffee.'

'Coffee, you say? Top man.'

While I put the kettle on he sat at the kitchen table poking his ears with an index finger and muttering to himself.

'Bad day?' I said.

'What's that?' he asked.

I put a cup of coffee down in front of him and put my face very close to his. He had those black Irish good looks and a long-term scruffiness, like a Kennedy who has just spent the summer sleeping in a doorway. And he seemed to be as deaf as a post.

'I said – what's wrong with your hearing?'

'Ah that,' he said. 'Let me explain about the ears thing. There's a posh place down in the West End where they fit hearing aids. But they also fit ear pieces – for television presenters. So their producers and directors can talk into their lugholes while they're presenting a programme. You might know the place.'

I knew it well. I remembered when Marty had been down there to get fitted for his ear pieces. That's when we knew we were really leaving radio.

'I just came from there,' Eamon said. 'Left in a bit of a hurry, as it happens. What the hearing man does when he is measuring you up, he pours some stuff like warm wax into your ears. Then you have to wait for a while until it sets. And then they know what size ears you have. For your ear pieces, that is.'

'I understand.'

'Except with me, he never got quite that far. He had just poured the hot wax into my ears and we were waiting for it to set when I thought – what the fuck am I doing here?' Eamon shook his head. Flakes of dried wax flew out. 'What makes me think that I can present a television show? What makes anyone think that I can present a television show? I'm a comedian. I do stand-up. Some people like it. But so what? Why does that mean I will be able to present a TV show?'

'So you were being fitted for your ear pieces and you got stage fright.'

'Before I got anywhere near a stage,' he said. 'I don't know if you could dignify it with the term stage fright. I suppose a bollock-shrivelling panic attack is probably more what it was. Anyway, I ran out of there with the wax still sloshing about in my ears. It seems to have set quite well.'

I gave him a tissue and some cotton buds and watched him scrape the hardened wax out of his ears. They always measure them for two ear pieces, one in either ear, although nobody ever uses more than one. Now I saw that it was just a ploy to stop you running away.

'I really wanted you to produce the show,' he said. 'I need – what do they call it? – an enabler. Someone to show me the way. Same as you showed Marty Mann the way when he left his radio show. I was disappointed when they said you weren't going to do it.'

'It's nothing to do with you,' I said. 'I'm looking after my son. Alone. I can't go back to work full-time. I need to be around for him.'

'But I notice he's wearing a uniform. Isn't the little feller at school now?'

'That's right.'

'So he's out of the house for most of the day?'

'Well, yes.'

'So – forgive me asking – what do you do all day, Harry?'

What did I do all day? I got Pat up, got him dressed and got him off to school. I shopped and cleaned. I was waiting for him at the school gates in the afternoon when he came out. Then I made sandwiches, read to him and got him ready for bed. What did I do all day?

'Nothing,' I said.

'Don't you miss it? Work, I mean?'

'Sure I miss it. I used to have quality time with my son – meaning I saw him for five minutes at the start and at the end of each day. Now I have quantity time instead. I didn't choose that change. That's just the way it has worked out. But that's why I can't produce the show for you.'

'But you could be the executive producer, couldn't you? You could come in a few times a week just to oversee the show? You could tell me what I need to do to stop looking like a complete eejit? You could help me play to my strengths, couldn't you?'

'Well,' I said. 'Maybe.'

I had never even considered the possibility that there was a compromise between working full-time and not working at all. It had never crossed my mind.

'Look, I admire what you're doing with your boy,' Eamon said. 'Believe me, you would go down a storm with the mothers of Kilcarney. But I need you. I'm here for really selfish reasons. I'm shitting coloured lights about presenting this show. That's why I'm dropping bits of hardened wax all over your kitchen floor. And I know you can get me through it without total humiliation. It might even be good.'

I thought about the long mornings and endless afternoons when Pat wasn't around. And I thought about my most recent meeting with the bank manager, who was impressed by my efforts to look after my son and less impressed by my expanding overdraft.

But most of all I thought about how good Eamon had been with Pat – admiring his light sabre, talking to him about Luke's home planet, telling me that he was a special kid.

I knew that at this stage of my life – and at all the future stages of my life, come to that – I would like anyone who liked my boy. When you are alone with a child, you want as many people rooting for him as you can get. This young Irish comic with dried wax in his ears seemed to be on our side. And so I found myself on his side, too.

I was ready to work with him on a part-time basis because

I was bored and broke. But most of all I was ready to work with him because he thought my son was going to make it.

'I need to see your act,' I said. 'I need to see what you do on stage so I can think about how it could work on the box. Have you got a show reel?'

'What?' he said.

twenty-two

Whatever the opposite of inscrutable is, that's what small children are.

Maybe in ten years' time Pat would be able to hide his feelings behind some blank adolescent mask and the old man – me – wouldn't have a clue what he was thinking. But he was four going on five and I could tell that the latest phone call from his mother had given him the blues.

'You okay, Pat?'

He nodded listlessly, and I followed him down to the bathroom where he squirted some children's toothpaste on his Han Solo toothbrush.

'How's Mummy?'

'She's all right. She's got a cold.'

He wasn't crying. He wasn't about to cry. His eyes were dry and his mouth was still. But he was down.

'You want to watch a video?' I asked him, watching him polish teeth that still looked brand new.

He spat into the sink and shot me a suspicious look.

'It's school tomorrow,' he said.

'I know it's school tomorrow. I don't mean watch the whole film. Just, say, the start of the first film up until the two 'droids get captured. How about that?'

He finished spitting and replaced his brush in the rack.

'Want to go to bed,' he said.

So I followed him into his bedroom and tucked him in. He didn't want a story. But I couldn't turn out the light knowing that he was depressed.

I knew what he was missing and it wasn't even what you could call a mother's love. It was a mother's indulgence. Someone who would tell him that it didn't matter if he couldn't tie his shoes up yet. Someone who would tell him that he was still the centre of the universe when he had just learned what we all learn on our first day of school – that we are not the centre of the universe. I was so desperate for him to make it that I couldn't be relaxed about him making it. Gina's indulgence. That's what he really missed.

'She'll be back,' I said. 'Your mother. You know that she'll be back for you, don't you?'

He nodded. 'As soon as she's done her work,' he said.

'We're okay, aren't we?' I asked him. 'You and me – we're doing okay, aren't we?'

He stared at me, blinking away the fatigue, trying to understand what I was going on about.

'We're managing without Mummy, aren't we, Pat? You let me wash your hair now. I make you things you like to eat – bacon sandwiches and stuff. And school's okay, isn't it? You like school. We're all right, aren't we? You and me?'

I felt bad about pushing him like this. But I needed him to tell me that we were doing all right. I needed to know that we were coping.

He gave me a tired smile.

'Yes, we're all right, Daddy,' he said, and I kissed him goodnight, hugging him gratefully.

That's the worst thing about splitting up, I thought as I turned out his light. It makes children hide their hearts. It teaches them how to move between separate worlds. It turns them all into little diplomats. That's the biggest tragedy of all. Divorce turns every kid into half a pint of semi-skimmed Henry Kissinger.

'I come from a little town called Kilcarney,' said Eamon Fish, removing the mike from its stand and gently tapping the transparent hearing device in his left ear. 'A quiet little town called Kilcarney where the girls are legendary.'

I was watching him on a monitor, sitting in the front row of the small studio audience that was facing the backsides of five cameramen. Although we were surrounded by all the usual paraphernalia of the television studio – lights burning in the rigging, cables snaking across the floor, the shadows beyond the cameras teeming with people whose jobs ranged from floor manager to working the autocue to pouring water, all of them wearing what we called 'blacks' – the director was shooting Eamon's act to make it look more like a stand-up routine than just another late-night chat show. There were already too many talk shows that looked like boot sale David Lettermans. But what would really make it different was the host.

'For those of you who have never been to that beautiful part of my country, you should know that Kilcarney has largely been untouched by the modern world. There are, for example, no vibrators in Kilcarney.' The audience tittered. 'It's true. The priests had them all removed. Because Kilcarney girls kept chipping their teeth.'

There was laughter from the audience, laughter which grew slightly nervous as Eamon ambled off the small stage and slowly came closer to us.

'I mean, I'm not saying Kilcarney girls are stupid,' he said. 'But why does a Kilcarney girl always wash her hair in her mother's sink? Because that's where you wash vegetables.'

The laughter grew louder. None of the studio audience

– the usual collection of the bored and the curious on the lam for a couple of hours of free fun – had ever seen this Eamon Fish before. But now they felt he was harmless. Then he turned on them.

'Actually, I'm making all this up,' he said. 'It's all bollocks. Kilcarney girls have the best exam results in western Europe. In fact, the average Kilcarney girl has more A levels than the average Englishman has tattoos. It's not true that the only difference between a Kilcarney girl and a mosquito is that a mosquito stops sucking if you hit it on the head. It's not true that Kilcarney girls only get fifteen minutes for lunch because any longer than that and you have to retrain them. It's not true that what Kilcarney girls and bottled Guinness have in common is that both of them are empty from the neck up. None of it is true.'

Eamon sighed, ran his free hand through his thick mop of black hair and sat down on the side of the stage.

'What is true is that even in this *Guardian*-reading, muesli-munching, politically correct age we seem to need someone to hate. Once it was the thick Irishman and the ball-breaking mother-in-law. Now it's blonde girls. Essex girls. Kilcarney girls.'

He shook his sleepy head.

'Now we all know in our hearts that geographical location and hair colour have got bugger all to do with sexual morality or intelligence. So why do we need a group of people who we can sneer at? What fundamental need in our pathetic souls does it fulfil? When we laugh about the blonde Kilcarney girl from Essex who turns off the light after sex by closing the car door, what's in it for us?'

It was only the pilot show, but I could already tell that Eamon was going to do it. After removing all the dried wax from his ears, he had crashed through the fear barrier and was learning how to be himself with five cameras watching. Fish was fine. I was more worried about the studio audience.

They had come in expecting to have their funny bones tickled, and had discovered that they were expected to defend their prejudices. They felt cheated, not good. It was a problem that we were always going to have with Eamon's show. As I saw it, the only way to solve this dilemma was to get them all pissed.

At our first production meeting after the pilot I told the AP to open a few bottles and cans and serve them to the audience while they were waiting in line to come into the studio. Everybody looked at me as if I were a genius.

That's what I love about television. You recommend opening a few cans of lager and they act as though you just painted the Sistine Chapel.

'So, it's a better job than the last one but they pay you less money,' my father said. 'How do they work that out then?'

'Because I don't work all week,' I told him yet again.

We were in their back garden, supposedly kicking a ball around with Pat, although he had retreated to the far end of the garden with his light sabre and dreams of conquering intergalactic evil. So that left me and two pensioners kicking a plastic football around between us in the autumn-tinged sunlight.

It was turning cold, but we were reluctant to go back inside. It was late September. The year was running out. There wouldn't be too many more Sunday afternoons like this one.

'If it really is a better job then they should cough up the readies,' said my dad, the international businessman, gently side-footing the ball to his wife. 'All these TV companies are loaded.'

'Not the ones Harry works for,' my mum said, thinking

she was being loyal, and trapping the ball under the sole of her carpet slipper.

'I go in for a couple of production meetings and I'm there when we record the show,' I said. 'And that's it. I'm not in the office all day, every day. I don't give them my life. I just go in twice a week and act like a big shot, bossing everyone around and coming up with brilliant ideas. Then I go home.'

'Home to Pat,' said my mum, knocking the ball to me. 'Your grandson.'

'I know who my grandson is,' my old man said irritably.

'Some people executive produce a whole bunch of shows,' I said. 'But I'm just going to do this one. I've worked it out. It's going to bring in less than we had before, but it will be enough.'

'This way he gets to pay his bills but he's there when Pat comes home from school,' my mum said.

My dad wasn't convinced.

He wanted me to have everything that life has to offer – the career and the kids, the family and the salary, the happy hearth and the fat pay cheque. He wanted me to have it all. But nobody gets away with having it all.

'Bobby Charlton,' he said, swinging a foot at the plastic football. It shot off his toe and into the rose bushes. 'Bugger,' he said. 'I'll get it.'

My mum and I watched him wander down to the end of the garden to retrieve the ball. He took the opportunity to put his arm around Pat and ask him what he was doing. Pat chattered away excitedly, his smooth round face turned up towards his grandfather, and my old man grinned down at him with eternal tenderness.

'Is he all right?' I asked my mum. 'He had a funny turn in the park the other day.'

'Fighting for his breath, was he?' she asked, not taking her eyes from him. And not surprised.

'Yes,' I said. 'Fighting for his breath.'

'I'm trying to get him to go to the doctor,' she said. 'Or the quack, as your dad calls him.'

We smiled at each other in the encircling darkness.

'He must be the last person in the world who calls doctors quacks,' I said.

'"*I'm not going to no quack,*"' my mum said. It was a pretty good impersonation of all the bad-tempered certainty my father was capable of summoning up. '"*I don't want no sawbones messing about with me.*"'

We laughed out loud, loving his old-fashioned distrust of anyone with any kind of authority, from the lowliest traffic warden to the most revered members of the medical profession, both of us taking comfort from the fact that my father was exactly the same as he always had been, even if we feared that might no longer be true.

He came back from the end of the garden with the ball and his grandson, asking us what was so funny.

'You are,' my mum said, taking his arm, and we all went back inside my father's house.

I didn't want it all. All I wanted was one more chance. One more chance to have a unified life, a life without broken bits and jagged edges. One more shot at happiness.

I didn't care how long it took before Gina came back from Tokyo. I was happy with Pat. And I wasn't looking for a brilliant career. All I wanted from work was a way to pay the mortgage.

But I wasn't ready to grow old and cold, hating women and the world because of what had happened to me. I didn't want to be fat, bald and forty, boring my teenage son to tears about all the sacrifices I had made for him. I wanted some more life. One more chance to get it right. That's what I wanted. That didn't seem like much to ask. Just one more chance.

Then the next day, Gina's dad came round to our place with his daughter Sally, the sulky teenage girl on the sofa, one of the many kids that Glenn had begat and abandoned as he moved on to sexier pastures, and it crossed my mind that what has truly messed up the lousy modern world is all the people who always want one more chance.

twenty-three

Glenn was dressed in his winter plumage – a ratty Afghan coat draped over a shiny blue tank top that revealed the hairs on his scrawny chest, and hipsters so tight that they made a mountain out of his molehill. He was so far out of fashion that he had just come back in style.

'Hello, Harry man,' he said, clasping my hand in some obscure power-to-the-people shake that thirty years ago probably signalled the revolution was about to commence. 'How you doing? Is the little dude around? All well? Sweet, sweet.'

There was a time when I wanted my old man to be more like Gina's dad. A time when I wished my father had appeared in glossy magazines in his youth, grinned on *Top of the Pops* once or twice in the early seventies and shown some interest in the world beyond the rose bushes at the end of his garden. But as I looked at Glenn's wizened old bollocks sticking up through his tight trousers, it seemed like a long time ago.

Glenn's youngest daughter was lurking behind him. At first I thought that Sally was in a bad mood. She came into the house all surly, avoiding eye contact by taking a great interest in the carpet, letting her stringy brown hair – longer than I remembered it – fall over her pale face as if she wanted to hide from the world and everything in it. But she wasn't really in a bad mood at all. She was fifteen years old. That was the problem.

I took them into the kitchen, depressed at the sight of two of Gina's relatives turning up out of the blue and wondering how soon I could get shot of them. But I softened when Sally's face lit up – really lit up – when Pat padded into the room with Peggy. Perhaps she was human after all.

'Hi Pat!' she beamed. 'How you doing?'

'Fine,' he said, giving no sign that he remembered his mother's half-sister. What was she to him? Half an aunt? A step-cousin? These days we have relatives we haven't even invented names for yet.

'I made you a tape,' she said, fumbling in her rucksack and eventually producing a cassette without its case. 'You like music, don't you?'

Pat stared at the tape blankly. The only music I could remember him liking was the theme from *Star Wars*.

'He likes music, doesn't he?' she asked me.

'Loves it,' I said. 'What do you say, Pat?'

'Thank you,' he said. He took the tape and disappeared with Peggy.

'I remembered how much he liked hip-hop when we were all staying at my dad's place,' she said. 'There's just a few of the classics on there. Coolio. Ol' Dirty Bastard. Tupac. Doctor Dre. Stuff like that. Things that a little kid might like.'

'That's really kind of you,' I said.

They sipped their drinks in silence – herbal tea for Glenn, regular Coke for Sally – and I felt a stab of resentment at these reminders of Gina's existence. What were they doing here? What did either of these people have to do with my life? Why didn't they just fuck off?

Then Pat or Peggy must have stuffed Sally's tape into the stereo because suddenly an angry black voice was booming above a murderous bass line in the living room.

'*You fuck with me and I'll fuck with you – so that would be a dumb fucking, mother-fucking thing to fucking do.*'

'That's lovely,' I said to Sally. 'He'll treasure it. So – you visiting your dad again?'

She shook her head. 'I'm living there now,' she said, shooting her old man a look from under her ratty fringe.

'A few problems back home,' Glenn said. 'With my ex-lady. And her new partner.'

'Old hippies,' Sally sneered. 'Old hippies who can't stand the thought of anybody else having fun.'

'Heavy scene with the new guy,' Glenn said. 'Bit of a disciplinarian.'

'That moron,' Sally added.

'And how's your boyfriend?' I asked, remembering the ape-boy smirking on the sofa.

'Steve?' she said, and I thought I saw the sting of tears in her eyes. 'Packed me in, didn't he? The fat pig. For Yasmin McGinty. That old slapper.'

'But we spoke to Gina the other night,' Glenn said, his foggy brain finally getting down to business. 'And we promised that we would look in on you and Pat if we were in the neighbourhood.'

Now I understood what they were doing here. No doubt they were responding to Gina's prompting. But in their own ham-fisted way, they were trying to help.

'Heard you've got a new gig,' Glenn said. 'Just wanted to say that the boy's welcome to crash with us any time.'

'Thanks, Glenn. I appreciate the offer.'

'And if you ever need a babysitter, just give me a call,' Sally said, hiding behind her hair and staring at a point somewhere beyond my shoulder.

It was really sweet of her. And I knew I needed a bit of extra cover with Pat now that I was working part-time. But Jesus Christ. I wasn't that desperate.

Cyd loved London the way only a foreigner could love it.

She saw past the stalled traffic, the dead pubs, the congealed poverty of the council estates. She looked beyond the frightened pensioners, the girls who looked like women, the women who looked like men, the men who looked like psychos. She saw beyond all of that. She told me the city was beautiful.

'At night,' Cyd said. 'And from the air. And walking across the royal parks. It's so green – the only city I ever saw that is greener than Houston.'

'Houston's green?' I said. 'I thought it was some dusty prairie town.'

'Yeah, but that's because you're a dumb limey. Houston is green, mister. But not as green as here. You can walk right across the centre of town through the three royal parks – St James's, Green Park, Hyde Park – and your shoes never touch anything but green, green grass. Do you know how far that is?'

'A mile or so,' I guessed.

'It's four miles,' she said. 'Four miles of flowers, trees and green. And people riding horses! In the heart of one of the biggest cities on the planet!'

'And the lake,' I said. 'Don't forget the lake.'

We were in a café up on the first floor of a huge white building from the thirties on Portland Place – the Royal Institute of British Architects, right across the street from the Chinese embassy, a monumental oasis of beauty and calm that I never knew existed until she took me there.

'I love the lake,' she said. 'I love the Serpentine. Can we still hire a rowing boat at this time of the year? Is it too late?'

'I'm not sure,' I said. It was the last week in September. 'We might be able to get a boat for a few more days. You want to try?'

Those wide-set brown eyes got even bigger.

'You mean now?'

'Why not?'

She looked at her watch.

'Because I've got to get to work,' she smiled. 'Sorry. I would have loved it.'

'Then how about tomorrow? First thing. Before the crowds get there. We'll get an early start. I'll meet you at your place after breakfast.'

I still hadn't seen her flat.

'Or I could come to your place after I get through at work tonight,' she said.

'Tonight?'

'That way we would really be sure of getting an early start.'

'You'll come to my place after work?'

'Yes.' She looked down at the clouds in her coffee and then back at me. 'Would that be okay?'

'That would be good,' I said. 'That would be great.'

Maybe the thing with Cyd had started off as some dumb infatuation when I was still reeling from Gina leaving me. But after we slept together for the first time it really wasn't like that any more. Because Cyd's mouth fit mine in a way that no other mouth ever had – not even Gina's mouth.

I'm not kidding – Cyd's mouth was a perfect fit. Not too hard, not too soft, not too dry, not too wet, not too much tongue and not too little. Just perfect.

I had kissed her before of course, but this was different. Now when we kissed, I wanted it to go on forever. Our mouths could have been made for each other. And how often can you say that? How often do you find someone whose mouth is a perfect fit for your mouth? I'll tell you exactly – once. That's how many times.

There're a lot of nice people in the world, a million people who you could fall in love with. But there's only one person out there whose mouth is a perfect fit.

And despite everything that happened later, I still believe that. I really do.

In the early hours I watched her while she was sleeping, loving it that she was on my side of the bed, happy that she knew so little about my old life that she hadn't automatically taken Gina's side.

I drifted off knowing that we had begun, and it was up to the two of us what side of the bed we slept on.

And then she woke up screaming.

It was only Pat.

Probably disturbed by drunks staggering home at the fag-end of a Saturday night, he had stumbled out of his bed and crawled into mine, never really waking, not even when he threw a leg over Cyd's waist and she woke up as if someone was kicking in the window.

She turned towards me, hiding her face in her hands.

'Oh God – I thought – I don't know what I thought. I could see you. But I could feel someone else.'

I put my arm around her shoulders, trying to comfort her. Pat was out cold on her side of the bed, his mouth open, his arms above his head, his smooth round face turned away from us, but one leg still draped over Cyd.

'I'm all right, I'm all right,' she said, gently removing Pat's leg. She slid over me and got out of bed, not sounding all right at all.

I thought she was going to the bathroom. But when she didn't come back after five minutes, I went looking for her. She was sitting at the kitchen table wearing a shirt of mine that she must have found in the laundry basket.

I sat down beside her, taking her hands. I kissed her

on the mouth. Softly, lips together. I loved to kiss her all different ways.

'I'm sorry he scared you,' I said. 'He does that sometimes. Climbs in my bed, I mean. I should have warned you.'

'I'm okay.'

'Are you sure?'

She shook her head.

'Not really.'

'Listen, I really am sorry he frightened you like that. I'll try to make sure it doesn't happen again. I'll put a lock on my door. Or tie him down. Or –'

'It's not Pat,' she said. 'It's us.'

'What do you mean?'

'We haven't really talked, have we?'

'Sure we have. I told you about Gina. You told me about the guy who was into the bamboo. The one who wasn't Rhett Butler. We talked a lot. We got all the sad stories out of the way.'

'That's the past. I mean we haven't talked about now. We don't know what the other one wants. I like you, Harry. You're funny and you're sweet. You're good with your boy. But I don't know what you're expecting from me.'

'I'm not expecting anything.'

'That's not true. Of course you are. Same as I am. Same as anyone is when they start sleeping together or holding hands in beautiful buildings and getting all dreamy over the coffee and all that. Everyone is expecting things. But I'm not sure if they're the same things.'

'How do you mean?'

'Well – do you want more children?'

'Jesus. We just slept together for the first time.'

'Ah, come on. You know in your heart if you want more children or not, Harry. I don't mean with me. I mean with anyone.'

I looked at her. As it happens, I had been thinking about it a lot.

'I want more children if the person I have them with is going to be with me forever. Okay?'

'But nobody can guarantee that they're going to stay together forever.'

'Well, that's what I want. I don't want to go through it all again. I don't like seeing all the pain and disappointment that you pass on to some innocent little kid who didn't ask for it and who doesn't deserve it. I didn't like going through all that with Pat and I'm never going through it again, okay? And neither is any child of mine.'

'Sounds very noble,' she said. 'But it's not really noble at all. It's just your get-out clause. You want more children, but you only want them if you're guaranteed a happy ending. Only Walt Disney can guarantee you a happy ending, Harry. And you know it. Nobody can ever give you that kind of guarantee. So everything just – I don't know – drifts.'

I didn't like the way this was going. I wanted more kisses. I wanted to watch her sleeping. I wanted her to show me beautiful buildings that I never knew existed. And the boats – we were still going on the boats, weren't we?

'You can't just transfer your heart to another woman after your marriage breaks up, Harry. You can't do it without thinking a little about what you want. What you're expecting. Because if you don't, then seven years down the line you will be in exactly the same place you reached with Gina. I like you, and you like me. And that's great. But it's not enough. We have to be sure we want the same things. We're too old for games.'

'We're not too old,' I said. 'For anything.'

'Too old for games,' she said. 'As soon as you've got a kid, you're too old for games.'

What did she know about having a kid?

'I have to go home,' she said, standing up.

'What about rowing on the lake?' I asked.

'Rowing on the lake can wait.'

twenty-four

'It's the ding-dong man,' Peggy said.

She was sitting on the floor playing with Star Wars figures, lost in some weird happy families game where Darth Vader and Princess Leia set up home on the Millennium Falcon and spend their evenings trying to get Harrison Ford to go to sleep.

Pat was standing on the sofa, massive headphones wrapped around his ears, groaning and rolling his eyes to the heavens and swaying from side to side as he listened to Sally's tape.

'The ding-dong man is coming,' Peggy said to no one in particular, lifting her head with a secret smile.

At first I didn't have a clue what she was going on about. Then I heard what her new five-year-old ears had picked up a lot earlier than my decrepit old lugholes – a chiming of distant bells that seemed to echo around the neighbourhood.

They didn't have the dull insistence of church bells. There was something tender and cheap and unexpected about them – they were an invitation rather than a command.

Naturally I remembered those bells from my own childhood, but for some reason I was always surprised to find that they still existed. He was still out there, still doing the rounds, still asking the children to put down their games and come into the street and stuff their happy little faces with sugar and milk. It was the ice-cream man.

'The ding-dong man,' Peggy said.

I pretended I hadn't heard her, turning back to the work that was spread out before me on the coffee table. Peggy wasn't even supposed to be here. This wasn't one of the afternoons when she came home with Pat. It was the day before the show and I had a shooting script to wade through, a task I found much easier when Pat and Peggy were not squawking on the carpet or listening to Sally's tape and those songs about bitches, gangsters and guns. Peggy was a sweet kid and never any trouble. But on a day like today, I preferred to have Pat squawking on the carpet alone.

Peggy was only here because her useless, chain-smoking babysitter had not been at the school to pick her up.

I had gone to meet Pat and found the pair of them holding hands at the gate, chatting away to Miss Waterhouse, their adoring faces lifted towards their young teacher.

Miss Waterhouse left us with a big grin and went off to do whatever primary school teachers do for the second half of the day, while we waited for Bianca's thin, sallow face to come coughing through the crowds in a halo of cigarette smoke. Except that Bianca didn't show up.

So the three of us waited at the school gates holding hands. And, as all those young mums swirled around us collecting their children, I stood among their bright chatter and car fumes feeling like the neighbourhood leper.

There were all kinds of young mothers outside those school gates. There were mums with Range Rovers and those waxed green coats that are made for the country. There were mums who caught the bus in ankle bracelets. And there were all the young mums in the middle who had enough sense not to have their partners' names tattooed on their shoulders, but who weren't rich or stupid enough to ferry around their five-year-olds in enormous four-wheel drives with bull bars on the front.

But whether they were in ankle bracelets or Alice bands, Prada or polyester, these young mothers all had one thing in common. They all looked at me as though I were the enemy.

At first I thought it was paranoia. I hardly had to explain that my marriage had broken up – just being there, a man alone, always without the company of a woman – unless it was my mother – was like drawing a diagram of our broken home and hanging it on the school gates. But these women didn't even know me or Gina – so why should they dislike me? I decided that I must be feeling thin-skinned and sensitive after all the changes of the last few months.

Yet as the term wore on and the days got darker and shorter, I came to realise that it wasn't paranoia at all. Young mothers didn't talk to me. They avoided my eye. They really didn't want to know. At first I tried to engage some of them in small talk, and they acted as if I had asked them for a blow job. So after a while, I didn't bother.

All those mums smiling sweetly at each other, they really would have preferred it if I weren't there. It got to the point where I tried to time my arrival at the school gates to the very second when the children were set free. Because I couldn't stand being around all those young mothers. And they couldn't stand being around me.

The teachers were always very friendly to me, and when I was talking to Miss Waterhouse it was easy to convince myself that I was part of the modern world where men could be single parents too. But that was proved to be a load of old bollocks any time I had to pause at the school gates.

Whether they were from the big white houses or the council flats, the mothers always gave me a wide berth. It had started on the first day of school, and it had somehow continued through all the other days.

The women in Alice bands had more in common with the women in ankle bracelets than they did with me. The women who were single parents had more in common with the women who had partners than they did with me. At least that's how they all acted.

It was all very English and understated, but there was no denying that the suspicion and embarrassment were always there. There might be understanding and enlightenment for a single father with a little kid out in the working world. But here at the sharp end of parenting, outside those school gates, nobody wanted to know. It was as if Pat and I were a reminder of the fragility of all their relationships.

But when Bianca failed to show up, and I stood waiting for her with Pat and Peggy, it felt like it was even more than that. Those mothers seemed to look upon me as a reminder of the thousand things that could go wrong with men.

Standing at those gates, I felt as though I was an ambassador for all the defective males in the world. The men who were never there. The men who had pissed off. The men who couldn't be trusted around children.

Well, fuck the lot of them. I was sick of being treated like the enemy.

It wasn't that I minded being considered an oddball. I expected that. After all, I knew I was an oddball. But I was tired of carrying the can for every faulty man in the world.

I loathed Peggy's babysitter – this girl who couldn't even make it to the gates of a primary school at an appointed hour, this useless coughing cow who couldn't even manage to get a phone call to the teacher to warn us that she wasn't coming, bloody Bianca with her modern name and her modern assumption that someone else would take care of her responsibilities.

But at least Peggy wasn't her child. And far more than the bitterness I felt towards Peggy's useless babysitter was the loathing I felt for Peggy's useless parents.

It's true that I didn't really know anything about them, apart from the fact that her father was out of the picture and that her mother worked strange hours. But in all the important ways, I felt that I knew everything about them.

Peggy's dad clearly took his parental responsibility about as seriously as he would a fortnight's package holiday in Florida. And it didn't really matter if Peggy's mum were some hotshot in the City or if she were supplementing her welfare state pocket money with a dip in the black economy. She obviously put her daughter's wellbeing at the bottom of her list of life's priorities.

They were typical modern parents. They were incapable of looking after this child. And if there was one thing that I had grown to hate, it was people who bring a kid into the world and then figure that the difficult bit is done.

Well, fuck the pair of them, too.

So after the crowds were starting to thin out, just when all the young mums had gone and the worst was over and I didn't actually mind standing at the school gates any more, we went into the front office and I told the secretary that Peggy was coming home with us.

Delighted at their unexpected chance to hang out together, Pat and Peggy squealed with delight as they crammed their little bodies into the front seat of the MGF. And I found myself making an effort not to cry, which was something I found myself doing every once in a while at those school gates. I felt sorry for Peggy, just as I felt sorry for Pat. We mess up our lives, and it is these forlorn little figures who pick up the bill.

Now I looked at her playing quietly on the floor, ignored even by Pat as he listened to Sally's brutal songs, the bells of the ding-dong man starting to fade away, and I felt a knot of regret and shame in my heart.

'Do you want an ice cream?' I asked her, feeling about as inadequate as I had ever felt in my life, feeling that I owed her some sort of apology.

Sorry about the collapse of the modern marriage, Peggy. Sorry that adults these days are so self-centred and dumb that we can't even manage to bring up our own children. Sorry that the world is so messed up that we think about our sons and our daughters about as deeply as the average barnyard animal.

But how about a Cornetto?

I was paying the ice-cream man for three 99s when Cyd came around the corner.

'You want a 99?' I asked her.

'What's a 99?'

'One of these,' I said. 'A cornet with a chocolate flake stuck in it. They're great.'

'No thanks,' she said. 'I think I'll keep a few teeth for dinner. How you doing?'

'I'm okay,' I said, leaning forward and kissing her on the mouth. She didn't make much of an attempt to kiss me back. 'I thought you were at work.'

'I got a call to come and pick up Peggy,' she said. 'Bianca couldn't make it. Sorry about that.'

I stared at her for a moment, unable to work out how these two worlds were connected.

'You know Peggy?' I said.

She shook her head. I didn't get it, did I?

'She's my daughter, Harry.'

We were standing outside the front door of my house.

She looked at me with those wide-set brown eyes. Waiting.

'Peggy's your daughter?'

'I was going to tell you,' she said. 'Honest.' She gave a little laugh that said she knew it wasn't all that funny. 'I was just waiting for the right time. That's all.'

'The right time? Why didn't you tell me straightaway? Why wasn't that the right time?'

'I'll explain later.'

'Explain now.'

'Okay,' she said, pulling the front door so that it was almost closed. So the kids couldn't hear us. Our kids. 'Because I don't want my daughter to meet strange men who might be out of my life very soon.'

'You don't want her to meet strange men? What are you going on about, Cyd? I'm not a strange man. She spends more time in this house than she does anywhere. Peggy knows me already.'

'She knows you as Pat's dad. She doesn't know you as my – well. What are you, Harry? I guess you're my boyfriend, aren't you? She doesn't know you as my boyfriend. And I don't want her to meet a boyfriend until I've been seeing him for a while. Okay?'

This didn't make any kind of sense to me. A blob of ice cream dropped on to my hand.

'But she had dinner here almost every night last week!' I said. 'She sees more of me than she does of that feckless bastard you married!'

'You don't know him.'

I loved that.

'Oh – good guy, is he?'

'Maybe not,' she said. 'But I don't want her to grow up

believing that every man is going to disappear the way her father disappeared. I don't want her finding strange men in my bed – and you *are* strange. In that way, you are, Harry. I don't want a strange man there when she wakes up. I don't want her thinking that it doesn't mean anything. And I don't want her getting attached to someone who might not be around that long.'

She was trying to be calm, but her voice was choking up a bit now and I felt like putting my arms around her. Which would have been very messy, as I was still holding three melting 99s.

'Because I don't want her getting more hurt than she has been already,' she said. 'I don't want her to give her little heart to someone and then he casually breaks it. Okay, Harry? Okay?'

'Okay,' I said. 'Okay.'

She blinked hard, tightening her mouth. I cleaned the ice cream from my hands. Then we went inside and I realised that nothing is extraordinary to a child.

Maybe when you are a kid life is still so full of wonder that there can be no real surprises, because almost everything is a surprise. Or perhaps children just adapt faster than adults. Either way, Peggy and Pat didn't faint with shock when Cyd walked into the house.

'Mommy,' Peggy said, and I thought – of course. Now I knew where I had seen those eyes before.

Cyd sat down on the floor and listened to her daughter explaining the domestic set-up on the Millennium Falcon. She took the headphones from my son and listened to a song he liked. Then, after we had all finished our ice creams, she told Peggy that it was time to go home.

'I'll call you,' I said.

'If you want to,' she said. 'I know this must be a bit of a shock.'

'You crazy or what? Of course I want to.'
'You're sure?'
'I'm sure,' I said, touching her arm. 'This doesn't change anything.'
It changed everything.

twenty-five

'Did you make love to the make-up girl?' I asked Eamon.

He looked at me in his dressing-room mirror and I caught a flash of something passing across his face. Fear maybe. Or anger. Then it was gone.

'What's that?' he said.

'You heard me the first time.'

The show was taking off. Ratings were good and the offers of lager commercials were starting to come in. But to me he was still a scared kid from Kilcarney with wax in his ears.

'Yes or no, Eamon? Did you make love to the make-up girl?'

'Why do you ask?'

'Because she's crying. We can't even get her to put some slap on the guests because she's sobbing all over her powder puff. It's gone all soggy.'

'What's it got to do with me?'

'I know she left the studio with you last week.'

He twisted on his little swivel chair, turning to face me with his head framed by the mirror's border of bare electric lights. He didn't look so scared any more, despite a shining trickle of sweat snaking through the thick layer of powder on his forehead.

'You're asking me if I made love to the make-up girl?'

'That's right,' I said. 'I don't care about your morals, Eamon. You can bugger the lighting director during the commercial break if you want to. I don't care what you do when we're off air. Just as long as it doesn't interfere with the running of the show. And a weepy make-up girl who can't do her job interferes with the running of the show.'

'You've been a big help to me, Harry,' he said quietly. Sometimes his voice was so low that you had to concentrate just to hear what he was saying. It gave him a certain power. 'From the moment we met, everything you've said to me has made sense. "*Remember – you're only ever talking to one person,*" you said. "*If you have a good time then they will have a good time.*" This stuff might not mean much to you but it's helped me to get through it. It's helped me to make it work. I couldn't have done it without you and I'm grateful. That's why I'm not angry that you're asking me this question, a question that – perhaps you'll agree? – would be a bit rude coming from my mother or my priest.'

'Did you make love to the make-up girl, Eamon?'

'No, Harry. I did not make love to the make-up girl.'

'Is that the truth?'

'That's the truth. I did not make love to the make-up girl.'

'Okay. That's all I wanted to know.'

'I fucked the make-up girl.'

'There's a difference, is there?'

'A big difference. It wasn't the start of a meaningful relationship, Harry. It was the culmination of something quite meaningless – that's what I liked about it. And Carmen – that's the make-up girl's name, Harry, she's called Carmen – might be a bit upset right now that there's not going to be a repeat performance, but I strongly suspect that's what she liked about it too. The very fact that it was a bit raw, a bit rough and for one night only. Sometimes a woman wants you to make love to her. Sometimes she just wants to get fucked. They are just the same as us, Harry. That's the big secret. They're just the same.'

'Why didn't anyone tell me before now? My life would have been so much simpler.'

'I'm getting a lot of offers at the moment, Harry. And not all of them are beer commercials. Carmen's a lovely girl. I'll treat her with respect. I'll be friendly to her. But she wanted exactly what I wanted and she got it. She can't expect anything more from me. And when she gets a grip of herself, she'll understand that.'

'You're not the first young guy who got laid because his ugly mug is on television once a week, Eamon. Just don't bring your personal dramas into this studio, okay?'

'Okay, Harry,' he said mildly. 'I'm sorry that this has been a disruptive influence, I really am. And I understand that you're my executive producer and telling me this stuff is why you're here. But I'm a man, okay?'

'Yeah? Really? You sound more like some old blues song. I'm a man. Spelt m-a-n. Christ, you're so fucking butch. You'll be advertising aftershave next.'

'I'm a man, Harry. And the reason I'm here is to plant my seed in as many places as I possibly can. That's why we're here. That's what men do.'

'Bollocks,' I said. 'That's what boys do.'

But later, as I watched him leave the studio with the show's cutest researcher, I thought – why not?

Why shouldn't he plant his seed in as many places as possible? What would he be saving it for? And what was so great about the solitary little flowerpot that I was cultivating?

Suddenly there were all these rules.

I could stay at Cyd's small, top-floor flat, but I had to be gone by the time Peggy got up. Cyd was happy to have me there when Peggy went to bed, and happy about me sleeping with her on the old brass bed under a framed poster of *Gone with the Wind*. But I had to be out of there before morning came.

Actually, there were not lots of rules. There was just that one rule. But it felt like a lot of rules.

'Maybe later it will be different,' Cyd said. 'If we decide – you know – we want to take it further. If we want to make a proper commitment.'

As soon as I stopped looking into her wide-set brown eyes and she had turned out the light, I didn't feel like making a proper commitment. To tell you the truth, what I really felt like was something a bit less complicated.

I wanted to be able to sleep in my girl's arms without being woken up and told it was time to go home. I wanted the kind of relationship where you didn't have to remember the rules. Most of all, I wanted things to be the way they were before everything got all smashed.

I was still dreaming when I felt Cyd's mouth on mine.

'Baby,' she whispered. 'Sorry. But it's time.'

It was still dark outside, but I could hear pigeons hopping around on the roof directly above our heads, a sure sign that it was time to put on my pants and piss off before the sun came up.

'Got it all worked out, haven't you?' I sighed, rolling away from her and getting out of bed.

'I wish you could stay, Harry. I really do.'

'So how long is it since you split up with Peggy's dad? Three years? More? And how many men have you introduced her to?'

'You're the first,' she said quietly, and I wondered if that was true.

'I just don't understand what harm it does if she sees

me eating a bowl of Cornflakes. Jesus – the kid sees me all week long.'

'We've been through all this,' Cyd said in the darkness. 'It's confusing for her if you're here in the morning. Please try to understand. She's five – you're not.'

'She likes me. And I like her. We've always got on fine.'

'That's all the more reason for going now. I don't want you to be an uncle to Peggy, okay? I want you to be more than that or less than that. But you're not going to be an uncle. She deserves better. So do you.'

'Fine,' I said. 'Absolutely fine.'

'You should love me for being like this,' she said, more angry than hurt. 'You should understand that I'm just trying to protect her and do what's best for her. You've got a kid yourself. You know what it's like. If anyone should understand, then you should understand.'

She was right.

I should have loved her.

For the first time in my life I could sort of understand why men of my age go out with younger women.

I never really got it before. Women in their thirties, their bodies are still springy and you can talk to them. They are still young, but they have seen something of life – probably quite a few of the same views that you have seen.

Why would any man trade that kind of equal partnership for someone with a pierced navel whose idea of a hot date is some awful nightclub and half a tab of something pretending to be Ecstasy?

If you can go out with someone who has read the same books as you, who has watched the same television programmes as you, who has loved the same music as you, then why would you want someone whose idea of a soul singer is the guy in Jamiroquai?

But now I got it. Now I could understand the attraction.

Men of my age like younger women because the younger woman has fewer reasons to be bitter.

The younger woman is less likely to have had her heart bashed around by broken homes, divorce lawyers and the sight of children who are missing a parent. The younger woman doesn't have all those disappointments that women – and men, too, don't forget the men – in their thirties drag around with them like so much excess luggage.

It was cruel but true. The younger woman is far less likely to have had her life fucked up by some man.

Men in their thirties and forties don't go out with a younger woman for her bouncy body and her pierced tongue. That's just propaganda.

They go out with her so that they can be the one who fucks up her life.

Heidi was a nanny from Munich.

Well, not exactly Munich – more Augsburg. And not exactly a nanny.

A nanny is a professional child minder who has made a career out of caring for small boys and girls. Heidi was a nineteen-year-old who was away from her parents for the very first time. She was just one economy flight on Lufthansa away from a bedroom full of stuffed toys and having her mum do her washing. She knew as much about child care as I knew about theoretical physics. Heidi was more of an au pair.

The plan was that Heidi was going to cook, clean and cover for me with Pat on the days I was working on the show. For this she would receive bed, board and pocket money while she studied English.

Pat was swaying on the sofa, listening to Sally's tape, when I took Heidi through to meet him.

'This is Heidi, Pat. She's going to stay here and help us around the house.'

Pat stared blankly at the big blonde German girl, his mouth lolling open, lost in the music.

'A lively and active boy,' Heidi smiled.

Trying to show willing, she asked me what I would like for dinner. I told her that I would grab something in the green room at the station, but she should fix something for her and Pat. She shuffled about in the kitchen until she found a big can of tomato soup.

'Is okay?' she asked.

'Fine,' I said.

Trying to let her get on with it, I sat at the kitchen table jotting down notes on next week's shooting script.

Pat wandered in to watch her, leaving the music still blasting from the living room, and I sent him back to turn it off. When he came back he started pulling at my sleeve.

'Guess what?' he said.

'Let Daddy work, darling.'

'But guess what Heidi's doing?'

'And let Heidi do her work, too.'

Elaborately sighing, he sat down at the kitchen table and idly fiddled with a couple of his little plastic men.

Heidi was clanking about by the stove, but I didn't look up at her until I heard the bubbles of boiling water. That was strange. Why was she boiling water to heat up a can of tomato soup?

'Heidi?'

'Is soon ready.'

She had placed the unopened can of soup in a saucepan of water and brought it to boiling point. She gave me a hesitant smile just before the can exploded, flinging steaming red gruel all over the ceiling, the walls and us.

Wiping the tomato soup from my eyes, I saw the livid

red slime slide down Heidi's face, her eyes staring through the oozing muck, mute with shock and wonder. She looked like Sissy Spacek in the prom night scene in *Carrie*.

Then she burst into tears.

'Guess what?' Pat said, blue eyes blinking in a crimson face mask. 'She can't cook either.'

So Heidi found a nice family in Crouch End.

And I gave Sally a call.

twenty-six

Auntie Ethel was on her knees in her front garden, planting spring bulbs for next year.

Auntie Ethel wasn't my real auntie but I had called her Auntie Ethel ever since we had moved in next door to her when I was five years old, and the habit had proved hard to break.

Auntie Ethel straightened up, squinting over her lawn mower at Cyd and Peggy and Pat and me as we climbed out of Cyd's old VW Beetle, and for a moment I felt as though I were a little kid again, asking Auntie Ethel if I could have my ball back.

'Harry? Is that you, Harry?'

'Hello, Auntie Ethel,' I said. 'What are you planting there?'

'Tulips, daffodils, hyacinths. And is that your Pat? I don't believe it! Hasn't he grown? Hello, Pat!'

Pat half-heartedly saluted her with his light sabre. We had never been able to persuade him to address Auntie Ethel by her proper title, and he clearly wasn't going to start now. Auntie Ethel turned her attention to Peggy, a cloud of confusion drifting across her familiar old face.

'And this little girl . . .'

'This one's mine,' Cyd said. 'Hi, Auntie Ethel. I'm Cyd. Harry's friend. How you doing?'

'Like Sid James?'

'Like Cyd Charisse.'

Auntie Ethel's eyes twinkled behind her glasses.

'The dancer,' she said. 'With Fred Astaire in *Silk Stockings*. A good pair of legs.' Auntie Ethel sized Cyd up. 'Just like you!'

'I *like* your Auntie Ethel,' Cyd whispered, taking my arm as we came up the drive. Then I felt her grip tighten. 'Oh God – that looks like your mother.'

My mum was standing at the door, all smiles, and Pat ran to meet her.

'Happy birthday!' she cried, sweeping him up in her arms. 'Five years old! Aren't you a big boy – ouch!' Still holding him under one arm, she pushed his Jedi weapon away with her free hand. 'Blooming light saver,' she laughed, looking down at Peggy. 'You must be Peggy. You haven't got a light saver too, have you?'

'No, I don't like Star Wars very much. I just play it because *he* likes it.'

'It's a boys' game, isn't it?' my mum said, never much of a one for breaking down traditional gender stereotypes.

Peggy followed Pat into the house and my mum smiled at Cyd, who was holding back, half a step behind me, still gripping my arm. I had never seen her looking shy before. My mum grabbed her and kissed her on the cheek.

'And you must be Cyd. Come in, dear, and make yourself at home.'

'Thank you,' Cyd said.

Cyd went into the house where I had grown up and my mum gave me a quick smile behind her back, lifting her eyebrows like a surprised lady in one of those old saucy seaside postcards.

It had been quite a while, but I had brought home enough girls to know what that look meant.

It meant that Cyd was what my mum would call a smasher.

And in the back garden was what my mum would call quite a spread.

The kitchen table had been carried out the back and covered with a paper tablecloth splattered with images of party balloons, exploding champagne bottles and laughing rabbits.

The table had been loaded with bowls of crisps, nuts and little bright orange cheesy things, plates of sandwiches with their crusts cut off, trays of mini sausage rolls and six individual little paper dishes containing jelly and tinned fruit. In the centre of this feast was a birthday cake in the shape of Darth Vader's helmet, with five candles.

When we were all seated around the table and had sung a few renditions of, 'Happy birthday, dear Pat,' my dad offered around the mini sausage rolls, looking at me shrewdly.

'Bet you had a job all getting into that little sports car,' he said.

From the living room I could hear one of his favourite albums on the stereo. It was the end of side two of *Songs for Swingin' Lovers!*, Frank breezing his way through Cole Porter's 'Anything Goes'.

'We didn't come out in the MGF, Dad,' I said. 'We came in Cyd's car.'

'Completely impractical, a car like that,' he continued, ignoring me. 'Nowhere for the children, is there? A man has to think of those things when he buys a motor. Or he should do.'

'My daddy's got a motorbike,' Peggy told him.

My father stared at her, chewing a mini sausage roll, lost for words. Her daddy? A motorbike?

'That's nice, dear,' my mum said.

'And a Thai girlfriend.'

'Lovely!'

'Her name's Mem.'

'What a pretty name.'

'Mem's a dancer.'

'Goodness.'

We all watched in silence, waiting for further revelations, as Peggy lifted open her sandwich and examined the contents. The further revelations didn't come. Peggy closed her sandwich and shoved it in her mouth.

I crunched my way through some bright orange cheesy things, feeling depressed.

My parents were trying as hard as they could. But this tiny little girl already had another life that they would never and could never be a part of. The all-consuming delight that they felt for their grandchild could never be felt for little Peggy. That kind of unconditional love was already impossible. She would always be too much of a stranger. I felt for them. And for Peggy too.

'Mem's not really a dancer,' Cyd said, watching my face, reading my mind. 'She's more of a stripper.'

My old man coughed up a piece of barbecue-flavoured crisp.

'Bit went down the wrong hole,' he explained.

My mum turned to Cyd with a bright smile. 'Jelly?' she said.

Once we had Mem's job description out of the way, the party settled down. And my parents liked Cyd. I could tell that they liked her a lot.

There were minefields to be negotiated – my dad had this thing about single mothers subsidised by the state and my mum had this thing about working mothers – but Cyd skipped through them without spilling her jelly.

'The state can never take the place of a parent, Mr Silver – and it shouldn't try.'

'Call me Paddy, love,' my dad said.

'Some women have to work, Mrs Silver – but that doesn't mean their children don't come first.'

'Call me Elizabeth, dear,' my mum said.

She talked to Paddy and Elizabeth about all the things they wanted to talk about – the kind of films that a five-year-old should be allowed to watch with my mum, the right time to remove the stabilisers on a child's bike with my dad.

And she made all the right noises – admiring my mum's sausage rolls ('Home-made they are, dear, I'll give you the recipe if you like') and my dad's garden ('Harry's never been interested in gardens – I can't understand that attitude myself').

But Cyd wasn't some little local girl who I had danced with a couple of times in a suburban club, one of the Kims and Kellys who I had brought home all the time until the day I brought home Gina.

Cyd was visibly a woman with a past – meaning a past that contained marriage, pregnancy and divorce, although not necessarily in that order. And it felt like the only way my parents could deal with that past was by ignoring it.

Their conversation lurched between her childhood in Houston to the present day in London, as if everything in between had been withdrawn by censors.

'Texas, you say?' my dad said. 'Never been to Texas myself. But I met a few Texans in the war.' He leaned towards her conspiratorially. 'Good card players, Texans.'

'It must be lovely having sisters,' my mum said. 'I had six brothers. Can you imagine that? Six brothers! Some women don't like watching football and boxing on the telly. But it never bothered me. Because I had six brothers.'

But Cyd's broken marriage was always there waiting to be confronted. In the end, Cyd dealt with it as casually as if it were just a stale sausage roll that had to be found and cast aside. She had never seemed more American.

'My family is like your family,' she said to my mother. 'Very close. I only came over here because Jim – that's Peggy's father – is English. That didn't work out, but somehow I never made it back. Now I've met your son, I'm glad I didn't.'

And that was it.

My mum looked at us as if we were Ryan O'Neal and Ali MacGraw in *Love Story*. Even my dad seemed to be brushing away a tear from his eye. Then I realised it was just a crumb from a mini sausage roll.

By the time Pat had blown out his five candles and we had cut the cake, my parents were acting as if they had known Cyd and Peggy all their lives.

If they were put out by the fact that the girl of my dreams had chosen someone else to share her dreams with before me, then they were pretty good at hiding it. This should have pleased me more than it did.

While Cyd was helping my mum clear the table and my dad was showing Pat and Peggy how he dealt with the menace of snails, I went into the living room and over to the stereo.

Songs for Swingin' Lovers! had stopped playing hours ago, but the cover of the record, an old vinyl LP – my father had never joined the CD revolution – was still propped up against the Sony music station.

That album cover had always been special to me. Sinatra – tie askew, snap-brim fedora on the back of his head – grins down at the perfect fifties couple, some Brylcreemed Romeo in a business suit with his suburban Juliet in pearl earrings and a little red dress.

They look like an ordinary couple – you can't imagine them hanging out with the Rat Pack in Vegas. But they look as though they have wrung as much joy out of this world as anyone possibly could. And I always loved looking at that couple when I was a child, because I always thought they looked like my parents at the exact moment they fell in love.

Someone called my name from the garden but I stared at the cover of *Songs for Swingin' Lovers!*, pretending that I hadn't heard.

They don't make them like that any more, I thought.

'Everybody had a good time,' Cyd said.

'It seemed to go very well,' I said.

We were back in London and up in her flat. Peggy and Pat were sitting on the sofa watching a tape of *Pocahontas* (Peggy's choice). Tired from a couple of hours in Cyd's wheezing old Beetle, they were starting to bitch at each other. I wanted to get home.

'Everybody had a good time,' Cyd said again. 'Pat liked his presents. Peggy ate so much that I won't have to feed her for a week. And I really loved meeting your mum and dad. They're really sweet people. Yes, everybody had a good time. Except you.'

'What are you talking about? I had a good time.'

'No,' she said. 'And what hurts me – what really hurts me – is that you didn't even try. Your mum and dad made an effort. I know they loved Gina and I know it couldn't have been easy for them. But they really tried to make it work today. You just couldn't be bothered, could you?'

'What do you want me to do? Start doing the lambada after a couple of Diet Cokes? I had as good a time as I could ever have at a kid's birthday party.'

'I'm a grown woman and I have a child, okay? You have to learn to deal with that, Harry. Because if you can't, we haven't got any kind of future.'

'I like Peggy,' I said. 'And I get on great with her.'

'You liked Peggy when she was just the little girl who

palled around with your son,' she said. 'You liked her when she was just the cute little kid who played nicely on the floor of your home. What you don't like is what she's become now that you've started going out with me.'

'And what's that?' I asked her.

'The reminder of another man's fuck,' she said.

The reminder of another man's fuck? That was a bit strong. You couldn't imagine Sinatra sticking that on one of his album covers.

twenty-seven

It was more than the reminder of another man's fuck.

If living alone with Pat had taught me anything, it was that being a parent is mostly intuitive – we make it up as we go along. Nobody teaches you how to do it. You learn on the job.

When I was a kid I thought that my parents had some secret knowledge about how to keep me in line and bring me up right. I thought that there was some great master plan to make me eat my vegetables and go to my room when I was told. But I was wrong. I knew now that they were doing what every parent in the world does. Just winging it.

If Pat wanted to watch *Return of the Jedi* at four in the morning or listen to Puff Daddy at midnight, then I didn't have to think about it – I could just pull the plug and send him back to bed.

And if he was down after a phone call from Gina or because of something that had happened at school, I could take him in my arms and give him a cuddle. When it's your own flesh and blood, you don't have to think about doing the right thing. You don't have to think at all. You just do it.

But I would never have that luxury with Peggy.

She was on the sofa, her little bare legs stretched out on the coffee table, watching her favourite Australian soap.

I was sitting next to her, trying to shut out the background babble of dysfunctional surfers who didn't know the true identity of their parents, as I read an article about another bank collapsing in Japan. It looked like complete chaos over there.

'*What do you mean – you're not my mother?*' somebody said on screen, and Peggy began to stir as the theme music began.

Usually she was off and running the moment the Aussies were gone. But now she stayed right where she was, leaning forward across the coffee table and picking up Cyd's nail polish from among the jumble of magazines and toys. I watched her as she began to unscrew the top of the small glass vial.

'Peggy?'

'What?'

'Maybe you shouldn't play with that, darling.'

'It's okay, Harry. Mommy lets me.'

She removed the lid with the small brush on and, very delicately, began painting crimson nail polish over her tiny, almost non-existent toenails and, I couldn't help noticing, all over the tips of her toes.

'Be careful with that stuff, Peggy. It's not for playing with, okay?'

She shot me a look.

'Mommy lets me do this.'

Globs of bright red nail polish slid down toes the size of half a matchstick. She soon looked as though she had been treading grapes or wading through an abattoir. She lifted her foot, admiring her handiwork, and a drizzle of red paint plopped on to a copy of *Red*.

With Pat I would have raised my voice or grabbed the nail polish or sent him to his room. I would have done something. With Peggy, I didn't know what to do. I certainly couldn't touch her. I certainly couldn't raise my voice.

'Peggy.'

'*What*, Harry?'

I really wanted her to do the right thing and not get nail polish all over her feet and the carpet and the coffee table and the magazines. But, far more than all of this, I wanted her to like me. So I sat there watching her small feet turning bright red, making doubtful noises, doing nothing.

Cyd came out of the bathroom wrapped in a white robe, towelling her hair. She saw Peggy daubing her toes with nail polish and sighed.

'How many times have I told you to leave that stuff alone?' she asked, snatching away the nail polish. She lifted Peggy like a cat plucking up a unruly kitten. 'Come on, miss. In the bath.'

'But –'

'Now.'

What made me laugh – or rather what made me want to bury my face in my hands – is that you would never guess that so much of our time was spent dealing with the fall-out of the nuclear family. Cyd's small flat was like a temple to romance.

The walls were covered with posters from films – films that told tales of perfect love, love that might bang its head against a few obstacles now and again, but love that was ultimately without any of the complications of the modern world.

As soon as you had come into the flat, there was a framed poster of *Casablanca* in the poky little hallway. There were framed posters of *An Affair to Remember* and *Brief Encounter* in the slightly less poky living room. And of course there was *Gone with the Wind* in the place of honour right above the bed. Even Peggy had a poster of *Pocahontas* on her wall looking down on all her old Ken and Barbie dolls and Spice Girls merchandise. Everywhere you looked – men smouldering, women melting and true love conquering.

These posters weren't stuck up in the way that a student might stick them up – half-hearted and thoughtless and mostly to cover a patch of rising damp or some crumbling plaster. There was far more than Blu-tack keeping them up. Placed behind glass and encased in tasteful black frames, they were treated like works of art – which I suppose is what they were.

Cyd had bought those posters from one of those cine-head shops in Soho, taken them to the Frame Factory or somewhere similar, and then lugged them all the way home. She had to go out of her way to have those posters of *Gone with the Wind* and the rest up on her walls. The message was clear – this is what we are about in this place.

But it wasn't what we were about, not really. Humphrey Bogart and Ingrid Bergman might have had their love affair cut short by the Nazi invasion of Paris, but at least Bogey didn't have to worry about how he should treat Ingrid's child from her relationship with Victor Laszlo. And it is open to debate if Rhett Butler would have been quite so keen on Scarlett O'Hara if she had been dragging a kid from a previous romance around Georgia.

I had never been around a little girl before, and there was an air of calm about Peggy – it was definitely calm more than sugar and spice or any of that stuff – that I had never seen in Pat or other small boys. There was a composure about her that you wouldn't see in a boy of the same age. Maybe all little girls are like that. Maybe it was just Peggy.

What I am saying is – I liked her.

But I didn't know if I was meant to be her friend or her father, if I was meant to be sweetness and light or firm but fair. None of it felt right. When your partner has got a child, it can never be like the movies. And anyone who can't see that has watched a few too many MGM musicals.

Cyd came back into the room with Peggy all clean and changed and ready for her big night out at Pizza Express with her father. The little girl climbed on my lap and gave me a kiss. She smelled of soap and Junior Timotei.

Her mother ruffled my hair.

'What are you thinking about?' she asked me.

'Nothing,' I said.

Peggy's eyes got big and wide with excitement when she heard the sound of a powerful motorbike pulling up in the street.

'Daddy!' she said, scrambling from my lap, and I felt a stab of jealousy that caught me by surprise.

From the window we all watched Jim Mason park the big BMW bike, swinging his legs off as if he were dismounting from a horse. Then he removed his helmet and I saw that Cyd had been right – he was a good-looking bastard, all chiselled jawline and short, thick wavy hair, like the face on a Roman coin or a male model who likes girls.

I had always kind of hoped that there was going to be something of Glenn about him – a fading pretty boy whose years of breaking hearts had come and gone. But this one looked as though he still ate all his greens.

He waved up at us. We waved back.

Meeting your partner's ex should be awkward and embarrassing. You know the most intimate details of their life and yet you have never met them. You know they did bad things because you have been told all about them and also because, if they hadn't done bad things, you would not be with your partner.

It should be a bumpy ride meeting the man she knew before she knew you. But meeting Jim wasn't that much of a problem for me. I got off lightly as there was still so much unfinished business between him and Cyd.

He came into the little flat, big and handsome, all gleaming leathers and wide white smile, tickling his daughter until she howled. We shook hands and swapped some small talk about the problems of parking in this neck of the woods. And when Peggy went to collect her things, Cyd was waiting for him, her face as impassive as a clenched fist.

'How's Mem?' she asked.

'She's fine. Sends her love.'

'I'm sure she doesn't. But thanks anyway. And is her job going well?'

'Very well, thanks.'

'Business is booming for strippers, is it?'

'She's not a stripper.'

'She's not?'

'She's a lap dancer.'

'My apologies.'

Jim looked at me with a what-can-you-do? grin.

'She always does this,' he said, as if we had some kind of relationship, as if he could tell me a thing or two.

Peggy came back carrying a child-sized motorbike helmet, smiling from ear to ear, anxious to get going. She kissed her mother and me and took her father's hand.

From the window we watched Jim carefully place his daughter on the bike and cover her head with the helmet. Sliding behind her, he straddled the machine, kicked it into life and took off down the narrow street. Above the throaty roar of the bike, you could just about hear Peggy squealing with delight.

'Why do you hate him so much, Cyd?'

She thought about it for a moment.

'I think it's because of the way he ended it,' she said. 'He was home from work – hurt his leg in another accident, I think he was scraped by a cab, he was always getting scraped by a cab – and he was lying on the sofa when I got back from dropping Peggy off at her nursery school. I bent over him – just to look at his face, because I always liked looking at his face – and he said the name of a girl. Right out loud. The name of this Malaysian girl he was sleeping with. The one he left me for.'

'He was talking in his sleep?'

'No,' she said. 'He was pretending to talk in his sleep. He knew he was going to leave me and Peggy already. But he didn't have the guts to look me in the eye and tell me. Pretending to talk in his sleep – pretending to say her name while he was sleeping – was the only way he could do it. The only way he could drop the bomb. The only way he could tell me that his bags were packed. And that just seemed so cruel, so gutless – and so typical.'

I had different reasons for hating Jim – some of them noble, some of them pitiful. I hated him because he had hurt Cyd so badly, and I hated him because he was better looking than me. I hated him because I hated any parent who breezed in and out of a kid's life as though they were a hobby you could pick up and put down when you felt like it. Did I think that Gina was like that? Sometimes, on those odd days when she didn't phone Pat, and I knew – just knew – that she was somewhere with Richard.

And I hated Jim because I could feel that he still mattered to Cyd – when she had said that thing about always loving his face, I knew it was still there, eating her up. Maybe she didn't love him, maybe all that had curdled and changed into something else. But he mattered.

I suppose a little piece of my heart should have been grateful. If he had been a loyal, loving husband who knew how to keep his leather trousers on – and if he wasn't into the bamboo – then Cyd would be with him and not me. But I wasn't grateful at all.

As soon as he brought Peggy back safely from Pizza Express, I would have been quite happy for him to wrap his bike around a number 73 bus and get his lovely face smeared all over the Essex Road. He had treated Cyd as if she were nothing much at all. And that was reason enough for me to hate his guts.

But when Peggy came back home with a phenomenally useless stuffed toy the size of a refrigerator, and pizza all over her face, I was aware that there was another, far more selfish reason for hating him.

Without ever really trying to match him, I knew that I could never mean as much in Peggy's life as he did. That's what hurt most of all. Even if he saw her only when he felt like it, and fucked off somewhere else when he felt like doing that, he would always be her father.

That's what made her giddy with joy. Not the motorbike. Or the pizza. Or the stupid stuffed toy the size of a fridge. But the fact that this was her dad.

I knew I could live with the reminder of another man's fuck. I could even love her. And I could compete with a motorbike and a giant stuffed toy and a prettier face than my own.

But you can't compete with blood.

twenty-eight

'Who do I look like?' Pat said when the trees in the park were bare and he had to wear his winter coat all the time and Gina had been gone for just over four months.

He tilted his head to stare up at the car's vanity mirror, looking at his face as if seeing it for the first time, or as if it belonged to someone else.

Who did he look like? People were always telling me – and him – that he looked like me. But I knew that wasn't quite right. He was a far prettier kid than I had ever been. Even if I had never had all my front teeth knocked out by a dog, he would still have been better looking than me. The truth was, he looked like both of us. He looked like me and he looked like Gina.

'Your eyes are like Mummy's eyes,' I said.

'They're blue.'

'That's right. They're blue. And my eyes are green. But your mouth, that's like my mouth. We've got lovely big mouths. Perfect for kissing, right?'

'Right,' he said, not smiling along with me, not taking his eyes from the little rectangular mirror.

'And your hair – that's very fair. Like Mummy's hair.'

'She had yellow hair.'

'She still does, baby,' I said, wincing at that past tense. 'She still has yellow hair. She's still got yellow hair. Okay?'

'Okay,' he said, flipping up the mirror and staring out of the window. 'Let's go.'

And your teeth are like your mother's – a little bit gappy, a little bit goofy, teeth that give every single smile a rakish air – but your sawn-off snub nose is like mine, although your strong, beautiful chin belongs to your mother and so does your skin – fair skin that loves the sun, fair skin that starts to tan as soon as it stops raining.

Pat didn't look like me. And he didn't look like Gina. He looked like both of us.

Even if we had ever wanted to, we couldn't escape his mother. She was there in his smile and in the colour of his eyes. I was stuck with Gina's ghost. And so was Pat.

'I don't understand what's going to happen to the kids,' my father said. 'The kids like Pat and Peggy. I can't imagine what growing up with just one parent around is going to do to them.'

He didn't say it the way he would have said it in the past – angry, contemptuous and with a mocking wonder at what the world was coming to. He didn't say it with his old loathing for single parents and all the changes they represented. He said it gently, with a small, bewildered shake of his head, as if the future were beyond his imagination.

'You grew up with two parents around,' he said. 'At least you had some idea of what a marriage looked like. What a marriage could be. But they don't have that, do they? Pat and Peggy and all the rest of them.'

'No. They don't.'

'And I just worry what it's going to do to them. If divorce is just something that everyone does, then what chance is there for their marriages? And for their children?'

We were on the wooden bench just outside the kitchen door, sitting in the three o'clock twilight watching Pat poke around with his light sabre at the far end of the garden.

'Everything just seems so . . . broken up,' my dad said.

'Do you know what Peggy said to me? She asked me if I would be her granddad. It's not her fault, is it? The poor little mite.'

'No, it's not her fault,' I said. 'It's never the child's fault. But maybe growing up with divorce will make them more careful about getting into a marriage. And more determined to make it work when they do.'

'Do you really think so?' my father said hopefully.

I nodded, but only because I didn't have the heart to shake my head. What I really thought was that his generation had faced up to its responsibilities in a way that my lot never could.

His generation had looked after their children, they had lots of early nights, and if they also had their own home and a fortnight in a caravan in Frinton, they had considered themselves lucky.

But my generation had grown up with our own individual little pile of happiness at the top of our shopping list.

That's why we fucked around, fucked off and fucked up with such alarming regularity.

My generation wanted perfect lives. Why should our children be any different? My dad had learned early on that nobody gets away with a perfect life.

'Yes, maybe it will be all right,' my old man said, thinking about it. 'Because every kid has got two parents, haven't they? Even a kid from – what do you call it? – a single-parent family. And perhaps Pat and Peggy and the rest of them won't grow up being like the parent who went away. Perhaps they'll be like the parent who stayed behind.'

'How do you mean?'

'Well, you're doing a good job with Pat,' he said, not looking at me. 'You work hard. You take care of him. He sees all that. So why shouldn't he be like that with his children?'

I laughed with embarrassment.

'I mean it,' he said. 'I don't know that I could have coped if your mother – you know.' His callused right hand rested lightly on my shoulder. He still wasn't looking at me. 'You're doing all right with that boy, Harry.'

'Thanks,' I said. 'Thanks, Dad.'

Then we heard my mother calling urgently from the living room, and when we ran inside she was standing by the window, pointing at my car.

'I saw the little bastards,' said my mum, who never swore. 'I saw the little bastards do it!'

The MGF's soft top had been repeatedly slashed with a knife. The ribbons of what was left of the roof had caved into the car, as if something had been dropped on it from a great height.

I stared at my mutilated car. But my father was already out of the front door. Auntie Ethel was on her doorstep.

'The alley!' she cried, pointing to the far end of our street, the rough end where there was a small cul-de-sac of council houses, like a ghetto for people who owned souped-up Ford Escorts and West Ham away shirts and didn't give a toss about roses.

There was an alley at this end of the street that led to a tired little string of shops where you could get your Lottery ticket during the daytime and get your face smashed in after dark. Two youths – the two who had tried to burgle my parents? or two just like them? – were legging it towards the alley. My father was chasing them.

I looked at the ruined roof and felt a surge of anger rise up in me. You stupid, spiteful little gits, I thought, furious at what they had done to my car and even more furious for taking my father from his garden.

I started after them, seeing them nervously glance over their shoulders as a murderous voice called after them, threatening to fucking kill them, and I was shocked to discover that the murderous voice seemed to belong to me.

The two yobs disappeared into the alley just as my dad suddenly stopped. At first I thought he had given up, but it was worse than that, because he sank to one knee and clutched his chest, as though he were suffocating.

By the time I caught up with him he was on both knees, holding himself up with one hand pressed flat on the ground. He was making a terrible, unearthly sound, his throat rasping with short, shallow breaths.

I put my arms around him and held him, smelling his Old Holborn and Old Spice, and he gasped for air, choked for air, his lungs fighting with all their might and yet still unable to suck in what they needed. He turned his eyes towards me and I saw the fear in them.

Eventually he managed to retrieve enough air to get shakily to his feet. Still with my arm around him, I led him slowly back to the house. My mother, Pat and Auntie Ethel were all by the front gate. Pat and Auntie Ethel were white with shock. My mother was angry.

'You *must* go to the doctor,' she said, tears streaming down her face. 'No more excuses.'

'I will,' he said meekly, and I knew he wouldn't try to get out of it. He could never refuse her anything.

'Aren't they evil little rotters?' Auntie Ethel said. 'It makes your blood boil, doesn't it?'

'Yes,' said Pat. 'They're motherfuckers.'

Black tie, it said on the invitation, and I always felt excited when I had to dig out my dinner jacket, dress shirt and black bow tie – a proper bow tie that you had to spend ages doing yourself, not the pre-tied dicky bow on a bit of elastic as worn by small boys and clowns.

I could remember my old man wearing black tie once a

year for his company's annual dinner and dance at some fancy hotel on Park Lane. There was something about the tailored formality of a tuxedo that suited his stocky, muscular frame. My mum always looked slightly amused by whatever ball gown she had climbed into that year. But my old man was born to wear black tie.

'Wow,' said Sally, shyly grinning up at me through a curtain of hair as I came down the stairs. 'You look just like a bouncer. Outside a, like, really, really cool club.'

'No,' Pat said, pointing his index finger at me and cocking his thumb. 'You look like James Bond. 007. Licensed to shoot all the bad people.'

But as I stood in front of the hall mirror, I knew what I really looked like in a dinner jacket.

More and more, I looked like my father.

Cyd wore a green cheongsam in Chinese silk – high-necked, tight as a second skin, the greatest dress I had ever seen in my life.

She hadn't done anything to her hair – just pulled it back behind her head in a ponytail, and I liked it that way, because that way I could see her face all the more clearly.

Sometimes we are only aware of how happy we are when the moment has passed. But now and again, if we are very lucky, we are aware of happiness when it is actually happening. And I knew that this was what happiness felt like. Not happiness in dewy-eyed retrospect or in some imagined future but here and now, in a green dress.

'Wait a minute,' I said to Cyd as our cab dropped us outside the hotel. I took her hands in mine and we stood there in silence, the rush hour on Park Lane roaring behind us, a frost on Hyde Park glinting beyond the traffic.

'What's wrong?' she asked me.

'Nothing,' I said. 'That's the point.'

I knew that I would never forget the way she looked that night, I knew that I would never forget the way she looked in her green Chinese dress. And I wanted to do more than enjoy it, I wanted to hold the moment so that I could remember it later, after the night had gone.

'Okay?' she said, smiling.

'Okay.'

Then we joined the laughing throng in their dinner jackets and evening dresses, and went inside to the awards ceremony.

'And the best newcomer is . . .'

The luscious weather girl fumbled with the envelope.

'. . . Eamon Fish.'

Eamon stood up, drunk and grinning, looking more pleased than he would have wanted to with all the cameras watching, and he hugged me with real feeling as he walked past.

'We did it,' he said.

'No,' I said, 'you did it. Go and get your award.'

Over his shoulder I saw Marty Mann and Siobhan at another table – Marty in one of those bright waistcoats worn by people who think that wearing black tie is like smoking a pipe or wearing carpet slippers, Siobhan slim and cool in some white diaphanous number.

She smiled. He gave me the thumbs up. Later, when all the awards had been handed out, they came across to our table.

Although Marty was a bit pissed and a bit pissed off – there were no awards for him this year – they couldn't have been more gracious.

I introduced them to Cyd and to Eamon. If Marty remembered Cyd as the same woman who had once dropped a plate of pasta in his lap, he didn't show it. He congratulated Eamon on his award. Siobhan congratulated Cyd on her dress.

Siobhan didn't say – *And what do you do?*, she was too smart and sensitive ever to ask that question, so Cyd didn't have to say – *Oh, I'm a waitress right now*, so Siobhan didn't have to get embarrassed and neither did Cyd, they could just get on with each other in that easy, seemingly natural way that only women can manage.

They began talking to each other about not knowing what to wear at these things, and Marty put a conspiratorial arm around my shoulder. His face was far heavier than I remembered it. He had the leaden, vaguely disappointed air of a man who, after years of dreaming, had finally landed his own talk show only to discover that he couldn't attract anyone who was worth talking to.

'A word?' he said, crouching down by my side.

Here it comes, I thought. Now he wants me back. Now he's seen how well Eamon's doing, he wants me back on the show.

'I want you to do me a favour,' Marty said.

'What's that, Marty?'

He leaned closer.

'I want you to be my best man,' he said.

Even Marty, I thought.

Even Marty dreams of getting it right, of finding the one, of discovering the whole world in another human being. Just like everyone else.

'Hey, Harry,' said Eamon, watching the weather girl cross the room, adjusting his weight as a ridge of high pressure passed through his underpants. 'Guess who I'm shagging tonight?'

Well, perhaps not quite everyone.

* * *

There were too many lights on in the house. There were lights upstairs. There were lights downstairs. There were lights blazing everywhere at a time when there should have been just one faint glow coming from the living room.

And there was music pouring out of my home – loud, booming bass lines and those skittering drum machines that sounded like the aural equivalent of a heart attack. New music. Terrible new music blasting from my stereo.

'What's going on?' I said, as if we had come to the wrong place, as if there had been some mistake.

There was someone in the darkness of the small front garden. No, there were a few of them. A boy and a girl necking just outside the open front door. And another boy lurking by the dustbin, being sick all over his Tommy Hilfiger anorak and his YSL trousers.

I went inside the house while Cyd paid the cab driver.

It was a party. A teenage party. All over my home there were youths in Polo gear snogging, shagging, drinking, dancing and being sick. Especially being sick. There was another couple puking their stupid guts up in the back garden.

In the living room Pat was in his pyjamas swaying to the music at one end of the sofa, while at the other end Sally was being groped by some fat boy. Pat grinned at me – isn't this fun? – as I surveyed the damage – lager cans with their contents spilled on the parquet floor and cigarettes stubbed out on their rims, scraps of takeaway pizza smeared on the furniture and God knows what stains on the beds upstairs.

There were maybe a dozen of them in all. But it felt like the Mongol Hordes had moved in. Worse than that – it was like one of those grotesque commercials for crisps or soft drinks or chinos, full of young people having the time of their life. Except that they were having the time of their life in my living room.

'Sally,' I said, 'what the fuck is going on?'

'Harry,' she said, and there were tears of joy in her eyes. 'It's Steve.'

She indicated the slack-jawed youth on top of her. He squinted at me with his cretinous porky eyes, eyes with nothing behind them but hormonal overload and nine cans of lager.

'He packed in that old slapper Yasmin McGinty,' Sally said. 'He's come back to me. Ain't it fantastic?'

'Are you crazy?' I said. 'Are you crazy or stupid? Which is it, Sally?'

'Oh, Harry,' she said, all disappointed. 'I thought you would understand. You of all people.'

The music suddenly died. Cyd stood there with the plug in her hands.

'Time to clean up this mess,' she told the room. 'Get rubbish sacks and cleaning stuff. Try looking under the sink.'

Steve climbed off Sally, adjusting his monstrous trousers, sneering at the grown-ups who had crashed his party.

'I'm out of here,' he said, as though he came from Beverly Hills instead of Muswell Hill.

Cyd moved swiftly across the room and clasped his nose between her thumb and forefinger.

'You're out of here when I tell you, elephant boy,' she said, making him yelp as she lifted him up on his toes. 'And it won't be until you clean up this mess. Not until then, got it?'

'Okay, okay!' he bleated, his fake American bravado melting in the face of the real thing.

I took Pat up to bed, turfing out a couple mating in the bathroom, while Cyd organised the cleaning detail. By the time I had read Pat a story and got him to settle down, Sally and Steve and their spotty friends were meekly cleaning the floors and the tables.

'Where did you learn to do that?' I asked Cyd.

'Texas,' she said.

It turned out that they were quite useless at housework, just as I imagine they will be useless at everything else they attempt in their brainless, designer-labelled lives.

Some of them were too sick. The rest of them were too stupid.

Steve squirted almost the entire contents of a bottle of lemon-scented, multi-surface liquid cleaner on the floor and then spent an hour trying to remove the suds as it foamed and spumed like a car wash gone mad. Cyd and I ended up doing most of it ourselves.

We kicked them out just after dawn. I kept Sally behind and stuck her in a minicab. She didn't apologise. She was still angry at me for not understanding that the course of true love sometimes leaves stains on the furniture.

'I hope you're satisfied,' she said as she was leaving. 'You ruined my chance with Steve, Harry. He'll probably go back to Yasmin McGinty. That slapper.'

Cyd brought me a cup of coffee when we were finally alone.

'Don't you wish you were still young enough to know everything?' she smiled.

I took her in my arms, feeling the green dress slide under my hands. I kissed her. She kissed me back. Then the telephone rang.

'Sally,' I said, 'calling to give me another piece of her mind.'

'She'll have none left,' Cyd laughed.

But it wasn't Sally. It was Gina, but without the usual little transcontinental blip before she spoke. That's how I knew immediately that Gina wasn't in Japan any more. This was a local call. She was back in town.

'I just realised something,' Gina said. 'This is the only telephone number in the whole world that I know by heart.'

twenty-nine

I arrived ten minutes early, but Gina was already there, sipping latte at a table for two at the rear of the café.

She was a little thinner from all that sashimi and sushi in Shinjuku and she was wearing clothes that I had never seen her in before – some kind of tailored, two-piece business suit. A woman of the working world.

She looked up and saw me and I could tell that she was still unmistakably Gina – the slightly goofy smile, the pale blue eyes – but a little bit older and far more serious than I could ever remember. The same woman, and yet changed in ways that I couldn't imagine.

'Harry,' she said, standing up, and we smiled nervously at each other, wondering if the correct form was to kiss or to shake hands. Neither of them really seemed right. Instead, I patted her quickly on the arm and she flinched as if she had been given a mild electric shock. That seemed to get us over the awkward moment.

'You look well,' she said, sitting down, smiling with a politeness that she had never bothered with in the old days.

And so did she – in her perfect face you could see the girl she had been and the woman she was going to become. Some people grow into their good looks and others grow out of them. And then there are people like Gina, who start turning heads as a child and never stop.

But like all the beautiful ones, Gina had always disliked excessive compliments, apparently assuming that they meant her worth was only skin deep. I guessed that she still felt the same way.

'You're looking well, too,' I said, not wanting to overdo it.

'How's Pat?'

'He's pretty good,' I laughed, and she laughed along with me, waiting for more. Except a waiter came and asked if he could get us anything, so we paused while we ordered another couple of lattes, and when he had gone, we talked about our son.

'A bit bigger now, I bet,' she said.

'Everyone seems to think he's really shooting up. Maybe I don't notice it so much because I see him every day.'

'Of course,' she said. 'But I bet I'll notice a difference. I mean, I haven't seen him for a couple of months.'

'Four months,' I said.

'Surely it's not that long.'

'Since the summer. It's four months, Gina. From July to October. Work it out.'

How could she imagine that it was only a couple of months? It was actually more than four. And it felt like far longer to me.

'Whatever,' she said, a little testy. 'Tell me about Pat. I can't wait to see him.'

What had changed? I looked around the café, trying to think what was different since Gina had gone away to Japan. And I was struck by the fact that the café hadn't changed at all.

It was one of those places that try to bring a touch of the Marais backstreets to the main drags of London – there was a big zinc bar, a blackboard with names of wines scrawled on it, a rack of newspapers on big wooden poles, and a scattering of chairs and tables on the pavement outside. They even called their full English breakfast something French.

It was a fairly typical café in our neighbourhood, and you might walk past it without even looking at it twice. But this place had meaning for us. Gina and I used to come here before Pat was born, back in the days when we were so close that we didn't even feel the need to talk to one another. And you can't get closer than that.

'School's going okay,' I said. 'That's changed. Nursery became a bit of a nightmare, but he's made a good friend at school and that's working well.'

'Why was nursery a nightmare?' she asked, looking all worried.

'He didn't like being left. It was just a phase he went through. A phase I thought might last until he was about eighteen.'

'But he has made friends with a little boy at school?'

'A little girl,' I said, and it seemed so strange to be talking about Cyd's daughter to her. 'Peggy.'

'Peggy,' Gina said, trying it out.

'She's got an English dad,' I said. 'And an American mum. From Houston.'

'And is he still crazy about Star Wars?' she smiled. Gina wasn't very interested in Peggy. 'Is it still Luke Skywalker and Han Solo around the clock?'

'Yes,' I said. 'That hasn't changed. But he's started to like other stuff, too.'

'Other stuff?'

'Well, he likes music,' I laughed. 'He likes gangster rap. You know, where they are always boasting about how they are going to shoot you in the head with their piece.'

Her face darkened. 'He likes listening to this music, does he?'

'Yes.'

'And you just let him, do you?'

'Yeah,' I said. 'I just let him.' I was a bit pissed off – she was acting as if I hadn't thought about this, as if I were letting him watch snuff movies or something. 'It's just something he's going through. It probably makes him feel tougher than he really is. Pat is a very sweet, gentle little kid, Gina. It doesn't do any harm. I can't see him getting involved in a drive-by shooting. He's in bed every night by nine.'

I could tell she didn't want to argue with me.

'What else?'

'He lets me wash his hair. He washes himself in the bath. He never makes a fuss about going to bed. He can tie his own shoes. He can tell the time. And he's started reading.'

The more I thought about it, the more I realised how much Pat had grown over the last few months. Gina smiled with what looked like a combination of pride and regret. I was embarrassed for her. She had missed all that.

'He sounds like a real little man,' she said.

'You should see him in his tie.'

'He wears a tie?'

'To school. They brought in a uniform because some of the kids were turning up in Polo gear and all that designer stuff. They thought it was unhealthy. So he has to wear a shirt and tie.'

'It must make him look really old.'

It didn't make him look old – dressing him up like a salary man actually made him look younger than ever. But I didn't feel like explaining all that to Gina.

'But what about you?' I asked. 'How long are you in town for?'

'Oh, permanently,' she said. 'Japan's over. For me and for everyone else. The days when some big-nosed pinky could go out East for adventure and a six-figure salary are gone. There's not much call for a translator when companies are going belly up. I got out before they threw me out.' She smiled brightly. 'So here I am,' she said. 'And naturally I want Pat.'

She wanted Pat? Did she mean she wanted to see him? To take him to the zoo and buy him a stuffed toy the size of a refrigerator? What did she mean?

'So you're not planning to live in Japan?'

'You were right, Harry. Even if the bubble hadn't burst, it would never have worked with Pat and me in an apartment the size of our guest room. I want to see him,' she said. 'As soon as possible.'

'Of course,' I said. 'I'm picking him up from my mum and dad this afternoon. You can wait for him at home.'

'No,' she said. 'Not at home. If it's okay with you, I'll meet you in the park.'

Stupid of me to suggest meeting at home. Because of course it wasn't Gina's home any more. And as I looked at the flashy new engagement ring where her simple little wedding band used to be, I suddenly realised that I had missed the really big change in our lives since the summer.

Pat lived with me now.

My Uncle Jack was at my parents' place.

Unlike Auntie Ethel from next door, Uncle Jack was my real uncle – my dad's brother, a dapper, wiry man who smoked his cigarettes by cupping them in the palm of his hand, as if protecting them from a fierce wind, even when he was in your living room dipping a ginger biscuit into his tea.

Uncle Jack was always in a suit and tie with some highly polished executive wagon parked outside. And on the passenger seat of the Scorpio or five series Beemer or big Merc or whatever it was, his chauffeur's hat would be resting.

Uncle Jack was a driver, ferrying businessmen back and

forth between their homes and offices to all the London airports. He seemed to spend more of his time waiting than driving, and I always pictured him hanging around the arrivals gate at Gatwick or Heathrow, fag cupped in hand, reading the *Racing Post*.

Uncle Jack was a gambler, like all my dad's side of the family, and as he grinned at me coming up the drive it seemed to me that all my memories of him revolved around betting of one kind or another.

There were the card schools at our house every Boxing Day. There were trips to the dog tracks at Southend and Romford, where my cousins and I would collect the big pink betting slips that had been discarded by all the unlucky punters. Even further back, when my grandmother was still alive, I could remember the bookie coming round to her house in the East End to collect her tiny daily bet on the horses. When did bookies stop making house calls to little old ladies?

There was another brother, the youngest, Bill, who had moved to Australia in the late seventies, but in my mind the three Silver brothers were together still – knocking back the scotch at Christmas and the brown ale at weddings, dancing the old dances with wives who they had fallen in love with as teenagers, playing nine-card brag into the early hours at Christmas with Tony Bennett singing 'Stranger in Paradise' on the music centre.

This was my father's family – a family of men, shrewd, tough Londoners who were sentimental about children and their suburban gardens, men whose old photographs invariably showed them in uniform, gamblers and drinkers, although neither to the degree where it was ever more than light relief, men who loved their families and looked on work as merely an unpleasant chore undertaken to support those families, men who prided themselves on knowing how the world worked. I knew that Uncle Jack was here for a reason.

'Saw you on telly the other night,' Uncle Jack said. 'At that awards do. Sitting at your table in your tux. He looks a bit of a lad, that Eamon Fish bloke.'

'He's a good kid,' I said. 'How are you, Uncle Jack?'

'I'm all right,' he said. 'Mustn't grumble.' He took my arm and pulled me closer. 'But what about your dad? I've seen him struggling for breath as soon as he gets out of his chair. But now he reckons he's seen the quack and he's been given the all clear.'

'He's okay?'

'So he says.'

My dad was in the back garden kicking a ball around with my mum and Pat. They were both wrapped up in thick coats and scarves, but my father was in just a T-shirt, seeming to take all the old pride in his hard, muscular body with its blurred tattoos and faded scars. As he tucked his T-shirt into his trousers I caught a glimpse of the big scar, the livid starburst on his side, and I realised that it still had the power to shock me.

'Dad? You saw the doctor?'

'Right as rain,' he said. 'Fit as a fiddle.'

'Really? What about your breathing?'

'He shouldn't be smoking, should he?' my mum said, but I could tell she was relieved that the old man had apparently been let off with a slap on the wrist. 'He wants to pack in the Old Holborn.'

'Bit late now,' my dad chuckled, enjoying his role as a dissenting voice in the muesli-sucking, low fat modern world. 'Bobby Charlton,' he said, blasting the ball into the wintry skeleton of the rose bushes. Pat went to fetch it.

'And the doctor really reckons that's the only thing wrong with you?' I asked.

My dad put his arm around Pat.

'Could go on for another twenty years,' he said defiantly. 'I'll tell you what – I intend to live to see this little fellow get married.'

Pat looked at my father as if he were insane.

'I'm never getting married,' he said.

I had forgotten to tell Gina that he could ride his bike.

I had forgotten to tell her that the timid little four-year-old who had tottered around the swimming pool with the aid of stabilisers had become a confident five-year-old who could zip around the park with a cavalier disregard for his safety.

So when Gina saw Pat pedalling towards where she was waiting by the swings and roundabout, she laughed and clapped her hands, laughed out loud with delight and wonder.

'You're so *big*,' she cried, her voice catching as she held her arms open to him.

Before he pulled away from me, I caught a glimpse of his face. He was smiling – but it wasn't the smooth, practised smile that I had grown used to, it wasn't the David Niven smile full of slick, shallow charm that he reserved for strangers and for reassuring me that everything was all right.

Pat saw Gina and he smiled without thinking about it, he smiled for real.

Then he was in his mother's arms, the hood of his anorak falling off his head as she lifted him up out of the saddle of his bike, and she was crying and getting tears on the top of his head and you could see that their hair was exactly the same colour, exactly the same burnished yellow.

'I'll bring him home in a couple of hours,' Gina called,

and Pat pedalled slowly away, her arm around his shoulder, nodding at something that Gina had said to him.

'Be careful on that bike, Pat,' I shouted. 'Don't go too fast, okay?'

But they didn't hear me.

thirty

My father had been lying.

He had been to see the doctor. But there had been no appointment that had ended with my old man being told to put his shirt back on, he was as fit as a fiddle, in remarkable condition for a man of his age, but – slap on the back, matey wink from the quack – he might like to think about cutting down on his roll-ups.

The doctor might have told him that there was no way of knowing how long he had to live. And he might have said that these things can drag out for years. But it is highly unlikely that the GP produced his NHS crystal ball and told my old man that he would live to see his grandson's wedding day.

The thing that was growing inside my dad had gone too far for all that.

My mother called me at work for the first time in my life.

He was in the hospital. The High Dependency Unit, she said, her voice breaking on those three clinically modern words.

He had been putting away the garden furniture that always sat in our garden until the middle of winter, storing the blue canvas deck chairs and stripy beach umbrella in the garage until next spring, as he did every year, and that's when he suddenly had no breath, no breath at all, and it was terrifying, absolutely terrifying, she said, and she had called for the ambulance but she didn't think they would get there in time. In time to save him.

'But what is it?' I said, still not understanding, still unable to comprehend that there could be a world without my father in it.

'It's his lungs,' my mother said, and her voice was a sick, shaken whisper. 'A tumour.'

A tumour in his lungs. She couldn't say the word, she couldn't name the thing that was stealing the very air that he breathed, and that terrible, dreaded word hung between us on the telephone line, as if it might go away if we didn't say it.

She didn't really have to say the word. Finally I was starting to understand.

It was a modern hospital, but in the middle of miles of farmland.

That was the thing about where I grew up, the thing about the suburbs. You could go from fly-blown concrete jungle to open rolling fields in just a short car ride. It was because of these fields – or fields just like them – that my father had brought his family out here a lifetime ago.

My mother was in the waiting room when I arrived. She hugged me and, with a kind of desperate optimism, told me that the doctor had assured her that there was lots that could be done for my father.

Then she went to get him, the Indian doctor who had given her this wonderful news, and when she came back she stood him before me. He was young enough to still look a little embarrassed at my mother's belief in his powers.

'This is my son, doctor,' she said. 'Please tell him that there's lots that can be done for my husband, please.'

'I was telling your mother that pain management is very sophisticated these days,' he said.

'Pain management?' I said.

'There's much that we can do to help your father breathe more easily, to help him sleep better and to relieve the pain that he has been suffering.'

The doctor told me about the oxygen mask that my father was already using. More obliquely, he talked about the benefits of a good night's sleep and the use of an effective painkiller.

'You mean sleeping pills and morphine?' I said.

'Yes,' he said.

There was lots that could be done, but they were all just things to make my father more comfortable. They were all just controlling the symptoms of what was growing inside him. None of it was going to make him better.

They could force more air into his poor, useless lungs and they could render his exhausted body unconscious for a while and they could pump enough opiates into him to fog his brain and make it blind to the unbearable pain.

There was lots that could be done.

But there was also nothing that could be done.

My father was dying.

We sat by his side, watching him sleep.

He was propped up in his hospital bed, a transparent oxygen mask strapped over his nose and mouth, a day's worth of stubble on his face, the face that he always liked to keep well-scrubbed and clean shaven.

There was a metal box with a button for calling for help by his side and a plastic sheet beneath him, and these little things clawed at my heart and made me feel like weeping. Already he seemed as helpless as a newborn baby.

He was in a ward with seven other beds containing men –

most of them old, but two of them younger than me – who all had the same thing wrong with them.

It might be in different parts of their body and it might be at different stages of development and some of them might go home and some of them might never go home. But they all had the same thing wrong inside them, that thing that we still couldn't say, my mother and I.

'He knew, didn't he?' I asked. 'He's known all along, I bet.'

'He must have known from the start,' my mother said. 'He went for tests when it all began, when he first started to lose his breath – I made him go – and he told me it was all fine.'

'I never knew,' I said, amazed that my parents could still keep a secret from me. 'I never knew he had any tests.'

'We didn't tell you because there didn't seem any point in worrying you. You had enough on your plate with Pat. And besides, he was fine. So he said.'

'But he wasn't fine,' I said bitterly, sounding like a small boy whining, *it's not fair, it's not fair*. 'He hasn't been fine for a long time.'

'He would have known from the start.' My mother's eyes never left his face as she spoke to me. 'I was talking to one of the nurses, and she said there's this thing called gradual disclosure – they don't give you the bad news all at once, not unless you make them, not unless you demand to know what's wrong.'

'And he would have wanted to know,' I said with total certainty. 'He would have made them tell him.'

'Yes,' my mother said. 'He would have made them tell him.'

'Then why did he keep it a secret for so long?' I said, already knowing the answer. 'He must have known that we would find out eventually.'

'He was protecting us,' she said.

My mother took his hands in her hands and held them to her cheek, and I looked away, fearing I might unravel at the sight of how much she still loved him.

'Protecting us,' she repeated.

That's right, Mum. He was shielding us from the worst this world has to offer, he was sparing his family some of the misery that was ahead, he was protecting us.

He was doing what he had always done.

'I'm so sorry about your dad, Harry,' Gina said. 'I really am – he always treated me with great kindness.'

'He was mad about you,' I said, nearly adding that it broke his heart when we broke up – but I managed to stop myself in time.

'I'd like to visit him at the hospital,' she said. 'If that's okay with you. And your mum.'

'Sure,' I said, not knowing how to say that it was already clear that he didn't like visitors, that he found it hard to deal with his own pain without witnessing everybody else's. But I couldn't say that to Gina without sounding as though she was being cut off.

'Will Pat see him?'

I took a breath.

'Pat wants to see him,' I said. 'But my dad's just too sick at the moment. If there's some improvement, maybe. But right now it would upset both of them too much.'

'What did you tell him?'

'Granddad's sick. Very sick. How do you tell a five-year-old that the grandfather who thinks he's the greatest thing in the world is dying? How do you do it? I don't know.'

'We need to talk about Pat,' she said. 'I know this isn't the best time and I'm genuinely sorry for what you're going through with your dad. But you should know that I want Pat back as soon as possible.'

'You want Pat back?'

'That's right. We don't need to have the arguments we had before, okay? I'm not taking him out of the country. I'm back in London. Richard and I are looking at places in the area. Pat wouldn't even have to change schools.'

'How the hell is old Richard?'

'Fine.'

'Still semi-separated?'

'Permanently separated. His wife is back in the States. And I know it seems fast, but we've been talking about getting married.'

'When?'

'As soon as our divorces come through.'

How I laughed.

'Fuck me,' I said. 'You're getting married as soon as your divorces come through? Ain't love grand?'

Gina and I hadn't even started talking about the mechanics of divorce. We had talked plenty about splitting up. But we hadn't discussed the paperwork.

'Please, Harry,' she said, a touch of ice coming into her voice. 'Don't get abusive, okay?'

I shook my head.

'You think you can just come back into our lives and pick up where you left off, Gina? You think that you can have Pat back just because the Asian economic miracle turned out to be not all that miraculous after all?'

'We *agreed*,' she said, suddenly angrier than I had ever seen her. 'You always knew that Pat was going to live with me. If I had stayed in Tokyo or come back here, I always intended to have him with me. What makes you think you've got any right to keep him?'

'Because he's happy with me,' I said. 'And because I can

do it. I can *do* it. It wasn't great at first but I learned, okay? It got better and now it's pretty good. And he's happy where he is. He doesn't need to be with you and some guy, some fucking guy you picked up in a Roppongi bar.'

Her mouth had a set to it that I didn't remember from before.

'I love Richard,' she said. 'And I want Pat to grow up with me.'

'We don't own them, you know. We don't own our children, Gina.'

'You're right – we don't own our children. But my solicitor will argue that, all things being equal, a child should be with his mother.'

I got up, tossing a few coins on the table.

'And my solicitor will argue that you and Richard can go fuck yourselves,' I said. 'And my solicitor – when I get one – will also argue that a child should be with the parent most capable of bringing him up. That's me, Gina.'

'I don't want to hate you, Harry. Don't teach me to hate you.'

'I don't want you to hate me. But can't you see what's happened? I've learned to be a real parent. You can't just come back and take that away from me.'

'Unbelievable,' she said. 'You look after him for a couple of months and you think you can take my place?'

'Four months,' I said. 'And I'm not trying to take your place. It's just that I've found a place of my own.'

Cyd took one look at me and told me that she was taking me out to dinner. I wasn't hungry, but I said okay because I was too tired to argue. And also because there was something I had to ask her.

I kissed Pat and left him watching *Pocahontas* with Peggy. Bianca hovered gloomily in the kitchen, chain-chewing

Juicy Fruit because she wasn't allowed to smoke in the flat.

'My car or yours?' Cyd asked.

'Mine,' I said, and we drove to a little Indian restaurant between Upper Street and Liverpool Road. The tape holding together the shredded roof of the MGF had dried, cracked and started to come apart, and it flapped like a ship's sails in a high wind.

The sight of the food repelled me and I half-heartedly pushed some chicken tikka masala around my plate, feeling as though everything was slipping out of focus.

'Eat what you like, honey,' she said. 'Just what you feel like. But try to eat something, okay?'

I nodded, smiling gratefully at this incredible woman who had lost her dad when she was half my age, and I almost asked her the question then and there, but I thought I would stick to my plan and ask her at the end of the evening. Yes, best to stick to the plan.

'We don't have to see this film tonight if you don't want to,' she said. 'It's not important. We can skip it and do whatever you feel like. We can just talk. Or we can do nothing. We don't even have to talk.'

'No, let's go and see it,' I said, so we drove into Soho to see an Italian film called *Cinema Paradiso* about a young boy's friendship with the old projectionist at the local movie house.

Cyd was usually good at choosing films she knew I would like if I gave them half a chance, films with subtitles and no star names which I wouldn't have even considered a couple of years ago.

But I found myself cooling towards this one at the end when the gruff old projectionist, now blinded by a fire in the cinema, tells the Bambi-eyed young boy, now a teenager, to leave their village and never come back.

The boy, Toto, goes away and becomes a famous film director and doesn't come back to his little village for thirty years, on the day that they are burying Alfredo, the old projectionist who taught him to love the cinema and then sent him away.

'Why did Alfredo send the boy away for good?' I asked as we walked through the crowds on Old Compton Street. 'Why couldn't they at least stay in touch? The way he told him to go away, this boy he had known all his life, it seemed cruel.'

'Because Alfredo knew that Toto would never find the things he needed in that little town,' Cyd smiled, happy to talk about it. 'He had to break free so that he could learn what Alfredo already knew. *Life is not what you see in films – life is much harder.*' She took my arm and laughed. 'I like it when we talk about this stuff,' she said.

The MGF was in the big carpark at the end of Gerrard Street, the one behind the fire station on Shaftesbury Avenue, Chinatown's carpark. We got in the car but I didn't turn on the ignition.

'I want us to live together,' I said. 'You and Peggy and me and Pat.'

Those eyes that I loved looked genuinely surprised.

'Live together?'

'Your flat is too small for all of us,' I said. 'So what would work best is if you moved in with us. What do you think?'

She gave a confused shake of her gorgeous head.

'You've had a really rough time,' she said. 'What with your dad. And Gina. You've really been through it.'

'That's got nothing to do with it,' I said. 'Well, maybe a bit. Maybe even a lot. But that's not all of it. I know what I feel about you. And I think you feel pretty much the same way about me. I want us to be together.'

She smiled, shaking her head again, more firmly this time.

'No, Harry.'

'No?'

'I'm sorry.'

'Why not?'

It was a pointless question, the kind of question a child asks. But I had to ask it.

'Because you want someone with a less complicated life than me,' she said. 'No kid. No ex-husband. No reminders of the past. You know you do. Remember how you felt on Pat's birthday? Remember that? You and I both know there's no future for us.'

'I don't know that at all,' I said.

'You think you want someone who can transform your life with love. But you don't really want love, Harry. You couldn't handle real love. You want romance.'

Her words were made worse, much worse, by the fact that they were said with enormous tenderness. There was no anger or malice in them. It was as if she felt genuinely sorry for me.

'And that's fine,' she said. 'That's the way you are and in a lot of ways it's a good way to be. But it would never work between us because you can't make the hearts and flowers stuff last for a lifetime. Not with kids around. Especially when they're not your own.'

'We could,' I insisted.

'No,' she said. 'We would end up in exactly the same place that you and Gina ended up. And I don't want that. I can't go through all that – not with Peggy. Sweet nothings are fine. Romance is fine. But I want someone who is going to rub my feet when I get old and tell me they love me even when I can't remember where I put my keys. That's what I want. I want someone I can grow old with. And – I'm really sorry – but I don't think that's what you want.'

She reached out to touch my face but I turned away,

wondering where I had heard all this before. We sat there in silence in that subterranean carpark, the whole weight of Chinatown above our heads.

'I thought you didn't want Peggy to get hurt by seeing you in a short-term relationship,' I said.

'I'd rather she saw that than a long-term relationship that goes wrong,' she said. 'And Pat and Peggy will still be friends. She will still see you. But this way you and I both get spared a lot of grief.'

'This way?' I said. 'You sound like you're ending it.'

'Not ending it,' she said. 'We can still be friends, too. But I looked at you at your son's birthday party and I realised that Peggy and I are not what you want. Not really.'

'I know what it means when a woman says we can still be friends,' I said. 'It means close the door on your way out. That's what it means, doesn't it?'

'Don't feel too bad, Harry,' she said. 'People break up every day. It's not the end of the world.'

The thing about cancer is that it can always exceed your worst expectations. There is something pornographic about cancer's ability to confound your imagination. Whatever new obscenity cancer comes up with to torment and torture you, it can always do worse tomorrow.

My father was shot full of morphine and his skin no longer had the colour of living skin and, even with the oxygen mask, his lungs strained and heaved to take in a pitiful amount of air that simply wasn't enough.

Sometimes the fog in his eyes would clear, that fog caused by the pain and the killers of pain, and when it cleared, I saw regret and fear in those eyes swimming with tears and I was convinced that this was it, this was the end, this was surely the end.

'I love you,' I told him, taking his hands, and saying those words that I had never said to him before.

And I told him because surely it could get no worse than this – but it did get worse, that's the thing about cancer, it can always exceed your blackest moment.

So the next day I went back to that crowded ward, sat by his bed holding his hand, and – crying harder this time – I told my father again that I loved him.

part three: *guess what?*

thirty-one

Eamon froze.

You would have missed it if you were watching from the cheap seats of the studio audience, what with all the cameras and crew obscuring your view. You might even have missed it if you were tuning in from out there in TV land, what with the television being just one more voice droning away in your living room, and this particular show not being central to your life in the way that it was to mine.

But I saw him lose it on one of the monitors up in the gallery and I knew that this moment could come if you had spent sixty years in front of a camera or sixty seconds. The moment that the autocue and the script and the rehearsal all mean nothing. The moment you lose it.

'Coming from Kilcarney, I'm shocked at all the divorce over here,' he said, and then he blinked twice, the panic flooding into his face. 'Very shocked . . .'

He stared into that unforgiving black eye with the red light above it, his mind blank, lost for words. It was more than forgetting the punch line. It was a complete failure of faith, like the tightrope walker who looks down and sees his own body smashed on the ground far, far below. In the studio audience, someone coughed. The silence seemed to hum with his fractured nerves.

'Come on, come on, you can do it,' I whispered, and he blinked, breathed and suddenly he was back on his rope.

'Over here, when a woman meets a guy now, she thinks – "*Is this the sort of man I want my children to spend their weekends with?*"'

The audience laughed and Eamon wobbled to safety on the other side. He told his next joke, still shaking with terror, trying very hard not to look down.

'It happens,' I said, taking him to a quiet corner of the green room. 'Just when you think that you're on top of this thing and stage fright is something that happens to other people, then it happens.'

Eamon sucked on a lager.

'I don't know that I can do this thing, Harry. I don't know if I can go out there every week knowing there's the possibility that my mind is going to suddenly seize up.'

'You just have to learn to live with the knowledge that your mind can go completely blank when a million people are watching you.'

'Fuck me.'

'You can do it.'

'But the point is – I can't. I might look confident and cocky to the folks back home, but it's all an act. It's not real, Harry. I throw up in my dressing room before I go on. I wake up at three in the morning dreaming that everybody's looking at me and I've lost my voice. I can't do it. I'm too nervous.'

'You're not nervous,' I said. 'You're excited.'

'What about when I puke my guts up before a show?'

'You're excited. You're about to go out there and entertain the country. Naturally you're excited. Who wouldn't be?'

'What about my bad dreams?'

'That's not nerves. That's excitement. Teach yourself the presenter's mantra and chant it again and again – *I am not nervous, I am excited.*'

'I am not nervous,' Eamon said. 'I am excited.'

'That's it.'

Someone came over with a sausage roll in one hand and a glass of white wine in the other and told Eamon that was the best show he had ever done.

'You want to get a real drink?' he asked me.

'Sorry, gents,' said a black bouncer the size of a skip, making us sound like a couple of public lavatories. 'It's dress corporate.'

'Dress corporate?' I said.

'Suits. Ties. Business garb.'

But then the other bouncer, a white guy the size of a skip, recognised Eamon's face.

'It's all right, Chris,' he said, lifting the red velvet rope. 'How you doing, Eamon?'

Smiles all round. Come in, come in. Me and my famous mate went into the darkness of the club and suddenly I had never felt more sober.

All over the bar there were beautiful half-naked girls – no, more like three-quarters naked girls, or nine-tenths naked girls – writhing and grinding and dancing in the faces of seated businessmen whose brows were beaded with sweat and whose paunchy bodies were immobilised by longing and lager. The girls all wore garter belts halfway up their thighs. The garter belts were stuffed with ten- and twenty-pound notes.

'Don't get too excited,' Eamon said. 'The penetration is all in your wallet.'

We went downstairs where a smiling black girl in a kind of little white tutu number greeted Eamon by name. She led us to a table by the side of a stage where more girls wearing only high heels and dental floss for underwear were sliding up and down poles.

They – and their scantily clad sisters torturing middle-ranking executives all over the room – were dancing to one of those American girl singers whose name I could never remember, the one who boasts about being both a bitch and a lover. One of the new songs. I realised that most of the songs I knew were old songs.

A bottle of champagne appeared. I told Eamon that I wanted a beer, but he said we could only get champagne at these tables. The champagne was compulsory where we were.

A statuesque blonde in a kind of disposable evening dress appeared. She smiled at me as if she had been looking for me all her life.

'I'm Venus. Would you like a dance?'

What the hell. I could probably use a dance.

'Sure,' I said, standing up and starting to jig around from foot to foot in that lame excuse for dancing that we have in this country. I felt good. This song about being a bitch and a lover wasn't so bad after all.

'No,' said Venus impatiently. I realised that she had a Birmingham accent. 'You don't dance. You just sit there.'

She indicated the poleaxed businessmen lusting silently in their chairs all over the room as girls bent double and winked at them from between their legs or almost grazed the broken veins in their boozy noses with a perfect nipple. '*I* dance for *you*, okay? You sit there and watch. No touching. One song for £10. Minimum.'

'Maybe later,' I said, sitting down and gulping some champagne. Venus disappeared.

'Relax, Harry,' Eamon smiled. 'You're not nervous. You're excited.' He slapped me on the back and roared. 'I love you, you fucking bastard. How the fuck are you?'

'Brilliant,' I said. 'My old man's in a cancer ward and my wife – my ex-wife – wants custody of our son.'

He looked at me with real concern. Not easy with a flute of champagne in your hand and naked dancing girls swarming all around.

'How is your dad?'

'He's stabilising,' I said. 'That's what the doctors call it. That means there's no marked deterioration. If he stays like this, maybe he can come home. But he wouldn't be coming home to get better.'

'Can I dance for you, Eamon?' said a young Asian girl with hair down to her waist.

She was the only Asian girl in the house. There were a few black women in here but mostly the girls were blondes, either by birth or bottle. It was a bit like flicking through *Playboy*. This was a place where blondes ruled the world.

'Later,' Eamon said, turning back to me as the Asian beauty disappeared into the gloaming. 'I'm sorry about your dad, Harry. And it's a drag that your ex-missus is cutting up rough. But cheer up, you miserable fucker.' He drained his flute and filled it again. 'At least you've got Cyd. She's a grand girl.'

'That's finished,' I said.

'Would you like a dance?' some pneumatic blonde asked me.

'No thanks,' I said. She went away, not taking it personally. 'Me and Cyd – we had our problems.'

'Problems?' Eamon said. 'At the award thing, you looked like you were getting on fine.'

'We got on fine when there were just the two of us. But she's got a kid. And I've got a kid. And they're great kids. But that means she's got an ex-husband and I've got an ex-wife. And it was all – I don't know – just so crowded.'

'And that was your problem?'

'Well, the biggest problem was that she dumped me. But she dumped me because I sometimes got depressed at how crowded it was. And because she thought I wanted – it sounds stupid – some kind of perfect love. And maybe she was right. She could handle things the way they were. But for some reason, I couldn't.'

'Because you're a romantic, Harry,' Eamon said. 'Because you believe in all the old songs. And the old songs don't prepare you for real life. They make you allergic to real life.'

'What's wrong with the old songs? At least nobody thinks it's clever to be a bitch and a lover in the old songs.'

'You're in love with love, Harry. You're in love with the idea of love. Cyd's a grand girl – but what's really special about her is that you can't have her. That's what really grabs you.'

That wasn't true. I missed her. I especially missed the way she put her arms around me when we slept. Most couples, they turn their backs on each other as soon as it's time for sleep. Not her. She snuggled and cuddled and tried to make us one flesh. That's ridiculous, I know, that's the impossible dream. But that's the dream she made me dream. And the thought that we would never sleep like that again was unbearable.

'She was special,' I said.

'Look around,' Eamon said, trying to fill my flute. I put my hand over the top of my glass. I'm not much of a drinker and I was pissed already. 'There's what? A hundred girls in here?'

I looked around. On the outskirts of the room where the girls in tutus waited with their torches and their trays, dozens of girls roamed the shallow waters of the club. Dozens more squirmed rhythmically in front of businessmen who leered and snickered when they were in their little gangs and then sat there all bashful and – yes – actually reverential when one of them bought a dance.

It's so easy to push our buttons, I thought, unable to imagine any woman melting – while simultaneously reaching for her money – at the sight of any man's buttocks.

Looking at the faces of the men looking at all that perfect female flesh – flesh toned by youth and gym, flesh that here and there had been enhanced by the surgeon's hand – it was easy to believe that being a man is like being chained to the village idiot.

'One . . . two . . . three,' said Eamon, knocking back the champagne as he started counting the girls. '. . . eight . . . nine . . . ten . . .'

'Yes,' I said. 'Maybe a hundred girls.'

'They're all special, Harry. So many special girls that I can't even count them. The world is full of special girls.'

'Not like Cyd,' I said.

'Bollocks,' said Eamon. 'Great big hairy bollocks, Harry.' He emptied his glass, tried to fill it again and seemed surprised to discover that the bottle was empty. He ordered another and put his arm around me. 'You love it, Harry. You love all this suffering. Because it's so much easier than actually living with a woman.'

'You're drunk.'

'I may be drunk, Harry, but I know women. You might know television – and may God love you and keep you for knowing television, for you have saved my Kilcarney hide on more than one occasion – but I know women. And I know you would change your mind about Cyd if you lived with her for the next seven years. *Because we always do.*'

'Not always.'

'Always,' he said. 'The old songs don't tell you that. The old songs talk about love found and love lost. Heroic love, eternal love, sweet and sour love. But they don't talk about love grown dull and old. They don't write songs about that.'

'Yes, they fucking do,' I shouted.

'Would you like a dance?' said some vision in a see-through nightdress.

'No, thank you,' I said. '"Where Did Our Love Go?", "You Don't Send Me Flowers," "You've Lost That Loving Feeling" – they write loads of songs about love going off the boil.'

'But they make it sound heroic,' Eamon said. 'And it's not. It's boring and stupid. Look around you, Harry, just look around this room – why would any man want to settle down with just one woman? It's not the way we're made.'

'It's not the way you're made,' I said. 'But that's just because all you care about is your nasty little knob and putting it in as many places as possible.'

'Not my knob, Harry.'

'Sorry, Eamon. I insist. Your nasty little knob.'

'Not my knob, Harry. My seed.'

'Okay, your seed.'

The Asian girl with hair down to her waist came over and sat on Eamon's lap. She placed a chaste kiss on his dark, unshaven cheek.

'I'm Mem,' she said to me, and I said, 'Harry,' and we shook hands, as though we were about to discuss some business deal. Funnily enough, in that room full of stale cigarette smoke and naked flesh and middle-aged dreams, there was a lot of formality going on, there was a lot of shaking hands and introductions and business cards quietly being handed over with the cash.

That was the genius of the place – the men were flattered into believing that they were really in with a chance, as if these girls were desperate to be bought dinner in some crap fake French restaurant when they could be in here turning every man into their own personal cashpoint machine with just a glint in their eye, a twitch of their hips and some new song about being a bitch and a lover.

Mem began to dance for Eamon, and as she pulled her dress over her head and began to slowly move her hard little body in front of his face, I could see why this small Asian girl – what was she? Indonesian? Thai? – managed to hold her own here on planet blonde.

'It's like the Heathrow Express,' Eamon said.

'What the fuck are you going on about now?' I asked.

'The Heathrow Express,' Eamon said. 'The train to the airport. Haven't you noticed? Just outside of Paddington, you pass this enormous great yard full of shining, brand new cars. And a little bit further down the line, there's another yard – but this one is full of rusting, rotting, burned out old cars all stacked on top of each other like the junk they are.'

'I think I'm missing something here, Eamon,' I said. 'You're saying that life is like the Heathrow Express?'

'I'm saying that relationships are like those cars,' he said, sliding the palm of his hand up one of Mem's golden young thighs, even though there was a strict no touching rule. An Indonesian thigh? A Thai thigh? 'They start off all shiny and new and looking like they're going to last forever. And then they end up as rubbish.'

'You're the devil,' I said, standing up. 'And I'm drunk.'

'Oh, don't go, Harry,' he pleaded.

'Got to pick up my boy from my parents,' I said. 'I mean, my mother.'

I kissed him on the cheek and shook Mem's hand – for some reason that seemed the right way round to do it, rather than kissing Mem and shaking Eamon's hand – and I was halfway to the door when I remembered where I had heard that name before.

And I knew that Eamon was wrong. If you are always

craving, always wanting, never satisfied, never happy with what you've got, you end up even more lost and lonely than you do if you are some poor sap like me who believes that all the old songs were written about just one girl.

The men who fuck around are not free. Not really. They end up more enslaved than anyone because they can never stop suspecting that the women they want are just the same as them. Just as unfettered, just as faithless, just as ready to move on or to make a quick detour as the hero of one of the new songs.

He was outside the club, waiting in the shadows with all the other boyfriends of the dancers. Somehow I knew he would be there.

And I knew he would look like all the rest of them, despite the flash cars – or in his case, the big BMW motorbike – that they had parked by the kerb. He didn't look happy. None of the boyfriends looked very happy.

They were standing behind the taxi drivers who were touting for trade. The cabbies were talking to each other and to the men who emerged from the club – need a taxi, sir? where you going? ten quid to Islington? – but the boyfriends of the dancers were silent and still and alone. They looked as though their dreams had come true, but all it had brought them was jealousy and disgust.

I saw him waiting, although he didn't see me, saw him stewing in the night with all the rest of the turbo-charged studs.

Jim Mason, Cyd's handsome ex, waiting for his Mem to finish work for the night.

thirty-two

Visiting hours were meaningless now. My father's waking moments were entirely dependent on the ebb and flow of pain and morphine.

You could sit with him all morning and he would sleep right through your visit – if you can dignify that drug-sodden rest in the hospital as sleep. And then as the opiates wore off, but before the tumour started to gnaw at him again, he might wake up and talk to you with eyes that were watery with suffering and an unendurable sadness. And that's when I would be waiting for him.

Halfway to dawn he stirred, his tongue flicking at his parched lips, waking me from my own fitful rest. The ward was silent apart from the snores of the old man in the next bed but one. I helped my dad to sit up, wetting his mouth with a pitifully small amount of water.

When he started to catch his breath – he would always catch his breath now – I helped him put the oxygen mask over his face and held his hand as he desperately sucked in some air. So little air, so little water. It broke my heart to see what he was surviving on.

He took off the mask, his face twisting with agony, and I thought again about how nobody warns you about this pain. But I still couldn't decide what was worse – seeing him in all that terrible suffering, or seeing him with his mind numbed by morphine, no longer truly himself. It was the pain, I decided. Seeing him in pain was worse.

He turned his eyes on me, shaking his head hopelessly, and then he looked away.

I took his hand in mine and held it tight, knowing his spirits were sinking. He was a brave man, but he couldn't fight this sadness which came in the middle of the night, this sadness which made you feel that nothing could ever be any good again.

And nobody warns you about the sadness. You are half-prepared for the pain. You can guess at the agonies of dying from cancer. But with all that physical suffering came a sense of loss that no shot of morphine could smother.

'The worst thing about it,' my father whispered in the darkness, 'is knowing what you will be missing. I don't mean the things that haven't happened yet – Pat's wedding day, seeing you finally settle down – but the things that you take for granted. Seeing Pat ride his bike, telling him a story, kissing him goodnight. Watching him running around the garden with his bloody light sabre. All those small things that mean more than anything.'

'You might come home soon,' I said, still clinging to hope because that is what we do, because there is no real alternative, still clinging to life even when life is full of torment. 'You might be doing all those things before you know it.'

But he was beyond kidding himself. Or me.

'I'll miss my garden. Your mother. Her cooking. Your television shows.'

I was flattered and embarrassed that he would put my work in the same league as his wife, his grandson and his garden. And I was a little ashamed too – ashamed that I hadn't done more in the time that we had, that I hadn't done more to impress him and win his approval. A couple of television shows and a broken marriage. That was about it.

But there was always Pat. And I knew that he loved his

grandson more than he loved anything in this world. It felt as though Pat was my only real gift to him.

My father wanted to sit up. I pressed the little metal box that controlled his bed and it whirred in the silence of the ward until the back was raised. Then he leaned forward and held on to me while I placed a pillow behind his back, his unshaven face rough against the skin of my cheek.

The old smells of Old Spice and Old Holborn were gone now and they had been replaced by hospital smells, the smell of illness and chemicals. There was no tobacco or aftershave in here. That was all behind him.

It still seemed strange to be physically helping him. The undeniable fact of my father's strength had been such a large part of my childhood and my youth that, now that his strength was gone, it felt like the world was ending, as though some immutable law of nature had been unceremoniously overturned.

And I could see for the first time that his strength wasn't the reason I loved him.

I had always believed that his toughness – that old world toughness which was endorsed by and embodied in his medal – was why he was my hero.

Now, as I helped him to sip water or to sit up in his hospital bed, I saw that I loved him for the same reasons that my mother loved him and my son loved him.

For his gentleness, for his compassion and for a courage that had nothing to do with physical strength.

'Don't say anything to your mother, but I don't think I'll be coming home.'

'Don't say that, Dad.'

'I don't think I will be. I can feel it. And I would like to see Pat.'

'Of course.'

He didn't say *one last time.* He didn't have to. And besides, there were some things that were too painful to say out loud. But we knew that we were talking about death.

'If that's all right with you,' he said. 'If you don't think it would upset him too much. You have to decide. You're his father.'

'I'll bring him the next time I come. But now try to sleep for a bit, Dad.'

'I'm not tired.'

'Just rest your eyes.'

Pat came out of school with a dark-haired boy who was swinging a battered Godzilla lunch box.

'You want to watch *Star Wars* at my house?' Pat asked him.

'Is it widescreen or pan and scan?' the boy said.

'Widescreen.'

'Okay.'

'Can he, Dad?'

I was searching the loud, laughing hordes for the one familiar face that I knew would be solemn and composed among all the high-pitched mayhem of 3.30. One little brown-eyed girl with a Pocahontas sandwich box. But she wasn't there.

'Where's Peggy?' I asked.

'Peggy wasn't in today,' Pat said. 'Is it okay if Charlie comes back?'

No Peggy? I looked down at Charlie. Charlie looked up at me.

'It's fine by me,' I said. 'But we have to clear it with Charlie's mum.'

Pat and Charlie began cheering and laughing and shoving each other. The sharp edge of a Godzilla lunch box smacked against my knee.

I missed Peggy already.

* * *

I opened the front door and Sally was standing there, warily peering up at me through her greasy fringe.

'Didn't think I'd see you again,' I said.

'I've come to say sorry.'

I let her in.

Pat and Charlie were bickering about *Star Wars* on the sofa. Charlie wanted to fast forward over the love scenes and moments of reflection and get straight to the combat. Pat – ever the purist – wanted to watch the film from beginning to end. Sally stuck her head around the door to say hello to Pat and then we went into the kitchen.

'I've been thinking,' she said. 'And I realise how dumb it was of me to let Steve's friends in.'

'It would have been helpful if you'd thought about it at the time.'

'I know,' she said, her sheepish eyes peering at me from behind a curtain of hair. 'Sorry. I was just – I don't know how to put it – so happy to see him again.'

'Well, I can understand that,' I said. 'My heart skips a beat whenever Steve comes into view.'

'You don't like him,' she said. 'You're making fun.'

'How's it going anyway? You and Steve, I mean.'

'That's all over,' she said, and, as her eyes filled with tears, I suddenly felt very sorry for this painfully shy kid. 'He gave me the elbow again. Once he got what he wanted.'

'Sorry,' I said. 'It's true Steve's not my favourite human being. But I know you liked him. How old are you now? Fifteen?'

'Sixteen.'

'You'll meet somebody else. I'm not going to tell you that you don't know what love is at your age, because I don't believe that's true. But you will meet someone else, I promise you.'

'That's okay,' she said, sniffing snot up her nose. I handed her a piece of kitchen towel and she honked on it loudly. 'Doesn't matter. I just wanted to apologise for that night. And to tell you that if you were to give me another chance at babysitting for you, it wouldn't happen again.'

I looked at her carefully, knowing that some extra help with Pat would be useful. The old support network had suddenly disappeared. My dad was in the hospital. Cyd was gone. I was even starting to miss Bianca. Now it was just me and my mum, and we were sometimes finding it a struggle.

'You're on,' I said. 'I could use a babysitter.'

'Good,' Sally smiled. 'Because I could use the money.'

'Still living with Glenn?'

'Yeah. But I'm sort of, well, pregnant.'

'Jesus, Sally. Is this Steve's kid?'

'There hasn't been anybody else.'

'And what does Steve have to say about becoming a dad?'

'He's not too keen. I think his exact words were – fuck off and die. He wants me to get rid of it.'

'And you want to keep it?'

She thought about it for a moment. Just a moment.

'I think it'll be good,' she said. 'I always wanted something that was only mine. Something that I could love and that would love me back. And this baby, this baby will love me.'

'Your dad knows about this, does he?'

She nodded. 'That's the one good thing about having a father who never stopped being a hippy,' she said. 'He doesn't get too upset by stuff like this. He was very cool when I had my stomach pumped when I was thirteen. Teenage pregnancy doesn't worry him. Although I think he's a bit shocked that I don't want an abortion.'

'But how are you going to support this child, Sally?'

'By babysitting for you.'

'That's not going to be enough.'

'We'll manage,' she said, and for once I didn't envy all the certainties of youth, I pitied them. 'Me and my baby.'

Sally and her baby.

They would manage all right, but only with the state playing surrogate daddy because Steve wasn't quite up to the job. I wondered why I bothered paying taxes. I could just stick the money in Sally's pram and cut out the middleman.

Christ. Now I was really starting to sound like my old man.

'A baby's not the same as a teddy bear, Sally,' I said. 'It's not just there to cuddle and make you feel good. Once you've got a kid, you're not free any more. I don't know how to explain it. But it's like they own your heart.'

'But that's what I want,' she said. 'I want something to own my heart.' She shook her head, gently chastising me. 'You talk as though it's a bad thing.'

Glenn came to pick her up, and they were just leaving when Marty arrived to talk about arrangements for his wedding day. I was about to make the introductions, but Glenn and Marty greeted each other like old friends. Now I remembered. They had met on my own wedding day.

So I made more coffee while they reminisced about *Top of the Pops* back in the glory days of the seventies, when Marty had been a fanatical viewer every Thursday night, and Glenn had briefly been a participant. Sally watched the pair of them with the smirking contempt of extreme youth. It was only when Glenn and Sally had finally gone that Marty told me he was having trouble sleeping.

'Everybody feels like that,' I said. 'A few doubts are natural before you get married.'

'I'm not worried about getting married,' he said. 'I'm worried about the show. Have you heard anything?'

'Like what?'

'Any rumours that the show isn't going to be recommissioned next year?'

'Your show? You're kidding. They would never drop *The Marty Mann Show*. Would they?'

'Sure they would. The word is that people shows are dying.' Marty sadly shook his head. 'That's the trouble with the world today, Harry. People are getting sick of the people.'

'Men die younger than women,' said my new solicitor. 'We catch cancer more often than women. We commit suicide with greater frequency than women. We are more likely to be unemployed than women.' His smooth, pudgy face creased into a grin, as though it were all a huge joke. His teeth were small and sharp. 'But for some reason I have never been able to fathom, Mr Silver, women are considered the victims.'

Nigel Batty was recommended to me by a couple of the boys on the show, the lighting director and the sound supervisor, who had both been through messy divorces over the last year.

A man said to have a messy divorce or two of his own behind him, Batty had a reputation for being fanatical about men's rights. For him all this stuff about long-term male unemployment and prostate cancer and men going into the garage and letting the engine run was far more than a sales pitch – it was the one true way, a new religion waiting to be born.

Despite his lack of height, the comfortable waistline concealed by a well-cut suit, and the milk-bottle glasses, Batty looked like a bruiser. I felt better already, knowing that he was in my corner.

'I warn you now that the law does not favour the father in cases such as this,' he said. 'The law should favour the child. And in theory it does. In theory, the welfare of the child should be the paramount consideration. But in practice it is not.' He looked at me with mean, angry eyes. 'The law favours the mother, Mr Silver. For generations of politically correct judges, the welfare of the child has been subjugated to the welfare of the mother. I warn you of this before we begin.'

'Anything you can do,' I said. 'Anything you can do to get me custody of my son.'

'It's not called custody any more, Mr Silver. Although the media still routinely talks of custody battles, since the Children Act of 1989, a parent no longer wins custody of their child. They are granted residency. You want to be granted a residence order in your favour.'

'I do?'

Batty nodded.

'Residency replaced custody as a way of removing the confrontational nature of deciding where a child lives. A residence order does not deprive any other person of parental responsibility. The law was changed to make it clear that a child isn't a possession which can be won or lost. Under the terms of a residence order, a child lives with you. But a child does not belong to you.'

'I don't get it,' I said. 'So what's the difference between trying to get a residence order and fighting for custody?'

'Not a damn thing,' Batty smiled. 'It's just as confrontational. Unfortunately it's far easier to change the law than it is to change human nature.'

He examined the papers on his desk, nodding approvingly.

'The divorce is straightforward enough. And it looks to me like you're doing a pretty good job with your young son, Mr Silver. He's happy at school?'

'Very happy.'

'He sees his mother?'

'She can see him whenever she likes. She knows that.'

'And yet she wants him back,' said Nigel Batty. 'She wants residency.'

'That's right. She wants him to live with her.'

'Is she cohabiting?'

'What?'

'Has your ex-wife got a boyfriend, Mr Silver? A boyfriend who lives with her?'

'Yes,' I said, grateful to him for downgrading Gina's relationship with Richard to something as grubby as cohabiting, grateful that the big diamond ring on the third finger of her left hand meant bugger all to Nigel Batty. 'She's living with some guy she met in Tokyo.'

'Let's get this clear,' he said. 'She walked out and left you with your son?'

'Well, more or less. She actually took Pat – our son – with her when she went to her father's place. But I collected him and brought him home when she went to Japan.'

'So, she abandoned the marital home and, to all intents and purposes, left the child in your care,' said Nigel Batty. 'And now she's back in town and decides that she would like to play mother for a while.'

'She says she realises how much she loves him.'

'We'll see about that,' said my solicitor.

thirty-three

The weight was falling off him. My father had never been a thin man in his life, but now his cheeks were hollowing and the skin under his neck was starting to hang in loose, unshaven flaps. More and more, he was looking like someone I didn't recognise.

Even his arms had lost their old beefy strength, and those tattoos proclaiming his loyalty to my mother and the Commandos were looking as faded as photographs from another century.

The flesh was slipping away and his bones were becoming more visible with every visit, pushing up through skin with its waning tan that I realised with a start would probably never see the sun again.

But he was smiling.

Sitting up in bed and smiling. And it was a real smile – not a being brave smile, not a smile that was forced or strained, but a smile of pure delight at the sight of his grandson.

'Hello, darling,' my dad said, as Pat walked up to his bed ahead of me, my mother and Uncle Jack. My father held up his right arm, the one where the intravenous drip was hooked to a vein in his wrist. 'Look at the state your old granddad's in.'

Pat had been full of life in Uncle Jack's car – excited to be awarded the special treat of a day off school, thrilled to be riding in the back of an executive saloon instead of the passenger seat of a vandalised sports car. But now he fell silent, warily approaching the bed and the sight of his grandfather's gaunt, stubbled face.

'Come here,' my father said, his voice gruff with emotion, holding out his free arm, and Pat climbed up on the bed and lay his head on my father's poor broken chest. They held each other in silence.

My mother shot a look at me. She had been against this visit.

There was no way of knowing if my father would be awake when we arrived. There was a very good chance that the pain could have been so bad that they would be pumping him full of opiates while we were looking for a parking space, and all Pat would have found was his grandfather lost and unknowing in some morphine fog. Or he could have been struggling for breath, his chest heaving, the oxygen mask over his nose and mouth, and his eyes wet with pain and fear. Or, although she didn't say it, he could have been dead.

All that was possible, even probable, and in the kitchen of her home, my mother had become angry and tearful with me at the thought of inflicting any one of those terrible things on Pat.

I had put my arms around her and assured her that it would be all right. And I was wrong. It was not all right – Pat was shocked and dismayed by the sight of his grandfather ravaged by disease, wasting away in a hospital bed in that room for dying men – the kind of dying that you never see on television or in the movies, the kind of dying that is full of agony and drugs and sadness at all that is about to be lost. I had been unprepared for the reality of death and there was no reason to believe that a five-year-old boy brought up on a diet of *Star Wars* would be any better prepared.

No, it wasn't all right. But it was necessary. My father

and my son needed to see each other. They needed to see that the bond between them still existed and would always exist. The love between them would always be there. They needed to know that the cancer couldn't kill that.

And I somehow knew – I just knew – that my father wouldn't be knocked out on narcotics or choking for breath if Pat was there.

There was no rational reason to believe that wouldn't happen if his grandson was there. It wasn't logical. Perhaps it was simply foolish. But I believed with all my heart that my dad would protect Pat from the very worst of it. I still believed there was a part of him that was invincible. I couldn't stop believing.

'Are you coming home soon?' Pat asked.

'Got to wait and see,' my father said. 'See what the doctors say. See if old Granddad gets a bit better. How's school?'

'Fine.'

'And the bike? How's old Bluebell?'

'Good.'

'A bit more fun without the stabilisers.'

'Yes,' Pat smiled. 'But I miss you.'

'I miss you too,' my father said, and squeezed him tight, Pat's blonde head pressed against his striped blue pyjamas, the kind of old man's pyjamas that he would never wear at home.

Then he nodded at me.

'Time to go,' I said.

That was my father saying goodbye to his beloved grandson. Propped up in his hospital bed, surrounded by people who loved him and yet ultimately alone. Had we been there for five minutes or an hour? I couldn't tell. But I knew he wanted us to leave him now.

And so we left my father fumbling with his oxygen mask,

hunched and stubbled and looking older than I thought he would ever look, a young nurse chatting breezily at the foot of his bed.

Here, finally, was the worst thing of all. The awful and complete isolation of death, the terrible loneliness of the terminally ill. Nobody warns you about that.

With his breath going and the pain coming, we left him in that overcrowded NHS ward with winter sunlight coming through the big unwashed window and the chipmunk chatter of daytime television in the background. We left him. In the end, it was all we could do.

And as we walked back to the car Pat fought back the tears, angry – no, furious – at something that he couldn't name. I tried to comfort him but he wasn't interested in being comforted.

My son looked like he felt he had been cheated.

There was a removal van outside Cyd's flat.

It wasn't one of those huge lorries that you can load with the contents of a family's lifetime, one of those massive trucks which can hold pianos and worn-out furniture that you like too much to throw away and all the accumulated junk of the years. It was from the kind of removal firm that advertises in the back of the listings magazines, perfect for a little family that was travelling light.

I watched two young men in T-shirts edging a child's single bed into the back of the van. Although Cyd and Peggy lived on the top floor, the men looked as though this was one of their easier jobs.

Peggy appeared at the front door, dragging behind her a stuffed toy the size of a fridge. She looked at me with her solemn brown eyes, not surprised to see me here.

'Look what I've got,' I said, holding out a leering male

doll in spangly silver trousers and what looked like a lilac tuxedo. It was a sex-change Barbie.

'Disco Ken,' she said, taking him.

'You left him at my house,' I said. 'I thought you might want him back.'

'Thank you,' she said, that beautifully behaved little girl. Then Cyd was behind her, a stack of paperbacks in her arms.

'Look what Harry brought me,' Peggy said. 'Disco Ken. I've been looking for him.'

Cyd told her to go up to her room and make sure she wasn't leaving anything behind. Peggy left the stuffed toy the size of a fridge on the pavement and disappeared into the house still clutching Disco Ken.

'How about you?' I said. 'You left anything behind?'

'No,' she said. 'I think I've got just about everything.'

The two removal guys brushed past us on their way back into the house.

'Moving without telling me?' I said. 'Some friend you turned out to be.'

'I was going to tell you. It's just – I don't know – it's easier this way. For everybody.'

'I looked for you at the café.'

'I quit.'

'So they told me.'

'We're moving across town. To Notting Hill.'

'*West* London?'

'Christ, don't look so shocked, Harry. I'm an American. Moving from one side of a city to another isn't quite as traumatic for me as it would be for you. Listen, I'm sorry but I'm really busy. What do you want? I can't believe that you came here just to bring back Disco Ken.'

'Disco Ken was part of it,' I said. 'But also I wanted to tell you that you're wrong.'

'About what?'

'About us. You're wrong about us. If we split up, then it's the end of the world.'

'Oh, Harry.'

'It's true. I know you don't believe in the one, the one person for someone in the whole world, but I do. You make me believe it, Cyd. And anyway, it doesn't matter what we believe. It's good between us. It works. And I've been thinking about it. There's not one more chance for me to get it right – you're it, you're my last chance for happiness, and even if there was another chance, I wouldn't want it. As Olivia Newton John said to John Travolta, you're the one that I want.'

'Wasn't it the other way round? Didn't John Travolta say it to Olivia Newton John?'

'Possibly.'

'Harry,' she said. 'There's something you have to know. I'm getting back with Peggy's dad. Jim and I are going to give it another go.'

I stared at her as the removal men carried a sofabed between us. 'Nearly done,' one of them said. They went back inside the house.

'Sorry,' she told me.

'But do you love him?' I said.

'He's the father of my little girl.'

'But do you love him?'

'Come on, Harry, you're the one who's always agonising about the break-up of the family. You're the one who is always complaining about how hard it is to compete with blood, about all the messy, broken bits of what you call the lousy modern world. You should be pleased for me. You should wish me well.'

'But you have to love him, Cyd. None of it means a thing if you don't love him. Do you love him?'

'Yes. Okay? I love him. I never stopped loving him. And

I want to give it a shot because he's given up his girlfriend, the Thai stripper, and he promises me that's all out of his system. The whole bamboo thing.'

'She's not a stripper. She's a lap dancer.'

'Whatever,' she said. 'But Peggy's thrilled that we're giving it another go. So even if you hate me, you should be pleased for her.'

'I don't hate you. I could never hate you.'

'Then please wish me well.'

'I wish you well,' I said, and I even sort of meant it. She deserved to be happy. So did Peggy. I kissed her quickly on the cheek. 'Just don't tell me I don't know you, okay?'

I let them get on with their moving. Anything I said now would have sounded empty and selfish, as if they were just weasel words designed to get her to come back to me.

Yet as she prepared to go back to her husband, at last I saw the limits of the nuclear family. Now I realised that dad and mum and the kids is all very well.

But if you don't love each other, you might as well be shacked up with Disco Ken.

'We've had a response from the other side,' Nigel Batty said. 'Your ex-wife says that she remained faithful to you throughout the duration of your marriage but that you committed adultery with a colleague from work.'

'Well, that's true,' I said. 'But it was just a one-night stand. I'm not saying it's nothing, but –'

'She also alleges that your son received a severe head injury while in your care.'

'What does that mean? That sounds like I beat him up or something. He fell, okay? There was an accident in the local park. He fell into an empty swimming pool and split his head open. And maybe I could have done more. Maybe I should have been watching him more closely. Does she honestly believe that hasn't crossed my mind again and again and again? But at least I was there for him. She was eating tempura with her boyfriend in Tokyo.'

The solicitor peered closely at the papers on his desk.

'And she seems to believe that you're not exercising proper parental control over what your son watches or listens to.'

'That's just crazy.'

'He's allowed to watch violent films unsupervised, she suggests. Videos with adult themes. And she says that on her last access visit she discovered that he had in his possession a music tape containing songs of a profane and adult nature.'

I could feel my face reddening with anger.

'That fucking . . . fucking . . .'

I couldn't find the word. There was no word strong enough.

Nigel Batty laughed out loud, as though I were finally starting to understand.

thirty-four

'Can I see the medal?' I asked.

'Of course you can,' my mother said.

She went to the cabinet where the stereo sat, and I could hear her shuffling through insurance documents, bank statements, letters, all the paperwork of a lifetime.

She came back with a small rectangular box which was coloured somewhere beyond claret, but not quite black. Inside, there was a silver medal, not that clean, resting on purple velvet. My father's medal.

The medal's ribbon was blue and white, two broad vertical white stripes with one thin vertical white stripe between them dissecting a blue background. 'For Distinguished Service,' it said on the medal, next to the image of the head of the King.

In the top of the box the maker's name was inscribed on white silk – 'By Appointment,' it said above the Royal Warrant, 'J. R. Gaunt & Son Ltd, 60 Conduit Street, London.' And I remembered how, as a child, the name of that company – did it still exist? would it be there if I looked for it? – had seemed like another part of the citation.

I gently took it out, as surprised by the weight of my father's DSM at thirty as I had been as a boy.

'Pat used to love playing with Dad's medal,' my mother laughed.

'You let Pat play with this?' I said, incredulous.

'He liked pinning it on me,' she smiled. 'I had to be Princess Layla at the end of that film.'

'Leia, Mum. She's Princess Leia.'

It was just past the middle of the night, and we were too tired to sit by his hospital bed any longer, but too restless to sleep. So we were going to have a nice cup of tea. Still my mother's answer to everything.

And as she went off to put the kettle on, I held the medal in my fist and thought about how the games I had played as a boy had prepared me to be the man my father had been, and the man his father had been before him – a fighting man, a man who kissed some tearful woman goodbye and put on a uniform and went to war.

Looking back on the games we had played in the fields and the backstreets of my childhood, they seemed to be more than childish pastimes lauding the manly virtues – they seemed to be preparing us for the next war, for our own Normandy or Dunkirk or Monte Casino.

My generation had played games with toy guns – or sticks pretending to be guns, or fingers pretending to be guns, anything could stand in for a gun – and nobody had thought that it was unhealthy or distasteful. But the only wars we saw as young men were small wars, television wars, as real and as life-threatening to the non-combatants as a video game.

My generation, the last of the generations of small boys who played with toy guns, were luckier than we knew. We didn't have a war waiting for us when we grew up. There were no Germans or Japanese for us to fight.

Our wives, that's who we fought with, this generation of men blessed with peace. And the divorce courts, that's where we fought our own grubby little wars.

I had seen the scars on my father's body enough times to know that war was not a John Wayne movie. But the men who survived – and who came home in more or less one piece – found someone to love for a lifetime. Which was better? War and a perfect love? Or peace and love which came in instalments of five, six or seven years? Who was really the lucky man? My father or me?

'You liked this girl, didn't you?' my mum said, coming back into the room with a steaming mug in each hand. 'This woman, I mean. Cyd. You liked her a lot.'

I nodded.

'I wish we could have held it together. Like you and Dad did. It seems impossible these days.'

'You're too sentimental about the past,' she said, not unkindly. 'You think it was all brown ale and red roses. But it was harder than that.'

'But you and Dad were happy.'

'Yes, we were,' she said, her eyes drifting away to some place where I couldn't follow her. 'We were happy.'

And I thought – I was happy too.

When I thought of my childhood, I thought of some sun-baked August – right at the start of the month, when the long six-week holiday was still stretching gloriously out ahead of me, and I knew there would be car rides to country pubs where my dad and my uncles would play darts and bring lemonade and crisps out to me and my cousins playing on the grass, our mothers laughing over Babychams at wooden tables, as separated from the men as Muslims.

Or it was some other holiday – Christmas, late at night with my uncles and aunts smoking and drinking in a card school, with football on Boxing Day at a misty Upton Park for the men and the boys.

Or it would be a Bank Holiday run to the coast, with huge pink clouds of candyfloss on a stick and the smell of the sea and frying onions, or to the dog track where my mum always bet on the number six dog because she liked the colours, she liked the way the red number looked against the black and white stripes.

I was grateful for that suburban childhood – for those memories of car rides and modest gambling and day trips – it seemed like a childhood crowded with life and love, a good time to be growing up, when Bobby Moore was at West Ham and Miss World was on the box and my mum and my aunts wore miniskirts.

And although my son's childhood had more material things, it also had the numbing bankruptcy of divorce.

With all the diplomatic skills and emotional armour that a five-year-old could muster, he now ricocheted between his mother and her boyfriend and his father and his badly bruised heart. A video recorder and the passenger seat of a flash car seemed like small compensation for all that.

It felt to me like Gina and I – and the million couples just like us – hadn't left much of an inheritance for the next generation.

'It worked between us because we made it work,' my mother said. 'Because we wanted it to work. Because – even when we didn't have money, even when we couldn't have a baby – we didn't chuck in the towel. You have to fight for your happy ending, Harry. It doesn't just drop in your lap.'

'You think I didn't fight for my happy ending? You think I haven't got enough fight in me? Not like Dad?'

I was curious to know what she believed. There was a time, when I was young and cocky, when I felt that my parents knew nothing of life beyond their well-tended garden and their overheated living room. But I didn't feel that way about them any more.

'I think you've got a lot of fight in you, Harry. But you beat yourself up sometimes. You can't be the same man your father was – it's a different world. Almost a different century. You have to fight different battles and not expect anyone to pin a medal on your chest. Looking after a child alone – you think your father could have done that? I love him more than my life, but that would have been beyond him. You have to be strong in a different way. You have to be a different kind of tough guy.'

I put the medal back in its box and the telephone rang.

My mother's eyes flicked to the clock and back to me, full of tears. It was just after four in the morning and this could only be my Uncle Jack calling from the hospital.

We both knew.

We held each other tight, the phone still ringing in the hall. Ringing and ringing.

'We should have been there with him,' my mother said, as she would say so many times in the days and weeks and years to come. 'We should have been there.'

Here's what a happy ending looks like, I thought bitterly. You spend your life with someone and then, if they go before you, you feel as though you have lost all your limbs.

At least my generation – the fuck around, fuck up and fuck off generation – would be spared the knowledge of exactly what that particular amputation feels like. Assuming that we don't have any happy endings of our own.

I picked up the telephone and my Uncle Jack told me that my father had died.

In the morning I went up to see Pat as soon as I heard his footsteps padding across the floor to the box of toys that my parents always kept for him in their second bedroom, the room where he always slept when he was here, the room that had once been mine.

He looked up at me from the toy box, a Star Wars figure in each hand, his eyes still puffy with sleep. I picked him up, kissed his sweet face, and sat down on the bed with him on my lap.

'Pat, your grandfather died in the night.'

He blinked at me with those blue eyes.

'Granddad had been ill for a long time and now he doesn't have to suffer any more,' I said. 'Now he's at peace. We can be happy about that, can't we? He's not in pain any more. He will never feel any more pain again.'

'Where is he now?'

This threw me.

'Well, his body is at the hospital. Later it will be buried.'

I realised that I knew nothing about the bureaucracy of death. When would they collect his body from the hospital? Where would they keep it before his funeral? And who exactly were they?

'We're sad now,' I said. 'But one day we will be grateful for Granddad's life. We will realise that we were lucky – I was lucky to have him as my father and you were lucky to have him as your grandfather. We were both very lucky. But we can't feel lucky today. It's too soon.'

Pat nodded, very businesslike. 'He's still at the hospital?'

'His body is at the hospital. But his spirit has gone.'

'What's his spirit?'

'That's the spark of life that made your granddad the man he was.'

'Where's it gone?'

I took a breath.

'Some people think the spirit goes to heaven and lives forever. Some people think that it just disappears and then you sleep forever.'

'What do you believe?

'I think that the spirit lives on,' I said. 'I don't know if it's in heaven or if it's somewhere else, some other place that I don't know anything about. But it doesn't just die. It lives on. Even if it's only in the hearts of the people we love.'

'That's what I believe too,' said my son.

With the slashed roof of the MGF cracking like a torn sail in a stiff gale, I drove slowly down the high street of the little town where I had grown up, not recognising the place.

Everywhere the shops and small cafés that I had known had become estate agents or the outlets of some big chain. No wonder the English have become so desperate to wave the flag of St George, to remind ourselves that our roots are just as deep and defined as those of the Irish or the Scots. This was my home town. But it could have been anywhere.

I didn't see a thing I recognised until I found my Uncle Jack in the snug of the old Red Lion, this pub seemingly the one part of the high street which was protected by an unofficial preservation order. He was in a fug of cigarette smoke, fag cupped in his palm, drinking a mineral water under the oak beams and horse brasses.

'Sorry about your dad, Harry.'

'Thanks, Uncle Jack.'

'You want one of these? Or shall we just do it?'

'Let's just do it.'

My Uncle Jack was at my side as I dealt with the bureaucracy of death. I was still numb from lack of sleep and the shock of knowing that my father was no longer in the world. But my Uncle Jack's craggy, chain-smoking presence made it a lot easier for me.

We drove to the hospital in the MGF and collected a pitiful little bag from the front office containing my father's belongings.

His wallet with his picture of his grandson inside, his reading glasses, his false teeth.

This was all that was left of him, handed over to me without sentiment or condolences. Why should they be sad for him? Or for me? They never knew my father. We moved on down the chain.

For some obscure administrative reason, we had to register the death in a small town that I had never been to before, although with its Burger King and Body Shop and estate agents, it looked depressingly familiar.

Part of the great procession of living and dying, we were behind a young couple registering their baby's birth and ahead of an old woman registering the death of her husband. And I wondered why Nigel Batty complained about men dying before their partners. What a relief not to have to visit this place, what a relief not to be condemned to living on alone.

Finally, we went back to my home town to see the undertaker. Like the pub, this was another place that had never changed in my memory – getting pissed and dropping dead, the two great perennials of the English high street.

With its gloomy window display of white headstones arrayed against acres of black silk, it had always looked closed when I was growing up, this boutique for the bereaved, and it looked closed now. When I was a child just discovering that I wasn't going to live forever, I used to walk quickly past this place. Now I went inside. And it was fine. Uncle Jack lightly rested a hand on my shoulder and I talked calmly to the undertaker about the funeral arrangements, as if this happened to me every day. With the death certificate between us, it seemed perfectly natural to be talking to this sombre old man in black about my father's burial. The only truly strange moment was when, almost apologetically, the undertaker produced a glossy brochure. I had to choose my father's coffin.

It was a brochure like any other – tastefully shot, beautifully presented – and the undertaker gently led me through it, starting with the cheapest, simplest pine numbers, going right up to the top of the range model, a large hardwood coffin lined with red satiny material and adorned with big brass handles.

My first instinct was to go for the most expensive one – let's push the boat out, nothing's too good for my old man. But my second instinct was that the top of the range coffin was just a touch too elaborate for my dad to sleep in for all eternity.

I hesitated, and told the undertaker that we would go for the second most expensive coffin. And when Uncle Jack and I were back on the street, I was pleased with my choice.

'Your old man would have had a fit at that posh coffin,' my Uncle Jack grinned.

'The most expensive one?' I smiled. 'Yeah, I thought that was a bit much.'

'Gold handles and a red velvet lining!' chuckled Uncle Jack. 'It looked more like a French knocking shop than a coffin!'

'Talk about turning in your grave,' I laughed. 'I know what he would have said if we'd gone for that one – "*Who do you think I am? Bloody Napoleon?*"'

I could hear his voice.

I would never hear his voice again.

I would always hear him.

thirty-five

'Two ducks check into a hotel,' said Eamon. 'Best hotel in Kilcarney. Big weekend for the ducks. But – no, listen – they get up to their room and they discover they don't have any condoms. No problem, says the man duck – I'll get room service to send some up. Call down to room service. Eventually the boy appears with the condoms. He says – Do you want me to put these on your bill, sir? And the duck, he says – Do I look like some kind of pervert to you?'

Eamon removed the mike from its stand in complete silence. They were going to put the laughter track on later.

'I feel for that duck,' he said, moving across a stage that seemed somehow brighter than usual, in front of an audience who were noticeably better-looking than normal. 'Because there's no real sex education in Kilcarney. My dad told me that the man goes on top and the woman goes on the bottom. So all through my first serious relationship, my girlfriend and I slept in bunk beds. You see, where I come from, sex is hereditary – if your mum and dad didn't have it, the chances are that you won't either.'

He placed the mike back in its stand, grinning into the lights.

'Luckily I'm a good lover now – but that's only because I practise a lot on my own. Thank you and goodnight!'

The audience applauded wildly as Eamon skipped to the side of the stage where a beautiful girl with a clipboard and headphones handed him a bottle of beer. Then he seemed to swoon, sinking to one knee, the bottle of beer still in his hand as he half-turned and retched into a sand bucket – a real sand bucket, not a pretend one.

'Cut, cut,' the director said.

I ran on to the set and crouched by Eamon's side, my arm around his shaking shoulders. Mem stood by my side, wide-eyed with concern and unrecognisable with her clothes on.

'Don't be afraid, Eamon,' I said. 'It's only a lager commercial.'

'I'm not afraid,' he said weakly. 'I'm excited.'

I wasn't excited. I was afraid. Very afraid.

My father – my father's body – was at the undertaker's. And I was going to see it.

The undertaker had mentioned the possibility of seeing the body – viewing the loved one at rest, he had said quietly, proud of this service they offered at no extra charge – and this meeting, this final meeting between my father and me, had assumed impossible proportions in my head.

How would I feel when I saw the man who gave me life lying in his coffin? Would I unravel? Could I stand the sight of my great protector waiting for his grave? I couldn't stop myself believing that it would be too much, that I would crumple and come apart, that the years would be wiped away and I would be a sobbing child once more.

When I saw him lying there, the brutal fact of his death would be beyond all lingering doubt and disbelief. Could I take it? That's what I wanted to know. I had learned that fathering a child didn't make you truly adult. Does a man have to bury his father before he feels truly grown?

My Uncle Jack was waiting for me in the snug of the old Red Lion. My mother had shaken her head and turned away when I had asked her if she wanted to come with me. I didn't blame her. But I needed to know if I could live with the knowledge that I was alone now.

Not alone, of course. There was still my mother, sleeping with the lights in her bedroom blazing all night long, bewildered to be alone for the first time in a lifetime. And there was Pat, bouncing between the joy of seeing Gina again and the suffocating grief in our own home. And there was Cyd – out there somewhere, lost in some other part of the city, sharing her life with some other man.

But with my father gone, there was a part of me that felt alone – at last and forever.

Even when relations between us had been strained, he had always been my shield, my guardian, my greatest ally. Even when we had bickered and fought, even when I had disappointed him or let him down, I had always been secure in the knowledge that he would still do anything for me. Now all that was gone.

Uncle Jack stubbed out his roll-up and drained his mineral water. We walked to the undertaker's, not saying much, although when we went inside and a little bell jingled announcing our arrival, Uncle Jack placed his hand on my shoulder. My uncle wasn't keen to see his brother's body. He was doing this for me.

The undertaker was expecting us. He led us into an antechamber which looked like some kind of changing room. There were heavy curtains on both sides, divided up into maybe half a dozen individual compartments. I took a breath and held it as he pulled back one of the little curtains to reveal my father in his coffin.

Except that it wasn't my father. Not any more. His face – the only part of him that was visible with the coffin lid opened just a shade – had an expression I had never seen before. He didn't look peaceful, or as though he were sleeping or any of death's soothing clichés. His face was empty. It had nothing to do with him any more, it was drained of identity as well as all pain and exhaustion. It was like knocking on a door and discovering that nobody was home. More than this – it was as though we had come to the wrong place. The spark that had made my father the man he was had gone. I knew with total certainty that his soul had flown. I had come looking for my father, to see him one last time. But I wouldn't find him here.

I wanted to see Pat. I wanted to hold my son in my arms and tell him that everything we had both tried so hard to believe was all true.

thirty-six

Usually I stayed inside the house, well back from the window, watching from behind the blinds as the silver Audi snaked down the street, looking for a scrap of parking space. But today I came out when I saw them coming – the now familiar car with the familiar configuration inside.

Pat's blond head in the back seat, looking down at some new trinket he had been given. Gina in the passenger seat, turning to talk to him. And in the driving seat, this unimaginable Richard, the semi-separated man, cool and confident at the wheel, as if ferrying Gina and Pat around town in his Audi were the natural order of things.

I had never spoken to him. I had never even seen him get out of his car when they delivered Pat back to me. He was dark, beefy and wore glasses – a suit that worked out. Good-looking in a Clark Kent kind of way. There was a tiny parking space just in front of the house, and I watched him expertly reverse the Audi into it, the bastard.

Usually Gina knocked on the door, said hello to me and quickly kissed Pat goodbye. The handover was done with minimum civility, which was about as much as either of us could muster. Still, we were trying. Not for our sakes, but for the sake of our child. But today I was waiting at the front gate for them. She didn't seem surprised.

'Hello, Harry.'

'Hi.'

'Look what I've got!' Pat said, brandishing his new toy – some scowling plastic spaceman with an unfeasibly large laser gun – as he brushed past me into the house.

'Sorry about your dad,' Gina said, staying on the other side of the gate.

'Thanks.'

'I'm really sorry. He was the most gentle man I ever met.'

'He was mad about you.'

'I was mad about him, too.'

'Thanks for Pat's toy.'

'Richard bought it for him in Hamley's.'

'Good old Richard.'

She shot me a look. 'I'd better be going,' she said.

'I thought you didn't like Pat playing with guns.'

She shook her head and gave a little laugh, one of those laughs that's meant to indicate that it wasn't funny at all. 'If you really want to know, I believe that there's enough violence in this world without encouraging children to think that guns are a form of light entertainment. Okay? But he wanted the gun.'

'I'm not going to give him up, Gina.'

'That's for the lawyers to decide. And we're not supposed –'

'I've changed my life to look after my son. I took a part-time job. I learned to organise things in the house, stuff that I never even had to think about before. Feeding him, clothing him, getting him to bed. Answering his questions, being there for him when he was sad or frightened.'

'All the things I did more or less alone for years.'

'That's my point exactly. I taught myself how to care for our child – the way you cared for him. And then you come back and tell me that's all over.'

'You've done a good job over the last few months, Harry. But what do you want? A medal?'

'I don't need a medal. I haven't done anything more than I should have done. I know it's nothing special. But you expect too much of me, Gina. I learned how to be a real father to Pat – I had to, okay? Now you want me just to act as though it never happened. And I can't do it. How can I do it? Tell me how I can do it.'

'Is there a problem?' Richard said, emerging from the Audi.

So he did have legs after all.

'Get back in the car, Richard,' Gina said.

'Yeah, get back in the car, Richard,' I said.

He got back in the car, blinking behind his glasses.

'You have to decide what you really want, Gina. All of you.'

'What are you talking about?'

'I'm all for men taking responsibility for their children. I'm all for men doing their bit in bringing up their kids. But you can't have it both ways. You can't expect us to take part in the parenting and then just step aside when you want us to, as if we were just like our dads, as if it was all really women's work. Remember that the next time you see your solicitor.'

'And you remember something, Harry.'

'What's that?'

'I love him, too.'

Pat was on the floor of his room, tipping a box full of toys on to the floor.

'You have a good time, darling? A good time with Mummy and Richard?'

I sounded ridiculously upbeat, like a game-show host when the really big prize is up for grabs, but I was determined to make Pat feel okay about these new arrangements. I didn't want him to feel that he was betraying me every time he went out to have a good time with his mother and her boyfriend. But I didn't want him to have too good a time either.

'It was all right,' he said. 'Richard and Mummy had a little bit of a row.'

Wonderful news.

'Why was that, darling?'

'I got some Magnum on the seat of his stupid car. He thought I shouldn't eat Magnum in the car.'

'But you like Richard?'

'He's all right.'

I felt a pang of sympathy for this man I had never met. Not much of a pang. Just a little one. But a pang all the same. The role he had chosen felt like an impossible part to play. If he tried to be a father to Pat, then he would surely fail. And if he decided to be just a friend, then that would be a kind of failure, too. But at least Richard had a choice.

Who asked Pat if he wanted to be eating a Magnum in the back of that silver Audi?

Cyd was working in one of those designer Asian restaurants that were starting to appear all over town, one of those places that sells Thai fishcakes, Japanese soba noodles and cold Vietnamese spring rolls as if they all come from the same place, as if that entire continent had been turned into one big kitchen for the West. It was bright and white, full of polished wood and gleaming chrome, like an art gallery or a dentist's surgery.

From the street I watched Cyd placing two steaming plates of what looked like Malaysian king prawn curry in front of a pair of young women who smiled their thanks at her.

Like every other waitress in there, she was wearing a starched white apron, black trousers and a white shirt. Her hair was cut shorter than I had ever seen it – it was almost boyish now, she had gone from an F. Scott Fitzgerald bob to a Beatle cut in just one trip to the hairdresser's. I knew it meant something important when a woman chopped off her hair, but I couldn't remember what.

She headed towards the back of the place, saying something to the young black guy behind the bar that made him laugh, and disappeared into the kitchen. I took a seat near the front of the restaurant, waiting for her to appear again.

It was after three, and the place was almost empty. Apart from me and the two young women eating their spicy prawns, the only other customers were a table of three well-lunched businessmen, empty bottles of Asahi Super Dry strewn in front of them. A young waitress placed a menu on my table just as Cyd banged back out of the kitchen doors.

At head height and balanced on the palm of her hand, she was carrying a tray holding three bottles of Japanese beer. She unloaded them in front of the drunken suits, not noticing me, ignoring their red-faced leers, not really aware of any of us.

'When do you get off?' one of them asked.

'Don't you mean how?' she said, turning away as they erupted with laughter, and seeing me at last. She slowly came over to my table.

'What would you like?'

'How about spending the rest of our lives together?'

'That's off. How about some noodles?'

'Okay. Have you got the thick kind?'

'Udon? Sure. We do udon noodles in broth with prawns, fish, shitake mushrooms and all that good stuff.'

'Actually, I'm not that hungry. But this is a coincidence, isn't it? Running into each other like this.'

'It certainly is, Harry. How did you know I was working here?'

'I didn't. This is the forty-second place I've tried over the last few days.'

'You really are crazy.'

'Crazy for you.'

'Just crazy. How's your dad?'

'The funeral's tomorrow.'

'God, I'm sorry. Is Pat all right?'

I took a breath.

'They were very close. You know that. It's a big loss for him. I don't know – he's dealing with it. Same as my mother. I'll be glad to get the funeral behind us.'

'After the funeral can be the worst part. Because everybody goes home and life starts to go on again. Except, for you, it doesn't. Is there anything I can do?'

'Yes.'

'What's that?'

'You can let me walk you home.'

'You've got to stop following me around,' she said as we walked through the silent white side streets of Notting Hill. 'It's got to stop.'

'I like your hair.'

She grabbed her fringe in her hand.

'It's no good for you and it's no good for me,' she said.

'Oh, I don't know. It doesn't look that bad.'

'You know what I'm talking about.'

'I want us to be a family.'

'I thought you hated that kind of family – the kind of family that is full of other people's children and ex-partners. I thought you wanted an uncomplicated life.'

'I don't want an uncomplicated life. I want a life with you. And Peggy. And Pat. And maybe a kid of our own.'

'One of those families? With your kid and my kid fighting

our kid? You'd hate it. You would really hate it, Harry. You'd last – well, I don't know how long you'd last.'

'I could never hate my life if it was with you. Listen, there was a tattoo on my dad's arm, some words written under one of those long, thin Commando knives. And it said – *United We Conquer*. And that's how I feel about us.'

'You're getting a tattoo?'

'No.'

'You're joining the army?'

'What I'm saying is that if we're together, then everything will be all right. I don't know what kind of family life it will be – because there have never been families like this before. But I know that it would be better than any other family we could ever have apart. Just think about it, okay?'

'Sure, Harry. I'll discuss it with my husband over dinner tonight.'

We had stopped outside an old white town house that had been chopped up into flats forty years ago.

'This is it, Harry,' she said.

And then Jim was suddenly bursting out of the front door, his arm in a plaster cast and a sling, screaming, 'Stay away from my wife, you bastard!' as he smoothly swung round in a full circle and his motorcycle boot exploded in my mouth.

I reeled backwards, my gums split and bloody, my legs gone to jelly, and two things were immediately clear.

Jim knew a bit about martial arts. And he had fallen off his bike again.

I bounced off some dustbins and lifted my fists as he came at me, but Cyd had moved between us and he howled with pain as she grabbed his broken arm.

'Leave him alone! Leave him alone!' she shouted at him.

'Watch my fucking arm, will you!' he shouted back at her. But he let her lead him back to the door. He turned to growl at me.

'If ever I see your face again,' he said, 'you lose all your teeth.'

'It wouldn't be the first time.'

I didn't explain that a friendly dog had pushed me on my face when I was five years old. That wouldn't have sounded quite so impressive.

He went back inside the house, holding his plaster cast.

They must have been living in the ground floor flat because I could hear what sounded a lot like Peggy crying. Cyd turned to look at me.

'Please leave me alone now, Harry.'

'Just think about what I said,' I slurred through my fat and bloody lips. 'Please consider my offer.'

She shook her head and – I know it's dumb – but I felt that she was starting to really like me.

'You don't give up, do you?' she said.

'I get it from my father,' I said.

Then she closed the door of the big white house and went back to her life.

thirty-seven

A mile from our family home, there is a small church on a hill.

As a boy, wandering where he wasn't supposed to wander on light summer nights, I had sometimes lurked in the graveyard of this church, drinking cider and choking on a Number 6 and peering down the sights of my friend's .22 air rifle.

We were not as cocky as we looked. At the slightest sound – the wind in the trees, the rustle of leaves across the cold stone of a grave, some ancient wood creaking inside the church – my friend and I would bolt in panic, terrified that the dead were about to reveal themselves to us. And now my father was going to be buried here.

I woke to the sound of the paper boy's bike, the *Mirror* roughly shoved through the letter box, the low hum of the radio coming from the kitchen. For one moment between sleep and waking, it felt like just another day.

But after breakfast we donned our bleak uniforms of mourning, my son and I, both awkward in our black ties and white shirts, and we sat on the floor of my old bedroom, thumbing through box after box of photographs, consoling ourselves with images of my father, his grandfather.

Time ran backwards, unravelled. There were bright colour pictures of my dad with Pat – opening Christmas presents, riding his Bluebell bike with the stabilisers still attached,

Pat as an impossibly blond toddler, and as a sleeping baby in the arms of his grinning grandfather.

And lots of pictures with the colours fading now – my dad and my mum with Gina and me on our wedding day, me as a smirking teenager with my dad, a fit fifty-odd, our arms around each other in our back garden – proud of his garden, proud of me – and still further back, me as a goofy eleven-year-old with my parents, still young, in the crowd shot of some cousin's wedding.

And all the way back to the beginning of memory and beyond – a black and white shot of me as a crop-haired child with my dad and the horses on Salisbury Plain, another black and white picture of my dad laughing as he lifted me up on some windswept beach, and pictures in shades of grey of him in uniform and my parents on their wedding day.

No pictures of him as a child or a baby. I knew it was simply because they had been too poor to have a camera, but it felt as though his life had only begun with our little family.

Downstairs the flowers had started arriving. Pat and I went to the window of my parents' room at the front of the house and watched the florist unloading them from his van. Soon the cellophane-wrapped bouquets covered all of the front lawn, and I thought of Princess Diana and the sea of flowers that had washed up against the black railings of the royal palaces. It was just another job for the florist, and the first job of the day, but he seemed genuinely moved.

'I wish I had known this man,' I heard him tell my mother, and I knew that he meant it.

We had a laugh when the coffin arrived at the church. It was a desperate laugh, one of those laughs that is there as a dam against tears which you are afraid will never stop if they are allowed to start, but a laugh all the same.

We were following the coffin into the old church, my mother, my son and I, but for some reason the four pall-bearers stopped at the entrance. Although Pat and I had her between us, our arms around her, my mother kept going, her eyes on the ground. And she only stopped when she smacked her head hard against the end of her husband's coffin.

She staggered backwards, holding her forehead, looking for blood on her fingertips, and then she looked at me and we both laughed out loud. We were both hearing his voice, that old London voice full of weary affection. 'What *are* you doing, woman?'

Then we went inside the coolness of the church and it was like stepping into a dream, a dream where everyone you have ever known – relatives, friends of the family, neighbours from the present and the past, men in Royal Naval Commando ties who had met as teenagers and were now seventy – had gathered together for one last time, row upon row of them, some starting to cry at the sight of my father's coffin.

The three of us were in the front pew. Once the three of us would have meant my parents and me. Now it was my mother, my son and me. Their heads were down, staring at the flagstones, the laughter all gone, but I watched the vicar as he began to quote from Isaiah – 'They shall beat their swords into plowshares, and their spears into pruninghooks: nation shall not lift up sword against nation, neither shall they learn war any more.'

His sermon was about the good soldier who became a man of peace – the warrior who learned to be the loving husband, the kind father, the caring neighbour. And I could tell that he had worked hard at this speech, that he had talked to my mother and my uncles and Auntie Ethel next door who wasn't really my auntie. But the vicar had never met my father, and so he could never really capture him and his life.

It was only when the old song that my mother had chosen echoed through the crowded church that I had to get a grip of my heart, that I felt the weight of all that we had lost.

More than the hymns or the sermon or the well-meant platitudes or the faces of all the people he had ever known, it was this old song that got to me. Sinatra's voice, very young, very pure, lacking all the swagger and cynicism of his later years. It rose and soared around that little church.

And my mother didn't move, but I could feel her holding Pat more fiercely, as if she were afraid of being swept to some other place and time, somewhere in the lonely future when she could only sleep with the bedroom lights blazing, or somewhere in the lost, unrecoverable past.

> Someday
> When I'm awfully low,
> When the world is cold,
> I will feel a glow
> Just thinking of you,
> And the way you look tonight.

And I could hear my father's voice complaining at the choice, his voice full of wonder at this woman he had shared his life with but who never ceased to amaze him.

'Not *early* Sinatra, woman! Not all that swooning bobby-soxer stuff he recorded for Columbia! If you've *got* to pick Sinatra, then pick something from one of the Capitol albums of the fifties – "One For My Baby", "Angel Eyes", "In the Wee Small Hours of the Morning" – one of the great saloon songs. But not that *early* stuff! And what's wrong with Dean Martin? I always preferred old Dino anyway.'

It was true. My father's favourite was Dean Martin. Sinatra, as much as he liked him, was a bit too much of the smooth romantic for my old man. He far preferred

Dean Martin's hard centre. But of course the song wasn't my father's choice. It was my mother's. It wasn't about how he saw himself. It was about how she saw him, knew him, loved him.

> But you're lovely!
> With your smile so warm
> And your cheek so soft
> There is nothing for me
> But to love you
> Just the way you look tonight.

The undertaker's men carried my father's coffin out of the church – gently, gently – and into the graveyard as we followed, dazed by the rituals of death, to the latest grave in a sloping field of headstones.

The freshly dug plot was at the end of a long line of graves, and one day, after this church had seen many more funerals, it would be difficult to find my father's resting place because it would be in the middle of a forest of headstones, just one among the many. But not now. Not today. Today my father was the latest arrival in this eternal place. It was easy to find his grave today.

And there was his headstone – white and new, my father's epitaph carved in gleaming black on the top half, leaving space for another inscription – for his wife, my mother, Pat's grandmother – to one day be carved.

PATRICK WILLIAM ROBERT SILVER, DSM, it said, a name from the days when ordinary families gave their children as many names as they could remember, as many names as they could carry, and below the dates of his birth and death, BELOVED HUSBAND, FATHER AND GRANDFATHER.

The vicar was talking – ashes to ashes, dust to dust, come, ye blessed children of my Father, receive the kingdom prepared for you from the beginning of the world – but all

I could hear was a scrap from one of the old songs, a song asking someone to never, ever change.

We were on the edge of the open grave, at the front of a large crowd of mourners. Some of them I didn't know. Some of them I had known all my life. And yet the faces that I knew were changed – I remembered laughing uncles and good-looking aunts in their middle years, the good years of new cars and bright clothes and summer days on the coast, their children growing or perhaps already grown.

Now these faces I knew were older than I had ever expected them to be, and the confidence of their thirties and forties had somehow slipped away with the years. They had come to see my father buried, the first of their generation to go, and their own deaths must have suddenly seemed very real. They wept for him and also for themselves.

In the distance I could see the fields where I had roamed as a boy, dark brown in mid-winter and as rectangular as playing fields, bordered by scrawny bare trees.

Did children still play on that ragged farmland? Somehow it seemed unlikely. But I remembered every brilliant stream, every muddy ditch, the stagnant pond inside the thick spinney, and all the farmers who chased us away, me and my friends, those city children with suburban lives.

Up here there was no sign of the housing estates and shopping centres that were very close by. Up here all you could see were fields. Up here this place felt like real country.

This was why my father had escaped the city. Those fields where I had played as a boy – that was what my dad had dreamed of, and now he was going to be buried among them.

There was crying all around now – louder, uncontrolled, more stung with grief – and I looked up and saw the tears on faces that I loved. My dad's brothers. Our neighbours. My mother and my son.

But I stood there dry-eyed as I watched them lower my father's coffin into the freshly dug grave, one arm wrapped tightly around my mother, who had her own arms around her sobbing grandson, and my free hand stuffed deep into the pocket of my black suit, my fist holding my father's silver medal as though I would never let it go.

thirty-eight

'The world is changing,' said Nigel Batty. 'It's not the seventies any more. This isn't *Kramer versus Kramer.* In residency disputes, the law still favours the mother – and it always will. But there's a growing awareness that not every lousy parent is a man.'

'I hate the thought of my son growing up around some other guy,' I said, more to myself than to my lawyer. 'I hate the thought of him being in the same house as someone who hasn't really got any interest in him at all. Someone who's only interested in his mother.'

'That's not going to happen. No matter what she says – she left both of you. And you've done a good job while your son has been in your care. No matter what she tells her solicitor.'

'I can't believe she's making me out to be negligent. If she kept it clean, I could respect her. But this – it makes my blood boil, you know what I mean, Nigel?'

'I know.'

My lawyer was no longer Mr Batty to me. Now he was Nigel. Now he had told me his story.

Seven years ago he had married a French woman who he had met while she was working for a barrister in London. They settled here and had twin daughters within a year of their wedding. But when their marriage came apart two years ago, his wife – soon to be ex-wife – decided she wanted to return to France. And with the Court of Appeal's approval, she had received permission to take their daughters out of the country. Nigel Batty hadn't seen them since.

'So my children end up losing one parent and no doubt loathing the other one,' he said. 'Thanks to some dumb fuck of a judge who thinks that the mother is the only parent who counts. And there's nothing special about me – plenty of fathers lose contact with their children. Because the women they married want to punish them.'

I made sympathetic noises. It was late in the evening and the cleaning staff were shuffling around his empty office in the West End. He sat on his desk and stared down at the traffic clogged up on Hanover Square.

'My children would certainly be better off with two parents. But working that one out – the impossible task of letting them keep both parents – that would have taken a degree of compromise. And residency disputes are not about compromise. And they are not about what's best for the children. They should be, but they're not. They are invariably about what the mother decides she wants.'

He took his glasses off and rubbed his eyes.

'Although the law tries to take the sting out of a residence order, it has to end in victory for one parent and defeat for the other. It *has* to. The one who loses is usually the man. But – and this is what has changed over the last twenty years – not always. And we can win this one. We deserve to win this one.'

'But she does love him.'

'What?'

'Gina loves Pat. I know that she loves him.'

Nigel shuffled some papers on his desk, almost embarrassed on my behalf.

'I'm not sure that's really relevant here, is it?' he said.

* * *

I watched them from the window. Gina emerged from the Audi's passenger seat and let Pat out of the back door – he had told me that Richard had fitted a child lock – and then, crouching on the pavement so that they were the same height, she wrapped her arms around him, burying his blond head against her neck, grasping her last few seconds with him before she gave him back to me.

Gina lingered by the car door – we couldn't talk any more, but she would wait until she saw me before she got in – and as I watched Pat run up the little path to our door, his eyes shining, I knew that he deserved to be loved as much as any child in this world is loved.

Later, he was playing on the floor of his room with his toys.

'Pat?'

'Yes?'

'You know Mummy and I don't get on very well right now?'

'You don't talk to each other.'

'That's because we're having an argument at the moment.'

He silently smacked Luke Skywalker against the side of the Millennium Falcon. I sat down on the floor next to him. He kept smacking Luke.

'We both love you very much. You know that, don't you?'

He didn't speak.

'Pat?'

'I guess.'

'And we both want you to live with us. Where would you prefer to live? With me?'

'Yeah.'

'Or with Mummy?'

'Yeah.'

'It can't be both of us. You understand that, don't you? It can't be both. Not any more.'

He came to my arms and I cuddled him.

'It's difficult, isn't it, darling?'

'It's difficult.'

'But that's what the argument is about. I want you to stay here. And Mummy wants you to stay with her. Her and Richard.'

'Yeah, but what about my stuff?'

'What?'

'All my stuff. All my stuff is here. What if I went over there to live – what about my stuff?'

'That wouldn't be a problem, darling. We could move your things. You don't have to worry about that. The important thing is where you live. And I want you to stay here.'

He looked up at me. They were Gina's eyes.

'Why?'

'Because it's the right thing for you,' I said, and even as the words were forming, I wondered if that were really true.

I had changed over the last six months, my months of bringing up Pat alone. The show with Eamon was just a way to pay the mortgage, not the way to prove my worth to myself and everyone else. Work was no longer the centre of my universe. The centre of my universe was my boy.

When I felt pride or fear or wonder or anything that reminded me that I was alive, it wasn't because of anything that happened at the studio, it was because Pat had learned to tie his laces or because he had been bullied at school or because he said something or did something which just stunned me with love, something that reminded me that my son was the most beautiful boy in the world. If he went away then I would feel that I had lost everything.

'I just want what's best for you,' I said, wondering for

the first time if I really wanted what was best for him, or what was best for myself.

'Your dad and I saw her at the Palladium when she was eighteen years old,' my mother said. 'They called her the Girl from Tiger Bay.' Her blue eyes became wide with excitement – why had I never noticed how blue they were in the past? In the gloaming of the Albert Hall, my mother's eyes shone like something in the window of Tiffany.

Although they had always spent most of their evenings at home, my parents always took in a show every six months or so – Tony Bennett at the Royal Festival Hall, a revival of *Oklahoma!* or *Guys and Dolls* in the West End – and so now I was taking my mother to a show at the Albert Hall. Her personal all-time favourite – the girl from Tiger Bay.

'Shirley Bassey!' my mother said.

I had been dragged to a few Shirley Bassey shows before I was old enough to protest. But when I was growing up, her audience hadn't been anywhere near as mixed as the crowd that confronted us inside the Albert Hall.

Impossibly handsome young men with little Uzbek caps and plucked eyebrows looked for their seats along with stolid elderly couples from the Home Counties, the men country-club formal in blazers, the women with that peculiarly frozen Maggie Thatcher hair-do that my mother's generation sport on a night out.

'I never realised that old Shirley was so big with the gay crowd,' I said. 'I guess it makes sense – the boys love that combination of showbiz glitz and personal tragedy. She's our Judy Garland.'

'The gay crowd?' my mum said, bewildered. 'What gay crowd?'

I gestured at the young men in Versace and Prada who

stood out so obviously against the wool and polyester of the suburban set.

'All around you, Mum.'

As if on cue, the boy next to my mother – a male model type who was simply too good-looking to be heterosexual – stood up and squealed with excitement as the orchestra struck up the opening chords to 'Diamonds are Forever'.

'We love you, Shirley! You're fabulous!'

'Well, *he's* not gay,' my mum whispered in my ear, totally serious.

I laughed and put my arm around her, kissing her on the cheek. She leaned forward excitedly as Shirley Bassey appeared at the top of the stage stairs – her evening dress sparkling with what looked like fairy lights, her hands tossed extravagantly in the air.

'How do you do it, Mum?'

'How do I do what?'

'How do you manage to carry on after losing Dad? I mean, you were with him all your life. I can't imagine what it must be like to try to fill a gap that big.'

'Well, you don't get over it, of course. You can never get over it. I miss him. I'm lonely. Sometimes I'm frightened. And I still have to sleep with the light on.'

She looked at me. Shirley Bassey was prowling the front of the stage to thunderous applause and showers of bouquets. Yes, she was definitely our Judy Garland.

'But you have to learn to let go,' my mother said. 'That's part of it, isn't it?'

'Part of what?'

'Part of what it means to love someone. To really love someone. If you love someone then you don't just see them as an extension of yourself. You don't just love them for what's in it for you.'

My mother turned back to the stage. In the darkness of the Albert Hall I could see that her blue eyes were shining with tears.

'Love means knowing when to let go,' she told me.

thirty-nine

'You're crazy,' Nigel Batty said. 'You're going to voluntarily give up your child? You're going to just hand him over to your ex-wife when we could fucking *beat* her? She's going to love this – you know that, don't you?'

'I'm not doing this for her,' I said. 'I'm doing it for him.'

'You know how many men would love to be in your position? You know how many men I see in this office – grown men fucking weeping, Harry – who would give everything they've got to keep their children? Who would give their right nuts? And you're just walking away from him.'

'No, I'm not walking away from him. I'm not giving up. But I know how much he loves to be with Gina, although he tries not to show it because he thinks it will hurt me or be a betrayal or something. And either they make some kind of connection again, or she's going to become someone he just sees at weekends. I can see it happening already.'

'Whose fault is that?'

'I know you're disappointed, Nigel. But I'm just thinking of my boy.'

'You think she thought of him when she walked out? You think she thought of him when she was in the cab to Heathrow?'

'I don't know. I just think that a child needs two parents. Even a kid whose parents are divorced. Especially a kid whose parents are divorced. I'm doing what I can to make that happen.'

'What about the guy she lives with? This Richard? You don't know anything about him. You're happy to turn your son over to him?'

'I'm not turning Pat over to anyone. He's my son and he will always be my son. I'm his father and I will always be his father. But I have to assume that Gina hasn't got completely lousy taste in men.'

'She seems to go for fucking fruitcakes, if you ask me. You know what's going to happen, don't you? You're going to become one of those weekend dads – sitting in Pizza Express on a Sunday afternoon trying to think of something to say to this stranger who used to be your kid.'

'Pat and I will never be like that.'

'Don't bet on it.'

'I'm not saying it's what I would have wanted. But don't you see? We fuck up our lives again and again and it's always our children who pick up the bill. We move on to new relationships, always starting over, always thinking we've got another chance to get it right, and it's the kids from all these broken marriages who pay the price. They – my son, your daughters, all the millions like them – are carrying around wounds that are going to last a lifetime. It has to stop.' I shrugged helplessly, knowing that he was disgusted with me. 'I don't know, Nigel. I'm just trying to be a good father.'

'By giving up your son.'

'It feels like the least I can do.'

'The way it's going to work,' I told Pat, 'is that you can leave as much of your stuff at our house as you want. Your room will always be your room. Nobody is ever going to touch it. And you can come back whenever you want. For a day, for a night, or forever.'

'Forever?' Pat said, pushing Bluebell by my side. His voice was very small.

'You're going to live with your mother. But nobody's going to make you live there. We are both going to look after you. And we both want you to be happy.'

'You're not arguing any more?'

'We're trying to stop arguing. Because we both love you very much and we both want what's best for you. I'm not saying that we will never argue again. But we're trying, okay?'

'Do you love each other again?'

'No, darling. That time of our life is gone. But we both love you.'

'Where will I sleep at Mummy's place?'

'She's preparing a new room for you. And it's going to be great – you can spread out your Star Wars toys all over the floor, turn on a bit of hip-hop, drive all the neighbours crazy.'

'And nobody's allowed to touch my old room?'

'Nobody.'

'Not even you?'

'Not even me.'

We were at the park now. The asphalt road winding around the lake spread out before us. This was where he loved to ride Bluebell, taking off at such a speed that the swans rose up from the water's edge when they saw him coming. But Pat made no move to get on his bike.

'I like it now,' he said, and it tore me up. 'I like it the way it is.'

'Me too,' I said. 'I like to make you breakfast in the morning. And I like to see you with all your toys spread out on the floor in the afternoon. And I like it when we get a Chinese takeaway or a pizza and watch a film together on the sofa. And going to the park together. I like all that stuff.'

'Me too. I like it too.'

'And we're still going to do all of that, okay? Nobody can stop us. That's never going to end. Not until you're a very big boy who wants to go off with his friends and leave his old dad alone.'

'That's going to be *never*.'

'But give it a good try, okay? Living with Mummy, I mean. Because she loves you very much, and I know that you love her too. That's good. I'm glad. I'm glad that you love each other. And although it makes me sad to see you go, it's not the end of anything. You can come back whenever you want. So try to be happy with Mummy. Okay?'

'Okay.'

'And Pat?'

'What?'

'I'm proud that you're my son.'

He dropped his bike and came to my arms, pressing his face against me, overwhelming me with what felt like the very essence of him. He filled my senses – his unruly mop of blond hair, his impossibly smooth skin, that Pat smell of dirt and sugar. My beautiful son, I thought, tasting the salt of our tears.

There was more that I wanted to say but I couldn't find the words. It's not perfect, I wanted to say. It will never be perfect. I'm not so dumb that I don't know that. But given the way that things have turned out, it's probably the best that we can do. It's not perfect. Because the only perfect thing in my life has always been you.

My beautiful boy.

My beautiful boy.

My beautiful boy.

Gina took Pat into his new bedroom and I stood there in the middle of their flat with a box of Star Wars toys in my arms, feeling as lost as I had ever felt in my life.

'Here, let me take those,' Richard said.

I gave him the box and he set it on the table.

We smiled at each other awkwardly. He was different from what I had expected – more self-effacing, gentler, less of the brash suit than I had imagined.

'This is a big day for Gina,' he said.

'A big day for all of us,' I said.

'Sure,' he said quickly. 'But Gina – well, as you know, she's a Libra. Home, family – it's all central to her.'

'Right.'

He wasn't quite what I had expected. But that didn't mean he wasn't a bit of a dickhead, of course.

'How about Pat?' he asked. 'What sign is he?'

'Please Clean Up My Room,' I said.

Gina came out of Pat's new bedroom and smiled at me.

'Thanks for helping him move.'

'No problem.'

'And thanks for everything,' she said, and for just a second there I recognised the Gina who had loved me. 'I know how much he means to you.'

'Love means knowing when to let go,' I told her.

I didn't see it coming. I swung the MGF on to the main road and suddenly the black cab was swerving to avoid me, horn blaring, rubber burning, the driver's face twisted with rage. Heads turned to look at the idiot in the sports car with the torn roof.

I pulled over to the kerb and sat there breathing deeply, trying to get my heart under some kind of control as the traffic ebbed and flowed around me. My hands were shaking. I gripped the wheel until my knuckles were white and the shaking began to stop.

Then I slowly started to make my way home, driving with

exaggerated care because I knew that my mind was on some other road, that it kept wandering away to a black and white image of a father and son glimpsed once in a photograph album, and the fragment of some old song about being a stranger in paradise.

'Anyway, Dad,' I said out loud, really needing to talk to my old man, really needing to know what he thought. 'Did I do the right thing?'

forty

We heard the church before we could see it.

The big black Daimler swung left into Farringdon Road, and as we trundled down that long narrow channel to the river, the bells were ringing for Marty and Siobhan.

We turned left again into the little Clerkenwell square and the church seemed to fill the big blue sky. In the back seat of the limo, Marty shifted uneasily inside his morning suit, squinting out at the guests being handed buttonholes at the entrance to the church.

'Should we go round a few times?' he said. 'Keep them waiting a bit?'

'That's what the bride does, Marty. Not you.'

'And are you sure you've got the –'

I held out the two gold rings.

He nodded.

There was nothing else to do but to do it.

We got out of the Daimler, the bells so loud now that they were all you could think about. Marty kept buttoning and unbuttoning his morning coat as we made our way up the steep stone steps to the church, smiling and nodding at the people we knew, and even the people we didn't know. We were halfway to the top when Marty trod on something and I had to catch his arm as he stumbled.

Marty picked up a nine-inch man made of moulded plastic. He was sporting a lavender jacket, spangly silver trousers and a white satin shirt. And he was either wearing a cummerbund or his stomach was heavily bandaged. He had lost one of his little white shoes.

'Now who the fuck is that meant to be?' Marty said. 'Liberace?'

'Not Liberace,' I said, taking it from him. 'That's Disco Ken.'

With the sun streaming through the stained glass windows behind her, a small girl came flying down the aisle of the church, holding on to her hat, which was the same colour as the yellow party dress she was wearing.

'Peggy,' I said.

'Disco Ken,' she said, taking him from me. 'I've been looking for him.'

Then Cyd was there, looking at me from under the brim of a big black hat. It was a little too big for her. Maybe she had bought it before she cut her hair.

'I'll be inside,' Marty said. 'On the altar.'

'At the altar,' I corrected him.

'I know where I'm going to be,' he said.

'Good luck,' Cyd smiled at him.

We watched him go, and then we looked at each other for a long moment.

'I didn't expect to see you here,' I said.

'I'm on the bride's side.'

'Of course. Siobhan really likes you. So – how's it going?'

'Okay, okay. Really okay. And how's Pat?'

'He's living with Gina now. It seems to be working out. You'll see him later.'

'Pat's coming?' Peggy asked.

'He's a pageboy.'

'Good,' she said, and ducked back inside the church.

'And he's happy?' Cyd said, and I knew it really mattered to her, and I wanted to hold her.

'There's a few teething problems with the boyfriend. He's a bit alternative. He doesn't like it when Pat hits him around the head with his light sabre. I keep telling him – no, no, Pat – if you're going to hit him, go for his eyes.'

She shook her head and smiled.

'Where would you be without your little jokes, Harry?'

'I don't know.'

'But you see him?'

'All the time. Every weekend and once during the week. We haven't worked out about the school holidays yet.'

'You must miss him.'

'It's like he's still there. I can't explain it. Even though he's gone, I feel him all around me. There's just this big gap where he used to be. It's like his absence is as strong as his presence.'

'Even when they're gone, they still hold your heart. That's what being a parent is all about.'

'I guess so. And Jim's all right?'

'I wouldn't know. That didn't work out. It was a mistake to even try.'

'Well, you tried for Peggy.' At least I hoped she had tried for Peggy. I hoped that she hadn't tried because she still loved him now the way she had loved him once before. 'It was worth trying for Peggy's sake.'

'You think so?'

'Definitely.'

She indicated a Daimler driving slowly past the church. In the back seat was a woman covered in white and a nervous middle-aged man. The car disappeared around the corner.

'We'd better go inside.'

'Well, see you later. We can share a vol-au-vent.'

'Goodbye, Harry.'

I watched her move off to take her place on the bride's side of the church, holding the brim of her hat as if it might fly away. Then Pat was beside me, tugging at my sleeve, dressed in some sort of sailor suit. He looked dapper in a maritime sort of way. I put my arm around him as Gina and Richard came up the church steps.

'I told you we wouldn't be able to park so close to the church,' he said.

'We did park, didn't we?' she said. 'Or did I miss something?'

They stopped bitching when they saw me, silently collecting their buttonholes from one of the ushers and passing into the church.

I smiled at Pat.

'I like your new suit. How's it feel?'

'Scratchy.'

'Well, you look great.'

'I don't like suits. They're too much like school.'

'I guess you're right. Suits are far too much like school. You still on for the weekend?'

He nodded.

'What do you want to do?'

He thought about it for a moment. 'Something good.'

'Me too. Let's do something good this weekend. But right now we've got a job to do, haven't we?'

'We're pageboys.'

'You might be a pageboy. But I'm the best man. Shall we go to a wedding?'

He shrugged and grinned.

My beautiful boy.

We stepped inside the church – it smelled of lilies, cool and dark apart from the shafts of honeyed light coming through the ancient windows, the women in their hats – and Pat ran ahead of me, the heels of his new shoes clicking against the flagstones.

And watching him run to where Marty was waiting for us

at the altar gave me a pang that was somehow very happy and very sad all at the same time.

I don't know. It sort of felt like he was already his own man.

The vicar was tall, young and nervous, one of those sweet-natured toffs from the Shires who the Church of England sends into the tower blocks of the inner city, and his Adam's apple bobbed up and down as he spoke of the day of judgement when the secrets of all hearts shall be disclosed.

He was looking at Marty, fixing him with a stare, asking his questions as though he really expected honest answers – Wilt thou love her, comfort her, honour and keep her in sickness and in health, and, forsaking all others, keep thee only unto her, as long as ye both shall live?

And I thought of Marty with his long line of opportunistic couplings that invariably ended up in the Sunday papers when the women he quickly humped and almost as quickly dumped realised that sleeping with him was not the first rung to a career in the entertainment industry.

And I looked at Siobhan standing with her father by her side, her pale Irish face impassive behind all that white lace, and – although it wasn't the time or the place – I couldn't help thinking of her weakness for married men and dodgy boyfriends who chained themselves to trees. But none of it seemed to matter very much today. Not the stung former lovers who gossiped about Marty, or all the wives who had eventually beaten Siobhan into bitter second place. It was all behind them now.

Both of them seemed redeemed today, renewed by these promises of love and devotion, by pledging their troth – even though I was pretty sure that Marty had absolutely no idea what a troth was or indeed how to pledge it. I felt an enormous affection for both of them.

And I couldn't find any cynicism left in me. Because this was what I wanted too. It was everything I wanted. To love and to cherish.

I turned to steal a look at the congregation. Cyd was staring at the vicar from under the brim of her hat. I could just about make out the top of Peggy's head. Pat caught my eye and smiled and I thought again what a great little kid he was. I winked at him and turned back as the vicar talked about remaining in perfect love and peace.

As the vicar asked his questions, I was forced to ask some of myself. Such as – can I truly be a positive thing in Peggy's life? And do I really think that I can make a good job of raising that little girl when I know for certain that we will never have the easy bonds of blood? Am I really man enough to bring up another man's child? And what about Cyd? Can we stick by each other for more than the usual five or six or seven years? Can we love and cherish as long as we both shall live? Will one of us – almost certainly me – eventually fuck up, fuck around or fuck off? Do I really believe that our love is big enough and strong enough to survive in the lousy modern world? Well, do I? Do I? *Do I?*

'I do,' I said out loud, and for the first time ever Marty looked at me as though I were the fruitcake.

I tapped a silver spoon against the side of my champagne glass and rose to give my best man's speech.

As all those relatives and friends and business colleagues looked up at me, content after the wedding breakfast and ready to be tickled, I looked down at my notes.

They were mostly jokes written by Eamon, scrawled on the back of postcards. They seemed quite useless now.

I breathed in and began.

‘One of the great thinkers once said – “You drift through the years and life seems tame, then a stranger appears and love is his name.”’ I paused dramatically. ‘Plato? Wittgenstein? Descartes? No, it was Nancy Sinatra. And she’s right, old Nancy. Life just seems so tame, so empty without the stranger. In fact, now I come to think about it, it’s worse than that.’

They didn’t know what the fuck I was talking about. I don’t think I knew myself. I rubbed my throbbing temples. My mouth was dry. I gulped down some water, but it was still dry.

‘Worse, much worse,’ I muttered, trying to work out what I was trying to say. It was something about the importance of Marty and Siobhan always remembering how they felt today. It was something about never forgetting.

I looked across the crowded room at Cyd, hoping for some sign of encouragement, but she was staring down at the remains of her dessert. Peggy and Pat were running among the tables. Someone coughed. A baby was grizzling. The crowd were getting restless. Someone went off to find the toilet. I quickly glanced down at my notes.

‘Wait, I’ve got some good stuff here,’ I said. ‘There’s the one about love beginning when you sink into someone’s arms and ending when you put your arms in someone’s sink.’

A couple of drunken uncles guffawed.

‘And there’s the one about the two inexperienced newlyweds who went to see their doctor for a demonstration of the sexual act,’ I said.

A tipsy auntie tittered.

‘The doctor made love to the woman and asked the groom if he had any questions. And the groom said – yes, how often do I have to bring her in?’

It got a laugh. Eamon smiled proudly. But I felt the postcards slipping through my trembling fingers. I didn't really need my notes any more. I couldn't use them.

'But what I really want to say is that I hope – I know – that Siobhan and Marty will remember that a life without love is no life at all. Nancy Sinatra said that. And if you find someone to love, then you should never let them slip away. I said that.'

I raised a glass to Marty and Siobhan. Cyd looked up at me and then ducked back down behind her hat.

'Ladies and gentlemen, boys and girls, please charge your glasses and drink a toast to the gorgeous couple.'

Eamon grabbed me as I came off stage. 'That was really great,' he said. 'But next time throw in a couple of jokes about the groom shagging sheep.'

It wasn't until the music started that I realised I had never seen her dancing.

I had no idea if she was a brilliant dancer – like her namesake – or if she was completely yet endearingly crap.

I didn't know if she twirled and glided with infinite grace, or if she just stood there taking those embarrassed little half-steps and wondering what to do with her arms. I didn't know if she danced like Cyd Charisse or Sid James. But I knew I didn't care.

Seeing Cyd dance badly would wrench my heart just as surely as seeing her dance brilliantly. I just wanted to dance with her.

The DJ was playing, 'Wake Me Up Before You Go-Go' and there was something about the goofy euphoria of that old record that filled the floor.

Marty and Siobhan were doing a dangerous-looking jitterbug, the groom's face turning coronary red as he attempted to lift his bride off the ground. Eamon was standing rooted to the spot and throwing his arms around as though he were rat-faced on Ibiza instead of half-cut in Clerkenwell. Mem slunk around him, pouting and grinding and looking dirty, doing the only dance she knew.

Gina was laughing with Pat and clapping her hands as he did this dance that he had just made up, which consisted of these strange little jumps that turned him completely around. Richard was slow-dancing with one of the bridesmaids. My mother was waltzing with the vicar.

And there was Sally, heavily pregnant now, shuffling from side to side in an ironic sort of way, because this was music to make old people feel young again.

And there was Glenn, his eyes closed and waving his arms around as if he was freaking out in the mud at Woodstock. Suddenly it seemed like a perfect party. Because Glenn danced in exactly the same way as Eamon.

But I couldn't see Cyd and Peggy.

When Marty put Siobhan down to take a breather, I touched her arm, shouting above George Michael's voice.

'Siobhan, where's Cyd?'

'They had to leave early to catch their plane. They're going back to America.'

'For how long?'

'For good. Didn't she tell you?'

I abandoned the MGF on the hard shoulder of the motorway somewhere west of the green suburban sprawl of Osterley Park. A few days later I tried to find the place in the *A to Z*, but it was too far out of the city to be included. It felt as though I dumped it at the end of the world. Or maybe the start.

But it was clear that I wasn't going to make it in time by car. The traffic on the road to Heathrow wasn't moving. Yet every few seconds another jet as big as an ocean liner roared off into the heavens above my head. It was no good. The MGF couldn't help me any more.

I got out of the car, realising that I didn't know what airline they were on. Virgin Atlantic left from Terminal 3 but British Airways were at Terminal 4. There wasn't time to go to both. What was it to be? Did I go for Richard Branson or the world's favourite airline?

I ran by the side of the motorway, the planes screaming into the blue sky above me, the tails of my morning suit flying.

In the end it didn't matter what flight they were on. The day's planes to America had all gone by the time I reached the departure hall.

The crowds were thinning out now. Those travelling were in the air. Those seeing them off were on their way home. By the international departure gate, sweating heavily inside my morning suit, I hung my head and sighed. I had been too late.

Then I saw him on the ground, a little lavender party man. Disco Ken. I picked him up. His silver trousers were filthy. He had lost his remaining shoe.

And then Cyd and Peggy were standing in front of me, their boarding passes still in their hands, their suitcases at their feet. They were both still in their party dresses.

'Great speech,' Cyd said.

'You don't think that it should have been a bit more traditional? You don't think I should have – you know – included some stuff about the groom and sheep?'

'No, it was good.'

'You missed your plane.'

'We let it go.'

I shook my head with disbelief. 'It's you,' I said.

'It better be,' she said.

Peggy took Disco Ken from me and looked up at Cyd, as if wondering what happened next.

In the early evening, the black cab headed slowly back towards the city. Cyd stared out at the first of the tower blocks along the Westway, lost in her own thoughts, and Peggy slept in my arms.

Sometimes this child could seem so grown up, so self-possessed and assured. But sitting on my lap with her head resting lightly against my chest, she felt like no weight at all. As though she were still a baby, with all her life still stretching out ahead of her, a life still waiting to find its shape.

She stirred in her sleep as she heard an ice-cream van ringing its bell somewhere in the endless streets of west London. More than any birdsong or blooming bud, this was the sign that the days of cold and dark were finally drawing to a close. Spring must be coming soon, because the ding-dong man was out there somewhere.

From the back seat of our black cab, I couldn't see exactly where he was in those quiet suburban streets that stretched out in every direction. But the echo of those chimes rang in my head like a memory of childhood, or a dream of wedding bells.

Inside:

Writing *Man and Boy*:
Q & A with Tony Parsons

Exclusive extract from *My Favourite Wife*

Don't miss Tony's other books

Writing *Man and Boy*: Q & A with Tony Parsons

What was the starting point for *Man and Boy*?

TP: The starting point was really feeling the two great roles that we play in a lifetime – the role of somebody's child, and somebody's parent. When you have a child, it feels as though they are going to be young forever, it feels like childhood will last a lifetime. And then suddenly the clock strikes midnight on their thirteenth birthday and everything changes. Suddenly they are accelerating towards being a grown-up. I saw that with my son as he became a teenager, and then a little while later my mother was diagnosed as having terminal cancer – and that is where *Man and Boy* began. Having a son who was growing up, and a parent who was dying.

It is seen as your most autobiographical book – why didn't you write it as non-fiction?

TP: But it is a novel. And no matter how much of my life I mined for *Man and Boy*, it is actually some distance from what happened to me when I was Harry's age. There's a lot of me in there, but a lot of my imagination too. The story would never have been written as non-fiction. I needed that distance that you get with fiction. In a novel you have the ability to change things, so that they work out as you would have wanted, or so that you can process the things that went wrong. You change things around – the wife in the book is based on a real woman, but she is not based on my first wife, for example. Somehow the freedom to change things – to invent, to make up – makes it more real than the mere facts would have. And although the character of Harry's father is very much based on my dad – old war hero, tough, patrician, sentimental – it wasn't really his spirit that drove *Man and Boy*. My father had been dead for ten years when I wrote *Man and Boy*. But my mother was dying when I wrote it. I would go from doctor's appointments with my mum, where I held her hand while the doctor told her there was nothing they could do, and then I would come home and work on *Man and Boy*. I was very aware that soon I would be in this world without either of my parents, and I was aware that soon my son would be a grown man. It is a book that anticipates loss – loss of a child, loss of a parent, loss of a family – and that gave it an emotional clout that it wouldn't have had if I had written it at any other time.

It has sold millions of copies all over the world – were you surprised by its success?

TP: Surprised doesn't begin to say it. I was shocked then, and I still am. You never really know what will be that kind of bestseller, but there was something in *Man and Boy* that people warmed to. I think it is quite a simple little story about some of the things that we all experience. I know that all those millions of readers didn't see my life in *Man and Boy*. They saw their own.

What were you expecting when you were writing it?

TP: Not much. I believed in the story. I felt I was onto something real and I hoped a few people would like it. But really it was written as therapy. More than anything, writing *Man and Boy* helped me deal with my mum's illness, and her death. If you are any kind of writer, then writing about these things somehow makes them slightly more bearable.

The benefits of that kind of commercial success are obvious – are there drawbacks?

TP: The only drawback is that you don't want to disappoint your readers. You want them to like every book as much as they liked that one. There's a certain pressure because you should never second-guess your readers about what they might like. You have to follow your heart. I am lucky because I always have one story in my head, but never more than one story. So the next book looks after itself. I guess the biggest pressure is wondering if you will ever have that kind of global success again, where even people who never buy books have read your book and come up to you in the street. I think I have written better books than *Man and Boy*, but I can't deny that's my greatest hit. And of course it means a lot to me. My mum died just before it was published, in the summer of 1999, and it is dedicated to her.

Did she get a chance to read it?

TP: No – but she knew I had dedicated it to her and said, "Ah, I must be on the way out if he's dedicated a book to me." That is what she was like. Brave and funny.

Why do you think it got the kind of response that it did?

TP: A lot of women bought the book. I wasn't expecting that. I thought it would be a book that was mostly read by men. Although there are women characters in the book, and a central love story, it is really about this guy and his relationship with his dying father and small son. I remember when we were having discussions about the cover, someone said how do we avoid having pictures of men all over the cover? I didn't think women would go for it, because it is about a man whose life falls to pieces after a one-night stand. I didn't think that women readers would forgive Harry for that. But they did. Somehow he redeemed himself. And I think people were surprised that a man could write about his child with such tenderness. But that seemed perfectly natural to me. I had been a single dad, just like Harry in *Man and Boy*, and all the usual parental emotions of love, tenderness and feeling fanatically protective are only heightened by the experience of being a single parent. Harry is a man who is redeemed by love. I think we always respond to a story like that because it gives us faith in the human spirit, and our ability to fix what is broken. Including ourselves.

What did your son think of the book?

TP: He was amused by it, more than anything. He liked how I stole his Star Wars obsession and put it to good use. And I think he was moved and touched by the scenes between the child and the grandfather. The final visit to the hospital, where Pat goes to see his granddad dying, and feels angry and betrayed and bewildered afterwards, was pretty much taken from real life. Sometimes you can't improve upon real life. But my son could also see all the things I had changed, and what made it a novel. That wasn't his mother in *Man and Boy*, and so he could never see it as a true story. It's more of a true story to me than it is to him.

As a general rule, how much of your life goes into your books?

TP: As a general rule, however much I need. I believe in the power of lived experience, but I also believe in the power of the imagination, and the value of research. Experience, imagination, research – these are the only tools that any writer has, and in every book you use them all. I use my own life when it works, but everything is a slave to the story. If you are going to make the personal into something universal, then that's what you have to do. Some scenes are taken directly from life. Sometimes the scenes that seem most obviously invented are the ones that actually happened.

In *Man and Boy*, you draw on experiences that had happened to you ten or fifteen years before the book was written – becoming a single parent, the death of your father, your career taking a downturn after some early success – why didn't you write it sooner?

TP: I didn't have it in me. Living through those things wasn't enough to make *Man and Boy*. I had to reach that point in life where I felt absolutely poised between the generation that came before me, and the generation that came after me. I needed big stuff to happen – profound changes, like a child growing up and a parent dying. Books are like babies – they come along when they are ready.

You wrote a sequel to *Man and Boy* with *Man and Wife* – will there be a third Harry Silver book?

TP: I think about it sometimes. It is almost exactly ten years since the publication of *Man and Boy*. Harry and Cyd have been married a long time. Pat is a teenager now. I wonder how they are all getting along.

Exclusive extract from *My Favourite Wife* – out now in paperback

He slept until first light and then abruptly he was wide awake.

He counted the things stopping him from going back to sleep. His body clock was pining for London time. Tomorrow morning at 8 a.m. the driver – Tiger – would take him to the Pudong offices of Butterfield, Hunt and West, and he would start his new job. He was curious to know where they were, and what their new life looked like in daylight. How could he possibly sleep with his head so full? As quietly as he could, Bill got up, got dressed and slipped out of the apartment.

The courtyard where the men in cars had waited for the girls was empty apart from Tiger. He was sleeping with his bare feet on the dashboard of the limo, his legs either side of the steering wheel. He jumped to attention when Bill walked past.

'Where to, boss?' he said, pulling on his shoes.

'It's Sunday,' Bill said. 'Don't they give you the day off on Sunday?'

Tiger looked blank. And then hurt. 'Where we going, boss?'

'I'm walking,' Bill said. 'And stop calling me boss.'

The Sabbath may have meant nothing to Tiger but out on the streets of Gubei New Area it felt almost like Sunday morning back home, with nobody around apart from the odd jogger and dog walker, the neighbourhood shuttered and still. It was early June, and the heat was already starting to build.

Bill walked. He was hungry to see what he thought of as the real China, the China that was nothing to do with plasma televisions and Dom Pérignon. The real China was somewhere nearby. It had to be. There were blocks of flats as far as he could see in a bewildering jumble of styles, but broken up with patches of manicured green and oversized statues. There were strips of restaurants – he could see Thai, Italian, everything but Chinese – a Carrefour supermarket, and a couple of international schools, including the one that Holly would go to in the morning. Little parks. A nice neighbourhood. Gubei was greener and cleaner than the grimy, crime-ridden patch of London they had left behind. His family could live here. His wife and daughter could be happy here. He felt a quiet satisfaction, mixed with relief.

He glanced at his watch and decided he had time to explore before Becca and Holly stirred. So he walked towards the rising sun and as he left Gubei New Area behind, the streets quickly filled. Women selling bruised fruit stared through him from shaded side streets. Someone bumped into him. Someone else spat at his feet. There were men in filthy, dirt-encrusted two-piece suits working on a building site. On a Sunday. And in the streets there were people. A tide of people. Suddenly there were people everywhere.

He stopped, trying to get his bearings. The roads were wide and traffic flew by, horns mindlessly beeping, ignoring red lights and pedestrians and the rest of the traffic. He saw a chic girl in sunglasses with her hair up behind the wheel of a silver Buick Excelle. There were flocks of VW Santana taxis. A muddy truck piled high with junk and men. And more trucks, lots of them, with their strange cargo of cardboard or orange traffic cones or pigs or yet more cars, so new they still shone with the showroom wax.

As the sun got higher, and Bill continued to walk east, the city got noisier, adding to his sense of dislocation. A woman on a scooter mounted the pavement and just missed him, beeping her horn furiously. Schools of cyclists with giant black visors over their faces swarmed past. Suddenly he was aware of the time difference, the light-headedness that follows a long-haul flight, the sweat of exhaustion. But he kept walking. He wanted to know something about this place.

He walked down alleys where thin men shaved over ancient metal bowls and fat babies were fed, and where ramshackle buildings with red-tile roofs were draped with drying laundry and satellite dishes. Then abruptly the jumbled blocks with their red-tile roofs suddenly gave way to the new shining towers and shopping malls.

Outside Prada men with their skin darkened by sun and grime tried to sell him fake Rolex watches and DVDs of the latest Tom Cruise movie. Young women hid from the sun under umbrellas. Naked Western models advertised skin-lightening products on giant billboards.

And as Bill walked on, he felt something that he had never felt in his life, and it was an awareness of the sheer mass of humanity. All those people in the world, all those lives. It was as if he truly believed in their existence for the first time. Shanghai gave him no choice.

Bill hailed one of the Santana taxis, impatient to see the Bund, but the driver didn't understand a word he said and dropped him by the river, glad to get rid of him. He got out next to a wharf with a ferry; not a sightseeing ferry but some kind of local public transport.

Bill handed over his smallest note, received some filthy RMB in return, and joined the milling mob waiting to cross to the other side. He tried to work out where the queue began. Then he realised that it didn't begin anywhere.

And as the ferry filled with people, and then continued to fill even more until Bill was hemmed in on every side, and fighting back the feeling that the ferry was overloaded, he saw that here, at last, was the real China.

The numbers.

It was all about the numbers.

He knew that the numbers were why he would be starting his new job in the morning, why his family's future would be decided in this city, and why all the money problems of the past would soon be over. They filled the dreams of businessmen from Sydney to San Francisco – the one billion customers, the one billion new capitalists, the one billion marketplace.

He struggled to move his arms and glanced at his watch, wondering if he could make it back home to his girls before they woke up.

The ferry began to move.

That afternoon they did the tourist thing.

The three of them joined the queues and took the lift to the top of the Oriental Pearl TV Tower where they stared down at the boats on the Huangpu River and saw that the city seemed to be without end.

On the other side of the tower they looked down at a park that was full of brides, hundreds of them, all in white, looking like a flock of swans as they surrounded the lakes, feeding confetti-coloured fish food to koi carp.

Bill lifted his daughter so she could see.

'New school tomorrow,' he said.

Holly said nothing, her eyes wide at the sight of all those brides.

'You're going to make lots of new friends,' Becca said, gripping one of Holly's ankles, and shaking it with encouragement.

Holly thought about it, chewing her bottom lip.

'I'm going to be very busy,' she said.

Although foreigners were a common sight in Shanghai now, Bill and Becca and Holly were the only non-Chinese at the top of the Oriental Pearl TV Tower that afternoon, and people stared at them.

The child and the woman were so blonde, their skin so pale, and their eyes so blue they looked like weather. The man holding his little girl and the child with her arms circling her father's neck and the woman with her arm draped around her husband's shoulders.

That's what was noticed about them – those gestures of child-like affection, the little family holding on to each other in their new home, as if the three of them could not exist without that physical contact, or without each other.

Everybody knew that Westerners didn't care about family in the same way that the Chinese did, especially not Westerners in Shanghai. But this man and woman and child seemed different.

Don't miss
Tony's other
books . . .

Man and Wife

Harry Silver is learning to juggle his many commitments – to his wife and his ex-wife, to his son, his stepdaughter and his mother, to his own work and his wife's career.

And then someone walks into his life who is going to make it even more complicated...

A sequel to the international bestseller *Man and Boy*, *Man and Wife* also stands on its own as a brilliant novel about relationships in the new century – about why we fall in love and why we marry – about why we stay and why we go.

978-0-00-651482-4 • £6.99

'Funny, serious, tender and honest... Tony Parsons is writing about the genuine dilemmas of modern life'
Sunday Express

Save 10%
when you buy direct from HarperCollins

Call 08707 871724
Free postage and packing in the UK only

Stories We Could Tell

Sometimes you can grow up in just one night

On a hot summer night in 1977, London rages around three young men who are about to learn the true meaning of friendship.

Hip young gunslinger Terry is basking in his scoop on rock star Dag Wood. But Dag has set his sights on a photographer called Misty – Terry's girlfriend. Who gets the girl?

Ray is about to be sacked from his music paper from crimes against cool and the only thing that can save him is landing an exclusive interview with John Lennon. Can he find his hero in time?

And Leon seeks sanctuary in a disco called the Goldmine as he goes on the run from the meanest gang in town and meets the dancing queen of his dreams. But are her dreams the same?

978-0-00-715124-0 • £6.99

'The trio's rites of passage are handled beautifully and poignantly and Parsons brilliantly captures a bygone era'
Irish Independent

Save 10%
when you buy direct from HarperCollins

Call 08707 871724
Free postage and packing in the UK only

My Favourite Wife

Into the booming, gold-rush city of Shanghai fly Bill and Becca Holden with their small daughter Holly – a young family seeking their fortune far from their north London home.

When tragedy forces Becca to return to London with Holly, the friendship between a lonely family man, working night and day, and a neglected second wife grows into something more – something that threatens to destroy all their lives. And when Becca and Holly come back, it is time for all of them to learn something about the meaning of love and the bonds of family.

978-0-00-722649-8 • £6.99

'His stories show all too well how we muddle along in search of love and fulfilment, and when we fluff it... sometimes that's just because it's easier'
Observer

Save 10%
when you buy direct from HarperCollins

Call 08707 871724
Free postage and packing in the UK only